"HELP! WE NEED HELP IN HERE!"

Violet pressed her hands as hard as she could to Chelsea's wound—it was all she could remember from the abbreviated first aid course they'd had in PE. She thought that maybe she should do something more, but she didn't know what that something might be.

And then Chelsea went still beneath her.

Not the kind of still that happens when someone falls asleep, when you continue to feel their breaths, when you know that their blood is coursing within them.

No, this was a different kind of still. The kind that Violet had only seen in death.

The final kind of still.

Also by Kimberly Derting

Kimberly Derting

DEAD
SILENCE

HARPER

An Imprint of HarperCollinsPublishers

Library of Congress Cataloging-in-Publication Data
Derting, Kimberly.
    Dead silence : a Body finder novel / Kimberly Derting. — First
edition.
        pages   cm
    Summary: "When Violet, a high school senior, learns that an
underground group has been carrying out murders on the order of their
Charles Manson-like leader, she is pulled into a deadly hunt, where even
her ability may not save her"—Provided by publisher.
    ISBN 978-0-06-208223-7 (pbk.)
    [1. Psychic ability—Fiction.   2. Serial murders—Fiction.   3. Dead—
Fiction.   4. Best friends—Fiction.   5. Friendship—Fiction.   6. High
schools—Fiction.   7. Schools—Fiction.   8. Washington (State)—Fiction.]
I. Title.
PZ7.D4468De 2013   2013007308
[Fic]—dc23   CIP
                                                                AC

Typography by Andrea Vandergrift
HB 09.26.2022
❖
First paperback edition, 2014

To Amanda, Connor, and Abby.
*For making me laugh and cry,
and everything in between.*

And to Mat—
welcome to the family!

PROLOGUE

JAY HIT THE DOOR WITH HIS SHOULDER, BUT IT didn't splinter beneath his weight or anything quite so dramatic. The handle, which was probably old and in disrepair anyway, fell apart on impact and the door shot open, banging against the wall on the other side. The crashing noise filled the dark house, echoing off the walls.

The sound of rushing water was stronger in here, as was the stink of urine. Violet recoiled from the smell, covering her face. She could only see fragments of the space around her, tiny pieces of the room: an old bureau with a cracked mirror, its jagged shards catching bits of light from outside and reflecting it around them; a window with dingy-looking curtains billowing in on either side of it; a mound in the center of the floor that could only be one thing.

"Chelsea," Violet whimpered, falling to her knees at the same time she caught a glimpse of another person—the killer—emerging from the darkened corner. Above his head there was something glowing, a blur of light that Violet couldn't make out . . . he was moving far too quickly now.

"Jay," she tried to warn, but it wasn't necessary.

Whoever he was, he was already launching himself toward the open window, throwing himself over the sill just as Jay was about to reach him. And with him went both the trickling of water *and* the stench of old urine.

Two of his imprints.

"We did it," Violet breathed. "We found her." Outside, the shrill sound of sirens came closer, and she no longer cared about anything except that they'd found Chelsea.

And then, before she could stop him, before she could even shout his name, she watched as Jay, too, hurled himself over the window's ledge.

She started to get up, to go to the window to see if he was okay. To see if he'd landed safely, but a hand stopped her. Chelsea's hand.

Relief rippled within her and spread outward.

"It's okay, Chels, I'm here now. I'm here."

She heard it then, a wheezing sound, and she felt frantically for Chelsea's face, her hands stroking her friend's cheeks. "It's okay," she repeated, but this time she was no longer sure. Something was wrong.

2

She kept going, her hands searching the girl beneath her as the sirens outside grew nearer and nearer. When her hands reached Chelsea's belly, she felt something warm and sticky and wet.

Her first instinct was to draw away. She didn't want to touch it. Not this. Not Chelsea's blood.

But that moment passed quickly, and then Violet was screaming as she heard the commotion below her, just outside the window. *"Help! We need help in here!"*

She pressed her hands as hard as she could to the wound, it was all she could remember from the abbreviated first aid course they'd had in PE. She thought that maybe she should do something more, but she didn't know what that something might be.

And then Chelsea went still beneath her.

Not the kind of still that happens when someone falls asleep, when you continue to feel their breaths, when you know that their blood is coursing within them.

No, this was a different kind of still. The kind that Violet had only seen in death.

The final kind of still.

She heard footsteps that seemed too far away. Voices that were disjointed and sounded nonsensical to her ears.

Nothing made sense. Nothing was real.

Hands pulled her off Chelsea and she struggled against them, fighting to stay with her, fighting to remain at her friend's side so she could save her. So she could protect her. To stop whatever was happening.

But when she first saw the smoke coming up from Chelsea, from her friend's hair, her skin, her mouth, as insubstantial and wraithlike as the air itself, she realized . . . she knew . . .

She was too late.

Heat . . . smoke . . .

This was Chelsea's echo.

CHAPTER 1

Almost Three Weeks Earlier

VIOLET AMBROSE COVERED HER HEAD WITH
her pillow and punched it, trying to drive her fist through
her ears—through her own skull if necessary—in hopes of
silencing the constant music-box sound that followed her.
Everywhere. Even into the depths of sleep.

It haunted her dreams and preoccupied her thoughts,
taking up every spare iota of space in her brain. And then
some.

Violet had never worried about the echoes of the dead
before. She'd never spent much time wondering why a

certain body carried the sensation that it did—the bold tastes, the intricate colors, the intense smells. She'd just accepted them for what they were. They were simply part and parcel of those who were taken away from this world too soon. She understood that those who were killed carried an echo, and that whoever was responsible for their deaths would carry his or her own matching imprint. End of story.

Except that now, Violet had her own imprint. And it was all she could think about. It was like she had become trapped in her own personal hell.

Because now she was a killer too. And in becoming a killer, she was now encumbered with a burden almost too great to bear.

Violet hated the song that echoed around, and above, her. Hated this particular echo of the dead like she'd never hated any other before.

Not because it wasn't beautiful or melodious or catchy. But because it was unending. A constant reminder of what she'd done.

You're a killer . . .

You're a killer . . .

You're a killer . . .

It never stopped.

She reached for her iPod and cranked up the volume until she was certain that everyone in the house could hear the music that erupted from the earbuds. She cringed against the metallic grate that meant she'd already turned it up way too high, and that the tiny internal speakers were threatening to blow. Only then did she press the button, letting the music fade . . . but only slightly.

She wanted to sleep. Wanted it so badly that her eyes burned and her head throbbed. But she knew it wasn't coming . . . not easily. Not this night.

There was a way though. Not one she liked, or even wanted to give in to. But there was a way.

Throwing back her covers, Violet jerked clumsily, getting out of bed and crossing her room. She kept her headphones on as she grabbed her purse from the dresser and dropped back onto her bed. Like the imprint, the purse was new, as was her cell phone and the alarm system for their house, all reminders of what had happened to her. She squeezed the stiff canvas between her fingers as she peeled the top wide, peeking inside.

It was in there—the bottle—and she reached for it tentatively.

Inside the brown plastic container, she could see one last pill, and she opened the top, letting the chalky capsule drop into her palm. Letting the weight of it sink in.

She hated how badly she needed it. And she hated that there was only this one remaining.

It meant she'd have to ask Dr. Lee for more.

The very thought made her shudder. It didn't matter to Violet that she'd been forced to see him on a weekly basis. During those visits she did her best to ask for nothing, and she offered less. She sat stiffly in his office, answering his questions as basically as was humanly possible.

He'd backed her into a corner by making it more than clear that her resignation from the team had been denied.

Not typical psychiatrist behavior, Violet thought—not that she'd had a lot of experience with psychiatrists—but she could only assume that they normally didn't threaten bodily harm to their patients' families.

At first she hadn't trusted any of them. Not Sara or Rafe, or even Krystal, Sam, or Gemma. She blamed them all . . . for everything. For Caine. For Dr. Lee.

For the nightmares and the imprint that kept her awake night after night.

That didn't last long, though, because she knew it wasn't their fault. Caine hadn't found her because of them. He'd found her because of her . . . because of what *she* could do. She'd wanted to be useful then, wanted to help stop killers like Caine.

And if she was being honest, she *still* wanted that. She just didn't want to be told she had no choice in the matter. But that wasn't her team's fault . . . at least not Rafe and the others. Sara, she still didn't know about, not really. She couldn't imagine a world in which Sara would force something like that on her.

Not the Sara she knew. Not the Sara who'd saved Violet's life, and now bore a frigid imprint of her own to prove it.

So for now, she blamed Dr. Lee. She kept her appointments with him, and she took the pills he offered her, but she gave him nothing in return. She hoped that maybe, just maybe, he'd grow bored by her insipidness, tired of hearing the tedium of her day-to-day life.

Maybe he'd become irritated with her and finally reveal his true intentions.

She knew it was foolish to hope for such simplistic solutions, but she couldn't stop herself from thinking that way. She hated that by taking this pill Dr. Lee would somehow know she needed him.

But the sad truth was, she *did* need him. The pills were the only things that seemed to help these days. The only way she could shut off the interminable imprint so she could sleep.

Check that, so she could drift into a comalike state—sensing, tasting, smelling, and hearing nothing at all.

It was bliss. Pure, unadulterated, drug-induced bliss.

She threw the pill into her mouth and swallowed, savoring the chalky feel against the back of her tongue. Relishing that soon—very, very soon—she'd feel nothing at all.

Even if it was only temporary.

Even if it meant going back to Dr. Lee for more.

"You excited about tomorrow? First day of school."

Violet pulled a clean mug out of the dishwasher and scowled at her mom's enthusiasm. "Seriously, Mom, take it down a notch. What's gotten into you, anyway? Shouldn't you still be in bed?" She frowned at the window, wishing the shades were still drawn against the glare of the morning sun.

Maggie Ambrose's expression shifted, contorting into a

mask of compassion. "I heard you last night. How late were you up?" She took a step closer, and Violet realized for the first time that her mom was already dressed, already wearing her paint-smeared smock, her hair pulled back in a messy bun. The only thing missing was a beret, perched just so, to complete the look of a picture-perfect artist.

"Are you going somewhere?"

Her mom's mouth twisted. "Stop deflecting and answer my question. Is it the imprint, Vi? Is it keeping you up?"

Wincing, Violet shook her head a little too quickly, pretending she couldn't hear the eerie plinking of the music box all around her. "Of course not." She hated that she was so transparent, and wished her parents would stop looking at her like that . . . like she was somehow broken. "It's . . . school. I'm just excited about school."

Her mom laughed, but there was no mistaking the sarcasm in her voice. "Yeah, right. You and school, you're like this." She held her fingers up, crossing them tightly together. But she didn't push the matter, even though that worried expression returned as she changed the subject. "I was thinking about taking a little field trip into the mountains, to see if I can find some *inspiration* up there. Maybe you should come with me," her mom suggested, watching as Violet's hand shot up to cover her eyes against the sunlight pouring in through the kitchen window. "The fresh air might do you some good."

Violet didn't doubt it, not that she thought a little fresh air could cure what ailed her. But she knew how she must look, standing there in the kitchen wearing her rumpled pajamas, her hair unbrushed in a tangled halo around her head. The pills had worked, maybe a little too well, because now Violet felt as if she were squinting out through a dense fog that clung to her—following her like a second skin and trying to dampen her mood.

She glanced down, scowling at the empty mug in her hand, suddenly remembering what she'd been planning to do with it when her mom had sidetracked her. She turned to the coffeemaker, thinking, *Caffeine. I just need caffeine to clear my head,* as she grumbled, "No thanks. I have stuff to do today."

"Like getting ready for school?" her mom inquired, still sounding skeptical.

"No, Mom, like stuff. Just stuff."

Her mom made a sound that might have been meant as a laugh, but by the time it reached her lips it came out sounding more like a strangled sigh instead. "Suit yourself, Vi. But I'm not wasting another minute of this glorious day." Violet watched as her mom gathered up her heavy canvas bag that was overflowing with brushes and charcoals, a sketchbook, and a small stretched canvas, as if she hadn't yet decided whether she'd be drawing or painting today. She wondered if there was clay in there too, in case the urge to sculpt struck her while she was on this little *field trip* of hers.

"Have fun with that," Violet quipped sullenly.

Pausing at the door, her mom met her gaze. "I can stay if you want me to. . . ."

11

Violet lifted her hand in a half wave, a puny effort to appease her mom since it wasn't her fault that Violet's head pounded or that she'd used up the last of her pills. "I'm fine. Go . . . enjoy your fresh air."

Violet leaned back and ran her hands over the top of the cool grass beneath her as she stared out at the chicken wire that ran around a small patch of earth in her backyard. Shady Acres. Such a strange name, she thought, considering that she and Jay had been kids when they'd come up with it. She couldn't remember why they'd decided to call it that in the first place, what exactly had inspired the cryptic name, but she remembered that when she'd heard it—whichever of them, she or Jay, had said it first—she'd known it was perfect. That it fit.

It was a good name for an animal graveyard.

It didn't look like much, really. Just a mismatched collection of sticks and rocks and clumps of dirt—some with grass growing over them, and some not—in long, irregular rows. All surrounded by the chicken wire her dad had helped her construct to keep the live animals outside from digging up the dead ones inside. To anyone else it was a mess, the remains of what might have once been a garden or a compost pile or just a dead patch of lawn.

Violet could remember a time, when she was in the sixth or seventh grade, when she'd worried that one of her friends—Chelsea or Jules or Claire—might figure out what it really was, that they might discover her darkest secret. She'd been so bothered by the idea, so tortured by the thought, that she'd saved her allowance to buy seed packets from the store and she'd carefully mounted them on old Popsicle sticks, setting them up in perfect lines in the graveyard, making it look like it was a garden. Making it look like something might actually spring up from the ground at any minute.

Like it was a place of life, rather than of death.

She probably shouldn't have worried; none of her friends had ever mentioned the place in her yard with the chicken-wire fence. None of them had ever seemed to notice its existence, except for Jay.

This had always been *her* place. Even now, sitting here and listening to it . . . *feeling* its staticky echoes reach for her, enfolding her, she felt at peace. She could almost forget she had an imprint of her own. As if those animals in there were offering her a brief moment of amnesty, repaying her kindness for giving them the peace they craved by covering her imprint.

Almost . . .

"Remember when you told your parents you wanted to be buried in there?" Jay's voice interrupted her thoughts, and a small smile tugged at her lips.

"I remember my dad spent like three hours explaining why I had to be buried in a *real* graveyard," she said, doing her best to mimic her dad's pragmatic tone. "And why 'proper channels' had to be followed when someone died. He told me that people can't just be buried in their own backyards. He even explained what embalming was, which totally grossed me out. I mean, I couldn't have been more than seven or eight, I think.

"And then my mom came home and I told her my idea about being buried in the backyard, and I think she said something like, 'What a lovely idea, Vi. Then you could be with your animals forever.'" Violet giggled. "My poor dad. I thought he was gonna lose it for sure. Sometimes I wonder how him and my mom ever hooked up in the first place."

Jay sat down in the grass next to her, their shoulders brushing. "And then you told *me* about '*em-bombing*.' Remember?" He raised his eyebrows when he said the word the way Violet had said it to him all those years ago. "You told me all about how they stick hoses inside your body and drain out all the blood, and then fill you back up with chemicals that keep your body from rotting. I think you actually said the word *rotting* too. And we made a pact that we didn't want anything to do with it. That *we* wanted to be cremated so we could have our ashes spread over the playground at school."

She burst out laughing then, leaning closer. "I wonder what the principal would have said about that. Can you imagine the other kids brushing our ashes off the swings?" She bumped her shoulder playfully against his. "We were kinda morbid when we were little, weren't we?"

"Better than being zombified forever in the ground, I guess." He grinned down at her, and Violet's mouth went dry. Even when he was saying things like "zombified" he could make her stomach do flips with just a simple glance. He

14

changed the subject then. "Are you excited about tomorrow?"

Violet's gaze narrowed, but she wasn't really upset with him. "Why does everyone keep asking me that?"

He shrugged, leaning closer, and she could feel his eyes settling on her lips, making them tingle in anticipation. "Because we'll be seniors tomorrow. Because it's our last year of high school. Aren't we supposed to be excited?"

"I suppose," she said, not really caring about the words coming from her mouth. She inhaled his breath, which was even with hers.

"But you're not?"

She studied his eyes, the flecks of gold and green and brown, pieced together like intricate bits of cut glass in a mosaic. She looked at his lashes, too long and thick for a boy's. And at his pupils, which grew larger as she drew nearer. "I didn't say that." Then she smiled. "But, no. Not really, I guess."

"Is that why you aren't at Claire's for the big back-to-school barbeque? I hear everyone who's anyone is there." His tone was mocking, but he wore the same concerned expression she'd seen on her mother's face just that morning.

Like she was broken.

"I'm okay, Jay. I promise."

He reached up and traced his thumb along one of the bruise-colored circles beneath her eyes. "The imprint?" he asked.

She nodded, but all she could think about was the feel of his touch.

15

"Have you slept at all?" His voice was lower, his mouth closer now.

Again, she nodded.

His hand cupped her cheek, cradling it. "They miss you, you know?" He didn't have to say who . . . she knew he meant Chelsea and Claire and Jules. It had been a long, strange summer as she'd tried to adjust to this new life of hers—the one that was never silent.

"I miss them too," she admitted. "I just . . ." She faltered, trying to come up with the right words and thinking it might be easier if Jay wasn't so close. If she wasn't staring into his beautiful eyes and breathing his tempting breath. "They act like, I don't know, like everything's the same as it's always been, but I feel like a stranger now. And whenever I'm with them, I feel like a liar too. They know I was abducted, but I can't tell them why. And every time Chelsea asks where I've been, and who I'm with, I have to make up some excuse so she doesn't know I've been at the Center. It's like I'm living two different lives." She nestled her face into the curve of his hand. "I don't know who to be."

His mouth quirked up into a sideways grin, and he reached for her, pulling her against him, and she could feel him shaking his head against the top of hers. "You're insane, you know that?" But his words were anything but critical. He drew back, watching her with the same amusement she'd heard in his voice. "You don't have to *be* anyone, Vi. Just you. They miss *you*."

She smiled back at him. He was right, of course . . . he

16

always was. And when he said it like that, so simply, it made perfect sense. Who was she kidding? Things had happened to her, things that had changed her to some degree—she'd be lying if she said she'd come out of the abduction unscathed. And it wasn't just the imprint that haunted her. But that didn't mean she wasn't the same girl she'd always been, did it?

Hadn't her friends tried to convince her of that very thing when they'd shown up at her house day after day? Hadn't they called and texted and cajoled her to come out with them, even after she'd turned them down time and time again?

Wasn't it Chelsea who'd finally worn her down by showing up every morning for a week, until Violet had had no choice but to agree to go to the lake with them?

And she'd had fun. She'd felt like her old self again, even if it was only for a day.

"We can still make it to Claire's if you want."

She shook her head.

"What would you rather be doing then?" he asked, his voice low and filled with meaning.

"If you have to ask . . ." Violet's words trailed away.

Jay's lips were on hers then. And that tingling of anticipation shot through her entire body, filling her with currents of pleasure that made her toes curl. She leaned into him, not thinking that her parents could look out the window any minute, or that they were kissing in front of a graveyard filled with dead animals, or that she should be getting ready for the first day of her senior year.

She thought of nothing but Jay. Nothing but his lips on her lips.

Nothing but the fact that everything was better when they were alone.

THE ROAD TO HELL

HIS FINGERS ACHED, AND HIS ENTIRE BODY WAS drenched with sweat, soaking his shirt all the way through. He was unable to stand still so he paced across the length of the stage, and then back again, clutching his guitar as he waited for the others to finish talking.

About him. To decide his fate once and for all. But it didn't matter, he knew he'd nailed it.

This time he was sure he'd nailed it.

Every once in a while he'd feel the weight of their eyes on him, scouring him in that appraising way that made him hyperaware he was under the most intense kind of scrutiny, and he'd stop, wondering if this was the time they'd tell him he was in.

This was the third time he was auditioning for them. His third time to stand on this stage, or one like it, and lay his soul bare as he played for them.

He knew what was holding them back, why they hadn't chosen him before. They were afraid, worried he would outshine them all. And they were right, he would. So this time he'd played it down a little. This time he'd played a little more clumsily, and he'd pulled back on his obvious charm, giving them just enough reason to think he wouldn't steal their spotlight.

Sure, they'd taken on other guys in the meantime—other guitarists, during those other two auditions—but they'd never lasted.

The first guy had been a bad fit, almost from the get-go, and there were rumors in the venues they played in of backstage bickering and out-of-control egos. One night, a fistfight had broken out onstage between the new guy and the bass player. It was unprofessional, but had made for a great show. He'd been there in the audience, watching every second of the brawl.

He'd never seen that guy again. That had been his last night with the band.

So they'd held auditions again. And again he'd been turned away, only to have the spot he so desperately craved filled by someone else.

And that guy had been a good match for the band, fitting in seamlessly. And, man, oh man, could he shred.

As much as he hated to admit it, the new guy had kicked ass up there, with the lights flashing and the girls screaming and the rest of the band at his back.

Only problem was, that was where he should've been standing.

That was his glory being stolen.

And this guy didn't seem to be going anywhere.

He'd had to force the situation.

Dude never even saw it coming. Never saw him coming . . . until it was too late.

Rumors flew after the new guy up and vanished. No one knew where he'd gone to. As far as they knew, he'd just left one night after a show and never come back. Maybe he'd gotten a better offer. Maybe he'd OD'd in a ditch somewhere.

Or maybe . . . just maybe he'd been stabbed thirty-three times and bled out in a storm drain in the middle of nowhere. Maybe the guy had screamed and cried, begging to be spared.

Maybe his body had never been discovered.

A sly smile touched his lips. And so what if it was? There was nothing to tie it back to him anyway. Nothing to make anyone think he might be the one responsible. He didn't know the guy, other than he'd been in the band—something he and about a thousand other people knew. Besides, he'd tossed the knife and his clothes. No one could ever link him to the body.

So here he was again, one hand resting on his axe, the other in his mouth as he chewed nervously at his ragged fingernail.

They had to choose him. They just had to.

This was his time.

This was his stage.

When they called his name he almost didn't realize they were talking to him at first. He blinked when he heard it again, louder this time.

"Yeah, yeah . . ." he said, dropping his hands and stepping

forward, back into the glare of the spotlight.

There was no postulating this time, no awkward explanations or excuses. He knew their answer when he caught that one simple phrase coming up from below him. "Dude, I'm sorry."

The words hit him hard, like someone had just bashed a hammer through the side of his skull.

For a moment he just stood there, not sure what to say or do. He was stunned, he'd been so sure this time, convinced that all his practice would pay off. His fingertips were still raw.

"Did ya hear me?" There was a soft round of laughter, and he wanted to tell them all where they could go.

They were the ones he'd followed from place to place to place. Their songs were the songs he'd memorized, note for note, and played over and over and over again.

They were his idols. There must be some mistake.

"What? But . . . why?"

The wooden chairs banged against the hollow wooden floor. "Man, I'm sorry. I hate to be so blunt, but you're just not good enough."

And then he heard another voice, not directed at him, filled with hostility, or maybe it was disgust. "Dude, he's just standing there."

He turned away then, unable to listen as their laughter reached up onto the stage and circled him. It ringed around him like the voices of schoolchildren, taunting and pointing and laughing some more.

He wasn't good enough.

He'd heard that before. From his father.

Rage burned the backs of his eyes, blinding him and making his shoulders shake all the way down to his fingertips. He didn't even realize what he was doing until he felt the heavy weight of the amp leaving his hands, as he hurled it off the stage and toward the place they were sitting.

From somewhere—above him or behind, or maybe from inside his own head—there was a loud electric popping sound, as the cord came tearing free from the wall and then the amp went silent, right before it crashed down on the table where they'd just been sitting.

Suddenly, all eyes were on him again, as he stood there above them, on the stage where he belonged.

He towered over them, still quaking. Still seething.

"It's a mistake," he finally muttered, his teeth gritted together. "You're making the biggest fucking mistake."

And then he shoved his way through the door at the back of the stage, before they had the chance to reconsider and beg him to stay.

Because he wouldn't give them a fourth chance.

CHAPTER 2

THE FIRST DAY OF SCHOOL HAD THAT TYPICAL chaotic, first-day feel. Like the inmates were running the asylum.

Keeping her headphones on, Violet bobbed and weaved her way through the pandemonium as best she could. She watched—rather than listened—as girls checked out what other girls were wearing, as boys checked out the incoming freshman girls, and as everyone compared their class schedules with everyone else's.

She managed to slip through the swarms of students relatively easily, avoiding fashion appraisals and obnoxious, overzealous greetings by kids who'd been going to school together since kindergarten but were now acting as if they hadn't seen each other in decades.

It was only school, Violet thought, feeling more irritable than she should on the first day of her senior year. But she just didn't get what all the fuss was about. She was probably just tired, she told herself. The pills might make her groggy, but without them the imprint made it nearly impossible to find deep sleep, leaving her with an ache in her head and a sting behind her eyes.

And, still, there was that tinkling echo that followed her everywhere.

Some of her irritability lifted when she saw Jay, waiting for her outside the door of her first-period class.

"Hey," he said, shoving away from the wall to meet her in the hallway.

She tugged one of the earbuds from her ear and let it dangle free. "Hey yourself." She smiled up at him, ignoring the headache—and the music-box chiming. "How'd you know what my first class was?"

The corner of his lip lifted. "I have my ways."

Violet shook her head. "It was Mrs. Jeffries, wasn't it?" she prompted, but didn't wait for his response. She knew Jay could get whatever he wanted out of the ladies in the front office. "You know she has a crush on you, don't you?"

"Gross, Vi. She's like my grandma's age."

Violet leaned in closer and nudged him with her elbow. "Doesn't stop her from flirting with you. And the sickest part is, I think you kinda like it. I think you encourage her

25

so you can find out things like . . ." She pursed her lips, watching him through appraising eyes. "Things like my class schedule. Any of this ringing a bell?"

He threw his arm around her shoulder, and everything inside her unwound as she leaned into him, letting him share a burden he didn't even realize was weighing on her.

She saw Chelsea then, shoving her way through a cluster of students who had gathered in the hallway, passing their schedules around to one another. One of the girls flashed Chelsea a dirty look as Chelsea elbowed past her, bumping the girl with her backpack. But Chelsea was oblivious to the girl's glare, and Violet wondered if she'd even realized the other kids were standing there at all.

"Oh my god, Vi! I've been texting you all morning. Don't you ever check your phone? What the eff?"

Despite her worries about being back in school, Violet couldn't help smiling at her friend's bulging eyes and breathless frustration. Some things never changed.

Violet reached into her pocket, digging for her phone, but Chelsea stopped her. "It's too late now. I just wanna know why you didn't tell me sooner," Chelsea reprimanded, her eyes level with Violet's as she gripped her arm. She leaned in close, ignoring the fact that Jay was right there. "How come you didn't say anything about your hottie friend comin' to White River."

Violet frowned at her friend. "I have no idea what you're talking about, Chels." She pulled her arm away and glanced up to see if Jay knew what Chelsea was rambling on about.

But he looked as perplexed as she was.

"Dude, whatever . . ." Chelsea's voice trailed off as her gaze shifted past Violet, to the hallway beyond. Her mouth curved, a sly, knowing smile parting her lips. "Are you trying to tell me you didn't know *he* was transferring here?" she muttered, and Violet realized Chelsea had spotted whoever it was she'd been talking about. Violet turned to look behind her. "You know, the brother of that lady who works with your uncle. The one you never want to introduce me to." She grinned knowingly. "I can totally see why, though. *Yum.*"

Violet was about to say that Chelsea was wrong, that she didn't know anything about a new kid in school, when her breath caught in her throat. She saw, then, who Chelsea was talking about. The "hottie" in question stood out like a sore thumb in his worn blue jeans and black leather jacket, especially amid the sea of freshly purchased mall clothes, some of which probably still had the tags on them, tucked conveniently inside the collars and waistbands.

"Jesus," Violet heard Jay breathe beside her, and she felt his arm stiffen around her neck as they watched Rafe approach. "You're kidding me, right? What the hell is he doing here? Tell me you didn't know about this."

"I—I didn't know about this," Violet tried to say, but she was sure that no sound had actually escaped her lips, that her words had gotten stuck, lodged against the stone blocking her throat. Because that was when she recognized who Rafe was with, the flawless blonde girl walking beside him.

It was Gemma—looking as out of place as Rafe did, but in an entirely different way. Even from the front, Violet knew the other girl's jeans were designer, and cost more than Violet's entire wardrobe. The heels on her boots were at least five inches tall, yet she walked as if she were wearing flats. Effortlessly. Gracefully. Her trendy bag was too big to be a purse, and Violet's throat tightened even more when she realized it was meant to carry books.

Rafe and Gemma stopped right in front of Violet and Chelsea and Jay. Violet was still speechless, unable to push her voice past the clog in her throat.

Chelsea had no such dilemma. "*Sooo . . .*" she said, looking from Violet to Rafe and back again. "This is sorta awkward." But there was nothing in her tone to indicate she was the slightest bit uncomfortable. She wrinkled her nose. "Well, since Violet seems a little . . . tongue-tied, let me be the first to welcome you. I'm Chelsea." She held out her hand, her grin extending to Rafe—and only Rafe—as if Gemma weren't standing there at all.

He cast an uncertain glance down at her hand, which wasn't held out for a handshake, but was palm up instead. Rafe turned to Violet, frowning.

Chelsea's brows rose impatiently. "Your phone," she explained, extending her hand even farther as she waited for him to hand it over.

An amused expression crossed his face, but he reached into his back pocket and dropped his cell phone into her awaiting hand. Her fingers moved quickly as she unlocked the screen and opened his Contacts list, deftly adding her name and number before handing it back to him with a satisfied grin. "There. That's better," she stated, as if he'd *asked* for her phone number. "Now I just need to know your name and we'll be all set."

"Rafe," he answered, a sly grin finding its way back to Chelsea, and something uneasy settled in the pit of Violet's stomach. The last thing she'd wanted was for these two worlds to collide, she thought, as she stood there in the hallway of her school and watched that very thing happening.

"So, Rafe," Chelsea drawled, making his name sound practically pornographic coming from her lips. "What made you decide to come to White River High?"

"He's not," Violet finally managed to choke out, but she wasn't really talking to Chelsea. She was glaring at Rafe now, her gaze intense and unwavering. "You can't just drop in and wander the halls of my school whenever you feel like it, Rafe. There are rules. You have to check in at the office first. You have to show ID and get a visitor's pass."

But Rafe just stood there, grinning back at her. It was Gemma, her eyes locked solely on Jay, who responded to Violet. "Mmm, actually, we can," she countered, raising her perfectly tweezed brows. "Your little friend's right. We're students here now. We can come and go as we please." She puckered her lush red lips as she shot a satisfied smirk in Violet's direction.

Fire crackled through Violet's veins as she scowled at the other girl, and then at Rafe, trying to decide who she was angrier at: Gemma for being such an ice princess, or Rafe for just standing there pretending to look utterly innocent in the matter. Violet knew better—Rafe was anything but innocent.

"And you are . . . ?" Chelsea cocked her head, appraising Gemma, in the same way a snake might appraise a baby mouse. "His sister?"

Gemma's lips curled and she glanced at Rafe, his black hair almost as far from her pale blonde as was possible. "Yeah," she agreed abrasively. "Something like that."

Violet looked at the two of them and wondered if there was a person alive who would buy that they shared a single strand of DNA. Chelsea appraised them suspiciously.

At the moment, though, Violet couldn't care less about that. "What is she talking about?" she demanded, ignoring both Chelsea and Gemma as she turned to glare at Rafe. "Why are you here . . . *really*?"

Rafe just shrugged, and Violet felt her blood simmer. "Gemma's right," he admitted, and then he pulled out a rumpled class schedule from his pocket and held it up, as if confirming Gemma's statement. "We're students. This is *our* first day too."

Violet grabbed his schedule and looked it over. She felt her stomach drop when she recognized four of the six classes. They were identical to hers. How the heck did Rafe—Rafe who Violet was pretty sure hadn't even *attended* school last year—get into AP Lit?

"Is this some kinda joke?" Jay asked, and Violet wondered

if he'd noticed the same thing she had—the similarities between the class schedules—or if he was just referring to the fact that Gemma and Rafe were actually planning to attend White River High.

Gemma looked dejected as she held out her schedule, not rumpled at all, toward Jay. "Look, we have classes together too," she said in a voice that Violet had never heard her use before. A soft voice. Almost a *nice* voice. She pouted, and Violet couldn't tell if it was calculated or genuine. "I thought you'd be happier to see us."

Jay hesitated, probably as taken aback by the switch he'd seen in her as Violet was—although probably not nearly as suspicious of it. And then his brows creased. "How did you know we had classes together?" he asked.

Gemma plucked the slip of paper from his fingers and tucked it into the pocket of her shiny patent leather book bag. She did a complete 180 then, her disposition changing from dejected to aloof in a matter of seconds. "You have your ways, I have mine." And then she wriggled her fingers at them in a wave that showed off her nails, which were flawless and glossy and as perfectly manicured as everything else about her. "I wouldn't want to be late on my first day!" she exclaimed before strutting away on her too-high-for-high-school heels, looking as if she were walking a Paris runway. Every male head in the hallway except for Rafe's and Jay's turned to watch her go. They were too busy having a good old-fashioned stare-down to notice anyone else.

"I hate her," Chelsea declared solemnly, and somehow

Violet managed to stop herself before she could agree.

Mostly because she didn't hate Gemma, even though she wanted to in that moment. But that didn't mean she didn't have every intention of finding out what she and Rafe were up to. Why they were suddenly enrolled at her high school.

"Come on, V. We should probably get going too." It was Rafe now, looking at her with smug confidence as he tapped his watch.

Violet's jaw clenched. "I'll be right there," she ground out, emphasizing each word, enunciating every syllable.

He shrugged once more and she watched as he sauntered through the classroom door, throwing the strap of his backpack carelessly over his shoulder.

Jay waited until he was gone and then he looked down at her. "You didn't know, did you?"

"I swear I didn't," Violet assured him, shaking her head. "Of course I didn't."

Inside the classroom, everyone had already taken a seat. Above the music box that no one else could hear, whispers filled the room as Violet stepped through the doorway, crowding the air and replacing the first-day exuberance.

There was a new kid in school.

Without meaning to, she found herself seeking him out the moment she stepped inside. He wasn't hard to spot though. He sat by himself in the back of the classroom, and all eyes were either already on him or were intermittently darting in his direction. Beside him, there was an empty desk with a backpack perched upon its chair.

He was saving her a seat.

Self-consciously, Violet searched for another opening before realizing that the one next to Rafe was the only one left. She'd lingered for too long in the hallway.

Rafe didn't seem to care that he'd managed to trap her, and that she had no other choice but to sit beside him. He only grinned when she rolled her eyes as she reluctantly made her way down the aisle toward him, listening to the barrage of whispered comments as she passed.

". . . did you see his hot sister . . ."

". . . different last names . . . must be adopted . . ."

". . . heard he was in juvie . . ."

". . . does Violet Ambrose *know him* . . . ?"

Violet ignored them all, keeping her gaze averted. She even managed to avoid looking at Rafe when she shoved his backpack onto the floor. It made a satisfying *thunk*, causing everyone in the class to turn and look at her as she took her seat. But instead of giving them the satisfaction of a response, she trained her eyes on the whiteboard at the front of the room, wishing their teacher, Mr. LeCompte, would stop dawdling in the staff lounge and get here already.

Mr. LeCompte was notorious for being late, she remembered that much from taking American Lit with him the previous year. But today, of all days, Violet wanted nothing more than for class to get started already.

She felt something tap against her elbow and saw Rafe from the corner of her eye, stretched all the way across the aisle, as he held something out to her. She jerked her arm away from him, and concentrated even harder on *not* looking at him.

"Psst." She heard it, almost unnoticeably at first. And then louder, so that everyone in the rows ahead of them could hear it too. *"Psst!"*

She turned then, concentrating on glaring daggers at him now. *"What!"* she whispered back.

He held out a piece of folded paper in her direction.

Her stern expression cracked as she bit back a smile. *Was he actually passing her a note in class?*

Swallowing her amusement so it wouldn't show, she snatched the paper from his hand and slipped it beneath her desk just as Mr. LeCompte wandered into the classroom.

"Happy first day of school, class, and welcome to AP Literature." The way he said "literature" made it sound distinctly like he had a British accent, despite the fact that everyone knew he'd only spent one year abroad during a teacher-exchange program. He dropped his crumbling leather satchel on his desk as he walked to the whiteboard to write his name with red dry erase marker. Below that he started itemizing their first-quarter reading list.

Violet glanced as surreptitiously as she could at Rafe when she realized that she'd seen those same books on the shelves in his bedroom. She remembered them all, *Catcher in the Rye, Heart of Darkness, The Handmaid's Tale.* His confident grin confirmed that he thought this class would be a piece of cake.

She, on the other hand, had only read one of the books on the list, *Lord of the Flies*, and that had been back in the eighth grade, so she probably wouldn't get away with skipping it this quarter.

Ignoring her impending workload, she unfolded the note hidden in her hand.

Don't be mad, was all it said in his blocky, boy handwriting.

Violet glanced over at Rafe, her head cocked challengingly. Why shouldn't she be mad at him? He should've at least called to warn her that he and Gemma were going to be there today. She deserved that much, didn't she?

She crumpled the note into a tight ball and shoved it into her backpack, which was on the floor by her feet.

Rafe shifted toward her, hanging from the side of his desk as he leaned all the way across the aisle. "Don't be like that," he insisted quietly. "It's not my fault, V."

She grimaced. "Stop calling me that."

"What? *V*?" Now he was the one who was confused.

"Fine. Whatever." He shrugged. "Then stop acting like I did something wrong."

"Ms. Ambrose? Mr. . . . ?" Mr. LeCompte interrupted them, and she could hear the warning in his fake-British drawl.

Rafe's eyes darted forward, but he didn't sit up. He stayed where he was, stretched across the aisle, practically sitting in Violet's desk. "Priest," Rafe answered. "Rafe Priest."

"*Mr. Priest*," Mr. LeCompte continued. "Since you two

have already started getting to know each other, you can go first." Violet felt her cheeks growing warm as she realized she had no idea what their teacher was talking about. Then, to the entire class, he explained, "Everyone will pair up, and you'll have five minutes to get to know your partner. After your five minutes is up, you'll each take turns introducing your partner to the rest of us."

There was a collective moan, and Violet sagged into her chair, not in the mood for this little getting-to-know-you exercise. But Rafe didn't seem nearly as reluctant as she was, and he dragged his desk closer, making Violet cringe against the screeching sound the legs made across the industrial tile flooring.

"Okay . . . go," Rafe said eagerly, watching her expectantly.

"Go? *Go what?*"

"Go . . . start telling me about yourself."

She half smiled. "How about *you* tell me what you meant when you said it wasn't your fault that you're here? Whose fault is it then? What the hell are you doing at White River, Rafe?"

He grinned back at her, a stupid grin. One that made her wonder what really went on inside that head of his. "Fine. Be that way, V, but this is gonna make for one awkward introduction. Consider yourself warned."

"You already know pretty much everything there is to know about me. Now stop avoiding my questions." She settled her chin against her palm, trying to look perky rather than peeved as she waited for him to get on with it.

He leaned closer, coming over the top of the wood laminate desk, so that she found herself staring directly into his deep blue eyes. She told herself not to be unnerved. It wasn't the first time she'd been this close to him. He was just trying to throw her, she was sure of it. His lips parted and her gaze shot down to watch them, her heart speeding up. "Sara," he said.

"Sara?" she asked. "Sara what?"

He let out a low chuckle, and she knew he was laughing at her but couldn't manage to be annoyed by it. "You asked whose fault it was. It was Sara's. She's the one who asked us to enroll this semester."

Violet frowned, trying to make sense of what he was telling her. "Why would she do that?"

His hand crossed the space then, settling over hers, and like so many times before, there was a sudden surge of warmth, like a microexplosion, from his skin to hers. Achingly familiar, yet disquieting at the same time. Like the music-box imprint that followed her. "She was worried about you, and she doesn't like the idea of us going to school in the city with metal detectors at the doors." He grinned then. "Plus, I think she's hoping some of your small-town charm will rub off on us."

Violet drew away, but not far enough, and their fingers still touched. "I'm fine. I've already told you that. All of you." She didn't know if he could tell she was lying. Honestly, she didn't even know *if* she was lying. She *was* fine, she supposed, as fine as she could be considering everything that had happened.

"Is that why you barely come to the Center?" He stared at her, unblinking as he studied her. "Is that why you avoid my phone calls?"

Violet glanced away. "I answer."

"Sometimes," he said, but there was a wistfulness to his voice now. "I get the feeling you wish I'd leave you alone though."

She swallowed, not sure what to say to that.

"I can't, V. And Sara's not the only one worried."

Her eyes shot back up to his, and she wondered if Gemma's empathic gift was wearing off on her, because she swore she could feel everything Rafe was feeling in that moment. Restlessness and fear and concern, all frenzied and tangled together like wings trying to beat their way out of his chest.

Or maybe those were her feelings.

"I—I'm telling you the truth. I'm better. I'm . . . *stronger* now."

Rafe just watched her, and then he shrugged. "Well, it wasn't up to us anyway. And we're not leaving, so you might as well get used to it."

Violet heard someone clear their throat, and she looked up to find Mr. LeCompte looming above them. She glanced nervously down at their hands, realizing that their fingertips were still pressed lightly together. She squeezed hers into a fist.

"You're up, you two," Mr. LeCompte said, and then

turned on his heel and left them sitting there, staring after him.

"Quick," Violet whispered. "Tell me where you were born."

Rafe got up, looking completely nonplussed by the panic in her huge green eyes. He bent down and whispered in her ear, "You were warned, V. This is about to get awkward." And then he grinned at her before following Mr. LeCompte to the front of the room.

"Hey, V! What's up?"

"Oh my god, will you please stop calling me that?" Violet complained to Chelsea as she dropped her lunch tray on the table with a crash.

Chelsea grinned back at her with absolutely zero remorse. "I think it's kinda precious. Besides, word on the street is you prefer it."

"Yeah, *V*," Jules chimed in, a similar unrepentant look on her face. "What I don't get is, why you never told us before. We're your friends—you can tell us anything."

"Can I tell you to shut your pieholes?"

"Uh-oh . . ." Chelsea mocked. "Someone's cranky."

"Maybe she's hungry. Her blood sugar's probably low," Claire offered. Jules and Chelsea started cracking up, while Claire just stared at them, trying to figure out what she'd missed.

"I'm *not* hungry," Violet retorted, just as she saw Jay coming toward her.

"Oh, snap! Check this out," Chelsea said conspiratorially, elbowing Jules. She pointed to Gemma and Rafe, who were also heading right toward them, drawing whispers and stares. "Jay doesn't like Rafe, but Rafe likes Violet—I mean, *V.* And the girl, the one who isn't really his sister—" She turned to Violet now, interrupting her narration. "Wait, what was her name again?"

"Gemma," Violet answered listlessly, giving up and letting her friends have their fun.

"Okay, yeah, Gemma. Gemma doesn't like Violet *or* Rafe as far as I can tell. She's kinda nasty, that one. But she *definitely* likes Jay, or at least I think she does. She was all over him in third period." Violet glanced up at them, suddenly more interested in Chelsea's running commentary than she wanted to be. Chelsea's voice dropped to an almost-whisper just as all three of the people she was discussing converged on the table at once. "This is about to get real."

They stood there, the three of them—Jay, Rafe, and Gemma—all looking down at the open spaces at the table as if deciding who would sit where. Violet reached for Jay's hand, making his decision for him as she pulled him down to sit beside her, scooting over to make room.

And then her mouth practically fell open when she realized that Gemma was actually trying to squeeze herself into the nonexistent space on the other side of him. Gemma smiled at the boy who sat on the long bench on the other side of her, batting her long lashes and puckering her lips, until he willingly made room for her. When he smiled back, he sheepishly revealed braces and could barely maintain eye contact with her. But he didn't seem to mind when she sandwiched herself between him and Jay. Why would he, Violet thought? Gemma was probably the hottest girl who'd ever pressed herself against him.

Violet, on the other hand, minded a great deal.

Rafe seemed oblivious as he rounded the table, to the other side, where Jules and Chelsea parted like the Red Sea to make a spot just for him.

Violet leaned forward on her elbows, hovering across the top as she narrowed her eyes on Rafe. "You realize everyone's calling me that now, don't you?"

"What? V? I thought you liked it."

She pursed her lips, counting silently to herself before responding. She didn't want to lose her temper. Not here, in front of everyone. "No, Rafe, you didn't. I told you I didn't, and you stood right up there in front of the entire class and told them it was my favorite nickname. And what was all that stuff about me playing the banjo?"

Claire stopped chewing long enough to ask, "So that's not true either? I thought that was kinda cool."

"You know we're probably getting an F, don't you?" Violet finished, ignoring Claire.

"An F . . . for introductions?" Rafe turned to Jay then, petitioning for an ally. "Come on, man. Help me out here. She's being a little dramatic, right?"

Violet glanced up at Jay and saw a flicker of something she recognized all too well, the hint of amusement. Her lips tightened as she locked eyes with him.

He raised his brows, holding up his hands in mock surrender. "Leave me out of this," he said to both of them, laughing just a little too easily. "I don't wanna get involved in your battles." And then he grinned at Violet, looking intentionally contrite. "That was the right thing to say, wasn't it?"

Across from them, Chelsea pretended to cough the word "whipped" while Gemma cupped her chin in her hands as she watched Jay and Violet with more interest than she should have. "Is she always this . . . controlling?"

Violet glared at Gemma, but it only made Gemma's lips bow upward. A smile that could pass for a sneer, depending on who it was directed at. And when she looked at Violet, it was definitely a sneer, no matter how pretty it was.

Inside, Violet felt her emotions churn at the prospect of spending even another hour, let alone a week or an entire semester, under the same roof as Gemma and Rafe on a daily basis. They were her teammates, sure, but they were also stirring up trouble in the part of her life she'd always considered her own. The one she tried to keep separate from the secrets of the team and her ability.

After stopping at the office to talk to the counselor about the possibility of changing some of her classes so she wouldn't have to spend the majority of her school day with Rafe, she reached the biology lab just after the bell sounded . . . which meant, on top of everything else, she was tardy.

It also meant there were only two seats still available by

the time she'd arrived. She was surprised to find that Gemma was in this class with her. She hadn't bothered to look at the other girl's schedule. In fact, it hadn't even crossed her mind they might actually share classes together.

The other thing that threw her off was that the seat next to Gemma was one of the two that remained vacant. Considering Gemma had been the star of the show today—at least where the boys were concerned—she would have expected to find them clamoring to sit beside her.

But when Violet glanced at the seat, she realized why it was still open. Gemma's designer book bag was already sitting there, and Gemma had already started unpacking her stuff and spreading out. It was clear she intended to take up more than her fair share of the lab table.

Gemma looked up as she opened the cover to her binder, which was an embossed alligator print that matched her book bag. Violet rolled her eyes and made her way toward the only other open seat in the lab.

But she faltered mid-step when she saw who was sitting in the spot beside it.

Grady Spencer.

Grady, who Violet had known since elementary school . . . who she'd played tag with on the playground and ridden bikes with and learned to skip rocks with at the lake.

He was all those things, and more. But he was also the same Grady Spencer who'd tried to kiss her last year . . . even after she told him she didn't want to be kissed. Even after she insisted he stop. He'd been aggressive and forceful, and had crammed his tongue inside her mouth. Even now the memory made her heart race and her palms sweat.

Seeing him there, she felt trapped.

Grady hadn't noticed her, as he dug through his backpack, his gaze down. But he would . . . any second now. And then he'd see the panic on her face, and he'd know that *he* was the one who'd caused it.

She wondered why she even cared what Grady thought. He *had* caused it. It was his fault she felt this way. His fault she stood frozen in the middle of the classroom, unable to take another step. Unable to even think.

Maybe he should know how she felt about him. How torn she was between the Grady he'd once been when they were kids . . . and the Grady who'd pawed at her, drunken and belligerent, refusing to believe she didn't want *him* the way he wanted *her*.

She looked around, sure that everyone must be watching her now. How could they not be? How could they not see the dread coming off her in anxious waves?

But they weren't. No one in the class even glanced her way.

Except for Gemma.

Gemma was watching her, her expression more intrigued than usual. Her lips taut and her eyes intensely curious.

And something else. Something *more* . . .

Violet wasn't sure what it was she saw there. If it had been anyone other than Gemma, she would've thought it was worry. But this was Gemma she was talking about.

Violet blinked, certain her imagination must be playing tricks on her. Certain it was merely the panic of facing Grady, distorting her perception and screwing with her mind.

But when she looked again, it was still there, the look. And this time she was convinced it had to be real.

And then Gemma did something else unexpected. Violet watched in disbelief as the other girl reached over and removed her book bag from the chair. After a moment, probably only the span of a breath really, when Violet didn't react, Gemma lifted her eyebrows and nodded toward the empty chair beside her.

And Violet knew: Gemma was telling her to sit in the open spot.

But why? Violet wondered, even as she backtracked in her own footsteps, trying not to breathe an audible sigh of relief that she wouldn't be forced to sit next to Grady.

It didn't matter really. Violet didn't have the luxury of being choosy; she took the seat wordlessly, not sure what she could say to the other girl.

She frowned as she pulled out her own spiral notebook—a plain one with a flimsy green cover—and dropped her backpack on the floor. She knew how Gemma felt about her.

What was it she'd said exactly, *that Violet reeked of the dead*? Was that how all empaths felt about her? That she carried the scent of death on her wherever she went? She supposed she'd have to wait until she met another empath, someone who could sense the emotions of those around them, to find out.

So far, Gemma was the only one she knew.

She glanced sideways at the blonde girl, who was staring straight ahead now, almost as if she were intentionally ignoring Violet. In spite of herself, Violet couldn't stop from asking, "Why?"

For a moment she thought Gemma wasn't going to answer her as she continued to look forward at the space where the teacher was already introducing herself and explaining the ins and outs of Anatomy & Physiology. But Violet didn't believe Gemma was as captivated as she appeared to be by the teacher's explanation.

Just when she'd decided it was pointless—the other girl wasn't going to answer her at all—she heard Gemma sigh and say beneath her breath: "Whatever that guy did to you, it must've been pretty messed up." She turned her pointed chin just the scantest amount to appraise Violet's reaction, and seemed satisfied when Violet's eyes widened. "I honestly don't think I could spend an entire semester in the same room with the kind of tension you were feeling. You were making *me* uncomfortable." She looked forward again, indicating the conversation was over. "And you're welcome."

CHAPTER 3

VIOLET SAT IN HER USUAL SPOT. THE SAME CHAIR she sat in every Monday afternoon. She listened to the ticking of the clock as she tapped the toe of each shoe to its rhythm. First one foot, then the other, then the first one again. She leaned forward and watched them, as if this were the most fascinating piece of choreography she'd ever laid eyes on.

It wasn't. In fact, she was bored to tears, mentally counting down the minutes until her session with Dr. Lee would finally come to an end and she'd be put out of this particular brand of misery.

Tap . . . tap . . . tap . . .

Is it possible to actually die of boredom? Violet wondered, as she fixated on the toes of her sneakers, forcing her gaze to remain down. But she could feel the good doctor looking at her. Watching her. Waiting for her to grow tired of this latest delay tactic.

Last month, during one of her sessions, she'd told him she had to use the restroom, and she stayed in there for almost the entire hour—longer than anyone should ever have to stay in a bathroom. He'd seen through her little ruse, of course, and at her next visit he told her, even before she'd made it out of the waiting room and had the chance to ask, that his restroom was "out of order." She hadn't tried that trick again.

She sighed as softly as she could. Her shoulders were starting to ache from hunching forward and she wanted to stretch them, just a little.

She waited for as long as she could, until the crick in her neck was screaming for relief, and then she decided to take a chance. She arched her back, rolling her neck ever so slightly from side to side, relishing the stretch in her sore muscles. Her mistake had been in miscalculating Dr. Lee's position. In not realizing that he'd shifted in his chair, so he was leaning toward her, and without meaning to, she accidentally made eye contact. It was fleeting, and Violet looked away again just as quickly as possible, but it was too late. Her reprieve had come to a bitter end.

She sagged, slouching back in her chair, not willing to admit how badly her back had been aching. "Fine," she told him, glancing at the clock. "We only have five minutes left anyway. Might as well get this over with."

Dr. Lee pressed his fingertips together, the way he always seemed to do when he was thinking about what he wanted to say. After a moment, he asked, "I take it you're sleeping better?"

Violet shrugged. "I sleep enough." But then she realized that her lie would get her nowhere; she needed him to give her another prescription. Her shoulders fell as she admitted, "But I could use a refill." She searched his face, looking for any sign that he was satisfied to have something she needed.

If he did, his smugness didn't show. "And what about echoes this week?" His bushy brows raised, same as always. He was like the clock in that regard—predictable. Tick-tick-ticking away.

She shrugged, a non-answer, knowing what was coming next: He reached up and tapped his lips. "Did you run across anything? Do you still feel like you have your impulses under control?"

Violet tapped her feet again. She knew what he wanted to hear. That she was doing great. That everything had changed since she'd met him.

Thanks to you, Dr. Lee, those pesky echoes never bother me at all. You're my hero! Or something to that effect.

Problem was, it was true . . . more or less. Dr. Lee was the one who'd made her ability bearable. He'd taught her the breathing techniques and meditation and had even used hypnosis, all of which helped her not just to overcome the

49

fog of depression and unease and just plain desolation that had once developed in the wake of discovering a body. That used to haunt her, making her drift through her days, as if she were a shell of her real self . . . until the body that was plaguing her was buried at last.

Until it found peace.

But now . . .

Now she felt something different. There was still a certain cloudiness, a sense of being weighed upon by the dead. But it was nothing like she used to experience. Nothing like before she'd met Dr. Lee.

And together with Sara, they'd taught her the importance of working as a team. Of not wandering into dangerous territory—even when the pull of an echo was strong—without waiting for backup.

Under any other circumstances, in any other lifetime, she would have praised him for that. Instead, she shrugged again, trying to look as taciturn as possible. "I can handle myself" was all she said.

"Good. That's good to hear," he said, smiling as if she'd just led a cheer in his honor. "I guess that's about it." He got up to go to his desk and Violet waited as he slid open the locked drawer where he kept his prescription pad. "Oh, and Violet? One more thing."

"Yeah?" she said absently.

"How was school? You started today, right?"

Violet cringed. She wanted nothing more than to get this appointment over with and get out of here, but there was something in the way he asked the question, in the way he'd kept his back to her as he'd posed it. "Fine. Why?"

He closed the drawer, sliding the key in the lock methodically, as if this were the most important task he'd ever taken on. And then he turned back around, his eyes boring into her. "I just wondered how it was having Rafe and Gemma there."

It took a moment for his words to sink in, but when they did Violet shook her head. "Was it you? Are you the reason they're at my school?"

When he nodded, Violet gripped the seat of her chair, her fingers digging into the upholstery. Her voice was filled with quiet disbelief. "But . . . *why*?"

"Because, Violet. You're not keeping up your end." His lips parted and he was no longer the benevolent psychiatrist he pretended to be here in his office. "Being part of the team isn't just about coming to your scheduled appointments and showing up at the Center when Sara calls you. I expect you to commit to this. Your team needs you." He held out the prescription for sleeping pills to her, and for a moment she just stared at it. Inside, she was shaking, and it took a moment to register that she was shaking on the outside as well. When she reached out to take the paper from him, her hands trembled violently.

But when their fingers brushed, his voice softened. "And whether you believe it or not, you need them too. Having Rafe and Gemma at your school is just another part of being on the team. It's our way of making sure you're okay."

She wasn't sure if it was his tone or his touch, or whether she was lapsing into some sort of shock, but she could practically *feel* the concern radiating from him, and it made her believe what he said as acceptance washed over her. His words made sense to her.

He was right, of course. She was being stubborn to believe otherwise. They were her team, and she knew they only wanted what was best for her. She nodded back at him, letting his conviction calm her.

He placed his hand on her elbow, and he patiently led her to the door.

"I'll see you next week," he said. "Let me know if you need anything before then. . . ." It was the same thing he'd said every time since the first time she'd come to see him.

She didn't have to respond because she was already in the waiting room, the door closing behind her.

Violet tried to shake off the feeling that she'd been played.

Sitting in her car in her driveway, parked far from Dr. Lee's office, she couldn't remember *why* she'd let him convince her it was okay for Gemma and Rafe to be spying on her at her own school.

It seemed they were there to stay. Whether she liked it or not. And she most definitely did not.

Chelsea didn't seem to mind though. It had been sort of weird to watch her friend in the halls between classes, focusing so much energy on Rafe. Watching as she held one-sided conversations with the less-than-chatty loner and then laughed giddily at his nonexistent jokes as if he'd just charmed the pants off her. It was even weirder though as, by the end of the day, Chelsea seemed to have drawn Rafe out of his shell. Rafe, who preferred to brood and be left alone. Rafe, who hated pretty much everyone.

Violet actually saw him smile at Chelsea. It was small, practically invisible unless you were looking for it, and maybe Violet shouldn't have been looking at all. But she had been . . . and she'd seen it.

The barest flash of teeth, the stark glint of amusement almost hidden behind his thoughtful blue eyes.

She'd turned away then, ignoring the pang, as the stone that had been there all day settled more heavily in her gut. She shouldn't care.

So what did she feel? she wondered. Certainly not the warm sense of acceptance she'd felt less than an hour ago, when Dr. Lee had assured her it was all for the best. She glanced at the brand-new bottle of pills she'd picked up from the pharmacy on her way home, wondering if Dr. Lee had somehow managed to drug her while she was at his office.

Whatever the sensation had been, it had worn off now.

She stepped outside, relishing the fact that although it was getting late, summer temperatures still lingered and she didn't need a jacket just yet. As it grew dusky, the sky was still tinged at the edges with fiery pinks and oranges that found their way up from the edge of the world, clinging to the undersides of the few clouds she could see, making them look like fat, sticky mounds of cotton candy.

"Vi?" She heard her mom call out to her as she slipped through the front door, and even though she'd meant to skulk up to her room and hide, she drew up short, knowing her mom would want to hear all about her first day back at school.

When she came into the family room, she saw her mother curled up on the sofa. "I made you some tea." She held her own cup, and Violet tried to recall a time when her mom wasn't drinking hot tea . . . even during the most sweltering days of summer. "It'll help you relax." Her mom smiled. "Maybe you'll even sleep better tonight."

"That must be some magical tea," Violet said, a devilish grin finding her lips as she leaned her shoulder against the wall. She watched her mom pour another cup and slide it across the coffee table toward her, inviting her to sit.

"Not magical, just chamomile," she answered, and Violet studied her mom's fingernails, the polish beginning to chip and peel. Violet curled her fingers, hiding her own bare nails as she wondered if her mom—or anyone else—had noticed that she hadn't painted them since her abduction. Since Caine had painted them for her. "And peppermint. It's good for your sinuses."

Violet smiled at her mother, shoving away from the wall and joining her on the couch. "My sinuses are just fine, thank you very much." She picked up the cup and inhaled the steam coming up from it, infused with the scent of mint and the sweet smell of chamomile leaves. She leaned back, putting the cup to her lips and sipping. She didn't tell her mom that she'd sleep fine tonight, that she had something stronger than tea to tide her over.

"So?"

"It's good. I'm sure I'll sleep great," Violet told her instead.

Her mom scoffed, but her voice was determined. "Not *that*. School. How was it?"

"Oh," Violet breathed. "Good." But she knew what her mom really wanted to hear, so she said it. "It was good to be back."

She saw the relief—the anxiety her mother had been shouldering—melt away in an instant with that simple statement.

"Rafe was there," Violet added, trying to make it sound like an afterthought. Like something that didn't really matter to her one way or the other. "He and Gemma are going to White River now." She shrugged nonchalantly, hoping she was convincing.

She still felt weird talking about them with her mom. It was bad enough that Violet had attracted the attention of a serial killer, but her mom had wanted her to quit the Center even before then.

Afterward, though, her mom's opinion had changed.

Afterward, her mom had left the choice up to Violet. All because it had been people from the Center who'd led the police to where the killer had been holding Violet. All because, in the end, they'd been the ones to find her.

Her mom lowered her cup, settling it on top of her lap as

she eyed Violet, that burden returning. "Really? They're at your school? As students?"

Violet nodded, wishing she couldn't hear the air of disapproval in her mother's words, echoing her own doubts.

"And you don't find that . . . odd?"

She shrugged again, repeating the word she'd said far too many times in the past few months. "It's fine." *It's fine. I'm fine. Everything's just fine.* She was starting to hate that word.

"What about Jay? What did he think about Rafe being there?"

This time it was Violet's turn to scoff, to make light of the matter, but she couldn't manage to make it as believable as she'd wanted. Maybe because she didn't believe it herself. "Why would he care?" she asked, taking a too-large gulp from her cup and wishing there was something stronger than just tea in there. She watched her mom's eyebrows inch up meaningfully. "Mom," she complained as if her mother had actually accused her of something. "We're just friends. Jay knows that."

But she could see her mom wasn't buying it.

She waited for her mom to say something else. But she didn't, and they just sat there, silently assessing what the other might be thinking.

Finally Violet got up to go to her room. As she set her teacup down, her mom perked up. "I almost forgot," she said, as if it were a natural transition in their awkward conversation. Her face twisted into a delighted grin. "I left something for you. On your bed."

Cocking her head suspiciously, Violet asked, "What is it?"

"I don't want to spoil the surprise . . ." her mom started, but Violet knew she would. Her mom hated keeping secrets almost as much as Violet hated surprises. "But I found a box of Grandma Louise's things in the attic this afternoon. I thought you might want to look through it."

At the mention of her grandmother's name, Violet's chest squeezed. She hadn't thought of her grandmother in months . . . far, far too long. She wished she'd had more time with her grandmother before she'd died, longer to get to know her, to swap stories about their shared ability, the one Violet had inherited from her.

Suddenly grateful for the change in atmosphere, and subject, Violet sighed, "Thanks, Mom."

Her mom shrugged, but Violet could see how pleased she was with herself. And suddenly Violet couldn't wait to get to her room.

Staring into the musty-smelling box, Violet frowned. She glanced at all the knickknacks, a box filled with treasures that looked a lot like junk. Things that her grandmother had once held dear enough to save, to store away.

She reached in reverently, her fingers brushing over a collection that included a book with a tattered cover, its binding nearly threadbare; a shoebox filled with photos and newspaper clippings and letters; a perfume bottle, mostly empty; and a small ivory box with delicate carvings.

57

Violet reached for the carved box and drew it out, holding her breath as she ran her fingers over it. It felt both delicate and solid, and Violet worried she might break something that her grandmother had once considered special. Important.

She studied the etchings engraved on its lid, a labyrinth of people, trees, and birds, each intricate and carefully crafted. She flipped it over, her breath catching as she recognized the mechanism underneath it.

It was a music box. A windup music box.

Violet's heart sped up as she wondered . . .

. . . if it were even possible that *this* music box and *her* music box—the one in her head—could possibly play the same tune. She knew there was only one way to find out.

She wavered for only a moment before winding the small silver dial, tightening the springs inside that would unleash the song within. Still, she didn't lift the lid right away. She paused, the air around her growing thick with anticipation, her own song buzzing in her ears as her fingers froze above it.

And then she opened it . . . and the first notes played.

Soft and tinkling, the sound filled her room, bleeding into the imprint that followed her everywhere, that filled her every waking—and sleeping—thought.

The two weren't a match.

She recognized the tune, though. She'd heard it before, the soft lilting of notes. Every child in the world would probably recognize that song.

Brahms Lullaby.

Violet could remember the song. She recalled hearing her grandmother hum it to her when she was small. She listened, letting the lullaby overtake the sound of her own imprint as she savored the bittersweet memories.

When the song ended, Violet closed the lid again, setting the box aside.

She began removing item by item, inspecting each one and then moving on to the next. It was fascinating to explore her grandmother's life, all packed into one place.

When she reached the bottom, she realized it was filled with books. She plucked one of them out and flipped through its pages.

No, she realized, they weren't just books. These were journals. There were at least fifteen of them, Violet counted, maybe more. Her grandmother had been a dedicated journaler, it seemed.

She felt strange just holding the private diaries that had once belonged to her grandmother, let alone contemplating opening one of them, peeking inside its cover.

But she felt like she *needed* to. Her grandmother was the only other person she'd ever known who could do what she could . . . find the dead.

Tentatively, falteringly, she flipped open the worn cover and looked at the scrawled, handwritten pages. The ink was clear and strong—not faded, as she'd expected it to be after so many years, and if Violet hadn't known better, she could've easily believed that this had been written just yesterday.

June 14, 1960
Ian was there again today and I'm starting to suspect
he might like me. I hope so anyway. After school, he
waited by Bobby DiMaio's locker, leaning against it and
pretending he wasn't there just to see me. Pretending that
he and Bobby have so much to catch up on, like there
aren't enough hours in the day to say all the things they
need to say. But I'm not buying it. It didn't used to be
that way. He never used to wait for Bobby, not until the
night Judy and I bumped into him after the game. Now he
waits at Bobby's locker every day, stealing glimpses of me
when he thinks I'm not looking. But I see him. And every
day when they walk by, he wears a smile that I'm sure is
meant for me.

Violet glanced up, her cheeks burning as if she'd just
been caught looking through someone's bedroom window.
Like she was some sort of Peeping Tom.

Still, it didn't stop her from reading the next passage.

June 16, 1960
Bobby wasn't at school today, but Ian was still waiting
anyway. Only this time he didn't stand at Bobby's locker,
he stood at mine. When he said "Hi, Lu," my stomach
did nervous flips and I was terrified to open my mouth
and try to talk, afraid I wouldn't be able to answer him.
How is that possible? How can a boy make me suddenly
speechless? He did, though, and I didn't even care. When

*he smiles at me, it's like staring into the face of an angel.
He makes me forget about all the things my mother taught
me . . . about being good and faithful and pure. I wonder
what it would be like to kiss him.*

July 3, 1960
*It happened! I can't believe it happened, but it did. Ian
Williams kissed me. Me! I let him, and I even kissed him
back. My mother would have a heart attack if she found
out. I'd never be allowed to leave the house again. But
I'd do it all over. A hundred times over! It was the most
amazing, wonderful, beautiful thing I've ever experienced.
I know I shouldn't say things like that. I know what that
makes me, but I don't care. Ian kissed me, and I kissed
him back.*

Violet covered her mouth, trying not to giggle at the
idea of her grandmother—a woman who'd always seemed
so . . . *so old* to Violet—having a crush on a boy.

She couldn't get over how old-fashioned it all was, the
notion that a girl wouldn't be allowed to kiss a boy.

Violet flipped through the pages, skimming the entries.

August 28, 1960
*We have to sneak around to see each other now. Mother
says Ian's not the right kind of boy for me, that he's not
good enough. I don't know what makes us any better than
him since Daddy works at the factory, same as Ian's father,*

*but that's what she says. I think she expected me to go to
college and find a husband, not to marry a local boy who
will likely end up at the factory too. I don't care though. I
want to be with Ian. Only Ian. Besides, I can still go to
college—Ian will wait for me. Who knows, maybe he'll
go to college too. Or maybe neither of us will. Maybe we'll
run away and get married before our parents can stop us.
<u>Mrs. Ian Williams</u>. <u>Mrs. Louise Williams</u>.*

September 6, 1960
*Ian's away with his father for the week. Hunting season
started and his daddy decided he was old enough to go
with the rest of the men. I miss the smell of him. I miss his
lips and his strong arms. I miss him.*

September 13, 1960
*I tried not to be alarmed when I saw him, but I knew
it the moment he came strutting down the hall at school
on Monday morning—he'd killed something. I hadn't
considered what his hunting trip might mean beyond the
two of us being separated for an entire week. I hadn't
thought about the consequences of him carrying a gun. He
may as well have come to school still wearing his bloodied
hunting gear—I could see it just as clearly. More so maybe.
It was revolting. The smell he was carrying was sickly and
sweet, like the decayed vegetation in my mother's garden
at the end of the season. Like rotting, rancid, moldering
fruits. Except that I was the only one who noticed it. I*

62

was the only one who'd known what he'd done to earn the mark he now wore. That he would always wear.

September 15, 1960
I've been avoiding Ian for two days, but I know he knows something's wrong. How do I tell him that it's not his fault . . . not really? I've tried to ignore it, but it's impossible, it comes off him in waves, like heat. Holding my breath only made me dizzy, but at least I could be with him, even if it was only for a few minutes. Until I let him kiss me. That was when I tasted it. It was on his lips, and then it was on mine. I actually gagged before I could push him away. I told him I had to go, that I had to catch my bus, and then I ran away. I can't avoid him forever, can I?

September 16, 1960
I've decided to tell him. I'm afraid. I haven't told anyone since I was a little girl, before I knew it was something to be ashamed of, when my parents made it clear that I was never to talk about it again. That, like my great-grandmother and my aunt Claire (who they pretend doesn't exist), I'm touched. <u>Touched</u>. I know what they mean when they say that. They mean crazy. It used to bother me that they felt that way about me, but I've learned to hide the things I see and hear and smell from them. I've learned not to tell them about the dead animals I sense. But now, with Ian, I feel like he needs to know,

63

otherwise he'll wonder why I've backed away from him.
Maybe together we can figure this out. Maybe we can find
a way to change it. Or at least to live with it.

Violet sat up, her heart racing despite the fact that she
was reading about events that had unfolded over fifty years
ago. She no longer felt guilty about reading her grandmother's private thoughts; she had to find out what had happened
next.

September 20, 1960
It was a mistake. I knew it almost immediately. I could see
it in his eyes, the way the spark that was always there, just
for me, flickered and then faded away, dying completely.
His expression went blank as I tried to explain—about
the bodies I could find, about the colors I would see and
the smells I would smell. About the smell I could smell
on him. No, he didn't go blank exactly—he went cold.
Cold as ice. I wanted to go back in time, to do it over and
not say anything, but it was too late. I'd already said the
words. It's been three days now and I haven't seen him
once. Not at school, not at the river where we used to meet
in secret, and not at his house when I ride my bike past.
Now he's the one avoiding me.

September 23, 1960
The whispers follow me everywhere, even into the stalls of
the girls' room when I think I'm alone, hiding, trying to

find some peace and quiet. But there is no peace for me. Everyone knows now. Everyone at school believes the same things my parents do, the same thing that Ian does. That I'm touched.

October 11, 1960
My mother says we're moving again. My own father no longer speaks to me. He can't even look me in the eye. I know he'll get over it, but for now, when I feel like I need my parents the most, the frosty look that passes over his face whenever I enter the room cuts worse than any blade ever could. My mother's not much better. She resents me and has a hard time hiding it. I'd rather have the silent treatment from her than listen to her offhanded comments about the friends she'll be leaving behind and the church groups she'll miss when we're gone. As if I haven't lost anything.

I've lost everything.

The first diary entries ended there, the rest of the pages in the book Violet was holding were blank, as if her grandmother had given up on her journal when she'd given up her secret. Violet tried to imagine what that must have been like for her, tried to reconcile the grandmother she knew—the one with quick-smiling eyes that could never decide whether they were blue or green—with the lonely girl in the pages of the diary. She must have been, what, fifteen . . . sixteen at the time? Young. And with no one to turn to.

Violet had no idea what that would be like; she'd always been able to count on her parents, and her aunt and uncle. She had Jay too.

She set the journal aside and climbed on her bed, bringing the music box with her and setting it on her nightstand. It was pretty, and it reminded her of her grandmother. It reminded her that her life wasn't so lonely.

She flipped it over and wound the silver key, opening the lid and listening to the sound of her grandmother's lullaby.

CHAPTER 4

"DID I MENTION I'M GLAD IT'S FRIDAY?" ROLLING over, Violet tried to ignore the protesting groan of springs whenever either she or Jay moved, making it sound like they were using his bed as a trampoline. She leaned up on her elbows and stared down at him, her lips curving into a lazy smile as she took in his disheveled hair and the uneven grin that met her. "I wish you didn't have to work tomorrow. You could go to the lake with us." She'd meant with Chelsea, Jules, and Claire, and probably everyone else from school who would be soaking up these last few days of summer.

Jay reached up and parted Violet's curls, moving them away from her face so he could study her, the way he always did—gazing into her eyes and making her feel like he could see inside of her, before finally settling on her lips. He looked at them too, making her stomach feel fluttery as her face flushed in anticipation. "You won't even notice I'm not there," he teased, his mouth almost to hers. "Did I mention how glad I am you suggested hanging out here tonight instead of at your house?" The low timbre of his voice made Violet's heart hammer against her chest as she leaned just the tiniest bit closer, so that his breath lingered with hers. "I mean, nothing against your parents, Vi, but this is *way* better than having your mom follow us around, asking if we need anything every five seconds. She might as well just say she doesn't want us messing around instead of trying to spy on us all the time."

Violet smiled back at him, but didn't disagree with his assessment. She must've asked her mom a hundred times to back off . . . just a little. She'd come to terms with the "no bedroom" rule where Jay was concerned, but her mother's constant hovering had reached the point that they had no space at all when they were at her house. It was impossible to even get through a movie without her mom offering to pop popcorn for them, or scoop them some ice cream, or order pizza, any excuse she could find to check in on the two of them.

"I thought things would get better once I turned seventeen, but I swear it's gotten worse. Worse than worse. She's making me feel like a prisoner on suicide watch."

"What'd you expect, Vi?" he asked, pulling her down

so she was nestled against him. The scent of his soap, crisp and fresh, filled her nose as she rested her head against his shoulder. His bed creaked again and Violet wondered what his mom must think. Then she realized that Ann Heaton wasn't like her mom. She wouldn't barge in on them, and probably didn't have her ear pressed against the other side of the door. "After everything that's happened? Your folks are just worried, that's all." His voice rumbled against her ear.

Violet reached up to find his hand at her shoulder. Her fingers danced and laced and moved through his, never settling in one place, and all the while his thumb traced her palm, her wrist, her pulse. She was amazed how such innocent gestures could make her hot and restless. "But that's the thing. I don't see how what you and I are—*or aren't*—doing has to do with . . . *that.* . . ." She faltered over the words. It was one thing to be aware of what had happened to her—the abduction, the fact that she'd had to kill the man who'd kidnapped her so she could escape—but it was another altogether to actually talk about it . . . even all these months later. She still struggled with that part. Even now, lying here with Jay, she could hear the constant reminder of what she'd done. "I just don't see how those two things are related at all. It's not like you were responsible for what happened to me. They can't possibly blame you—you weren't even there."

Jay's hand went still, and he stiffened beside her.

"Jay . . ." Violet frowned, squeezing his fingers with hers. "I didn't . . . you know what I meant." She peeked up at him. She wasn't the only one bothered by this subject. Jay

69

still blamed himself for not getting to her house sooner, and her parents felt as if they never should have left her alone in the first place. "It wasn't your fault, you couldn't have known he was there. No one did."

She thought of Rafe and Gemma and Krystal, even Sam. None of the members of her team, even with all their special abilities, had been able to predict that the killer was coming after her. None of them had been able to stop it from happening.

He dropped her hand and pulled her close, protectively. "I know," he sighed. "It's just . . . I'm sure they feel the same way I do, that they wish you hadn't had to go through any of that. I'm sure they just want to make sure it never happens again, even if that means they're a little overprotective."

Violet decided she was tired of pretending that every nerve in her body wasn't straining to be closer to him. She rolled on top of him, so that her chest was pressed against his. "And you know what I think?" she asked with a wicked smile as she stared at his lips, thinking how warm and soft they looked. How badly she wanted to taste them. "I think they just want to make sure we don't do this." She lowered herself then, letting her mouth softly graze over his as a tremor rocketed along her spine, making her flesh prickle. She drew back, just enough so she could speak. "I gotta say, though, I kinda want to."

His breath gusted against her lips as he grinned back at her, pulling her down so she was no longer teasing, tempting him. When her mouth parted for him, her pulse exploded, and suddenly she was aware of nothing—not the music-box imprint or the creaking of the bedsprings or her looming curfew. All she cared about was Jay, and the fact that their hearts were beating in time, and she was kissing him. She just wanted to keep kissing him.

His lips were soft and salty and tasted like shelter from the storm that raged inside her. His unintelligible words, as he whispered them against her mouth, were like a melody all their own, drowning out all else.

She pressed herself closer . . . as close as she could get. In Jay's arms, she felt alive. And free.

At peace.

Violet squinted against the sun that came in through her windshield as she reached the stop sign, and then she turned, if for no other reason than to avoid the glare. She knew the wrong turn would delay her arrival even more, but she didn't care at the moment. She wasn't lost or anything—she knew exactly where she was—yet she was in no hurry to get to her destination.

She was already late, there was no changing that fact now.

Still, she felt bad she wasn't making more of an effort to meet them on time. It wasn't their fault her head was ringing. Literally.

She continued to drive like that—with no real plan in mind—turning, and turning again, winding along side roads, and then back roads, until she could see glimpses of the lake between the houses lined up along the opposite side of the street. Turning up the radio, she was able to drown out the other song that was in the car with her, the one she wasn't in the mood to listen to.

It wasn't until she felt the familiar quivering beneath her skin that she realized she hadn't been driving without a purpose after all. That at some point, her course had begun to mean something . . . at least to her.

She didn't have to distinguish an echo to recognize its presence. And it didn't take more than a second to realize it wasn't the one she carried with her.

These vibrations reached into the center of her body and tugged at her, telling her there was a body out there . . . calling to her.

She came to a fork in the road, one she'd passed before—dozens, maybe hundreds of times—one she'd never even considered before this very moment. Normally, she would veer right, following the main road as it continued, eventually winding away from the lake and heading into town.

But this time she pulled her steering wheel in the other direction, to the left. It was just the slightest variation, requiring the barest touch, so it was strange to feel so much change all at once. That's how she knew she was close.

Behind her eyes, colors began to pop and flash, becoming something vibrant and viral, closing in on the periphery of her vision, almost as if her windshield were cracking from the outside in, morphing into some sort of strange psychedelic optical illusion.

At the same time, she could smell coffee. Not warm and fresh brewed, like coffee should smell. But cold and bitter and stale, like old grounds that had been left sitting in the trash for too long.

She pulled to a stop in front of a closed gate that was set between two massive stone walls that stretched around the grounds of an impressive lakefront estate. Violet could see the house that stood beyond the wrought-iron spindles of the gate. It was large and imposing with an enormous circular driveway out front . . . everything you'd expect of a private, gated home.

Whatever, or whoever, had summoned her, lay beyond that gate, she was sure of it. Yet she had no idea what to do as she watched the firework-like display of colors bursting at the corners of her eyes, spreading and parting and then coming together again in entirely different formations.

Most visual echoes remained fixed—attached—to the body, making it impossible for Violet to recognize them until she was just steps away. It was unnerving the way this one behaved, less like a visual echo and more like a tactile one . . . becoming a part of her. Attaching to her from the inside out, making it seem as if she were looking at the world through a kaleidoscope.

Every nerve in her body sang in anticipation and she could feel the magnetic pull to be closer, nearer to the body. Or bodies, rather, since she'd sensed two distinctly different echoes, noting the coffee-grounds smell that hovered in the air.

"You can't do this. You have to wait for the police," she told herself, thinking that if she said the words aloud they might mean more, might carry more weight. She tried to remind herself of the things Sara had tried to teach her, and even the techniques Dr. Lee had offered, to help her contain her impulses . . . so that she could avoid situations like this. So that she wouldn't wander into dangerous situations on her own. But her words sounded hollow and robotic in her own ears, and she knew she didn't mean them, any more than she meant to stay in her car and call for help.

She couldn't help herself.

She *had* to go in there.

Turning off the ignition, she stepped outside her car. The sun beat down on her from overhead, reminding her that she should be elsewhere. With her friends, she thought vaguely. Having fun.

Not here.

She tucked her phone into her pocket, maybe the only intelligent thing she could think to do at the moment as she raised her hand to her eyes and searched for signs that someone was out there, on the grounds beyond the closed iron bars of the gate.

But it was just her . . . and the flashing colors and the decayed coffee grounds.

She wasn't sure what she should do next.

Pacing in front of the entrance, she eyed the wall. It was too high to scale, at least without help. On impulse, she pressed the button on the intercom that was attached to a stone post.

She waited for a long moment, and then pressed it again. After the third buzz, she realized no one was going to answer.

The edginess inside of her was building, the call of the dead had reached a fevered pitch as the echoes grew. The sensation caressed her skin and rattled her bones, alternately seducing and terrifying her.

It was strong, this need to be found. So very, *very* strong.

Violet edged closer to the gate once more and gripped the iron rails in her hands. She strained to see to the other side of the grounds, to the waters beyond. That was when she realized the flaw in the wall surrounding the home. The lake. The tall stone fence line ended where the shoreline began. Where the water met the shore, she could get around the wall.

That realization set her in motion, propelling her into action.

She began moving, slowly, uncertainly at first, but soon she was running, following the tall stone barrier. She stopped when she reached yet another obstacle. The next-door neighbors had a similar fence surrounding their house. Also tall and also imposing, and also blocking her way.

But she was determined now, and she went around to the other side of the house. Her body was tingling everywhere, her vision disrupted by the shattering colors. Her breath hitched when she reached that side of the property, where still another house stood.

A house *without* a fence of its own.

Violet sighed out loud as she started running again, racing now toward the water's edge. When she reached it, she didn't stop, or even slow, she just stumbled into it, letting it splash all the way up to her knees until she'd rounded the end of the stone wall and had made her way back up onto the firm green lawn on the other side.

She didn't stop to think about what she was doing . . . and what might await her if she didn't turn back.

Her wet feet plodded over the grass as she ran up the sloped yard toward the house. She had no plan, no idea what she'd do if the bodies that beckoned her turned out to be human. All she knew was that they needed her.

She passed flowered gardens that had been pruned to perfection, and a detached garage with four regular-sized car doors and one oversized one. Through a window in the side of the structure, she could see a polished boat with bright red stripes parked inside.

When she came around the front corner of the house, reaching the entrance, she stopped dead in her tracks, suddenly feeling the gravity of her situation as a cold tingle of apprehension crept down her spine.

The front door stood open, and from where Violet stood, the colorful explosions were moving, drifting from her periphery and crowding her line of sight.

This was it. This was where the bodies were.

And what if it wasn't just the bodies in there? What if

whoever was responsible for the echoes was still inside as well?

She held her breath and strained, trying to decide if she could distinguish imprint from echo . . . if she could tell if there was a killer in her midst. She listened, trying to hear beyond her own imprint, but all she could hear were the sounds coming from the lake beyond: splashing and waves lapping, shrieks of laughter, boat engines that seemed to blur, one into the next.

And still, the bodies begged to be discovered. And still, her body ached to answer them.

She took one cautious step forward, her self-control teetering on the edge as the toes of her wet shoes abutted the front step. She stood there, letting the coffee-grounds smell and the medley of shapes envelop her, letting them overshadow all else.

Even common sense.

And then she stepped again.

It was the third step that led her across the threshold—of both the house and of reason—and into the darkened entryway.

The first thing she was aware of was the air-conditioning. It was set entirely too high despite the outside temperatures. The second thing she noticed was the smell. A real one that pierced even the bitter coffee-grounds scent that had been suffocating her. She knew now, more than ever, that she was in the right place.

It was the scent of death. Of newly decaying flesh.

Bodies.

She strained toward it, like a ravenous predator. Her hand closed around the phone in her front pocket now as her heart raced and she bit back her breath, afraid it might disturb the air around her and give her away.

But if someone was in there with her, it was already too late. Her shoes were still wet, and they squeaked across the tiled entry, giving her away the moment she'd stepped inside. She slipped one foot out of her shoe, and then the other, leaving the shoes beside the front door as she crept inside on bare feet.

She wasn't afraid. She should be, she knew. But she couldn't find the fear to hang on to.

The entryway was dark, but only because the lights were out, and as she slipped past the wall, Violet could see the sunlight trying to strain through the narrow opening between the heavy curtains that were drawn in front of a large picture window.

She went there first, her fingers clutching the soft fabric as she began to peel them apart, pulling them back along the curtain rod. Light washed the living room in its golden glow.

It would have been a beautiful setting, if not for the blood. And if not for the victims.

Violet gasped, choking on her scream as she staggered backward, falling against the window. She hit the glass hard—too hard—and she held her breath as she waited, listening for the sound of breaking glass to fill her ears.

It won't hold. She'd hit it too hard.

Any moment it would shatter beneath her and she would just keep falling, all the way through it to the lawns below. And then to the water. And even then, she'd keep falling.

Falling . . .

But the sounds never came, not even a crack, although she couldn't help wondering if it wouldn't have been preferable to what she now witnessed.

She'd known there would be bodies. Of course she'd known it, she told herself, as she shoved her palm against her mouth to keep from screaming out loud.

She stayed frozen like that, with her hand pressed to her lips as she leaned against the window for several long seconds . . . minutes . . . or possibly hours.

She couldn't tear her gaze away from them.

All three of them.

Her vision was nearly blocked now as the colors of the kaleidoscope echo swirled and whorled and erupted in front of her eyes, leaving only gaps through which she could see.

But it was enough.

She could make out their sightless eyes. And their gaping wounds. And exposed throats.

I have to get out of here, Violet realized, coming to awareness only as her stomach recoiled violently. She eased away from the glass, testing her legs and her balance for only a second before she started running, scrambling to get to the front door again on feet that felt suddenly slippery beneath her.

Outside the door, she bent over one of the large potted plants that stood on either side of the entry and retched, clutching the sides of the ceramic planter and vomiting until her stomach was empty. Then she vomited some more, tasting the stomach acids that filled the back of her throat. And when her body had finally stopped convulsing, her head felt clearer. *Too clear.*

She was alone in a house with a dead family.

And that's what they were, a family. A mother and a father and a boy—ten, maybe eleven, years old.

They'd been seated on the couch, although Violet couldn't imagine that that was where they'd died. Their placement was too peaceful, the setting too serene. This whole thing looked . . . *planned.* Posed.

No, she was certain they'd been placed there.

Afterward.

She fumbled with her cell phone, her hands shaking so hard that she nearly dropped it. She had to try three times to get her Contacts list up, and even then she struggled to scroll through it. She searched for her uncle's number, listed only under "Stephen." He was the chief of police in Buckley, and although she might be outside his jurisdiction here on this side of the lake, she knew he'd be there in a flash. Less than a flash, if she called him for help.

Her thumb hovered for several long seconds before she changed her mind and called someone else instead.

When he answered, she whispered into the phone, her

voice raw and her throat sore from throwing up. "I need you," she pled almost silently. "Hurry."

Even when she'd called him, Violet had known that calling Rafe meant she was inadvertently calling Sara too. Sara was the team's leader after all. But more than that, she was also Rafe's sister.

Violet hadn't waited for them at the house, despite the nearly irresistible pull that continued to tug at her, trying to draw her back inside. Instead, she'd stumbled back around the stone fencing that surrounded the estate until she reached her car, where she huddled inside and shivered, even as the temperatures climbed to nearly ninety degrees. Sweltering for the Northwest.

This kind of heat kept the lake beyond busy and crowded, and Violet was forced to listen to that same constant drone of boats and jet skis out on the water, until finally she'd pulled out her iPod and turned up the volume. It took nearly an hour for Rafe and Sara to come all the way from Seattle, but the moment she saw Sara's car, Violet felt something she hadn't felt in ages.

She felt understood.

Rafe, more so than even her own uncle, knew what she was going through right now, since he too had an ability that allowed him to glimpse the world beyond their own. To see—and sense—things no one else could.

She'd been so annoyed to see him and Gemma at her

school, in a place she'd tried to keep free from that part of her life, but now, today, she needed him.

And here he was.

Violet practically fell out of her car when she got her first glimpse of Sara, and it was Sara who rushed to Violet, gathering her in her arms as she assured herself that Violet was safe before either of them spoke. Violet had nearly forgotten how cold Sara's touch could be and she shivered once more. Behind Sara, Violet noticed Rafe glancing at her, scrutinizing her with his curious blue gaze, and she wondered if she looked half as frazzled as she felt.

"What's happened exactly?" Sara was asking, still holding her, hugging her. "Are you all right?" Steam gusted from Sara's blue lips as she gripped Violet's shoulders with fingers that were icy, despite the summer heat, and all thoughts that Sara wasn't entirely on her side evaporated just like that.

Violet had grown accustomed to seeing Sara's imprint, the one she'd earned when Violet had been attacked outside the Center—the day Sara had saved her life. But she'd never stop thinking that the imprint was probably the most fascinating one she'd ever seen.

A fine layer of frost coated every part of Sara's skin, making Sara glisten like an icy sculpture, making her look as if she'd been carved from a glacier. Behind that chilly facade, she studied Violet with eyes that were eerily similar to her brother's.

"I'm fine." Violet turned her head and nodded toward the house. "They're in there, three of them. All dead."

Sara looked past the gate, at the stately house overlooking the glittering waters of Lake Tapps. Her hands fell away from Violet and Violet wrapped her arms around herself. "How did you—?" Sara started to ask, and then reformed her question. "Did you know them?"

Violet shook her head. "I was just driving by. . . ." She wiped the corners of her mouth with her thumb and forefinger, realizing she hadn't bothered cleaning up after she'd puked, and wondering if they could see just how affected she'd been. "I *felt* them."

"Damn," Rafe muttered, moving forward now, and Violet took a step back from him. She didn't want to be comforted, not now. Not by him.

She glanced at him, nodding. "It's bad," she breathed.

"Who else did you call?" Sara asked, and Violet knew that what she really meant was had she called her uncle yet?

"No one. Just you."

Sara reached for her cell phone. "I'll call it in," she said, breath gusting as she turned away from them. "You two wait here."

The police arrived in far less time than Sara and Rafe had, her uncle among them. He greeted her like her uncle, hugging her so tight she felt like she'd get lost in his arms, whispering quiet questions that only she could hear as she nodded assurances against his chest.

Then, he transformed, slipping into his official role as chief of police, and Violet became an unintentional bystander, a witness to a crime. She watched as he interacted with the other officers, always fascinated by this no-nonsense side of him. Rigid, bordering on militant. So different from the carefree uncle she'd grown up with, the uncle who was always teasing and laughing and playing with her.

She expected to be shuffled away shortly after giving her statement, taken home to face her parents, but instead she and Rafe had been left outside to wait for Sara and her uncle. They stood on the fringes of the scene, not really a part of the investigation but not forbidden from it either. Ignored was more like it.

Or forgotten.

She watched in silence as officers moved in and out of the house, unable to stop thinking about what was in there.

But not about the bodies so much, and not about the blood either. Although both were forever seared into her memory, permanently etched into her mind's eye.

It was something else that bothered her, niggled at her.

Something wrong about what she'd seen.

Something was . . . off.

She chewed the inside of her cheek, replaying the scene in her head once more. She thought of the word *staged*, and realized it fit the scene. The father had been placed beside the mother who had been placed beside the son. The only thing missing was a family dog.

Violet's head snapped up as she realized what was bothering her. Not the dog at all, but what was absent from the scene.

"Rafe," she said urgently, reaching for his sleeve and pulling him from his own quiet reverie. She knew where he'd been, what he'd been thinking about. Rafe had his own skeletons, and dead families played right into his deepest fears. "Where's Sara? Do you know where she went?"

Rafe looked at her, his eyes still glazed. "No." He shook his head. "Inside, maybe . . ."

Violet sprinted toward the house, but Rafe caught up to her, grabbing her arm to stop her. "Jesus. What's up with you?"

"Something's wrong. I need to go in there."

"There's a lot wrong in there, V." He frowned back at her.

"No. I mean, I know . . . but there's something I need to see . . . feel . . ." She trailed off, unable to explain what she was thinking. And then she looked past him. "Uncle Stephen!" She waved at her uncle who had just emerged from the front door.

He was rubbing his eyes when he looked up at her, and his expression, that look of worry on his face, deepened. "What are you still doing here, Vi?" he asked, pulling her aside. "I thought you'd left—"

"Uncle Stephen, I need to go back inside," she insisted, cutting him off.

But he was already shaking his head. "That's not possible. You should go home. I'll come by later and we can talk then."

She stepped closer, clutching his hand in both of hers,

her voice dropping all the way. "I don't need to talk. I need to go back in there." She met his eyes determinedly. "Please. Just for a minute. There's something I have to know."

For a moment she thought he would continue to deny her, and she tightened her grip. But then his shoulders sagged and she knew he was giving in. "Is it that important?" He didn't ask her *why* she needed to go inside.

She nodded. "It is. At least . . . I think so."

He sighed. "Okay, here's what we'll do. I'll take you in, but you can't touch anything, Violet. I mean it. Stay right with me, and when I say it's time to go, we go. Got it?"

Violet nodded again, and when her uncle started leading her toward the house, she saw Rafe, his forehead creasing as he watched her, behind the spectacle of flashing colors that crowded her periphery as she left him behind on the lawn.

Inside, there was that same over-air-conditioned feel, and that same smell of moldering coffee grounds.

Violet walked exactly where her uncle did, following in his footsteps as if she were walking on stepping-stones. They passed Sara, who had stopped talking to one of the officers—or maybe detectives, Violet didn't know for sure—as she watched the two of them with thoughtful consideration, her icy brows raised inquisitively.

Violet was prepared this time for the explosion of colors that burst behind her eyes, and for the disturbing image of the family spread out before her on the couch, bloodied and gashed. They reminded her of flowers—fragile and delicate. Like death in bloom.

Her suspicions were confirmed as she focused on the colorful explosions and the smell of old coffee.

One of these bodies had no echo. At least none that she could discern.

She took minuscule steps, moving closer to the family, until she was standing near the end of the couch where the man had been propped up, set up to look as if nothing were out of place, as if he were spending an ordinary evening with his family.

Bending at the waist, Violet leaned in, keeping her gaze directed solely on him.

The result was instantaneous. The kaleidoscope of colors exploded behind her eyes, blinding her and making it impossible for her to know if anyone was watching her. Blocking out all else.

That echo belonged to him.

She flinched, drawing away, and bit by bit her vision gradually returned, clearing with each millimeter of space she put between them. Then she turned to the woman beside him.

She almost didn't need to approach the woman to know . . . the coffee grounds were most definitely hers. But she did so anyway, tilting toward her ever so slightly, in the same way she had the man. And in that instant, the smell became so overpowering that Violet nearly gagged from the stench alone. She pulled back, more slowly this time, shuddering as she tried to find a breath of uncontaminated air in the too-chilled room.

There was only one body remaining. The boy.

Violet approached him more tentatively. Her music-box imprint seemed to swell in her own ears, but it had nothing to do with the boy. Likely it was only her imagination that made her more conscious of it.

She wanted to glance around her, to know who was still in the room with her because it felt like she was all alone now. Just her . . . and the bodies. Somehow, though, she couldn't manage to turn her own head. She couldn't stop watching the child with his lifeless eyes.

The echoless corpse.

She crept nearer to him and felt her heart stutter. At any other time she'd have felt something by now. At the very least, her skin would have prickled, her nerves tight with the awareness that she was so near a body. Even if the echo was faint and hard to find.

But not now.

Now there was nothing.

She turned to her uncle and dropped her voice until it was almost nonexistent. "I know you said I couldn't, but . . . can I try . . . I just need to touch him. I promise I won't disturb anything." She couldn't imagine how much more *disturbed* the scene before her could possibly be.

Her uncle looked around, considering her request uncertainly. Then he reached into his pocket and pulled out a pair of latex gloves—the kind she'd seen at other crime scenes on the people gathering evidence.

It was all the confirmation she needed and Violet slipped

her hands into them before he could change his mind. She took another short step, watching her feet as she closed the gap. She didn't *want* to touch him, but she wasn't sure she had any other choice.

She watched her own fingers, thinking how stiff and cold they looked—so very much like the ones she bent forward to touch. Hers brushed across his, and she could feel the bloodless sensation despite the latex that separated them, yet the only thing she was aware of was the glaring absence of anything from him.

She stared at his blood-soaked T-shirt, noting the way his head slumped against his mother's shoulder, and she knew that what she felt wasn't possible. She knew this boy hadn't died of natural causes. He had been killed, just like his parents had been. He *had* to have an echo.

Yet . . .

She shook her head as she drew her fingers away, wrapping her other hand around them. Fingers that felt as if they'd just betrayed her. Lied to her.

It wasn't possible.

Still . . .

"What's the matter, Vi?" It was her uncle, standing at her back now and staring at the same thing she was but seeing something entirely different.

She stepped back, bumping into him. "I—I don't . . ." But she wasn't sure how else to say it. "He doesn't have an echo."

She felt her uncle's hands close around her upper arms

and then his voice was at her ear, reminding her that there were others there with them, those who didn't know what she could do. "Are you sure?"

Half nodding and half shaking her head, so that she looked like some sort of deranged bobble-head, she whispered back, "I've never been more sure of anything."

CHAPTER 5

VIOLET LET HER UNCLE LEAD HER AWAY FROM the bodies. She felt staggered by her discovery; she'd never imagined that a body—especially one that had so obviously died at the hands of another—could be missing its echo.

Yet it was true. The silence, the total dead space around the boy, was proof.

The impact of that fact had yet to sink in.

They'd almost reached the kitchen, when something else stopped her. Something that penetrated the near-blinding explosions behind and around her eyes.

She turned toward the wall, which was tall, reaching up

91

two stories, and she marveled at how she'd ever missed this in the first place.

"What is that?" she asked, taking in the strange design as best she could. Taking in, too, the fact that, whatever the pattern was it had been drawn in blood . . . most likely blood taken from the very family who'd lived here. Who'd died here.

She blinked, trying to clear her vision.

The crimson smears were wide, too fat to have been made by any brushstrokes. No, whatever made this was misshapen and soaked in blood, as drops had oozed down the walls, gravity pulling them away from their intended formation.

But the shape itself could still be distinguished, despite the dribbles and streaks and smears.

If she were to describe it, she supposed she might call it a cross of sorts. Like the ones you'd see in church or on the Bible. But that wasn't right, because it wasn't a cross exactly. At its base, there was a strange, sideways figure eight, almost like a pedestal that it sat upon. And there was a second line, smaller than the one that generally intersects the cross, just beneath its top . . . perched above the other.

"We don't know yet," Uncle Stephen said, drawing her attention as he pulled her away from it.

But Violet kept it in her sight for as long as she could. Her eyesight cleared a little more with each step she took away from the man on the couch . . . and his kaleidoscope echo.

The kitchen was spacious and overly bright, and Violet blinked as she stared at the granite countertops, with their swirled and flecked patterns. They seemed to blend with the swirls and flecks that were gradually receding to her periphery.

"I don't understand," he was saying. "I thought all bodies had echoes. Everyone who's been murdered anyway."

She nodded hesitantly. "They . . . do . . . at least they always have . . ." she said slowly, but then moved her head side to side, just as uncertainly. "Until now." She frowned, feeling foolish for asking her next question. "And . . . and you're sure that he was . . . you know . . . murdered?"

Her uncle's brows rose and she could feel the are-you-really-asking-me-that look he shot her way. Of course they'd been murdered. All of them, the boy included. Violet knew as much, she'd seen him with her own eyes. Felt his lifeless body even.

"I don't get it," she admitted. "There should be . . . *something*."

"But the others?" her uncle asked. "The mom and dad . . . ?"

"Yeah. Both of them. Clear ones."

Violet leaned back, trying to make sense of it herself as she stood propped against the edge of the counter. But she paused as she glanced at the refrigerator, her eyes skimming the array of photos taped to the face of the stainless steel door. They were cluttered and disorderly, lending it a homey feel.

She saw a picture of the boy pinned up there, suited up in his Little League uniform. His smile revealed his two missing front teeth and he held his bat at his shoulder, as if preparing to swing at the next pitch. Beside that was a photo of the couple—the husband and the wife—taken in some tropical locale. Both of them were wearing flowered leis, and he had on a garish Hawaiian shirt—the kind tourists wear. Among the images, there were report cards and colored drawings, and a birthday card that read: *Who's Ready for a Fiesta???* with a Chihuahua wearing a sombrero perched eagerly in front of a birthday cake.

At the top right of the refrigerator, there were twin school photos with the same bland gray backdrops, one was of the boy—taken several years earlier, when he was probably in the first or second grade. The other was a girl, several grades older than the boy. She had braces and freckles and wore a T-shirt with a rainbow emblazoned across the chest.

She's cute, Violet thought, stepping closer to examine the images. She looked like she could be the boy's sister.

Her eyes moved over a collection of magnets and a Crock-Pot recipe for chili. And then she froze and her heart hammered against her breastbone like it was trying to punch its way out.

There was a photograph, buried amid the others, almost unnoticeable at first.

She took a step closer, until her nose was practically pressed against the image, and she lifted her fingertips to brush across the stippled surface of the photo paper.

She stared at the couple, all dressed up. He, in his jacket and tie, a boutonniere pinned to his lapel. And she, wearing a short white dress with black ribbon trimming the hemline and tied around her waist. It had a dramatic effect. Her hair was pinned up and tiny curls fell strategically to frame her face. Balloons fashioned together in the shape of a giant heart created a whimsical backdrop to the vignette.

It wasn't the picture, though, that made bile rise into the back of Violet's throat all over again. It was *who* she was looking at in the image.

The girl was the same girl from the school picture. She was older in the dance photo, but it was most definitely her.

"Holy . . ." Her uncle breathed from between gritted teeth, and Violet guessed that he was thinking the same thing she was: That the girl belonged here. In *this* house. With *this* family.

Violet nodded, unable to tear her gaze away from the image, because there was more. The boy in the dance photo with her . . .

She knew him better than she probably wanted to. And she hated that he was there, standing next to the smiling girl in her prom dress, while Violet had to be here . . . in the girl's house . . . with her murdered family.

"We need to find her," her uncle said now, reaching over Violet's shoulder and snatching the picture off the fridge. "We need to make sure she's safe."

Violet stumbled after him, realizing she was losing him— her uncle. That he was already disappearing into police chief mode. "Uncle Stephen," she called, before he was too far gone.

He stopped at the kitchen door and turned to her. "What is it, Vi?"

"That's Grady," she said, nodding toward the picture in his hand. "The boy with her, at the dance, it's Grady Spencer. You know him, don't you?"

Her uncle glanced down at the image, and Violet saw a quick flash of recognition before he slipped back into the living room, leaving Violet to decide whether or not to follow. She lagged behind, her hand hovering over one of the other pictures, the school photo of the girl in her braces.

As she plucked the image from the fridge, tearing the tape that held it, she heard her uncle on the other side of the wall. "We need to find the girl in this picture. Go up and look through her bedroom. Look for anything to tell us where she might be. In the meantime," he added, his voice lowering, but not so much that Violet still couldn't hear him, "start with a kid named Grady Spencer. He might have some idea where she is."

Violet stood at the living room window and stared out at her driveway, her impatience mounting with each passing second. "What's taking him so long? Shouldn't he have at least called by now?"

She knew it was pointless to ask her dad, he had no way of knowing where her uncle was or what he was doing, any more than she did. But she couldn't help it; all this waiting was driving her crazy.

Especially with these new echoes weighing on her.

She supposed she should be relieved there hadn't been a third one to deal with, but instead, its absence was making her edgy, making it even harder to sit still. *To relax*, as her dad kept trying to tell her.

Relax? Was he kidding? She felt like jumping out of her skin, not soaking in a bubble bath.

"You know, it won't do you any good to pace. Why don't you just sit down and rel—"

Violet held her hand up. "Please. Just don't say it." She blew a curl out of her eyes. "Fine. I give up." She marched over to the couch, where her dad had been sitting, doling out words of wisdom, and she flopped down beside him. Letting out an exaggerated sigh, she complained one more time, "I just wish he'd hurry up already. I hate not knowing if the girl's okay. I hate the idea of her being out there some-where . . . alone." Her eyes burned and her dad reached over and squeezed her leg.

"She'll be okay, Vi. Uncle Stephen'll find her."

She nodded, her eyes still stinging. "I know, it's just . . ." She couldn't imagine what that would be like—losing her parents. She couldn't imagine having the police come to her with the kind of news they'd be bringing to this girl.

His arm slipped around her. "It's not your fault. There's nothing you could've done."

"How does something like this happen? How are people not safe in their own homes?" It wasn't like Violet didn't know it was possible. It wasn't like she'd never seen the news before, or watched a movie or TV show about home invasions. But the idea of it happening so close to where they lived. To someone she shared a connection with . . . even someone as unsavory as Grady Spencer.

It wasn't the first time she'd known someone who'd died—not that she actually knew this girl or her family. But even then it had seemed so foreign to her, somehow detached. Like something that only happened to other people.

Yet she knew better.

She'd seen it with her own eyes.

The front door opened, and Violet's heart shot into her throat as she jumped up, expecting to see Uncle Stephen standing on the other side. She was halfway across the room when she saw her mom instead, her expression harried.

"Violet," she gasped, completely unaware of the disappointment on her daughter's face. She dropped her purse on the floor as she reached for Violet. "Your father told me what happened," her mom said. She drew back, her eyes raking over her daughter. "You're okay? You weren't hurt at all?"

"Mom, stop." She wriggled out of her arms. "I wish everyone would just stop asking me that. Yes, I'm fine. Nothing happened. . . ." And then she added, her voice quieter, "At least not to me."

"I thought you were learning not to do that. I thought

that was the point of seeing that psychiatrist, so you wouldn't put yourself in danger like that anymore." Her voice rose, a hysterical edge creeping into it.

"Maggie." Her dad's voice was quiet, reasonable. "She said she's fine."

But Violet didn't care that her dad was calm. She was too tired to pretend, too tired to act like today hadn't been a strain. "I thought so too. It's not like I didn't try, but clearly, it didn't work. Is that what you want to hear, that I'm too messed up to be fixed? I couldn't help myself. I knew they were in there, and I told myself I should call for help, and I didn't. You know why? Because some things can't be fixed, that's why."

A single tear of frustration slid down Violet's cheek as she glowered at her mom, angry at her for forcing her to say that everything wasn't okay after all. For making her admit—out loud—that she really was broken.

"Vi." The edge had left her mother's voice, and now she just sounded . . . sorry.

"I'm going to my room," Violet shot back before her mom had the chance to say anything else.

Violet wasn't alone for long before she heard the slight tap at her door, right before it slid open. She didn't look up from where she was thumbing through the pages of one of her grandmother's journals, not really able to concentrate.

From the doorway, her mom sighed, but Violet kept her gaze fastened on the pages spread open on her lap. "I'm sorry,

Vi. I didn't mean—" There was a pause, and then without realizing her mom had bridged the gap between them, the bed beside Violet dipped and she felt her mother's leg against hers, their shoulders brushing. "No, that's not true. I meant to ask if you were okay. I can't help it. I'm your mom. It's what I do."

She bumped Violet, and even though Violet wanted to stay mad—and she managed to keep her expression stern—inwardly, she cracked . . . just a little. She didn't expect them not to care, and she supposed it was unfair to ask them not to worry either.

She just wanted them to stop acting like she was something fragile. Delicate.

"Aunt Kat called," her mom told her, and she suddenly had Violet's attention as her head snapped around to face her.

"What'd she say? Does she know anything? Has Uncle Stephen come home yet?"

Her mom was shaking her head before Violet had even finished asking. "She said he's still out, but she wanted to make sure you were okay. She's been getting calls from people who've heard about what happened. She said they're asking if it's true, that the bodies were found by a student from White River."

At the mention of her high school, Violet stiffened. If word was already spreading, she wondered what else they knew. She wondered how much longer she'd be able to keep her name, and her ability, a secret.

Her mom tried to smile, but it was weak and uninspired.

100

"Don't worry," she assured her. "They didn't know who you were. And even if they did, they'd just assume you were there because of Uncle Stephen." But then her expression became more serious, and Violet saw the worry she tried to mask. "So can I at least ask why you were there, Vi? Who are . . . Who *were* they?" she corrected herself.

Violet just shook her head. "I—I don't know who they were. I didn't mean to find them. I just . . . I followed . . . well, you know . . ."

Her mom nodded. Of course she knew. "Was it . . . ? Was it as bad as Aunt Kat said it was?"

Violet shrugged, not sure how much detail her mom really wanted. Or how much she could handle, for that matter. Her mother wasn't like her. She wasn't accustomed to seeing bodies, and even those of the animals Violet used to carry home when she was little had made her mom squeamish. "What did she say?"

There was a long silence, and then her mom said, "That they were slaughtered."

Violet thought about that, the description. She imagined the scene she'd walked into, even as she tried to purge it from her mind. *Slaughtered* was a pretty accurate word. "Yeah, it was that bad. They were in their own home, Mom. Even the little boy . . ." She nodded, her focus distant. "It was really, *really* bad," she repeated in a whisper.

"Sara Priest was there?" her mother asked, her words experimental now, as she tested the waters of their truce. "And Rafe?"

101

"I called him." There was no point dancing around the truth.

"And were they able to help?" her mom continued to probe, as she tried to be casual about it. She rubbed at some charcoal residue on her fingers—a sure sign she'd been sketching that day. "Could they tell *anything* . . . about the family?"

Violet was cautious now. She had to be vague, even with her parents, about what the other team members could do. Discretion was the first rule of being part of the team. She shook her head. "Not yet. But I think there was an older daughter who wasn't there . . . when they were killed." Violet turned to face her mother. "And she and Grady Spencer know each other. Maybe even dated . . ."

Her mom stopped scraping at the black stains beneath the edges of her fingernails. "Grady Spencer?" she breathed, meeting Violet's gaze now.

Violet nodded. "The one and only."

"But you didn't recognize her? She doesn't go to your school?"

"I only saw a picture of her, but I don't think I've ever seen her before. Uncle Stephen's looking for Grady now. Maybe Grady knows where the girl is. Or maybe he can tell them something about her." Behind her eyes, a throbbing pain pounded in time with her heart. "Do you mind if I lay down for a little bit?" She closed the journal and set it on her nightstand. "I'd kinda like to be alone for a while."

102

This time Violet didn't try to ignore the anxiety she saw in her mother's expression. She could no more ask her mom to stop caring than she could will away the imprint that clung to her. "Go ahead." The strained smile was back, but her kiss was gentle and spoke volumes about how hard she tried. "I'll tell you if Uncle Stephen calls, 'kay?"

THE TIES THAT BIND

HE THREW HIS FOOT DOWN ON THE BACK OF HIS
skateboard, forcing its nose up to his hand. Lifting it, he tucked it
beneath his arm just before he ducked, slipping inside the opening
of the wide-mouthed sewer drain. Even if it had been tall enough
to stand in, the corrugated sheet metal beneath his feet would have
made it impossible to ride his board through the tube. It didn't matter
though; he preferred to sneak inside noiselessly. It was better for all
of them if no one heard him coming.

He emerged from the other end to face the grungiest apartment
building in the entire city. There were only six units in the building,
but he doubted there was water or power running to any of them.
Most of the windows had been broken out at some point, only to

104

be repaired by cardboard and duct tape, if they were repaired at all. What made matters worse was that there were actual tenants living in some of those units, people who handed over their welfare and disability checks to some slumlord who could give a rat's ass about their living conditions.

He wasn't one of those suckers, of course. None of his people were. They were squatters, crashing in one of the vacant apartments for as long as they could go undetected.

Slowly, he approached the main floor slider—the one that didn't lock, but still closed at least—and he pressed his ear against it, listening. Inside, he could hear the low hum of Boxer's voice followed just a moment later by the sound of Kisha . . . not quite a giggle, but an attempt to laugh.

He rapped once at the door, signaling he was there before letting himself inside.

Kisha was crouched on the stained mattress that the two of them shared in the middle of the living room floor. She wore just his T-shirt over her plain white underpants, and he could see how thin she was, as her arms wrapped protectively around her bare legs. There was a half-burned candle on a plate littered with discarded matches beside her, making the sheen of sweat on her face glisten and glow in the light from its flame.

Her eyes lit up when she saw him, and Boxer turned to glance over his shoulder.

He lifted his chin in a silent greeting. "Where's Bailey?" he asked, after doing a quick head count.

As always, Boxer was quick to respond. Faithful and diligent. He cocked his head toward the closed door, a bedroom the size of a closet. "Sleeping. She's crashing pretty hard."

But it was Colton who narrowed his gaze at him, scrutinizing his face and drawing attention to something he'd just as soon ignore. "I thought you weren't going home. You said you were just gonna sell the stuff and get our shit. What the hell happened to you?"

He turned his still-throbbing cheek away from them. He didn't want to answer their questions about the bruise forming beneath his eye. "Don't worry about me, I'm fine." Nodding toward the door again, he steered the conversation back to Bailey. "I got what she needs." And then he smiled temptingly. "I got enough for everyone."

He pulled out a plastic bag, showing them the fine brown powder inside.

Colton's eyes went wide. "How much did you score? I knew we had a lot'a shit to sell, but I bet there's enough there to keep us high for a year." As always, it was Colton, wearing that stupid grin of his. Boxer knew better. He knew when to keep his mouth shut.

"I got enough. Bailey won't be dope sick for a while." He dropped down in front of Kisha. He reached out to stroke her gaunt cheeks, wondering when she'd last eaten. She stared back at him dreamily, trustingly, and his chest swelled with pride.

Kisha blinked, her eyes never leaving his. "Can I have some? Just a taste?"

He knew what she really meant, just enough to take the edge off, and he wondered if he should tell her no. He didn't need the drugs to keep her, or any of them, in check. They would stay with him—follow him—regardless. But he liked being the only one who was clearheaded. He liked the way they had to lean on him to make decisions, even simple ones like what to eat . . . and when.

He cupped her chin, turning her face one way, and then the other, inspecting her even though there was nothing new to see. The smudges beneath her eyes were still the same, as was the devotion in them. With the slightest nod, he gave Kisha the permission she was waiting for, and she practically squealed, dragging the dirty sleeve of her T-shirt up and holding out her arm to him.

He handed the bag to Boxer and watched. Boxer worked methodically, squeezing her emaciated arm as he tried to find a vein that hadn't long since collapsed. It took longer than it should have, but eventually he looked up triumphantly.

Kisha's eyes widened as she watched Boxer draw the needle. The vein was small and it rolled when he tried to jab it, but after several attempts the point of the needle finally found its way inside, releasing the drug into her system.

After that it was only minutes—seconds, really—before she was transformed, her eyes too bright.

She blinked, as if trying to clear her drug-blurred vision. "Baby," she whispered, allowing herself to be more familiar now that her inhibitions were down. She reached out to him, her voice hoarse. "Thank you."

"Told you I'd take care of you," he said, letting Kisha's arms fold around his neck, her fingers burrowing into his hair. Her lips were soft and moist and fervent.

He pulled Kisha onto his lap and he watched while the others took their turns, feeling satisfaction swell inside him as his sense of control was secured with each thrust of the plunger. They needed him. These were his people, his real family.

When Boxer had taken his fix and was leaning back against the wall, his head lolling lazily to the side, he lifted his brows, glancing at the girl in the corner. "What about her?"

The girl didn't look up when she was mentioned. She hadn't said anything, hadn't made a peep since he'd gotten there. But her eyes were round as she clutched her knees, her fingernails digging into her elbows, and he knew her drugs had long since worn off. He wondered what she remembered, whether she even realized what they'd done—what she'd helped them do.

"I don't know, Boxer, you tell me. You plannin' to keep her?"

Boxer's glazed eyes wandered to her. With some effort, he licked his fat lips. "She's real pretty," he said, his words becoming lazy. And then to her, "Come here, girl."

She didn't move, didn't even blink.

He decided to help Boxer out, because that's what leaders did. That's what family did.

Still on his knees, he crawled toward the girl. Behind him, he heard Kisha giggle—a real giggle this time. He waited for the vacant eyes in front of him to register that he was there at all, and he reached out and lifted her chin, more roughly than the way he'd handled Kisha, forcing the girl to at least face him.

"Hey, Butterfly," he whispered, hoping he sounded comforting, reassuring. He knew that wasn't her name, but to be fair, he couldn't remember what her real name was. "You in there? You still with us?" He squeezed her cheeks, just enough to get her attention when she refused to respond. "Colton, hand me that shit." He held out his hand impatiently. He didn't like to be the one to give it to her, but she needed it. Otherwise they'd have to get rid of her, and Boxer seemed to have taken a liking to her.

It wasn't hard to find a vein in her arm; hers were still fat and unblemished.

It also didn't take much of their stash to get her to return to them.

After a few minutes, she met his gaze, as if noticing his presence for the first time. He smiled at her, silently welcoming her back.

"Here, Boxer," he said, shoving the girl toward him. "Take her. She's yours. But you need to take good care of her. She's your responsibility now."

"Come here, Butterfly," Boxer cooed as the girl staggered into his arms. She curled into his lap, resting her head on his shoulder as he petted her, the way he might pet a kitten. She never seemed to notice the blood that was still on her hands.

Colton was lying on the floor now, staring up at the water-stained ceiling, wearing that same grin he always wore. The younger boy's enthusiasm was irritating at times, but there were worse things than enthusiasm, he thought, feeling the throb of his swollen cheek pulsing.

Besides, that's what families did, they put up with one another's quirks and faults.

"What about me? When do I get a girl?" Colton asked into the dim space of the apartment.

He didn't answer Colton right away; instead he settled down beside Kisha, letting his hand move slowly up and down her arm as she finally found a peaceful kind of sleep. The kind that wasn't riddled with nausea and night sweats.

After several quiet minutes he whispered softly, his voice spinning the same tale he'd told them a thousand times before, "Be patient, man. Big things are comin' our way. When I'm famous—when we have more money than we know what to do with—you can have all the girls you want."

CHAPTER 6

"VIOLET, WAKE UP. UNCLE STEPHEN'S HERE." IT was her dad's voice, finding her in the darkness of her room. Automatically, she reached for her cell phone, checking the time and realizing it wasn't even midnight yet. She hadn't meant to fall asleep.

Still groggy, she nodded and rose up on her elbow. "I'll be right down," she managed to croak.

She waited till her dad left the room before throwing back her covers and grabbing a pair of sweatpants. She pulled her hair into a ponytail, not bothering to check the mirror. There was no point.

In the kitchen, the lights seemed too bright and Violet

111

could smell the fresh coffee brewing in the pot. But more than that she could taste the presence of her uncle—his own unique imprint—the dandelion taste that coated her tongue whenever he was around. All eyes shot her way when she staggered in and she glanced around at them—her mother, her father, and her uncle—while the repeating music-box loop played in her head.

"So?" Violet asked, pulling up a chair at the table and joining the rest of her family. "Did you find her?" She leaned across the table expectantly.

There are pauses people take when you know that what they'll say isn't what you want to hear. For Violet, this was one of those moments. She knew, even before her uncle opened his mouth, the news wasn't good. His pause was exactly that long.

"I'm sorry, Vi." He shook his head woefully, and Violet wondered if he'd had to practice that expression, that look of patient sympathy. If this was the same look he gave others when he had to deliver bad news. Even his voice sounded too smooth, too practiced.

Violet turned to her dad, and then back to her uncle. She hated the knot of confusion that coiled in her gut, warning her there was more to this visit than just that denial. It was too late to drop by if he didn't know *something*.

"Well," Violet started, "if you don't know where she is, then what do you know? What about . . ." She choked on the feel of his name, bitter on her tongue. "What about Grady? Did you talk to him?"

Her uncle's expression cracked, just slightly, and he gave a slight nod. He glanced down at his coffee mug, staring but not drinking. He just watched the steam rising up from it. "We did. He didn't know where she was either."

"*And . . . ?*" There was definitely more. Violet's Spidey senses were tingling off the charts. She knew her uncle was holding back.

"We found his prints all over their house," her uncle admitted, still not meeting her eyes.

Violet relaxed a little. "So what? Is that so weird? Wouldn't that make sense if they were dating or whatever?" She'd seen the picture. Most girls didn't go to the prom with someone they hadn't spent at least a little time with.

But then her uncle went on, "He also had some of her things in his possession. An iPod, a bracelet . . . things he admitted belonged to her. And we think there might more, things that were missing from the house, but we haven't been able to get an accurate inventory just yet."

"Again . . ." Violet hedged, thinking of all the things she'd left at Jay's house, all of the things that were probably there now. "If they were dating, wouldn't that kind of explain her stuff being there?"

Her uncle cleared his throat. It was strange to watch him shift and squirm in his chair, like a schoolboy who'd been caught cheating on a test.

"Violet," her mom interjected. She cast a meaningful glance at Stephen, reproachful almost. "They think Grady might've had something to do with what happened to the girl's family." She continued, a heavy sigh buried behind her words. "They found some strange pictures at his place."

Violet's heart felt like it was jammed in her throat. "What . . . ?" She swallowed, trying to clear a space for her words. "What are you talking about? What kind of *strange pictures*?"

Her uncle nodded, as if he hadn't just chickened out and had delivered the news himself. "Photos of the girl," he said, sounding like himself again. "Veronica, by the way. Her name is Veronica Bowman." He kept going, while Violet let the name sink in. She didn't recognize it, not that she'd expected to. "The pictures were . . ." her uncle continued, stopping for just a moment to chew the inside of his lip. "Well, they were mutilated. The girl's eyes had been gouged out, and he'd drawn horns on her—"

Violet interrupted then, trying to give them a rational explanation. Surely even that could be explained. "Okay, so maybe they broke up. Maybe he was pissed and he ruined some pictures. That's not a crime—"

This time it was her uncle who interrupted her. "There were red slash marks drawn on her neck and wrists."

Violet's mouth was still open. She'd been ready to argue, to take up Grady's defense, when her uncle's words had caused it to go bone dry. She thought about the bodies of the girl's—*Veronica's*—family, of the way their throats had been sliced open.

She thought too about the way Grady had groped her last year at the party they'd been at, when he'd backed her against his car and tried to kiss her, putting his hands all over her. He'd been drunk and stupid, but he'd also been aggressive. "What did he say?" she finally managed to ask, her voice sounding far less confident. Far less outraged. "When you asked him about it, what did he say?"

Her uncle ran his hand through his hair, looking weary. Her mom put a hand on his shoulder.

"He said what you said, that they'd had a fight and he was mad at her. That the pictures didn't mean anything."

Violet wasn't sure what to think now. "Maybe they didn't. Did you find other fingerprints at the house?"

Stephen nodded, but it wasn't a convincing nod . . . not to any one of them sitting at the table. "Of course we did. Several of them. Most are being processed now, but in the meantime Grady is a suspect."

"*Grady*—" Violet sputtered. "Are you serious?" Even though Grady had made mistakes, and was probably a first-class jerk, that didn't make him a killer. The idea made her stomach twist.

"What we're sure of, Vi, is that we have a family who's been murdered, a girl who's still missing, and an ex-boyfriend who's harboring a grudge. Right now he's all we have, and until he can convince us that we *shouldn't* be looking at him, we're looking." Her uncle's chair scraped across the floor as he got to his feet. He looked like her uncle again, Violet thought, examining him more closely, only a wearier, more exhausted version. His eyes were red-rimmed, and his shirt was wrinkled and untucked. "Now, it's late and I'm tired, and I'd like to get home."

Violet wanted to nod, to give him some signal that she'd understood what he'd said, and that she was okay with his decisions. But she couldn't . . . because she wasn't. Because no matter how much time she'd spent avoiding Grady, she just couldn't accept that he was the cold-blooded killer her uncle insinuated he might be.

Instead, she listened while her parents walked her uncle out . . . and then she heard the deadbolt sliding into place and the beeping of the new alarm system being set for the night. More reminders that there'd been a time she wasn't safe in her own home.

After her mom came back in and kissed her good night, her dad lingered behind in the kitchen. He sat beside her at the table, in the seat her uncle had just occupied. "He did the right thing, you know?" he told her, his voice soft and comforting. "They'll question your friend and they'll figure out he didn't do it. But they have to pursue every possible option. It wouldn't be fair to the girl if they didn't."

Violet gritted her teeth. She knew her dad was right, that they all were, but it didn't change things. It didn't make her feel better that someone she knew, someone she'd once considered a friend, was the prime suspect.

Violet went back to her room, but couldn't sleep. She couldn't stop thinking about Grady.

She couldn't stop thinking about the girl . . . and her family.

She thought about calling Jay, to see if he was still up. But she knew it was too late for that.

She glanced at the box, still on the floor, still filled with her grandmother's journals. She settled down beside it and reached inside, pulling out diary after diary, trying to find where her grandmother had picked up writing again.

She began sorting them into chronological order as she drew each one out, flipping through the pages and searching for dates. She found entries from her grandmother's later years, which she placed near the end, and those from her early married life—with mentions of her husband, Violet's grandfather, whom Violet had never known—which she placed near the middle. Finally, after searching through several of the journals, she found the one she'd been looking for, from when her grandmother had started writing again.

There was a significant gap in time. There were no more entries from her grandmother's high school years. They didn't resume again until *after* she'd moved away to start college. She'd left home, Violet read, deciding to leave her parents in Michigan, where they'd settled after the incident with Ian, so she could start anew at the University of Washington, in Seattle.

It was a big change for her grandmother, being on her own, but as Violet flipped through the pages, she realized that she'd seemed happy then, maybe for the first time in her life. She was free from the parents who'd looked down on her, who had hidden both her and what she could do. She'd made friends in college. She'd taken classes in psychology, religion, art, and history, exploring worlds and ideas she'd never even considered before.

And she'd met a man.

Violet ran her finger over the page when she read his name. John Anderson. Such an ordinary name. If she were to look, there were probably hundreds of John Andersons in the phone book at this very moment.

But this John Anderson was different. This was Violet's grandfather.

Violet awoke the next morning surrounded by her grandmother's words. She smiled at the journals covering her bed as she stretched. Pushing them aside with her feet, she had to climb over them to get up. She quickly reorganized them, tucking them safely away in their box, careful to keep them in order now that she'd sorted them, and she gently placed the box in the bottom of her closet, like they were rare, irreplaceable treasures.

All but one. The one she'd fallen asleep reading. The one in which her grandmother wrote about falling in love with her grandfather.

Violet knew it was cheesy, but she couldn't help herself, it was better than any romance novel ever written. Her grandmother wrote so eloquently about him, and Violet found herself feeling sorry that he hadn't lived long enough for her to know him in person. She was certain she would have loved him as much as she'd loved her grandmother.

She set that particular journal aside, not yet ready to tuck it away.

And then the memories of the day before settled over her, crushing her chest and making it suddenly hard to breathe.

The family at the lake. The missing girl.

Grady . . .

She knew what she had to do. It was the only way to clear his name.

Violet rapped softly on the front door, mentally preparing herself for the possibility that she'd been wrong about all this. That Grady *was* responsible for killing that family after all, and that he'd be wearing the imprints that would condemn him—the stale coffee grounds, the menagerie of colors, and the missing echo that belonged to the boy.

His mother answered, looking like she hadn't slept all night.

"Violet Ambrose?" She sounded as surprised as she looked. "I'm afraid Grady's not really up for visitors, dear."

As if on cue, Grady appeared in the hallway behind his mother. There was a time when Violet had believed Grady was handsome—in a goofy, boyish sort of way. They'd spent enough time together over the years that she hadn't always noticed it, the way friends sometimes did, but it was there all the same. Now, however, he looked pale and tired and skittish.

"Violet?" He blinked as he realized who had come to see

119

him. "What are you doing here?"

Violet started to rush toward him, not sure whether she should hug him . . . or hit him for making her care. But even after everything he'd done, she *did* care.

He wasn't a killer. That much she knew.

That much she was 100 percent certain of.

"How are you?" she asked, cringing to be asking such a stupid question. She could see just by looking at the dark circles beneath his eyes how he was.

Grady just stared at her, as if she'd grown a second—or third—head. "I don't get it. What are you doing here?"

"I . . . I just wanted to see if you're *okay*." She wondered how many times she'd been asked that very thing. It felt strange to be standing here, practically begging for his response.

Grady watched her, and for a moment Violet thought he wasn't going to answer at all. Then his face softened, transforming into the old Grady, the boy she'd climbed trees with in the fourth grade, as he smiled at her. A slow, wistful smile. "I'll be okay, Violet," he said, his voice low and rough. "Thanks for . . ." Emotion choked his words. "Thanks for coming by."

After dinner, which was takeout from her favorite Thai restaurant, and dessert, cupcakes that her dad had picked up from the bakery in town, Violet retreated to her bedroom. It wasn't that she didn't appreciate the extra effort her parents were making in the wake of what had happened at the lake house . . . especially their attempts to bribe her with baked goods. But it was too much like a flashback of the days following her return home after the kidnapping, when every conversation had had an edge of forced cheer, and when an almost endless stream of neighbors and acquaintances had come to the door, bringing with them cookies and pies and casseroles.

Like she'd died rather than survived.

Even her friends had been awkward around her at first, not sure how to act when she'd finally relented and invited them over for a girls' night to watch a movie. Like everyone else, Chelsea seemed to think that food solved everything and had shown up with a grocery store cake decorated with pink and yellow roses, and pink piping that spelled out the word *Congratulations* on it.

Congratulations. Violet had stood there staring at the cake Chelsea had thrust out to her, wondering what she was being congratulated for exactly. *Congratulations on being the lone survivor of a serial killer?* Or just your average, everyday *congratulations-for-killing-a-guy?*

If it hadn't been for Jules, who'd shoved Chelsea and called her an "inconsiderate A-hole," and then scooped up a piece of the pretty white cake with her bare hand and smooshed it in Chelsea's face, it probably would've stayed awkward. As it turned out, it's not food that fixes things, it's *food fights.*

Violet had been more than happy to stand in the corner of her kitchen and watch as Jules and Chelsea, and even

121

Claire, had demolished the cake, smashing and shoving and squishing it all over one another, until they'd all had to change clothes, and had spent the rest of the night digging frosting out of their ears and noses.

That had been the first time Violet had laughed—really laughed—after coming home.

This wasn't quite the same, but there was still that strange awkwardness about it. So, for now, she much preferred the less awkward peace of her bedroom.

The first soft *ping* blended in with the sounds of her imprint, and was easy enough to ignore. But it persisted— the pinging that struck the side of her house—once even hitting her window with a sharp crack.

Violet didn't have to look to know who it was, or that if she didn't stop him, her parents would.

She opened her window, leaning over the windowsill on her elbows. "You're either going to break the window," she whisper-shouted down to Jay, whose arm was cocked behind him, ready to launch another pebble, "or get arrested for being a nuisance."

He wiped his hands on his jeans and grinned up at her, a grin that was equal parts wholesome and predatory. "Come down here and I'll stop throwing rocks at your house," he taunted.

She didn't answer, just shut her window and stole out of her room. Jay was probably the only person who could've coaxed her out tonight, the only person she actually wanted to see.

Violet shook her head as she hopped down her front steps. "What are you doing here?" She stopped just before she reached him and put her hands on her hips. She didn't tell him that perched against his car like that, he took her breath away, or that she was thrilled to see him. Instead, she tried to glare. "It's kinda late, isn't it?"

Jay grinned, looking for all the world like he had no place better to be than standing there, in her driveway, waiting for her. He shrugged at the same time, his easygoing stance never shifting. "Violet," he explained, reaching out and looping his finger into the top of her jeans. He tugged, dragging her the rest of the way to him. The feel of his chest beneath hers made it even harder to breathe. "It's only nine."

"But it's a Sunday," she offered.

"*Mm-hmm . . .*" he responded, his voice distracted as he leaned down and nuzzled the side of her neck. His lips brushed playfully over her earlobe, as the soft stubble on his chin grazed the sensitive skin of her shoulder.

"It's a school night." She almost didn't get the words out as she stopped caring what she was saying. As she stopped caring about anything but his touch. She closed whatever space remained between them, and her fingers curved up to his shoulder and around his neck, slipping into the back of his hair so she could anchor herself. Everything inside of her reacted to him, like he'd flipped a switch, awakening her in all the right places as she ached for more. The evening air was thick and warm, and smelled like grass and cedars and Jay.

123

Whatever spell they were under didn't last nearly long enough, however, and with a shaky breath Jay drew his mouth away from her neck, resting his cheek against hers. It seemed to take all the effort he had just to stay like that. "If we don't stop now, your parents are going to make the driveway off-limits too." He remained frozen against her, his breathing harsh and uneven for several long minutes.

Violet couldn't quite gather her thoughts. Instead she concentrated on the beat of his heart beneath hers and the fact that they were separated by only two thin T-shirts. "Is there somewhere we can go?"

She knew he wanted it too, but he just shook his head. "I wish, Vi." He turned, just enough so his lips could leave the promise of a kiss on her cheek before he drew away completely . . . unsteadily. "It is a school night, you know?" he mocked, but he didn't fool her with his forced smile. He was as shaken as she was.

Violet sighed, leaning her head against his shoulder. "I saw Grady," she blurted out unexpectedly.

Jay paused, looking down at her. "You did? When?"

"Today. I went by his house." She tried to decipher what she saw in Jay's face. She knew how he felt about Grady after what he'd tried to do to her at the party last year. But she also knew that he and Jay had once been friends—there was no way Jay wanted the accusations to be true. "He didn't do it, Jay. He didn't have an imprint."

Jay studied her, as if he could uncover the answers to all his questions hidden in her expression, buried in her features.

And then he asked, "What'd your uncle say? When you told him?" Violet was silent for too long, and Jay squeezed his eyes shut before sighing. "You *did* tell him, didn't you?"

She chewed on her lower lip as she dropped her eyes. "Not *exactly*," she ground out. But before Jay could interject, telling her it was foolish to keep things from her uncle, she tried to explain. "I know it was the chicken's way out, but you weren't here last night. You didn't see the way Uncle Stephen looked. He's not gonna be happy when he finds out I went to see Grady by myself."

"When will you start trusting other people?" His words were harsh but his tone was so tender that Violet turned to watch his face. His eyes told her all the things his words didn't—that he was worried for her, and fearful of losing her. That he loved her.

"I trust you," she tried, but even she knew that wasn't what he meant.

Wrapping his arms around her, his muscles tensed, consuming her in his silent oath. "I do my best, Vi," he said against the top of her head. "But I can only do so much to keep you out of trouble."

She laughed, but she knew he was being at least semi-serious. He wanted to protect her, like some sort of knight in shining armor. The thing was, she wasn't a damsel, at least not the kind who needed saving from dragons and whatnot. Her worst enemy, as it turns out, was herself.

"Oh, and now you're laughing at me. Great." He groaned as he released her. "You're not a walk in the park, you know?" His head was tilted to the side as he considered her thoughtfully. "You know what I think? I think you don't even deserve the present I got you."

"Present?" Violet exclaimed. "For me?" She pulled away, a tiny thrill shivering through her as she stared into his flecked eyes. "You're wrong, I totally deserve it," she exclaimed. She playfully walked her fingers up his chest, puckering her lips and batting her eyes at him.

"You're ridiculous," he scoffed, but he was laughing at her.

Giggling, Violet glanced down at his empty hands, her brows arching. "*Well* . . . you know I hate surprises."

Without turning, Jay reached one hand behind his back, through the open window of his car to the seat below. When it came back he was holding a small, gold-colored bag with gold tissue sticking up from inside of it.

Violet recognized the name on the bag, even though she'd never gone into the shop. It was a store in the mall, the kind of place that sold jewelry and picture frames and collectibles. Not exactly a store where she imagined Jay would shop.

"Jay," she breathed, not sure how to feel about this. First her parents, and now Jay. "What's it for?"

"Just because." He shrugged. "I saw it and it reminded me of you. I hope it's not too weird."

Weird? Violet thought, wondering what kind of "weird" thing could possibly be contained in this beautiful bag.

He waited while she reached inside, excavating the

diaphanous paper, and took it when she handed it to him. When she peeked inside, she looked back up at him, confusion painting her expression. "A turtle?" she asked, wrinkling her nose. "*Okay*, maybe it's a little weird."

"Not the turtle . . ." He pushed the bag toward her again, prodding her to keep going. "Take it out."

Violet reached inside and lifted out the heavy silver turtle. She looked dubiously from it to Jay and back again. "It's . . . *cute* . . . ?" She didn't mean for it to sound like a question, but it totally had. She tried to rack her brain for reasons that Jay might think she wanted a turtle, or to think of something she'd done to make it remind him of her.

"Yes, Violet, it's cute," Jay sighed. "But that's not why I got it for you. Open it."

Violet looked again, and realized he was right, there was a tiny silver clasp she hadn't noticed before, just beneath the edge of the embellished shell. Pushing it, the shell popped open, and Violet's breath caught.

The inside was lined with black velvet, and Violet ran her finger over its soft silken surface.

She picked it up and turned it over. Engraved on the bottom were the words: *Moonlight Sonata.*

That was it, just *Moonlight Sonata.*

Violet looked back to Jay for a clue. "I still don't get it. I mean, I like it, I just don't get it."

Jay exhaled and took it from her hands. "It's a music box, Vi. You have to wind it up." He flipped it over and wound the almost unnoticeable silver key she hadn't seen before.

And that's when it started . . . the music.

The music.

She knew within two notes which song it was, and because of the engraving on the bottom, she also now knew the name of it: *Moonlight* Sonata.

It was haunting, hearing it played out loud and out of sync with the version in her head. Knowing that Jay could hear it too. Haunting and hypnotic and terrifying.

"How . . . ?" she breathed, not even able to finish that single thought.

"It's the right one, isn't it?" He was watching her expectantly, eagerly.

She wanted to tell him yes. She wanted to ask him how he'd known what was buried—hidden—deep inside her head. She wanted to wrap her arms around him and smother him with kisses for giving her this one tiny, probably insignificant piece of the crazy puzzle that had become her life.

Instead, she nodded. Slowly.

He shrugged again, looking so pleased with himself that Violet had to wonder if someone could actually burst from pride. "I heard you humming it," he explained, answering the question she'd been unable to ask. "You do it, when you think no one's listening. Thing is, I always listen, Vi."

It was possibly the sweetest thing she'd ever heard. His words . . . lingering with the sound of the music that now had a name.

How had she gotten so lucky? What had she done to deserve someone like Jay, someone who paid attention to the little things? Even something as trivial as which tune she hummed.

"And it's not too weird? You know, that it matches your imprint?" He looked uncertain now, his eyebrows drawn together in the center of his forehead, his lips pursed.

Violet reached up and settled her hand against his jaw. "It's *so* not too weird, Jay. I mean, yes, it is, but this is me we're talking about here . . . weird is relative." She sighed. "I love you," she vowed. "And I love my turtle. . . ." She let out a choked laugh and then she hugged it to her chest, even as the last notes wound down. "You, Jay Heaton, are the best boyfriend ever."

In her room that night, Violet played her new music box again and again. She memorized every detail of the silver turtle, each etched groove and flat polished plane. She silently repeated the name of the song too.

Moonlight Sonata. *Moonlight* Sonata. *Moonlight* Sonata.

The name was as beautiful as the tune.

She played her grandmother's music box too, the one with Brahms Lullaby, setting them side by side, until all three songs blurred together—the two music boxes and the imprint in her head—creating a dissonant sound that probably only she could appreciate.

That only she thought was beautiful.

She listened to the last notes as she curled beneath her blankets to read her grandma's scrawled handwriting.

July 13, 1971

Maggie is the perfect child. I'm sure every mother says that about her baby, but I'm certain that in this case it must be true.

Violet grinned, fascinated by the notion of her mother as anything but a grown-up. It was strange to consider her mom through her grandmother's eyes. She kept reading, enthralled.

I can't stop looking at her, studying her, trying to see who she is . . . and who she will be. She has curls and the unmistakable green eyes of her father. She has my lips though. It's too soon to know what else she might have of mine, what else she might have inherited. I can only hope she doesn't have it. I want nothing more than to know that Maggie will live in peace, never tasting or smelling or hearing the dead.

Violet's chest ached as she gripped the pages, recognizing what her grandmother meant. She knew she shouldn't let it bother her, that her grandma had wished for her mom not to share her ability—the ability that Violet herself had. But she couldn't help it. It stung that the woman who she'd inherited it from hadn't wanted it. Hadn't wanted her daughter to have it.

Where once Violet had believed that she and her grandmother had shared a bond, she now realized they shared an

130

affliction. Like a birth defect. At least in her grandmother's eyes.

Still, Violet kept reading the passages, knowing that somewhere along the line something must have changed, because the woman she remembered hadn't felt that way at all.

> *John says even if she has it, it won't matter. He tells me it makes me who I am and he wouldn't change a thing about me. He's sweet that way, always trying to assure me that I'm normal, good even. If only I felt the same.*

> *October 25, 1971*
> *Winter's coming, but Maggie and I bundle up whenever possible and head outdoors. She can't tell me so, but I'm sure she likes our adventures as much as I do. I watch her closely whenever I feel them coming on, one of those echoes from the dead. So far she doesn't seem to be aware of them. She looks safe and peaceful there, inside her stroller. She smiles and coos blissfully as they call to me.*

> *But that doesn't mean she doesn't feel it. Maybe she's sensing something different from what I do. Hopefully, though, she feels nothing at all.*

Violet tried to remember the first time she'd ever heard the word *echo*. It's what she'd always called the sensations she felt, but she'd never really considered where the term had come from. It never dawned on her that it might have been her grandmother who'd come up with it. It was strange to think how easily she'd accepted it, how it had just become part of her everyday vocabulary, like *apple* or *cat* or *school*.

She kept reading, page after page of entries about her mother's first words and her first steps. She learned more about her grandfather—her mom's dad—a man Violet was sure she would have liked, probably loved even. She saw the gradual change in her grandmother's passages as, over the months and years, she'd learned to believe her husband's words about her being a good person, a worthy person, until eventually she'd accepted her ability. She'd even begun to call it a gift.

Like Violet, her grandmother spent as much time outdoors as possible, so there were numerous accounts of the animals she'd discovered. Several times her grandmother had used her garden as an excuse for why her fingernails had dirt caked beneath them. But in the privacy of her journal she told another story. A tale of giving those animals the peace they craved.

Of silencing their echoes.

Violet knew what that was like. She had Shady Acres, where she'd buried more than her share of the animals she'd come across. Her way of finding her own silence.

If only it were that easy now, she thought, listening to the imprint that clung to her.

She learned too that it hadn't been a secret in her grandparents' household, much like it wasn't in Violet's.

It wasn't until she came to a passage written during the spring of 1976—over thirty years earlier—that Violet sat up in her bed, every part of her body singing with awareness. She reread her grandmother's entry, which had been written hastily, as if she couldn't get the words down fast enough:

March 23, 1976

I'm not sure what it means that a body doesn't have an echo. None at all. I wasn't even sure the poor little mouse was dead when I first saw it, curled in a ball in Maggie's hands. I told Maggie to drop it, afraid it was just stunned, that it might come to at any second and bite her in an effort to escape. I almost didn't realize I'd yelled at Maggie until she started crying. But I didn't go after her, not right away. I had to be sure about the mouse.

It was dead though. Dead as dead. I uncurled its body, which was already cold and stiff, so I had to pry it apart. Its chest had been ripped apart. Mauled was more like it. But the strange part was the emptiness surrounding it, the lack of . . . anything.

I have a theory. John's going to help me find out if I'm right.

April 1, 1976 (April Fools' Day)

This is probably a good day for my experiment because surely I'm wrong and then the joke will be on me. I'm dying for John to get home.

April 1, 1976

It worked! Which means I was right. I'm not sure whether I should be so elated by this revelation, but I am. Probably because it means I understand one more thing about my gift, one more thing I didn't before.

Tonight, John brought home a live chicken. We had to wait until Maggie had gone to bed and then one of us had to kill it. I thought he'd want me to do it, since it was my idea. Instead, he did it. I told him he didn't have to, that I didn't need an answer that badly, but he could tell I was lying. I did want to know. I can't explain why.

Before he did it, I almost changed my mind again. I thought about Ian and how he smelled (and tasted) after he'd gone hunting with his daddy. I was worried about what might cling to John in the wake of the chicken's death. But somehow, I couldn't tell him that. I wanted to know that badly. I was willing to take that risk.

He didn't make me watch, but I was sure he must have cried. His eyes were red when he came back and the chicken was limp in his hands. Its head was hanging at a strange angle and there was a scent of chicory coming off it . . . and off John. Chicory! I could live forever with chicory!

Turns out, the heart was the key. It seems like such a simple solution now, like something I should've known all along. The mouse's was gone, torn out when whatever killed it was trying to eat it, I assume, since most of its chest was missing. As soon as I removed the chicken's heart the chicory scent vanished. It was just a chicken then. A dead chicken.

The strange part was, the scent didn't just vanish from the chicken, it vanished from John too. Whatever chicory I'd smelled on him was gone now. Forever, I suppose.

Violet read the entry again and again, her own heart pounding in her chest now. When she was certain she hadn't misread it, that she understood exactly what her grandmother was saying, she reached for her cell phone.

Sara answered, her voice sounding thick and bleary. Violet glanced at the alarm clock on her nightstand. It was 1:04.

"Sorry, Sara, I didn't mean to wake you." Suddenly she wished she'd waited till morning, but she wasn't sure she'd be able to. She had to know.

She heard rustling, and Sara cleared her throat. "It's okay, Violet. What's going on?"

"I had to ask you something. The boy, the one from the lake house . . . his body, was there anything *strange* about it?"

A brief pause, and then, "Strange how?"

Every muscle in her body tensed, as if this was the moment of truth. "His heart . . ." Violet said, thinking how weird this might sound if she was wrong. That maybe she'd awakened Sara for nothing. "Was it . . . *missing*?"

There was another pause, but this time there was no rustling sound coming from the other end. "How did you know that? How could you possibly know that?"

"So it's true then?" Violet relaxed, practically sighing into the phone.

"I got a call from someone at the medical examiner's office today. But I still don't understand . . . *how did you know?*"

"It's *why* he didn't have an echo." She explained what she'd read in her grandmother's journals. "It's why I couldn't *feel* anything from him."

"Holy crap," Sara breathed softly, absorbing the information Violet had just given her.

Violet nodded. "I know, right?" Mentally, she added this to the ever-changing list of rules she'd created in her head.

No heart, no echo.

CHAPTER 7

VIOLET CLIMBED INSIDE JAY'S CAR, TURNING around just in time to see her mom still standing at the doorway, wearing the same I-don't-want-to-let-you-out-of-my-sight expression she'd been wearing all weekend. Just the fact that she was up this early told Violet how worried she was.

Oblivious to her mother's concerns, Jay leaned over Violet and waved, "Hey, Mrs. Ambrose!"

"Will you stop calling her that?" Violet complained, pushing him out of her way so she could close her door. "She's probably told you a million times already to call her Maggie."

Her mom made a pinched face and waved back, but it was more like she was waving him off before she turned to go back inside, closing the door behind her.

"See? Told you so," Violet insisted.

Jay handed her one of the Starbucks cups that had been sitting in his console.

"Wow," she said, delighting in the feel of the warm cup, and sniffing the small opening in the lid. "This whole stumbling-onto-a-crime-scene thing is really starting to pay off. Last night a present. Now this." She grinned as she took a sip of the vanilla latte.

Jay rubbed his jaw nervously. "Yeah, I wasn't really sure what the protocol for 'freaked out by dead bodies' was. You're not sick, so bringing you soup was out the question. And you didn't know the people, so giving you flowers seemed *wrong*."

Violet pursed her lips, considering his dilemma. "I see what you mean. Jewelry maybe? Or cash?"

Jay laughed. "Sorry, just a turtle. And some coffee." He raised his eyebrows. "But at least I went to Starbucks."

Since there wasn't a real Starbucks in Buckley, Violet knew that meant he'd driven all the way to the next town to get it.

She shrugged, biting back a grin. "I guess coffee'll do. Until you find the right diamond, or maybe something designer."

Jay started his car. "You're starting to be sorta high maintenance, Violet Marie." He backed out of the driveway.

"I remember when you were happy if I gave you the better stick to play with."

She giggled. "Um, yeah, I was nine then!"

"Yeah, well *that* Violet wouldn't have complained if her boyfriend had driven all the way to Enumclaw to get her a coffee before school."

"Yeah, well *that* Violet," Violet added, taking another sip of her latte and raising her brows defiantly, "would have gagged on the coffee and then punched you in the nose for trying to poison her."

Jay glanced at her over his shoulder as they hit the main road. "Touché, Vi! Touché!"

Violet leaned back and tipped her head to the side, watching Jay as he drove. Sunlight poured in through the car's windows and glinted off his face, catching the strands of his hair and casting his skin in a soft golden glow. It was the way she always saw him, golden and sun-kissed and beautiful. She took a sip of her coffee, feeling warm from more than just the drink.

Without meaning to, the tinny plinks of her imprint drew her thoughts to a darker place, as she remembered what she'd read in her grandmother's diaries. As always, her first instinct was to keep the information to herself, to hide it from Jay, and her parents, and from everyone else who mattered. Ferreting the knowledge away and doling it out only on a need-to-know basis.

It was a lonely way to live. And she was getting sick of it.

"Hey, you know those journals I told you about? The

ones my mom gave me that belonged to my grandma Louise?"

His eyes stayed trained on the road as they pulled into the student lot. "Uh-huh."

"I read something in them last night. Something interesting."

Jay cast a quick glance her way. "Interesting how?" he asked.

Violet lips curved upward. It was a lazy smile, but a satisfied one. "She knew why a body wouldn't have an echo."

"You mean she'd seen that before? Like the boy you found at the lake house?" Jay pulled into a parking spot and turned to stare at her. She nodded. His expression was incredulous, and she thought it was exactly the way she'd felt when she'd first read the entry.

"I know," she agreed, even though he hadn't said a word.

When they got out of the car, Jay groped for his backpack in the backseat and punched the alarm button on his key fob several times more than he needed to before rushing to keep up with Violet.

By the time he caught her, Violet was halfway across the parking lot. "So," he asked, reaching out to stop her before they reached the school. "What was it? Why was the boy missing his echo?" He cocked his head to the side, still looking too golden for his own good.

"His heart," Violet offered quietly. "It had been cut out."

But before he could respond, Violet tasted the familiar tang of dandelions and glanced up to see a car parked in front of the school—one she recognized all too well.

"Uh-oh," Jay said from beside her, seeing the same thing she had. "Looks like someone's in trouble."

Her uncle was there, leaning against the side of one of his police department vehicles with his arms crossed in front of his chest. He spotted her immediately, and she recognized the look on his face. He was fuming.

"Wait here," she told Jay, deciding she might as well do this on her own. No point dragging him into this too.

Her uncle's stance didn't ease, even as she came nearer, closing the gap between them. If anything, he looked sterner. Angrier. Violet's insides felt like Jell-O the closer she got to him.

"When were you planning to tell me?" He stood up, his actions tense and jerky as he yanked open the back door of the cruiser, telling her without words to get inside.

She frowned at him, but followed his lead. "Soon," she said as she slid inside the cool interior of the police car. She would have shivered even if the plastic seat wasn't cold from the AC. Her uncle's glower was downright frosty.

He got in the front seat, and Violet did her best to ignore the strange looks she was getting from the other students as they walked past. She was sitting in the back of a police car, after all. No doubt they were thinking she was in some sort of trouble—at least those who didn't realize right away it was her uncle behind the wheel.

She kept her gaze averted, not sure where she should look since she didn't want to look at her uncle either.

"You saw Grady after I expressly told you not to get involved," Uncle Stephen accused. There was a pause and she knew he was waiting for her to look up. Instead, she concentrated on her bare fingernails, which were short and ragged, in desperate need of a manicure, she thought idly.

Guilt flushed her cheeks. "Actually, you didn't," she said, feeling like she was on shaky ground now. She glanced up nervously to see him watching her from the rearview mirror.

"Didn't what, Vi?" he snapped, his voice not sounding nearly as unsure as hers had.

"Didn't say not to get involved," she answered, trying to be bolder now. "You didn't really say anything." She watched as his face turned an unnatural shade of red.

She waited for him to say something. To argue that she was wrong, and insist that he *had* told her to mind her own business. But he couldn't because he hadn't. She saw the moment he realized the truth as his shoulders fell and he sighed, a long, deflated sound.

For a long time there were no other sounds, no words between them. And then he turned around in his seat, no longer staring at her from the mirror.

When he faced her, she could see the shadowed stubble along his jaw and the even darker shadows beneath his eyes. "I might not have said it, but I should have." His voice was softer now, less accusatory and more thoughtful. "I didn't want you to see Grady, but not because I think he's a killer. I don't. At least not anymore. The evidence is back, and we

142

won't be charging him. There's nothing that shows he was there the day of the murder. Even his alibi checks out.

"The real truth is, it's hard for me to stand by and watch you go through this again and again. It can't be good for you, seeing the things you see. Being around bodies and killers." He shook his head. "What I should have said that night is that I didn't want you to get involved any more than you already are because I'm worried about you. I know I can't protect you, Vi, but it doesn't stop me from wanting to."

Violet choked on the lump that formed in her throat. She hated how much she'd already put her family through by being different from everyone else. And she hated even more that it wasn't going to end anytime soon. "I'm okay, Uncle Stephen. I can handle it." It was true. She'd realized that much, at least, over the past months . . . the past year. "I *want* to help. I only went to see him, to see if . . . you know, if he was the one you were looking for."

"I know," he said, nodding, and looking worn-down. "Sara called me this morning; she said you told her he didn't do it. It was just one more reason to believe the evidence. Dammit, Vi. When did you get so grown up? When did you stop wearing princess dresses and begging me for piggyback rides? When did you stop needing me to look out for you?"

Violet grimaced. "Okay, one . . . I don't think I ever wore princess dresses, even when I was Cassidy's age, but I'll cop to the piggyback rides. And two . . ." Her eyes stung as she blinked hard against the tears building behind her eyes. "You know I'll always need you to look out for me." She let out a watery laugh. "I mean, you have met me, right? I'm sort of a danger magnet."

She heard a sniffle from the front seat, and then her uncle was getting out of the car and opening her door. "Come here, you," he said, and he was reaching for her before she could even get out on her own. "I really just want you to be happy. I want everything to be rainbows and sparkles for you, Vi."

Violet grinned against his chest, where he had her wrapped in one of his famous bear hugs. She hoped she never outgrew his silly sayings. "I know, Uncle Stephen. I'm just not that girl, I guess."

He shrugged, not letting her go right away. "Doesn't mean I can't try, does it?"

She was about to tell him that she loved how hard he tried. That, or that she couldn't breathe, when she heard Jay, his voice finding its way inside the wall of arms her uncle had her buried in. "Does this mean everyone's all good? There's been a truce?"

Her uncle released her and Violet fought the urge to gasp for breath.

"It's fine. It's fine," Uncle Stephen said, sniffing again. "I should get going anyway. There's still a lot to do."

"I have to go too," Violet agreed, peering up at Jay. "You know, school and all?" And then she paused as she turned back to her uncle. "So, what about the evidence? Did it show who *was* there? You said it cleared Grady, but did it give you an idea who might have done it? Any leads on Veronica?"

Her uncle rubbed his eyes, and this time it had nothing to do with princesses or piggyback rides or family bonds. He shook his head, looking weary once more. "Not yet. But I promise I'll tell you if we find something. Deal?"

Violet smiled at him. "Deal." He turned, but before he could get in his car, Violet called after him, "I love you, Uncle Stephen!"

He didn't turn back, but lifted his hand in a wave. "Rainbows and sparkles, Vi. Rainbows and sparkles."

School was as bad as she'd expected it to be. Worse even.

As soon as she entered the hallways, Violet could hear everyone around her talking about the family who'd been killed over the weekend, each with their own dramatic interpretation about how it had happened . . . each with their own version of the gory—if incorrect—details of the murder scene itself.

In some it was a straight-up home invasion–style shooting. Others claimed it had been a stabbing. Still others claimed murder-suicide. A few gave detailed descriptions of the bodies having been "chopped to bits."

And almost all mentioned Grady.

She hated hearing him accused of crimes she knew— without a doubt—he hadn't committed. Yet she was unable to defend him, no matter how riled she got.

How could they be so ignorant? So insensitive? This was

145

one of their own classmates they were talking about. In some cases, he was their friend.

"You hear about Grady?" Chelsea sidled up next to Violet and started talking before Violet even had a chance to open her mouth. "I hear they think he offed an entire family. It was some girl he was dating who went to Riverside High. And she's missing now. Her picture is all over the television." Violet searched for Jay, wishing she hadn't decided to wait while he dropped his books at his locker. "Dude, Grady Spencer? I never would've pegged him as the cold-blooded-killer type."

Violet's stomach dropped as she wondered how much she should—or was even allowed to—reveal. But this was Grady they were talking about. "He isn't," she told Chelsea, mildly annoyed that this was the kind of talk she was hearing from her own friends.

"You know what they say about these guys? You never see it comin'. They're the perfect neighbor, then one day . . ." Her eyes widened exaggeratedly. "*Bam!* They just . . . snap."

"Okay, crazy." Violet let out a shaky laugh. She felt bad for even joking when they were discussing something so serious, so disturbing, but Chelsea looked as if she were telling a ghost story in front of a campfire, her eyes all wild and her statements outlandish. "Take it easy. Even if I thought you were right, my uncle told me he didn't do it."

But Chelsea wasn't finished just yet. "Know what else I heard?" Her face hovered just inches from Violet's and her eyes narrowed mistrustfully. "I heard that it was someone from White River who found the bodies." Her voice dropped. "And maybe, just maybe, *that someone* never showed up at the lake to meet her friends."

Violet could hear the blood rushing past her ears, and she reached up to grip the strap on her backpack, her fingers going numb. She prayed Chelsea didn't notice how pale she'd gone, and she let out a laugh—a nervous high-pitched sound. "That's ridiculous, Chels," she said, trying to sound as carefree as she could manage. She started weaving her way through the crowded hallway.

Chelsea kept up with her easily though, watching her out of the corner of her eye. "Really? Because we waited for hours and you never even called." Her words were heavy with meaning. "You *know* something, don't you, V?"

Violet smoothed her features as best she could and shrugged. "There's nothing to know."

But Chelsea refused to drop it. "Bull," she countered. "I know you've been through some serious shit, but there've also been a lot of times when you've just . . ." She snapped her fingers. "Vanished." Her gaze turned momentarily thoughtful and she pulled Violet to a stop. "And I'm not talking about when you really . . . you know, vanished. I'm talking about all the times no one can reach you, all the times I've stopped by your house and your mom says you're at the 'library' or at 'Jay's house'"—she emphasized the words with air quotes, making it clear what she thought of the excuses she'd been given—"but here's the deal, you were never at any of those places. I know because I checked." Before Violet could say anything, Chelsea went on, "Yeah, that's right." Her eyes tapered to slits. "I'm watching you."

Violet didn't have to pretend to laugh this time as she pushed Chelsea away from her. "Oh my god, Chels, you've been watching *way* too much *CSI* or *Law & Order* or whatever. Get a grip." She brushed past her friend, trying to drop the subject. "And stop calling me V. I mean it this time."

"You ready?" Jay asked when he found them, and Violet lifted her eyebrows at Chelsea, silently asking her if she was through.

Glaring, Chelsea made a disgusted sound and studied Violet with pinched lips, but she didn't say anything else.

Then, just as she was about to leave them, to go the opposite direction toward her class, Chelsea lifted her first two fingers up to her eyes and then pointed back at Violet, the universal sign for *I'm watching you*.

Jay looked confused. "What was that all about?" he asked.

Sighing, Violet leaned into him as they walked, feeling the burden of too many secrets weighing on her. "Chelsea thinks I'm hiding something from her."

He snorted and pointed out the obvious. "If she only knew." But before Violet could punch him in the arm, they reached her classroom and he stopped short. He scowled, but not at Violet; it was meant for Rafe, who was waiting for Violet, leaning against the wall, wearing a smug grin on his face.

Jay had accepted the fact that Rafe would be at their

school every day, but she knew it bothered him. How could it not? It bothered her, and he was her friend.

"You okay?" Violet asked, shifting on her feet to block his view of Rafe, forcing him to look at her instead.

Jay exhaled noisily. "Everything's . . . fine." He smiled at her, and Violet's heart shuddered. She didn't try to stop him when he closed the gap between them, his lips finding hers in a deep—and territorial—kiss.

When he was finished, she couldn't find her voice for a long, breathless moment. "That was for him, wasn't it?"

"The kiss? Nah, that was for you, Vi. Only for you."

She giggled. "I feel like I'm stuck in the middle of some kind of tug-of-war. Only I'm the rope and you two are trying to pull me apart."

"Don't kid yourself, you're not the rope, you're the prize." Jay's lazy grin reached all the way to his eyes. "And, for the record, I've already won."

Violet shook her head. "It's not a contest, Jay," she replied as she started to walk away.

But Jay put his hand over hers, pulling her back for one final kiss. "I know, Vi."

When she passed him on her way into the classroom, Rafe scowled. "Nice show," he bit out acerbically. Violet tried to pretend she didn't know what he was talking about as she headed down the row of desks to her seat.

"Whatever," Violet answered, not wanting to have this discussion.

Guys are ridiculous, she decided as she kept walking, glad Rafe was behind her and couldn't see the scowl on her face.

If only it were that simple, because then it was Rafe stopping her. Rafe with his electric touch, and when his fingers reached for hers, she couldn't help jolting. "Sara told me," he said, his voice so quiet Violet could barely hear it above her music-box imprint. "About what you read in your grandmother's diary." His eyes were deep and mesmerizing, and Violet told herself it didn't matter because Jay already had her. "She also said you told her your friend didn't do it," he whispered.

Violet glanced around, wishing that everyone had heard the truth in those last words, but knowing they couldn't. Yet all she could say was, "He's not my friend."

Through the cafeteria window, Violet could see Chelsea and Rafe sitting on the grass in the quad, rather than at their usual table. While the weather cooperated, the grassy area out in the courtyard, and benches surrounding it, was crowded during the lunch hours. After that, when the rain returned, or when it was too cold to be comfortable, only the loners—either by choice or by circumstance—would continue eating out there, sitting alone and thumbing their noses at the rest of the school for forsaking them.

But for now, as the sun beat down, and students crowded every open space, eating outside didn't seem like such a bad idea.

Violet had expected to interrupt another lopsided conversation, in which Chelsea talked and talked, and talked some more, while Rafe only half listened, nodding occasionally so she wouldn't think he was a total D-bag. As far as Violet could tell, that was about as far as his social charms extended . . . to attempt to tolerate those around him.

Except that wasn't what she walked into at all. It wasn't until that very moment, when Violet approached the two of them, Chelsea sitting with her legs crossed in front of her, and Rafe sitting up, leaning one elbow on his knee, that she realized just how chummy the two of them had gotten. So much so, that she heard Rafe, his voice as low as ever, actually responding when Chelsea asked what he was reading.

When he told her it was *Catcher in the Rye*, Chelsea cast him a knowing grin and said boldly, "'In my *mind*, I'm probably the biggest sex maniac you ever saw.'"

Rafe laughed then, and Violet froze in place, trying to figure out what had just happened. Trying to unsort the jumble of emotions that knotted tightly in her chest, making it nearly impossible to breathe.

Rafe's laugh was such a foreign sound. Of course Violet had heard him laugh before, but never that kind of laugh. An encouraging one. A flirtatious one. And that's what that laugh had been, Violet was sure of it. They were sitting there, in the quad at school . . . flirting. With each other.

Violet took an uncertain step backward, thinking that

sitting outside might not have been such a great idea after all. Suddenly all this fresh air was making her woozy. Or possibly it was the company. Either way, her head was spinning and she felt like she might be coming down with something.

Rafe glanced up then, at that very moment, and saw her standing there gaping at them. And she saw something cross his face, something dark and unexpected, filling her with guilt. It was a look so close to longing it made Violet wince. "Violet?" he said, his voice no longer flirtatious and teasing, and she thought she might have actually heard a note of regret, buried in the deep timbre of her name.

Violet wanted him to stop looking at her like that, and she certainly didn't want Chelsea to see him doing it, so she dropped her gaze to her friend, ignoring Rafe altogether. "Did . . . did you just quote *Catcher in the Rye*?" She couldn't help asking the question any more than she could stop the incredulity that saturated her voice. Since when did Chelsea quote anything from the required reading list at school? Or more importantly, since when had Chelsea ever *read* anything from the required reading list?

Chelsea's smile was mischievous as she glanced up at Violet, admitting, "It's the only line I know. And that's probably the only chance I'll ever have to use it." She turned back to Rafe, her grin widening lasciviously. "Or maybe not."

But Rafe was no longer flirting with her, and Violet's legs felt unsteady, and all she wanted to do was turn and run away. Because standing there, with Rafe's blue eyes boring into her, she felt far too vulnerable . . . far too exposed.

And far too confused.

When she felt a hand at her elbow, she jumped and spun nervously to face whoever had just grabbed her.

Jay was there, staring back at her with his warm, faithful eyes and a crooked smile on his lips. Gemma stood beside him, looking like they'd just arrived together.

"You aren't serious, are you? We aren't really going to eat our lunch in the dirt, are we?" Gemma folded her arms across her chest and eyed the grass as if Chelsea and Rafe were rolling around in an oozing pile of sloppy mud.

"You don't have to sit here at all," Chelsea told her, lifting her chin defiantly. One thing about Chelsea, she either liked you or she didn't, and you didn't have to guess which side of the line you fell on. And Gemma, for whatever reason, had landed on the wrong side. "We were doing just fine before you got here."

Violet was still dazed, and then Jay's hand slid down to hers, his palm settling lightly, gingerly over her own. For several seconds their hands stayed like that, their fingers lined up in perfect rows, from thumb to pinkie, his dwarfing hers. She savored the feel of his rough skin sliding over hers. It was electric, his touch, but not in the way it was when Rafe touched her. This kind of electricity started inside of her, filling her up and spreading to every fissure, making her feel connected. Whole.

Rafe glanced away, and she could feel him withdrawing once more, disappearing inside himself. A different kind of guilt stabbed her; she didn't want to be responsible for hurting him.

But Jay's fingers were still there, and when he finally slid them in and through and between hers, Violet felt the knot in her chest loosen. She could breathe again. And more than that, she could feel the rush of her own pulse pumping blood past her ears. Without saying a single word, Jay drew her down onto the grass, and Violet followed, letting her knees fold beneath her as she stayed right by his side . . . where she belonged.

Gemma, still standing above them, rolled her eyes and exhaled dramatically. "Fine," she snapped, just as Claire and Jules came out into the quad, joining them. "I guess I'd rather sit in the dirt than sit alone."

She scowled at each and every one of them in turn, but most especially at Chelsea, who smirked as the blonde girl tried to find some position that would keep both her and her clothing from touching the ground at all. Ultimately, Gemma ended up using her fancy new book bag as a cushion of sorts, keeping her knees bent so that her jeans didn't so much as graze the tops of the grass. She brushed obsessively at nonexistent pieces of dirt or pollen or whatever else it was she thought might be landing on her, and she barely touched her lunch.

But it was Jay who had captured Violet's attention, when he leaned across her shoulder, his breath finding her ear and sending shivers along the length of her spine. "What do you say we spend some time together tonight? Maybe do some homework?"

By the time she reached Anatomy & Physiology, the class where Violet had spent the entire first week of school pretending Grady didn't exist—trying not to look his way or draw attention to herself—she'd nearly allowed herself to forget what happened. But now that she was standing inside the classroom they shared, Grady was all she could think about. Even though it had only been a week since school had started, the seat he'd occupied during that brief time had indisputably become his. And now it sat empty. Untouched. A shrine of notoriety.

Violet slumped solemnly in the chair next to Gemma, who'd fled from lunch early so she could wash her hands— and probably everything else she could reach—after being subjected to the "filthy outdoors." Violet didn't bother trying to contain the conflicting emotions she felt toward her classmates: anger, unease, disgust, worry—all coiled together in one enormous mass that had turned her into a time bomb of sorts. Even if Gemma hadn't been an empath, she probably would have sensed something was wrong.

Turning an exasperated glance at Violet, Gemma scooted her chair a little farther away.

Violet just shrugged, not bothering to apologize or explain as she pulled out her notebook. She didn't care whether she was making Gemma uncomfortable or not.

"Oh, for god's sakes," Gemma huffed. "It's so hard to make you miserable if you don't give a shit. Fine, I give up." Her voice shifted, becoming . . . almost nice. "I'm sorry you had such a craptastic weekend. And . . . sorry about that guy, even thought you sorta hated him." She nodded toward the empty chair. "If it makes you feel any better, I think everyone else hates him now too."

Violet's jaw tensed. "It doesn't. And I don't hate him. I just . . . we just . . ." She didn't owe Gemma any explanations. "We weren't friends anymore, but that doesn't mean he deserves this."

"So it's true then? What Sara said about him not being guilty?"

Sometimes Violet forgot that Gemma lived with Sara and Rafe, that they were the only family she had, and that she knew what they knew.

She nodded. They might not be friends—she and Gemma—but it was nice to have another person she could confide in. Or rather, not have to lie to all the time. Not to have to hide her ability from.

She wished it could be this easy with her *real* friends.

"Hmm," Gemma exhaled. "I sorta pegged him as an ass." When Violet turned in her chair to gape at her, she lifted her shoulder. "*What?* I did."

"Well, just because someone's an ass doesn't make them a murderer."

Gemma's lips twisted into a meaningful smile. "You got

that right, sister," she said. "If that were the case, Rafe would definitely be a serial killer."

Violet couldn't help the smile that slid over her lips. Gemma was right. She thought of the way Rafe generally kept others at a distance, ensuring that no one got too close or became too attached, by offending everyone. In that sense, it almost seemed logical that he'd be drawn to Chelsea. She was sort of offensive herself.

But Violet knew there was another side of him too, he'd shown it to her. He'd told her how he felt.

Unfortunately, Violet couldn't share Rafe's feelings.

Couldn't, she thought, turning the word over in her mind. It was a strange way to phrase it. Hadn't she meant *didn't*? That she *didn't* share Rafe's feelings?

It didn't matter though, she had someone. She had Jay.

She and Rafe could only ever be friends.

"People are talking, you know?" Gemma said, interrupting Violet's thoughts and dragging her back into the classroom.

"About Grady? I know."

"No. About you." She shrugged. "I mean, not about you, really. But about the person who found the bodies. They know it was someone who goes to school here. There's a lot of guessing going on about who it could be."

Goose bumps broke out over Violet's skin. "Have they . . . ? Did they . . . ? Has anyone said my name?"

Gemma made a face, dismissing the notion as absurd.

"Of course not. They point at each other mostly, trying to get someone to admit it was them. Really, they have no idea who it was."

Violet looked around her, at the other students in her class, most of whom she'd known her whole life. Somehow, Gemma's assurance, even with her empathic abilities, didn't make Violet feel any more secure.

By the end of the day, Violet was exhausted. What she wanted was to go home and flop on her bed. To read through more of her grandmother's journals. To sleep.

But it was Monday and she had an appointment, one she wasn't allowed to miss. After Jay had dropped her off at her house so she could get her car, she made the long drive into the city, trying to give herself every reason to cancel her weekly meeting with Dr. Lee, but knowing, no matter how good the excuses she came up with, it was against the rules he'd laid out for her. And the last thing she wanted to do was to put her family in harm's way.

Instead she concentrated on the fact that he might actually be able to help her this time. As much as she hated to admit it, he had a way of making her feel better when an echo—or in this case, *echoes*—weighed on her.

She was doing okay. Better than okay, really. By comparison to how it used to be after she'd found a body, the dull headache and the sluggishness she felt now were a cakewalk. She could manage through this like a champ.

Still, that didn't mean it couldn't be better, which was

where Dr. Lee came in. He had ways . . .

Ways of stilling her mind. Ways of easing the tension. Ways of chasing away her demons.

And for that, she almost hated him more. For making her lean on him, even when he was twisting her arm and forcing her to do things.

She barely said two words during the entire first half of the session. It wasn't until Dr. Lee asked her about the events of the weekend that she—reluctantly—allowed him to walk her through a breathing exercise.

Of course, it worked. And of course, inwardly she cursed herself for letting him be so useful. But she did feel better, despite herself.

As she slipped out into the waiting room, a familiar voice startled her. "Violet! *Hey! How are you?*"

She glanced back, checking to see if Dr. Lee was watching, but the door to his office was closed, giving them a few minutes of privacy. Sam didn't seem to notice her guardedness as he stepped forward and wrapped her in a hug that was too tight.

Violet laughed, momentarily forgetting her silent vow to be sullen and brooding whenever she was in Dr. Lee's presence. "Sam . . ." She could feel his ribs poking out beneath her hands as she shoved out of his grip. "What are you doing here?"

Sam's skinny arms fell away, but his smile stayed firm and affixed on his face. She still had a hard time with the notion that Sam was some sort of super genius—or at least *self-professed* super genius. She knew it must be true, though. He wasn't even sixteen and already he was a sophomore at the university. Hard to imagine since he barely had his learner's permit and still had to take the bus and get rides from his parents everywhere he went.

He tapped the side of his head. "You know, psych checkup. Makin' sure all the cogs are still in working order."

Violet scrutinized Sam, trying to decide if he was being forced here the same way she was. But he stared back at her with his usual unreserved, too-eager expression, the one that looked like he had nothing in the world to hide.

Sometimes Violet forgot there'd actually been a time when she *wanted* to be here, when her visits to Dr. Lee were less than obligatory. "Yeah. Me too," she said, knowing she couldn't tell anyone else about the doctor's coercive tactics.

"Man, I heard about the righteous crime scene you stumbled on. I'm so jealous. I heard it was disgusting."

"Um, yeah," Violet agreed. "It was pretty gross. And you're pretty twisted if you're jealous."

He lifted his scrawny shoulders. "Duh," he said, like that much was obvious. "Never said I wasn't. So? Any suspects yet?"

Violet shook her head, thinking about Grady being cleared, and her uncle's promise to let her know if he learned anything new. "Not yet."

Sam glanced over his shoulder, making sure they were still alone before he leaned closer. "Man, I wish I could'a been there. That's my favorite part . . . being at the scene

160

itself. Touching things that belonged to the . . ." He shifted nervously on his feet, as if what he was saying was disrespectful, and then he shrugged. "Victims and whatnot. I love that flash . . ." His eyes lit up then, filled with wonder. "When I know I've got something. When I know I can help. Hopefully Sara can snag us some of their things. I hear the girl's still missing. Hopefully it's not too late for her."

Violet felt a sudden jolt at Sam's words, and wondered how she'd nearly forgotten that Rafe wasn't the only one who could glean information by touching objects. Sam had the gift of psychometry too.

"Sam, Sam, Sam . . ." She flashed him a knowing grin as she reached for her backpack. She fumbled around inside it for a second, her fingers closing around the leather-bound journal that had once belonged to her grandmother.

She felt giddy, as she opened the front flap of the journal and reached for the photograph she'd hidden there, the one of the missing girl—the school picture Violet had lifted from the crime scene. Violet wasn't sure it would work, but they could try at least. Maybe someone had handled it enough, maybe it had meant enough to one of them, that something could be read from it.

"Here," Violet said, handing it over to him. "Keep it safe. And, please, don't tell anyone I gave it to you. I don't want anyone to know I took it."

Sam watched her, his eyes wide as if she were presenting him with a work of art, rather than something she'd stolen off someone's refrigerator.

"You can count on me," he breathed, pressing it against his chest and closing his eyes.

Dr. Lee opened the door to his office then, pausing as he looked at each of them slowly, his face masked of all expressions. "Sam? Are you ready?"

Sam nodded, as he slid the picture discreetly into his back pocket. "Coming."

Dr. Lee stood there a second longer, and then vanished inside to wait for Sam.

Sam winked at Violet, keeping his voice quiet. "I'll let you know if I sense anything," he said. Then he, too, disappeared into the doctor's office.

Violet suddenly felt better. She may have a lead at last.

BLOOD IS THICKER THAN WATER

"I THOUGHT YOU WEREN'T COMING BACK THIS time." There was a mocking quality to his father's words that he'd grown accustomed to over the years. He'd expected it from the old man.

"I'm not. I just need to grab a few things, then I'm outta here." He'd hoped to get in and out without running into his dad, especially since the old man's piece of shit car wasn't parked out front. But even he'd known that had been hoping for too much. His dad rarely left except to make a run for more cigarettes or booze. Which is probably where his car was now, stranded somewhere on the side of the road . . . out of gas.

163

His dad barely looked up from the TV. "Don't be like that. Stop being such a pansy and get your ass home. I got shit needs to be done around here." The SOB had been drinking, and his words were sloppy. To an unaccustomed ear, it sounded like he'd said, "I go' shi' nee's be done 'roun 'ere."

Evan's stomach clenched, but he managed to keep his mouth shut.

"Oh, I know. Yer too good for us, isn't that right, boy? Yer gonna run off and be a rock star."

"I just need to get some things," he repeated as calmly as he could manage, leaving the room while the miserable bastard still ranted behind him. He needed to pack his shit and get out of there before the old man's words morphed into full-on rage.

He passed a darkened bedroom, the door slightly ajar, just like it always was, and he hesitated. Something inside of him stirred, something small and childlike. Something he didn't want to acknowledge. "Ma," he breathed almost soundlessly into the still room.

There was no response but he knew she was in there; he could smell the fetid stench of her waste and her unwashed body. Smells that no child should ever have to smell. And along with her scent, he could hear the slight rustling of her sheets.

"It's just me," he said, louder this time. "I . . . I just stopped by. . . ." He didn't know how to tell her he wasn't staying. That he was leaving her alone—once and for all—with her husband.

But then there was another smell, the caustic stench that made the hairs on his arms stand on end, disclosing his father's presence even before he spoke. He knew it had been a mistake, coming here.

164

He knew he should've waited, till he was sure his old man wasn't home.

"You think she needs you, boy? You think she gives a flyin' fuck"—he could feel spittle shower the back of his neck—"that you're here? She doesn't even know where she is. She doesn't even know who you are," his father spat. "She's a junkie. No better'n that girl you got yerself hooked up with."

Evan turned as fury uncoiled, making his hands ball at his sides even though he told himself not to do it. Even though he begged himself to stop.

His father saw too. "What're'ya gonna do, boy? You think you can take yer ol' man?" His mouth split into a hideous grin, baring teeth that were decayed and gums that festered, swollen and red. "Try it."

He thought of Kisha and Bailey and Boxer and Colton—Butterfly, too—all waiting for him. All counting on him. He couldn't do this. He knew he was outmatched. His father outweighed him by at least fifty pounds, and drunk or not, he'd once gone toe to toe with some of the best amateur fighters in the circuit. He could throw a punch as naturally as he could polish off a fifth of bourbon.

He loosened his fists and tried to duck around the bastard. "It's not worth it," he muttered.

But it was too late. His father was already raring for a fight, he'd already pushed the old bastard too far.

He felt his dad tackle him from behind and instinctively his arms shot up, covering the back of his head as his face slammed against the ground. That was the first line of attack—always was—his head.

His dad landed a couple of solid blows, making his arms ache where they tried to shield him, but he already knew the rhythm of the punches—right, left, right. He dragged himself to the left, just as a hard right was coming at him, and he heard his father's fist slam the hardwood just beside his ear.

There was a pause, and then his father's shrieks—outrage mixed with pain—rumbled off the wall of the house. "Son of a— You mother fu—"

But Evan was already rolling away, taking advantage of the fact that he'd thrown the old man off kilter by fighting back. He kicked behind him, just once, and managed to catch his father in the gut. He heard the bastard land on the ground with a satisfying whomp!

He wouldn't have long, he knew, and he scrambled to get to his feet, knowing his only chance was to get the hell out of there. He could get his shit later, when his dad ran out of booze again and had to make another liquor run.

He was almost to the door when he felt his feet jerked out from beneath him and he landed on his knees. His head reeled as he struggled to figure out what had just happened. He rolled onto his back, still trying to figure out why he'd fallen, only to see the old man waving something at him. His dad looked like a demented matador in a bullfight. Except that instead of a red cape, he was brandishing a floor mat. One Evan had walked on thousands of times before.

His father had literally pulled the rug out from underneath him.

"Nice try, fuckwad." He threw the rug down and closed the distance in two strides.

The first fist his dad landed was a hard left, and it hit him so hard his teeth clattered together. He might have bitten his tongue, or maybe it was his cheek, but he definitely tasted blood. The second was a right hook, coming up just beneath his jaw. He saw stars or fireworks or whatever you called it when white hot flashes exploded behind your eyelids making it impossible to see.

Glancing around, Evan searched for something, anything, that could be used as a weapon. Something that might stop, or even just delay, his father long enough so he could escape.

There was nothing. Just an array of bottles and an overflowing ashtray and enough Playboys to make the old man look like some kind of perv.

He reached for the nearest bottle, barely noticing that the lid wasn't screwed on, and he felt the cheap whiskey dribble down his arm as he waved it in front of the old man. "Get away from me, you prick. Stay back."

His dad's vision cleared slightly as he fumbled for the bottle. "Hey, knock it off, you idiot. That's perfectly good scotch. Put it down or I'll beat your ass."

Evan laughed as he staggered to his feet, still letting the contents of the bottle spill all over the floor. "Really, you stupid bastard? You'll beat my ass?" He wondered what the miserable drunk thought he'd already done to him . . . this time, and a thousand times before. He threw the bottle down, feeling a sense of satisfaction as it shattered on the floor, sending shards of glass spraying everywhere.

And then he reached behind him, while the old man was busy trying to figure out if there was any way to salvage the booze spreading outward around the broken fragments of glass—to mop it or sponge it up probably, possibly even to get on his hands and knees and lick it up if necessary.

Evan's fingers closed around the baseball bat that was propped there by the door, the one meant for protection from anyone who might dare to break in, might try to rob the old man of his precious stash.

Now, however, it would simply be used against him.

The first blow, when he delivered it, was a right. It hit his father square in the left temple, causing his knees to buckle as he reached for the wound, which was already oozing blood. The second was a line drive to the right side of his skull, and this time he heard—or maybe felt—the bone give beneath the wooden bat.

This time, the old man shrieked, his mouth wide, until no sound was coming out. He stared at his son, blinking in disbelief, right before he tumbled forward, falling on his face.

The next three blows were rights—his strongest hand—and came from above as he stood over his father's slack form. Gratification surged through him each time he heard the sound of the bat crushing bone.

It wasn't until his arms ached and he was breathless that he stopped. He wiped his hands on his pants before throwing the bloodied bat on the ground.

Panting, he waited until he caught his breath again before making his way back to the bedroom.

This time he didn't call out to her, he just slipped inside without a sound.

He stood at her bedside, waiting for his eyes to adjust, until he could see the gray outline of the woman who'd once been his mother. The woman who'd lost herself, first to the pipe, and then to the needle. The woman who'd left him in the care of that bastard.

"I'm sorry," he said at last, as he tried to make himself feel something.

And then he lifted the pillow and covered her face.

She didn't struggle or fight to try to live, not the way a normal person would have. Instead she just lay there, letting her only son steal the air from her lungs.

Letting herself die.

When he felt her body shudder, a tremor he'd felt before, he knew she was gone. He lifted the pillow and set it aside.

"I'm sorry," he said again, before smoothing a hand over her cheek.

He went to the cupboard then, to where the old man kept the lighter fluid, the kind that normal families used to start charcoals when they barbequed in their backyards, but that his own dad had used to refill his stupid D-Day lighter that he claimed had belonged to his dad—the miserable drunk who'd come before him. He pulled off the stopper and squeezed, dousing his father until the stream of butane made the blood watery, spreading the pool.

He pulled a pack of matches from his front pocket, then changed his mind and went back to the littered coffee table, where the ashtray spilled over with cigarette butts and ash. Beside it, he picked up the lighter his dad used to scold him for touching.

He stood at the door, surveying his handiwork; glad the prick could never hurt him again. Glad his mother wouldn't have to spend

169

another day suffering because she needed her fix.

Then he lit the flame, mesmerized by the dancing blue and yellow blaze that flickered and flashed.

He threw the lighter down, into the pool of bloody lighter fluid and watched as the old man went up in flames.

And he closed the door behind him.

CHAPTER 8

VIOLET STRETCHED OUT ON HER STOMACH, flipping through the pages of her grandmother's diaries. Immediately, she was cocooned in the warmth of her grandma's words, and even though she couldn't eclipse her own music box, she reached over to her nightstand and wound the ivory box she'd found that first day, getting lost in the reassuring sounds of her grandmother's lullaby.

The entries would have been dull to anyone else . . . stories about her grandma Louise's married life, their family, and anecdotes from her mother's childhood. But to Violet they were a treasure trove. She learned that her mom had sprained her ankle and skinned both knees when she was twelve, trying to impress a boy at the roller rink. She laughed out loud when she read another entry about her mom, when she was a teenager, getting busted for sneaking out with her friends in the middle of the night. She'd even taken the car—something she would've skewered Violet over, especially since she was only fourteen at the time. It was hard to imagine her mom causing trouble or having crushes on boys—anyone other than her dad. But there it was, in black and white.

Reading the journals was soothing, and she stretched again, until her toes were dangling over the edge of her bed.

She was about to call it a night, when one of the entries caught her eye:

March 4, 1987
A man came to the door today. At first I told him my
usual "no thank you," certain he must be a salesman
even before he'd opened his mouth. It was the suit.
No one in our neighborhood wears suits. Not unless
they're selling something. But he assured me that wasn't
the case. He said he was here to see me, and then he
lowered his voice and told me he knew what I could do.
I almost slammed the door in his face, then and there.
But then he said a name that I hadn't heard in years—
Ian Williams.
Ian . . .

I think I was too stunned, hearing that name after all this time to even react at first, giving him enough time to say what he'd come to say. Giving him more time than I probably should have.

Whatever would have possessed Ian to tell someone about me all these years later? Whatever possessed me to listen to the crazy tale this salesman spun at my door?

I probably should've closed it after all.

Curious now, Violet rolled onto her back and kept reading, no longer sleepy. She scanned ahead, skipping past all the Maggie-this and Maggie-that entries that riddled this part of her grandmother's life.

Then another one caught her attention, this one dated just three weeks later.

March 27, 1987
Maggie's been gone all week, spending her spring break in Palm Springs with Sabrina Luddy's family. I would be worried, except that Sabrina's father is as strict as they come. Still, it probably couldn't hurt to worry a little, she is sixteen after all. But I've been too preoccupied to worry. The man in the suit has come back twice. I still haven't told John about him, although I'm not sure why. I've meant to, plenty of times. I've opened my mouth to tell him everything, but each time I close it again, feeling like this is something that needs to be kept to myself. At least for now. The man always wears

the same dark suit, and he's tried and tried to convince me
that he understands what I've gone through. He's told me,
too, in far-too-mysterious terms, that I'm not alone.

Not alone? Even though he hasn't answered any of
my questions, I think I understand the implications of
what he's saying: He knows others who can do what I do.
He knows people who have "gifts" like mine. Still, it's
hard to trust anyone, so I can't bring myself to actually say
the words to him. To admit that he's right about me, that I
can do the things he says I can.

But I listen. And I desperately want to know if there
are others.

Violet sat up now, chewing the side of her fingernail, tugging at the skin with her teeth. She knew exactly how her grandma felt. She knew what it meant to no longer be alone, to realize that there might be someone out there who understands you.

She kept reading.

April 6, 1987
I'm not even sure I should be writing this down, but I
feel like my world has just been tilted upside down. The
man—I know his name is Ari Espinda now—has finally
persuaded me to come to where he works, although I'm
not sure I'd call it work, exactly. This time, he made clear
what I'd already suspected in my heart: that I shouldn't

tell John anything about him or our meetings. I suppose this should be a red flag to me, a clue that something might be wrong about this whole situation, but I'm so ~~curious~~ lonely. The idea of meeting someone else like me is seductive. I'm certain that was his intention. Either way, I've agreed to meet him. Tomorrow . . . after Maggie leaves for school.

April 7, 1987
It wasn't the building that impressed me, although it was impressive, in a strange sort of way. There's more security than I'd expected (cameras that moved whenever I did), almost like visiting some secret government facility. It wasn't though—I'm almost sure of it.

It was the people I met today that impressed me most. They weren't exactly what Ari said they'd be—they weren't like me. But how could they be? I'm not sure anyone else can do what I can. But that doesn't mean they didn't have their own amazing abilities. The best way I can describe those I met was to call them psychics. Real ones. Not like the ones who advertise on television, charging people by the minute for relationship and career advice. No, these were the kinds of psychics who truly can communicate with a world beyond our own.

I'm generally not a skeptic—someone in my position has no right to be. But I couldn't help having reservations. Or at least I did, until Ari introduced me to a woman named Muriel. She was intense—maybe it was her penetrating eyes. When she focused them on me I felt as if she were looking inside me. It turns out, she was. Ari used her to allay my doubts by asking Muriel to "read" me.

At first the reading felt generic, like I could've been at the carnival having my palm read. But then . . . then she started to tell me things that were intimate and detailed. She said Maggie's name, which could have been easy enough to find out, but she told me other things too. She knew about the miscarriages. And how later, after Maggie was born, I'd lain awake night after night worrying that she might have inherited my ability. She knew, also, that she hadn't. She told me the names of my childhood pets, and that I'd once dreamed of being a ballerina (although what girl didn't?), and that I secretly wished I could see my aunt once more, so I could tell her that what we can do isn't so bad after all.

By the time she was finished, I was exhausted, as if her gift had used up every ounce of energy I had. And then they invited me to join their group.

I have no idea what I've agreed to, but for the first time in my life, I feel like there might be others who know exactly what it's like to be as different as I am.

April 21, 1987
Ari insists we meet almost daily, which means I have to hurry downtown as soon as I see Maggie off to school.

Since I'm home before she is, John never even realizes I've been gone.

We've spent most of our time so far testing what I can do. Strange, since I've never really known myself. The hardest part has been the bodies. <u>Human bodies</u>. It took some getting used to, and it helped to hear them being referred to as "cadavers." Somehow the word dehumanizes them for me, at least a little. The autopsies were tough too, but they were necessary, to help us understand how exactly the "echoes" work.

The two things I've learned so far:

First, I was right about the heart. It must remain with the body in order for the echo to stay intact. During the autopsies I've witnessed, the heart is actually removed from the cadaver. First it's weighed, and sometimes tissue samples are taken to test for drugs or toxins or anything else they can think of. It's then that the body stops emitting an echo. It just goes . . . silent, so to speak. But once the heart is replaced—and it's almost always placed back inside the chest cavity—the echo returns, exactly as it was before. I'm stunned every time this happens.

Second, cremation changes nothing. That caught me completely off guard. I thought for sure that once the body—including its heart—was turned to a pile of ash and bone, it would eliminate the echo altogether. How could it not?

How indeed? I have no idea, but the echo was still there. Still strong.

And what I know more than anything else:

*Everything remains a secret. This fact is constantly drilled
into me, although I have no idea why. I have to assume
that the others are as worried about their privacy as I have
been. It's the only explanation that makes sense.*

Violet thought about what she'd always known about
echoes and imprints. She'd known that people in law enforce-
ment and military could carry imprints as could those like
her—people who'd killed in self-defense.

She'd also learned from seeing the corpse of Mike and
Megan's father that a suicide could cause someone to bear
both their own echo *and* imprint.

She turned back to the journal, wanting to know more.

May 5, 1987
*We're calling ourselves the Circle of Seven, our strange
little group. Ari isn't a part of the Seven since I now
know he has no ability. Apparently, his true skill lies in
recruiting. The rest of us, however, those who do have
gifts and were brought together because of them, have
forged a bond of sorts. A camaraderie like nothing I've ever
experienced before.*

Violet felt herself nodding along with her grandmother's
words as she read them. Yes, she thought, camaraderie. That
was exactly the right way to describe it.

She was intrigued by the way her grandmother depicted
this group, these people who reminded her so much of her

own team, right down to the fact that none of the others could find bodies the way she did. In that, she was unique.

She was restless now, and she sat up, so she was on her knees, knowing she'd have to stop reading soon. It was late and she needed to sleep. Tomorrow she had school.

But she couldn't stop herself, she had to know more.

May 29, 1987
I'm fascinated by one of the Seven, a young man named Jimmy. His ability isn't like the others, he can't read the future or tell your past. Like me, his gift is distinctive.

He's been harder to get to know than the others. He's quiet and reserved, but gentle too. I can tell just by watching him. He's got a stillness about him, a certain tranquility. It's not real, though . . . or so I'm told. It's part of his ability. He makes others feel at ease. He takes away their worries and fears and anxieties, replacing them with . . . calm.

I'm not sure how I feel about that, being forced to feel serene. But I'm certainly not immune to it, that much I know.

June 28, 1987
I've made a terrible mistake. It's not the fault of any of the Seven. Or maybe I'm just naive. Maybe every one of them knows—has known all along—what the group has been up to. Maybe I'm the only one who has qualms about what we're being asked to do.

*I still don't know, exactly, who's behind our
operation . . . who's pulling our strings. But we're just
part of some larger organization, and for whatever reason,
they've decided we might be useful. Ari becomes tight-
lipped whenever I ask.*

*Some of the others have been working on projects
already, which we all assumed would happen eventually.
We couldn't be tested forever with no outlet for our skills.
Muriel said something about doing background checks,
which I assumed had something to do with prospective
employees or investors, since she was giving a detailed
history—more detailed than a standard credit report or
criminal record check could be. My guess is that the kind
of information she can dig up could be invaluable to a
corporation.*

*There was one name I kept hearing, again and again.
<u>Jack Hewitt</u>. It wasn't just Muriel who mentioned him. I
heard two of the others talking about him as well. I didn't
give it much thought really, I didn't consider who he was
or why I'd heard his name on more than one occasion.
Until two nights ago, when John and I were watching the
news.*

*A man's face flashed up on the television screen, but it
was his name—Jack Hewitt—that made me take notice. I
knew immediately it was the man the others in the Seven
had been investigating. John said he'd been in the news for
several days. He'd been involved in a financial scandal,*

accused of embezzling almost half a million dollars from his company. On the night I saw the news story though Jack Hewitt had finally cracked under the pressure and shot himself. Right after he'd killed his wife and his two young boys.

Still, I might not have questioned the circumstances of his death if it hadn't been for the redecorating of our government-like office. Almost overnight it was transformed into the kind of luxurious workspace that could have belonged to any head of state. It was as if the sky had opened up and rained money down on our group.

With a little digging, it wasn't hard to discover that Jack Hewitt's death facilitated one of the largest mergers in corporate history. That he'd been the majority stockholder in Hewitt and Sons, a company that had been in his family for generations. He hadn't wanted to sell the business, but his brother had.

I can't prove it, but I'm sure that somehow we were involved in his downfall, and the merger that followed. I'm sure that the others had been used to gather information about him, information that had been used against him. Maybe he was blackmailed. Maybe he was just plain threatened. Like I said, I can't prove anything. All I have are a handful of personal trinkets belonging to a dead man, items that mean nothing . . . unless you have the ability to tell someone's past just by touching them.

July 1, 1987

I confided my suspicions in Muriel, and she confessed that she had concerns as well. She confessed, too, that she'd been asked about Jack Hewitt's personal life—things that should have remained private. In searching his past, she'd discovered infidelities, including the name of a mistress he'd had for years, and had even given them information about a love child he'd been hiding, filtering money to through the company. Things that might destroy a man's family, as well as his career.

Together, we decided to dig for more information, to see if we could connect what she'd found to those who were behind the Seven, all of whom still remained anonymous.

Jimmy was the one who caught us as we were searching through the files. We told him what we suspected.

Muriel said she was thinking of quitting the Seven. All the while I was calm, almost too calm, as if Jimmy were manipulating me. Then he said that she couldn't quit, they wouldn't let her.

<u>*They*</u>*, he said. It was ominous, and my feelings were exactly what they should have been. Fear. He told us that no one leaves the Circle.*

He didn't say "the Seven," which is what the rest of us call ourselves. He said, "the Circle," as if the number changes. As if we weren't the first group they've assembled.

182

July 15, 1987
Muriel is dead. And I know why. She tried to quit the
Circle.
I have to find a way out.

Violet sat back on her heels, as the goose bumps that had started at the base of her neck bloomed outward, spreading over her body, until she was covered in them.

The Circle of Seven. They'd been just like her team. Just like Rafe and Gemma and Krystal and Sam. And whatever phantom organization had directed the Seven, from behind the scenes, assembling them and then giving them tasks, was so eerily similar to whoever was running the Center—it made Violet's head spin.

What if those similarities weren't just a coincidence? What if there was some connection between the group her grandmother had belonged to and the team she was on now?

Except, how was that even possible? The members of the Seven had been asked to participate in corporate espionage—even if it was of the psychic variety. Their skills had been used to manipulate financial dealings, had been utilized for personal gain and wealth. Violet's team wasn't like that.

They were helping to find missing persons and stop killers. There was nothing selfish about that, nothing materialistic about what they did.

Besides, that was almost thirty years ago.

Yet . . .

She thought of the Center, where her team met. She pictured the state-of-the-art facility and the high-tech feel, with the computers and LCD monitors . . . and yes, even the security. The cameras and the keypads at every entry. Hadn't her grandmother mentioned the security?

She thought too of the fact that her mom had always told her that her grandma had never found a dead person before, not the way Violet had. That the echoes she'd discovered had always been limited to animals she'd come across.

Lies, Violet knew now. Lies that her grandmother had been forced to tell to protect her family, to keep them safe from a group she suspected were capable of murder.

How many other secrets had there been? How many other lies?

Still reeling, Violet was about to close the journal when she saw something sticking out from between the pages. A slip of paper, maybe. She stuck her finger between the pages of the journal, and just as she was opening the book, a photograph drifted out, floating to the floor in front of her.

She didn't have to pick it up to realize what she was looking at. *Who* she was looking at. All she had to do was count.

They were all there, the Circle of Seven.

Gingerly, she plucked up the image, holding it close and inspecting it. She recognized her grandmother right away. She was younger than Violet remembered her, and smiling, making Violet think this picture had been taken before she'd known what the group was all about. Before she'd grown to fear them.

Her eyes roved over their faces, and she realized that all of these people were older than the members of her own team—even Krystal, who was their oldest member at twenty-one. These were adults, all of them. Most closer to her grandmother's age than to her own.

And then she felt the floor drop out from beneath her as all of her doubts evaporated in a single instant.

Dr. Lee . . .

Violet looked at the picture again, letting her finger wander over the faded paper—but not so faded that she couldn't see him, couldn't recognize his face. Even thirty years younger, she knew it was him.

She tried to recall whether any of the entries she'd read in her grandmother's journals had named him, but then realized that they had, she just hadn't put two and two together. Why would she? Jimmy, or James rather, was a common-enough name.

He was the young man who could make others feel calm.

Violet crossed her arms in front of her, trying to ward away the chill that enveloped her, cupping her elbows and drawing her arms against her chest. She took that in as she thought about the visits she'd had with Dr. Lee.

How much of what he'd taught her was truly technique—meditation, hypnosis, breathing—and how much of what she'd felt was simply the result of his own unusual ability to make those around him relax? To take away their stress, their discomfort?

But for someone who could put others at ease, he certainly hadn't always used it. He'd let her be angry and suspicious in the days and weeks since he'd forced her hand. He hadn't calmed her when she'd been sullen or disrespectful during their mandatory sessions.

She supposed he had no reason to stop her from feeling those things; she wasn't hurting anyone really. She'd never actually left the team, despite all her frustration and fury with him.

But then she remembered . . .

He had used it on her, she was sure of it . . . when she'd asked him about Rafe and Gemma coming to her school. The way she'd blindly accepted his explanation, and his involvement in the decision to have them attend White River.

She remembered, too, how she'd felt later, when she'd gone home and thought about it; she'd been frustrated with herself for not questioning him further, for not arguing with him. Suddenly she questioned everything. Everyone.

She wondered if it had really been the dead boy on the waterfront—the one she'd discovered all those months ago—who had brought her to the attention of Sara Priest in the first place. She wondered if she hadn't been on their radar all along. She *was* the granddaughter of one of the Seven, after all. Surely they knew . . . or at least suspected what she could do.

And her grandmother had been trapped, just like she was.

When you grow accustomed to something, when it becomes part of your everyday life, you notice when it suddenly vanishes.

That was what happened when Violet sat bolt upright in the middle of the night. At first she didn't understand why her pulse was racing even before she was fully awake. She had no idea why her ribs ached as her lungs struggled and gasped for breath, or why she couldn't see or hear.

I'm dead was the first thought that found its way through her awareness. It was jarring to consider, but it made a certain amount of sense. *This is what it feels like to lose consciousness and succumb to death.*

She blinked, searching for some sort of bright light, or a tunnel that would lead her to *the other side*, the kind you always hear about in people's near-death experiences.

But there was . . . nothing . . .

Nothing.

She blinked once . . . twice . . . and then her eyesight adjusted. She was still in her bedroom, and it was still the middle of the night.

Her breath finally found a place in her throat, and she felt the hitch as she gasped, a long choking sound . . . one that she most definitely heard. Her heart hammered too hard against the walls of her chest and she realized she must've been dreaming. That had to be it, she assured herself, it was all a bad dream.

But it was still eerily quiet around her. Spookily, frighteningly quiet.

And then she realized why that was.

It was gone. Her music-box imprint . . .

It was gone.

She shook her head, because surely her sanity had slipped, if only a notch. It wasn't possible for an imprint to just . . . vanish. It wasn't something you could just *lose*.

Yet here she was. Sitting alone in the dark, in total, complete, utter silence.

The phone, when it vibrated on the nightstand beside her, made her jump and caused her heart to start racing all over again. She lunged for it, pressing her hand against her chest as she took another breath and glanced at the screen.

"Rafe?" she whispered, her voice unsteady. "What's wrong?"

Static poured through the line from the other end, and she thought at first he might not hear her, that they had a bad connection. Then his voice reached through the phone, finding her. "Hopefully nothing. That's why I was calling. I wanted to see"—he paused—"how *you* were."

"I'm . . ." She swallowed her word. She'd started to say "fine," something she'd said so many times before it was nearly automatic now. Yet here she was, no longer sure whether that was true or not. Under the circumstances, *I'm losing my effing mind* might be more accurate. Instead, she settled for "confused."

In the background she heard noises: metal banging against metal, maybe; the clang of buckles, probably. What was he doing?

"But better, right?"

"Bett—" Her mind whirled as she tried to make sense of their strange conversation. "What have you done? Did you . . . *do this*?"

She heard the distinct whooshing sound of a zipper. "Look, I only have a minute. I probably should've waited to call, but I wanted to see if it worked or not."

Violet lifted her hand to her lips. "I don't understand . . . how . . . ?" And then stopped pretending, because she did understand. She understood entirely too well. "You didn't . . . ? You didn't just dig him up, did you?" She lowered her voice to barely a breath. "You could get in so much trouble."

Rafe actually laughed. "Well . . . I didn't *just* dig him up, I had to do some other stuff too. Really gross stuff. And since you haven't said otherwise, I assume it worked. You can thank me later. But for now, I'm cold and I'm dirty, so I'm gonna go."

She tried to imagine Rafe going to the graveyard at night and digging up a body—*Caine's body.*

She squeezed her eyes shut, wondering whatever had possessed him to do such a thing, to take such a risk.

But she knew. "This doesn't change anything, you know?"

There was another brief pause, right before she heard him say, "Oh, I don't know, V. I think it changes everything." And then he hung up.

CHAPTER 9

WAKING UP THE NEXT MORNING HAD BEEN strange. And quiet.

And . . . well, strange.

Violet hadn't slept much after hanging up with Rafe, but this time it had nothing to do with the ghostly imprint she'd become so accustomed to. Or rather it had everything to do with it. Its absence was palpable, and Violet kept waiting for it to reappear, kept searching for it in the darkness of her mind.

Odd how something she'd once thought she hated had become such an integral part of her daily life. Like breathing.

And without it, peace was nearly as hard to find as it had been with it.

But not impossible, and eventually Violet had found the silence comforting, letting it wrap around her, swaddling her in solitude.

In the morning, she thought about other things. Like Rafe, and what he'd done to make the spectral sounds vanish for good.

She wanted to tell everyone—or at least Jay and her parents. She wanted them to know what he did, that her imprint had been silenced. But she wasn't sure she could . . . or should. What Rafe had done was criminal.

So she said nothing, pretending instead that everything was the same as it always had been. That the music-box imprint still followed her. Haunting her.

Marking her as a killer.

"I think we should talk," Rafe told her as he scooted his chair across the aisle so their desks were lined up side by side.

Violet peered toward the front of the classroom, knowing that if Mr. LeCompte caught them like that, they'd be in trouble. Again.

Rafe was continually breaking the rules in class, but it was Violet who Mr. LeCompte always seemed to catch. So far this year, she'd been reprimanded for talking, passing notes, and for pushing the perfectly aligned desks out of order—all because of Rafe. Just once, Violet wanted to see Rafe take the blame.

"Stop it," she hissed, scooting her desk away from his, but knowing that wasn't the solution. She'd only be scolded for disfiguring her row too.

He reached across, surprising her when he captured her hand with his, and she felt that far-too-familiar jolt. "I mean it, Violet. You can't just pretend I didn't"—his eyes held hers, and everything around her went still—"*do what I did* last night. We need to talk about it."

She started to draw away from him, to tell him where he could go—in terms that weren't exactly ladylike, either. But something about his expression stopped her.

She looked at him, really looked at him, and thought about all the secrets—and the pieces of the puzzle that still didn't fit. Maybe she *did* need to talk to him.

Overhead the class bell rang, and before Violet could change her mind, she nodded. "Fine. But not here," she insisted, staring at the students who were still settling into their seats. "Grab your backpack and let's get out of here."

Rafe looked confused at first, like he hadn't really expected her to take him up on his offer. Like she'd just said the very last thing on earth he'd expected her to say. But it only lasted a second, that stunned expression, and then he was lifting his backpack off the floor and his desk screeched as he stood too abruptly. Too impatiently.

Violet stood too, just as Mr. LeCompte sauntered into the classroom, wearing a self-righteous smile on his face, ready to teach thirty-three high schoolers the finer points of AP Lit.

193

His pointed gaze fell on the two of them as they stood in the aisle, but ultimately landed on Violet, giving her his signature reproachful shake of the head. "Tardy again, I see," he drawled in his pretentious, false accent.

She opened her mouth to respond, even though she had no idea what she actually planned to say, but Rafe didn't give her the chance. He dragged her, instead, down the row as every student in class watched them head to the front of the classroom. "Actually, we *are* late. But not for class," he explained as they passed the smug instructor on their way out the door.

"Well, I—you can't just . . ." Violet heard Mr. LeCompte sputtering behind them, but it was too late. They were already halfway down the hallway. She thought she heard him bellowing something about the principal's office and detention—or maybe it was *suspension*—but she couldn't be sure. Rafe didn't slow down, and neither did she.

He led her past the front office, out the entrance, and through the parking lot. It wasn't until they were standing in front of his motorcycle, and he was handing her a helmet—a sweet bubble-gum-pink number that could only belong to Gemma—that she realized his intention.

"Oh no." She threw her hands up in front of her, warding off the offensive fiberglass helmet. "Not in a million years. I saw what that thing did to you. There's no way I'm getting on it." She still couldn't look at his new bike without remembering the way his old one had sounded as it had skidded across the concrete—metal against asphalt. Without imagining Rafe lying in the center of the intersection, looking hopelessly broken. "I can't believe Gemma agrees to ride it at all."

Rafe grinned slyly. "She only gives me one day a week. The rest of the time I have to ride in that little Barbie-mobile of hers. I'm likely to get my ass kicked just for being seen in that thing."

Violet had seen Gemma's car, a Mini Cooper that was just a few shades lighter than the pink helmet Rafe was holding now. She'd wondered how Gemma could afford a car like that, especially knowing Gemma's background as a foster kid, but she'd held her tongue. Asking questions insinuated curiosity, and curiosity might be misconstrued as caring.

And she definitely didn't want Gemma to think she cared.

"If it makes you feel any better, this isn't the same bike," Rafe offered, still trying to persuade her to get on. "If you recall, that one was totaled."

"Is that seriously supposed to make me feel better?" She reached out and punched him in the arm. "You can be a real ass, you know that?"

"So I've been told. Come on, V. It's safe, and I'll drive real slow. I promise." He held Gemma's helmet out again, and this time Violet's resolve cracked. Not because she wanted to ride his stupid death-mobile, or because she trusted his word necessarily, but because she could see Mrs. Jeffries from the office coming out the front entrance to investigate. She wondered if Mr. LeCompte had made good on his threat to call the principal.

She wrenched the pink helmet from his grasp and forced it over her head, realizing too late that her head must be at least two sizes larger than Gemma's as the helmet crushed her skull. She tried to make herself feel better by telling herself it was probably just because she had so much more hair than Gemma.

Rafe secured their backpacks using bungee cords, while Violet kept checking over her shoulder. So far, Mrs. Jeffries was just watching them, but she was positive the office lady knew who they were, and she was equally sure they could expect letters in their permanent files when they returned to school. When Rafe reached out for her, Violet let him help her climb on clumsily behind him.

She felt wobbly on the bike, and she waited for Rafe to give her a quick lesson on how this would work, explaining to her where she should put her hands and her feet . . . to give her some instructions about motorcycle etiquette. Instead, he started the engine. It rumbled up through her entire body but was muffled through the thick layers of foam that lined her helmet.

"Hold on," he called over his shoulder, his only piece of advice before he hit the accelerator and took off, leaving the school and Mrs. Jeffries behind.

She was surprised when they pulled to a stop in the nearly empty parking lot of Wally's Drive-In, not that she'd given a lot of thought to where, exactly, they were headed. She sort of thought they'd go to the Java Hut, where other kids from school would go if they were ditching class. Rafe didn't exactly seem like a Wally's kind of guy.

Violet turned around to squint at the restaurant behind her. Java Hut might be where all her friends hung out, but if Buckley had a tourist attraction it was definitely Wally's. People came from all over to eat at the drive-in burger joint. There wasn't a kid in town who didn't love pulling up to one of Wally's menu boards, which were set up in each individual parking space, then having their food delivered right to their car.

Rafe pulled off his helmet as he dropped the kickstand in place. From behind, Violet could see that his dark hair was rumpled, but after he ran his fingers through it a few times, it fell into place, as if on command.

Violet wished her hair would be so manageable. She knew what hers must look like as she stripped off her own helmet. She could feel her curls twisting and coiling, tickling her cheeks and standing up riotously all over her head.

"I hear this place has great shakes," Rafe said, stepping off the bike gracefully and leaving Violet feeling somewhat trapped on the machine. He reached out to give her a hand.

She stared at him, suspicious of his words. "Who told you that?"

Rafe just shrugged. "Everyone says it. I'm surprised you haven't heard. I figured it was something everyone here in Podunk knew." He spent extra time saying the word *Podunk*, making it more than clear what he thought of her hometown.

He was right, of course. Everyone *did* know about Wally's shakes. But it was hard to imagine Rafe carrying on an entire conversation with *anyone* about milk shakes.

She took his hand and eased off the motorcycle. It hadn't been bad, the ride. Not nearly as perilous as she'd imagined it would be. If she was being honest, and she supposed she could be—at least in the privacy of her own thoughts, right?—it had even been sort of fun. Sort of. In an I-can-barely-breathe-because-I'm-a-little-terrified kind of way.

And if she was being *completely* honest, she might even admit there were moments there when she'd allowed herself to relax—brief snippets of time when she hadn't been thinking about the accident, or about whether she was holding on tight enough, or too tight, or listening to the whine of the engine—when she'd felt sheer exhilaration as they whipped down the highway. When she felt free.

Although she'd never admit as much out loud. And never to Rafe.

They went inside and ordered—a chocolate shake for him and a peanut butter chocolate chip one for her. The woman behind the counter gave them a strange look, probably because it was only eight in the morning and milk shakes weren't much of a breakfast. Or maybe because it was obvious they should've been at school.

Either way, they took a booth as far from the counter as possible. The red vinyl booths were retro-style, looking like they were made from vintage car seats, and there were pictures of icons like Marilyn Monroe, Marlon Brando,

James Dean, Elvis, and even some of Betty Boop plastered all over the walls. With the black-and-white-checkered tiling on the floors, it was like stepping into an old-fashioned soda shop.

Rafe, never one to mince words, got straight to the point. "It's been months since the kidnapping, and you still don't seem like yourself." Stony-faced, he watched Violet as she toyed with her straw, swirling it through the thick ice cream. When she didn't answer, he tried again. "I thought that, maybe, getting rid of that *imprint* thing might make things better for you."

She glanced up, shrugging noncommittally. "I don't really know yet," she told him truthfully. "It wasn't just that," she admitted, but it wasn't an easy subject for her. "Don't get me wrong, I'm glad it's gone. I hated being reminded of what I'd done—"

"Of what you *had* to do," he interrupted, his jaw tight and his voice filled with emotion. "No one blames you for that. You did what you had to do, V. If you hadn't, you'd be dead."

"Right. I had to," she agreed, sounding less than convinced. "But it was still hard to be reminded all the time." She took a breath. "Getting rid of the imprint doesn't change the fact that when I close my eyes . . ." And she did then, she closed her eyes. ". . . he's still there."

She felt his fingers cover hers, and her eyes flew open once more. "V . . . I . . . I'm so sorry. . . ."

Like before, when he'd caught her watching him and

Chelsea in the quad, she saw longing in his expression, and she recoiled inwardly, her stomach tightening. She didn't want him to look at her like that.

"I know," she said, pulling her hand away.

They sat there in silence—the kind of uncomfortable silence Violet hadn't experienced in a long time. She didn't want to push him away, but she couldn't encourage him either.

She thought of what he'd said last night, right before hanging up, *I think it changes everything*, and she wondered if there might be just the tiniest grain of truth in those words. She couldn't help feeling some gratitude, and even a sense of obligation for what he'd done. But was that all she felt?

She shook her head. *Of course that was all*, she reprimanded herself. She was just confused. This was a lot to process.

Besides, she had other things to tell him, other things she wanted to talk about than her imprint. She leaned forward on her elbows. "What do you know about Dr. Lee?" she finally blurted out. "What has Sara said about him?"

Rafe stared back at her, confused. "Dr. Lee? What's he got to do with this?" He frowned, but he answered anyway, hesitantly, as if he wasn't quite sure what he was walking into. "I know that he's a psychiatrist. And that he works for whoever runs the Center. I think Sara trusts him, she's never really said she doesn't." He paused. "Come to think of it, she's never really said much at all about him. Why are you asking? What do *you* know about him?" And then his lips tightened as a thought occurred to him. "Has he done something to you? Has he . . . has he acted *inappropriately* with you?"

Rafe's meaning was crystal clear. He wanted to know if Dr. Lee had made some sort of unwanted advance on her. The idea was almost laughable, partly because it was hard to imagine the rigid Dr. Lee doing anything "inappropriate," at least of the sexual nature. He seemed like the sort of guy who went home to his stark, spotless apartment and hung his perfectly starched black suit in a row of identical perfectly starched black suits, all on hangers that were equidistant from the next.

Truthfully, she had no idea who the *real* Dr. Lee was. Not even after reading her grandmother's journals.

"God, Rafe, are you kidding? No. At least not the way *you* mean."

Rafe relaxed, if only a little. "What, then? Why are you asking?"

She remembered the way Dr. Lee had warned Violet about telling anyone about their "arrangement." And she remembered her grandmother's handwriting, scrawled on the pages of her diary: *Muriel is dead. And I know why. She tried to quit the Circle.*

Was this the same as quitting, revealing a secret she'd been cautioned to keep? Could the consequences be just as deadly?

But she knew she couldn't remain silent forever. She didn't want to. "Remember when I told you I didn't want to be on the team anymore, that I was quitting?"

Rafe's eyes fell away guiltily as he cleared his throat, and Violet could practically read his thoughts. He still blamed himself. He still believed she'd been leaving because of him. "I remember."

She was the one who reached over then, her fingers hovering near his—not quite touching, but almost. He watched them. "It wasn't your fault," she told him in a voice that was infinitely quieter than it had been before. "It wasn't about you. It was me. I felt like I needed some distance, from you *and* from the team. That's when I told Sara I was quitting." She paused, waiting for him to look up again. When he did, at last, she continued, "But I didn't change my mind about that, Rafe. *I* wasn't the one who decided to stay. It was Dr. Lee. He told me I couldn't quit. He said there were others . . . those higher up than him in the organization who wouldn't allow me to just *leave*." She whispered now, her words barely a breath as she voiced them aloud for the very first time. "He threatened my family."

Rafe's scowl was intense as he sorted through what she'd just revealed to him, and Violet waited for him to say something. She thought he seemed closer to her now, but she'd never noticed him move. It felt as if he'd stretched all the way across the tabletop, until he was somehow sharing her very breath.

He wasn't, though. He was right where he'd always been. Sitting in the booth across from her, his eyes sliding over her face as he absorbed the accusations she was making.

She waited for him to say she was crazy, that she'd lost her mind. That the imprint she had listened to on a daily basis had finally—completely—driven her mad.

But that wasn't what he said at all. He just nodded, a brief and decisive gesture. "If this is true . . . if what you're saying is true, we need to find out what he's up to."

Blinking, Violet shifted in the booth. "There's more," she explained, reaching into her pocket and sliding the picture across the table. "That's him," she told Rafe as she tapped the picture of a younger Dr. Lee—James Lee. "And that," she said, moving her finger over less than an inch, "is my grandmother."

He looked up at her, and then back at the picture in front of him.

She nodded. "They knew each other, Rafe. They were on a different team, sorta like ours. They called themselves the Circle of Seven."

He took a breath, his shoulders tense as he hunched forward, studying the picture. "Your grandmother's not the only one," he said at last, and then his finger touched the image too, landing on a girl, probably the youngest in the entire group. She had dark, shoulder-length hair. "That . . ." he said, his voice a whisper, "is my mom."

Dumbfounded by his words, Violet sat there. She let them sink in, waiting until her brain had sorted them through, making them find a place in the puzzle that was growing more complicated with each passing minute. "Was she"— she lifted her eyes to his—"like you?"

"No. I mean . . . I didn't think so, but I guess I don't really know. She never said anything. Sara never said anything." And then his lips tightened. "I'm sure Sara doesn't know anything about this." Violet wasn't sure if he was trying to convince her . . . or himself now. "She'd never have kept a secret like this, not from me."

"No," Violet agreed. "You're right, I don't think she would." Her eyes widened as she reached for him again, this time clutching him like a lifeline. And he was, in a way. He was the only thing standing between Dr. Lee and her family's safety. "Rafe, he told me not to tell anyone. Ever." Her voice wavered. "I'm afraid of him, of what he'll do if he finds out you know."

Unflinchingly, Rafe nodded, making her a vow. "He won't find out. I won't tell anyone. Not even Sara."

Violet's grip on him eased. She reached out and pulled her milk shake closer and took her first taste of the creamy concoction, letting the peanut butter ice cream melt over her tongue as she thought about what she'd just done and about what Rafe had revealed. The shake was cold and sweet, but did little to calm her churning stomach. "So how will we find out what he's up to . . . if we can't talk to Sara about him?" she asked at last.

Rafe leaned back now, looking more like himself again, like he belonged in a place like this, his leather jacket making him look like he was one of the props. He could definitely give James Dean a run for his money. "I don't know exactly," he said, lifting his own straw to his lips as he rested his arm over the back of the bench seat and studied her. "But give me some time and I'll come up with a plan that'll blow old Dr. Lee outta the water."

Violet smiled, wishing she felt half as cocky as Rafe did—or at least half as cocky as he appeared. "So basically you have no idea."

He lifted his chin and grinned at her. "Exactly."

Since they were already in trouble for ditching school, Violet suggested they might as well go back to her house after finishing their shakes so she could show Rafe her grandmother's journals.

He'd been at her house a few times before, but having him at her house then wasn't the same as having him in her bedroom now.

She'd been in his bedroom once. And like that time, when she'd seen the place where he slept, and where he spent most of his downtime, it felt too *personal*. Sharing this part of herself made her feel exposed.

Rafe's eyes moved over her patchwork quilt, which suddenly seemed more girly now that she was looking at it from his point of view. He surveyed her oversized corkboard, the one plastered with ticket stubs, birthday cards, ribbons she'd collected from spelling bees and sack races, photo booth strips—all depicting her, Chelsea, Claire, and Jules crammed into the tight space and vying for the camera's attention—along with other mementos she'd accumulated over the years.

It was like a scrapbook of her life, hanging right there on the wall . . . in plain sight.

"They're over here," Violet said, trying to draw Rafe's attention away from the collection of memorabilia. Knowing what he could do—his ability to glean information from a simple touch, especially from items of importance or with sentimental value—made her uneasy about his being in the presence of such intimate details of her life. Like he might uncover her most personal thoughts and feelings and secrets.

"I never realized you were so talented with your tongue." His voice was subdued, but she heard a hint of amusement.

"Excuse me?"

He reached out and tapped one of the pictures. In it, Violet and Chelsea were flanking Jules, squishing her between them, and each of them had their tongues sticking all the way out, as if, at any moment, they were planning to assault her by licking her cheeks. Jules, on the other hand, looked typically bored by their antics, and Claire was crammed all the way to the back of the booth so that only her hair was visible behind the rest of them.

Violet grinned, puckering one side of her lips. "You don't know all my tricks."

He rolled his eyes and came over to inspect the box of journals she'd set on her bed for him.

He watched thoughtfully as she reached inside and handed him a single diary. "Here," she told him. "Maybe you can figure something out."

Rafe took it, his expression uncertain. "What about the rest?"

Violet wasn't ready to part with all of them, not now that she'd just gotten to know her grandmother . . . *really know her.* Besides, he only needed the one that had entries about the Circle of Seven . . . it was the only one that was relevant. She still didn't know what happened beyond that last entry she'd read, the one in which Muriel had died. "I'll give them to you after I'm finished."

He hesitated, and then his eyes shifted, as if searching for something. Violet followed his gaze until it landed on the ivory music box on her bedside table. "She loved that song, you know?" he told Violet. "She bought it for your mother . . . when she was just a baby."

A lump formed in Violet's throat. "How could you . . . ? You didn't even touch it—" She stopped herself, because the answer was so obvious. "It—it doesn't say that in there." She pointed to the book in his hand, still amazed by what he could do, and knowing that one thing didn't have to have anything to do with the other. Rafe's ability was about "reading" things that were important, and the journal must have triggered something for him . . . something about the music box. "It's just that easy for you, huh?" she said instead.

His lips pressed together, not an unpleasant gesture. "Yep. Sometimes things are just that simple."

"Let's hope you get more than just a feeling about a music box," Violet said.

Even though school had just let out, by the time they got back to campus, the lot was practically deserted. That was the thing about the last bell of the school day, it was like signaling the start of some sort of race, and the students couldn't clear out fast enough. Rafe had to go back to pick up Gemma, and Violet needed to get her car before heading back home to power through more of the journals, searching for clues as to how Dr. Lee, her grandmother, and Rafe's mother all fit together.

But when they got there, Jay's shiny black Acura was parked beside Violet's car, and Gemma was perched against it, her arms folded and her lips pursed in a sulk. But even without Gemma's pout, the fact that Jay was actually *letting* her lean against his car indicated something was wrong, since he generally parked his car in the back forty so no one could even breathe on it.

Violet glanced his way and realized that his expression didn't match Gemma's at all. He didn't look annoyed the way she did . . . he looked pissed.

Her stomach plummeted, dropping all the way to her toes, as Rafe pulled his motorcycle to a stop in front of them. Jay shoved away from the bumper of Violet's car, where he'd been waiting for her.

Rafe didn't help matters though. From behind her, Violet heard him chuckle. "This looks like a personal issue," he said. And then he called to Gemma. "You ready?"

Coward, she thought spitefully, although she was partly

208

grateful he and Gemma were leaving. And when she finally heard the drone of his motorcycle behind her, growing farther and farther away, she let out the breath she'd been holding.

"So not only did you skip school to hang out with . . . *him*," Jay ground out, his eyes scouring her face as he glared down at her, searching for something . . . bits of truth he thought she was hiding from him. "But you didn't bother to tell me where you were going or what you were doing? Isn't it bad enough you lie to your friends? I mean, I get that; I know you have to. But now you're lying to me too?" She tried to reach out to him, but he jerked away from her touch as if it repulsed him. As if *she* repulsed him, and Violet withered inside, her knees suddenly unsteady beneath her as she struggled to remain upright.

"Jay . . ." she said. "It's not like that."

"Right." He squared his chin, his words cutting through her like icy blades. "I guess I just don't know what to believe anymore, Vi. I guess I don't know how many more secrets I can handle."

Violet recoiled, his meaning finding its mark. It was the one thing she'd always worried about, that the secrets would get the best of her. Bury her.

He was right, it was bad enough that she lied to everyone else . . . that she'd spent an entire lifetime lying. She shouldn't be lying to him too.

She opened her mouth to tell him as much, but he was already walking away from her.

"Jay, wait!" she called after him, her voice sounding far too quiet coming from her mouth.

She heard the slam of his car door as he shut her out, right before he peeled out of the parking lot, and she knew . . .

He was tired of waiting for her to figure things out.

Violet replayed that moment over and over *and over* again. She and Jay had argued before. Heck, they'd even fought once in the third grade, throwing unsophisticated punches and pulling each other's hair. Their parents had grounded both of them for a week after Violet had given him a black eye, all because he'd said that Justin Timberlake lip-synched all of his songs. He'd never dared to say it again.

But this was so much different from some stupid childhood spat. This was serious and real, and Violet worried that, because Jay was right this time, because she'd lied one too many times, it might be irreparable as well.

She'd tried calling him again and again, but he was ignoring her calls and sending them straight to voice mail. If he'd been working, it would have been easy for her to force him to at least hear her out; he'd have been a captive audience at the auto parts store. But it was his day off.

She went to all their usual places: Java Hut, the park where they used to hang out, the library (even though they hadn't been there in ages), the lake, Wally's, and even to the school to see if he'd gone back there. But he was nowhere, making it even clearer to Violet that he had no intention of being found. At least not by her.

210

Making it clear to Violet that she'd made an utter and complete mess of things.

When she'd finally given up and gone home, she was in no mood for chitchat about her day, so she'd stalked up to her room and slammed her door. When her mom had asked if she wanted dinner, she insisted she wasn't hungry—which was another lie, but one she was prepared to live with if it meant not having to explain why she didn't want to talk, or why her eyes were uncharacteristically red and puffy.

Instead, she burrowed into her bed, and into her grandmother's journals, searching for information.

CHAPTER 10

VIOLET HAD HOPED TO TALK TO JAY AT SCHOOL
the next day, and she would have even if it meant stalking
him and forcing him to face her . . . except Jay didn't show
up at school. She'd waited all day, thinking at first he was
just late. And then later, when he still wasn't there, that he
must've had a doctor or dentist appointment he hadn't had
the chance to tell her about . . . you know, since he wasn't
talking to her and all. But by lunchtime Violet was convinced he was skipping school in order to avoid her.

It made her day tick by painfully . . . *excruciatingly* slow,
as she worried more and more about just how much damage

she'd actually done, and whether or not it could be fixed this time.

Rafe, of course, was his usual tactful self, asking her if she'd finally dumped her *backwoods boyfriend* and was ready to "trade up." Instead of giving *him* a black eye, which Violet seriously considered, she decided it was best if she steered clear of Rafe for the time being. They might be working on uncovering a mystery that only the two of them knew about, but he was annoying as hell.

And clearly, he was toxic to her relationship.

When Jay didn't show up for a second day of school, Violet felt physically ill, her stomach churning uncontrollably as she tried to choke down her sandwich at lunch and pretend it didn't bother her that her boyfriend was willing to ditch school just to avoid her.

After throwing most of her food away, Violet escaped to the girls' room, locking herself in one of the stalls as she took out her cell phone, knowing that calling Jay again was pointless. She opted instead for a text. A simple message that she meant more sincerely than she'd ever meant anything in her life:

No more secrets, ever. I swear.

She tucked her phone back into her pocket and leaned her forehead against the cool metal of the stall door. Hopefully he'd understand just how hard this was for her, making a promise to open up to him in every way. It wasn't like her to bare all to anyone . . . even to someone she trusted with her life.

Even to Jay.

But if that's what she had to do to keep him, then so be it. Because she didn't want to do this . . . any of it . . . without him. She didn't want to *be* without him.

She knew it meant telling Jay about her imprint, and what Rafe had done to get rid of it. Telling him everything Dr. Lee had said and done to make her stay on the team and the months she'd kept it from him. And explaining her grandmother's and Rafe's mother's roles in the Circle of Seven.

All of it.

And it was worth it. If only he'd forgive her.

If only he'd call her back.

CHAPTER 11

VIOLET STOOD IN FRONT OF THE MIRROR AND appraised the indigo blue maxi dress that swished around her ankles, wishing she had something a little more funeral-y to wear. Eventually she'd decided that with her mom's cardigan it at least looked church-ish, which would have to be good enough. Besides, she reminded herself, it wasn't like she was actually planning to attend the funeral. She was simply planning to spy on it.

But she still didn't want to be disrespectful, not this day of all days. Not to the family being put into the ground. This was their time to find peace, and Violet didn't feel like a pair of jeans and a T-shirt were appropriate attire, even from a distance.

Jay had skipped school for two days, which had made it nearly three days since she'd seen him. She wanted to convince herself that she was numb about it, that she hadn't cried herself to sleep the past three nights, but she'd be lying . . . again. And the new, more honest Violet was trying not to do that. Least of all, to herself.

But today was Friday, the day of the funeral, and now she was the one playing hooky. She grabbed the directions off the printer and stuffed them into her purse before slipping on some flats and rushing out the door. She didn't want to be late.

The sight of a car parked in her driveway brought her up short, nearly causing her to trip down her own front steps.

She tried to think fast, to come up with an excuse for the way she was dressed since she'd texted her friends to tell them she was staying home sick today, but it was too late. Chelsea was already slamming her driver's-side door behind her, a look of single-mindedness on her face. Jules was right behind her, and Claire, not to be outdone, but also not willing to get out of the car, unrolled her window from the backseat.

"Where the heck are you going in *that* getup?" Chelsea asked.

"Um, I . . ." Violet faltered, coming up blank. She tried to turn the conversation around as she glanced at Claire, who'd pulled out a compact and was dabbing at her lip gloss.

"Shouldn't you guys be at school?"

"Yeah," Chelsea stated. "But it's lunchtime, and since Jay wasn't at school again, and you've been all Mopey McMoperson lately, we thought we better stop by to make sure everything was okay. Clearly, it is, and you're off to some big shindig at the local feed store." Chelsea pointed at her dress. "Hope you get there before all the good hitchin' spots are gone."

"It's not that bad," Violet said, defending her fashion choice.

Jules snorted. "Yeah. Yeah, it is, Little House on the Prairie. You and Pa gonna rustle up some vittles for supper?"

"At least lose the sweater," Chelsea offered. "You look like your mom."

Claire, still sitting in the car, glanced up. "She's right, V. You totally do."

Violet glanced down at the dress, thinking how much she'd liked it when she'd tried it on. Remembering, too, that it had been Chelsea who'd talked her into buying it in the first place, telling her how the halter top showed off her shoulders. Of course that was before she'd covered them up with her mom's oversized cardigan. "Sorry, guys. I . . . gotta run. I'll call you later."

"So you're really not gonna tell us what this is all about, are you?" Chelsea drawled as if she wasn't at all surprised by Violet's secrecy.

Violet felt a stab of guilt as she turned her back on her friends and climbed into her car. *More secrets*, she thought regretfully, trying to squelch the feeling as she pulled out of her driveway and watched her friends disappear in her rearview mirror.

While she was driving, she reached for her purse, digging around for the directions she'd printed, but couldn't find them. It didn't matter, though. She knew the general direction, and even before she'd reached the gates of the cemetery, she knew she was in the right place. She had to blink several times as colors began to blot her vision. And, of course, there was the smell.

This was definitely it, she thought, pulling her car to a stop behind a large procession that was already parked up and down the narrow road. She had to get out and walk the rest of the way, picking her way past the grave markers and headstones as other—less familiar—sensations pricked at her.

Most were dull, the way they always were once they were buried . . . staticky and bleeding into one another. Like the animals buried in Shady Acres. But some managed to find their way above the rest, demanding to be noticed.

A ripping sound, like paper. Tear after tear after tear.

The smell of laundry detergent, strong enough that it nearly made her eyes water.

And then there was the one that made Violet turn around, more than once, checking to make certain there was no one standing behind her. The feel of warm air—like someone breathing too near the base of her neck. It persisted even when she tried to rub it away.

But she continued to follow the smell of coffee and the

218

trail of cars that led her toward the service, which was already underway in the central part of the cemetery.

Far off, she could hear a man's voice, speaking in the resonant tone of a minister or a priest—someone reading passages and trying to give comfort to those who were grieving. Violet hadn't been to many funerals, but she imagined they were all sort of alike in that regard.

She stood back, keeping her distance as she spied on the funeral from behind both a tree that blocked her from view, and the medley of colors that clouded her eyesight.

There were three coffins, one much smaller than the other two, and Violet wondered if it was strange that they were holding the service without the daughter being present . . . without even knowing where she was, or whether she should be joining her family in the ground today. She supposed they had to have the funeral eventually, and that those left behind deserved their closure too.

There were flowers everywhere, making it look more like a garden show than a funeral. And behind the caskets, there was an easel with a blown-up family photograph propped up on it—one that included the girl.

They were a lovely family, Violet couldn't help thinking, as she gripped the rough tree bark, trying hard not to look too long at the little boy with freckles splashed across the bridge of his nose.

She turned instead to the people in attendance. There were so many of them, far too many to simply be family members. But Violet's attention was drawn by a couple sitting in the front row, closest to the three caskets. They were older, much older than the couple being buried, and she watched as they leaned into each other. Or rather, as *she* leaned into him. She blubbered mournfully against his shoulder, while he did his best to maintain a stoic expression. His lips were pressed so tightly they were nearly bloodless.

Parents, Violet thought, guessing at their relation to either the man or woman in the caskets.

Beside them, two women squeezed hands, each pressing tissues to their mouths. One cried soundlessly as the other sniffled and choked loudly on her sobs. From their resemblance, Violet thought the two might be sisters.

When the man speaking, the minister or preacher or priest or whoever he was, finished, he asked if anyone wanted to share stories of the family. He said their names, and even from where she stood, Violet could hear them: Brian, Dawn, and Tyler.

Tyler. The little boy with the freckles was Tyler.

Her chest constricted as she thought of all the things Tyler would never get to experience, of all the things he'd miss out on: kissing a girl, driving a car, getting married, watching his children grow old.

She wondered if his sister missed him. If she'd be crying too if she were here.

She felt the hot air on the back of her neck again and she brushed at it, trying to make it go away.

"I knew you were up to something," the voice behind her said. Violet jumped, whirling to stare into Chelsea's

I-told-you-so expression. "I knew I'd catch you eventually. So what's the deal, V? Why are you all dressed up like you're going on a job interview or something? You applying to be a gravedigger?"

Violet just stared at her friend, her throat constricting as she tried to come up with a reasonable explanation for why she was standing in a cemetery, hiding behind a tree.

"Yeah, I didn't think so," Chelsea said when Violet didn't answer right away. Couldn't answer. "So what is it then?"

Violet blinked, mustering up the only words she could manage, "Where are Jules and Claire?" She looked past Chelsea, still trying to figure out what her friend was doing here, how she'd found her. "Are they . . . are they here?"

Chelsea shook her head. "I dropped 'em off at school. But after I saw you, I decided I had better things to do than learning inverse trig functions." She wiggled her eyebrows, letting Violet know that *she* was that better thing. "Oh, and you dropped this." She waved a piece of paper in front of Violet, the printed directions she'd been searching for.

They stared at each other for several long seconds, neither of them speaking.

Chelsea looked past Violet then, to where the funeral was still underway. To where the three caskets were lined up perfectly, ready to be lowered into the ground. Her brows drew together, and Violet could see her working it out, piecing it all together, and then she turned back to Violet, her expression clearing. "Oh my god," she breathed. And then again, as she squeezed Violet's arm. "Oh my god." She

221

looked at Violet with eyes that were wide and lucid. "It *was* you, wasn't it? It was *you* at the house on the lake."

Violet's heart crashed in her chest, but she didn't answer. Chelsea didn't seem to notice. She looked at Violet like she'd never looked at her before, with a mixture of shock and awe. "*You* were the White River student who found the bodies. And now you're here, watching their funeral." She frowned, confused all over again. "Why? Why would you come here?"

Violet reached up to cling to the tree for balance. Her head was spinning, and she was choking on the accusations her friend threw her way. As if somehow the truth was filling her lungs, making it impossible to breathe.

She looked at Chelsea, a girl she'd known her entire life. Someone she'd grown up with, someone she'd laughed with and leaned on. This was her friend. One of her *very best* friends in the entire world. Why shouldn't she tell her? Why shouldn't she know what Violet could do . . . and why she was here now?

She thought of Jay, and how he wasn't talking to her because he was sick and tired of all the lies.

And then she thought of her grandmother, and how she'd once tried to confide in someone she'd cared about. Ian. How he'd turned on her and told others her secret. How she'd been considered a freak . . . and had been ostracized by her entire community. By her own family, even.

But this was Chelsea, Violet told herself, looking into her friend's expectant eyes. Eyes that begged for an explanation.

"Come on," Violet said abruptly, making her decision as she reached for Chelsea's hand and dragged her away from the shelter of the tree.

"I don't get it. What are we doing out here?" Chelsea complained for the millionth time. "When are you going to talk to me?"

Violet lifted her skirt as she picked her way along the overgrown path. It was cooler here, beneath the canopy of trees, and there were mosquitoes to contend with. She was glad for the sweater she'd swiped from her mom's closet. "Just wait," Violet told Chelsea, concentrating on her steps. It was harder to walk in the girly flats than she'd realized it would be this deep in the woods.

It was easier to concentrate now, though, since the bodies had finally been lowered into the ground and the first soft shovelfuls of dirt had been tossed upon their caskets. The bodies had said good-bye to the earthly world. They had their peace.

And so did Violet.

She hadn't realized just how much tension she'd been carrying until that moment, until the last body had let go. It was almost hard to believe she hadn't noticed it sooner, the way the muscles of her shoulders had felt bunched and tight, the way her jaw had clenched.

Everything unraveled now, freeing her as well.

"How much farther?" Chelsea asked from beside her, swatting at a bug on her arm. "I'm getting eaten alive here."

But they were close now . . . very, very close. Violet could feel the vibrations just beneath her skin. Rippling outward as the tiny hairs all over her body stood on end, alert.

Violet stepped off the path, reaching for Chelsea and dragging her with her. Chelsea stumbled but caught herself before she actually fell. She even managed not to complain about the detour, and instead remained silent as Violet lost herself in the sensation that tugged her . . . reaching into her gut and propelling her forward.

Ahead of her, Violet could see a soft red radiance, the echo that came up from the ground, near the base of a gnarled pine trunk. A glow that existed only in that single space on the forest floor.

"Here," she whispered reverently, bending down and scooping the soil with her bare hands. "I told you it wouldn't be far."

"Um, okay . . ." Chelsea said dubiously, as she fell back and watched, like Violet had lost her mind.

And maybe she had. Maybe this was all just a huge mistake.

It only took a second to uncover the body. A dead possum.

It was ugly and partially decayed and its teeth were still exposed as if it had died trying to defend itself.

Chelsea staggered backward. "Gross, Vi! What the *frak*? That's disgusting!"

But Violet wasn't deterred. She stood up and brushed her hands on her skirt. "You asked if it was me who found those bodies at the lake that day . . . ?" Violet said, speaking slowly now, carefully. She paused only for a moment and then plunged ahead. "It *was* me," she confirmed, watching her friend closely for signs that this might be too much information to take in at once. "It's kinda what I do, Chels."

"*What you* . . . ? What do you mean, it's what you do?"

Violet pointed at the possum and Chelsea glanced down too, flinching before she looked away again, acting as if she might puke. "I find bodies," Violet told her.

She waited for Chelsea to say something, to tell Violet she was crazy or to warn her to stay away from her. Instead Chelsea looked stunned as she glanced first to Violet and then back to the dead animal, and then back to Violet again. Doubt gradually transformed her features.

And then she pretended to cough the word *bullshit*, as she propped her hands on her hips. "No one *finds* dead bodies."

Violet shrugged, her brows raised as she did her best to emulate the same cocky gesture she'd seen Chelsea pull off a thousand times before. "*I* do."

"You could've planted that." Chelsea nodded toward the possum, barely able to look at its decomposing form.

Violet thought about that for a minute. "Really, Chels? Why would I do that? On the off chance that you discovered my little secret and decided to call me on it? And how would I know when that might happen? Wouldn't I have to plant a dead possum, like, every day or something?"

"Didn't say it had to be a possum." But then Chelsea stopped to consider Violet's explanation. "So, if you didn't

225

plant it, find another one," she challenged.

Violet shrugged. Cynicism was way easier to deal with than straight-up disbelief. At least Chelsea wasn't shutting her out. "Fine, but I can't promise how long it'll take."

"Course you can't," Chelsea chided, making it clear that she doubted Violet would ever "find" another body again. At least not the way she'd just found this one. Still, she followed as Violet moved back toward the path that was overrun with branches and roots.

It didn't take as long as Violet thought it might. There was another echo nearby, not as strong as the first one, but noticeable nonetheless. It reached into Violet's gut and tugged her, a sensation she doubted she'd ever really be able to explain to anyone, as if her body were no longer moving of its own accord. As if she were possessed.

She answered the call, straying from the path, and she could hear Chelsea right behind her, saying nothing at all. The only sounds were the twigs that snapped beneath Chelsea's sneakers—shoes that were far more suitable for this terrain than Violet's.

At first, Violet thought the echo was faint, but she soon realized she was mistaken. It wasn't faint, it was just . . . melodic.

This echo was a sound.

A sound that made Violet grin as she drew nearer, and it grew clearer, louder. It was like she'd stumbled into a carnival, the music lilting and rising.

No, Violet thought. Not like a carnival, like a carousel.

The music reminded her of riding the colorfully painted wooden horses when she was a little girl.

She stopped suddenly, every nerve in her body telling her she was in the right place. She turned to Chelsea. "This is it."

Chelsea gave her a look that told her what she thought about her proclamation: Violet was full of crap.

But Violet was already turning away from her, falling to her hands and knees as she began brushing away the thin layer of rotting leaves and needles and twigs. Her heart was beating harder than it should, almost as if some part of her worried that Chelsea might be right. That there might not be anything there at all.

But then she felt it. She let the carousel sound overtake her, relishing this song, one that was so different from what her own imprint had been, with its notes rising and falling over her like a nostalgic rainstorm, drenching her. She smoothed the remaining dirt away, creating a small circle on the ground so Chelsea could see what Violet saw.

"*Holy* . . ." Chelsea breathed from over her shoulder now, looking down at the animal—a squirrel, or maybe a rabbit. Something too small and too far decomposed to be recognizable any longer.

Violet turned back, a sly smile finding her lips. "Bang," she said. "I just blew your mind." But she said it quietly, as if she were afraid she might disturb the animal beneath them.

Then Chelsea leaned away from Violet—and her discovery—as she lifted the hem of her shirt up to cover her nose.

"Oh my god!" she gasped. "Do they always smell this bad?"

"Sometimes it's worse," Violet admitted. And it was. Sometimes it was almost unbearable.

Chelsea took a couple of steps back, and Violet watched her as the color drained from her face. "So, are you telling me this is for real? This *body-finding stuff*?" Her face had gone chalk white. "This is freaking me the hell out, Violet."

Violet reburied the animal, gently mounding the leaves and dirt back in place before standing up again. "Yeah, Chels. It's for real," she said. "And no one knows about it. You have to promise me you won't tell anyone. It has to be a secret. *Our* secret." Violet waited for Chelsea to meet her gaze. "Promise," she coaxed her friend.

Chelsea nodded, but it was slow . . . the exact opposite of her usual unflappable determination. Her hesitation made Violet uneasy. But then she recovered, and she clutched Violet, gripping her upper arms and leaning so close that Violet could smell peanut butter on her breath. "I promise," she swore without a trace of doubt. "Whatever you want." Her eyes were shiny and filled with utter confidence now—just like the Chelsea that Violet needed her to be. "Dude, you know I love you. I'll do whatever you need me to do. Consider it in the vault."

Violet smiled—both on the outside and on the inside. Everything about her felt better . . . lighter. Why had she waited so long to share this? Why had she thought she needed to keep this a secret for so long?

Chelsea could handle this.

She could handle this.

Chelsea's eyes continued to glitter as she clutched Violet. "You know what this means, don't you? It means you're some kind of superhero or something."

The smile slipped from Violet's lips, even as nervous laughter bubbled up her throat. "Uh, no, Chels, it doesn't."

But she could see the wheels in Chelsea's head already turning. "Think about it, Vi. How many people do you think can do this? I've never heard of it before, have you?" She didn't wait for Violet to answer, she could carry this conversation on her own. "None. And you know why? Because you're special. Like Superman or Spider-Man or Batman." She stopped. "Scratch that, not like Batman. He was just some dude with a bunch of cool gadgets on his belt. But you know what I mean, *you have a power*. A power, Vi." Her eyes got wide then . . . like, lunatic asylum wide. She was grinning now. "You know what you need, don't you?"

Violet groaned, wondering how this conversation had gone sideways. She answered hesitantly, worried about what she might hear next. "What's that, Chels?"

"A sidekick!" Chelsea announced, beaming back at her, and suddenly Violet realized why she'd been so worried. Because Chelsea *was* a lunatic. "And who better to be your Robin than me? Not only can I keep your secret, I can help you."

This time it was Violet grabbing Chelsea's arms. She gave her a brisk shake, trying to snap her back to reality. "I'm. Not. A. Superhero," she insisted, enunciating each word carefully.

"And what, exactly, would you help me do? Comb the woods searching for dead animals? I seriously don't think we need capes and secret identities for those kinds of adventures."

Chelsea deflated beneath her, but she shot Violet a withering stare. "Buzz kill," she accused. "Fine. No capes . . . got it. But I have, like, a million questions. I don't even know where to start."

Violet just smiled. That, she could totally understand. It was a lot to take in, a lot to process. Chelsea had just discovered that her best friend was some sort of freak of nature.

She dragged Chelsea over to where there was a large boulder covered with sprinkles of soft green moss. "Here," Violet told her, waiting till Chelsea got settled. "Think about it for a minute. Then you can ask me whatever you want, 'kay?"

Violet kept a watchful eye on Chelsea as she sat down. She was glad when the color returned to her friend's cheeks, and it didn't take long for Chelsea to gather her thoughts, sounding more like herself again. Flippant, but rational . . . *ish*. "So, you're definitely not some kind of necrophiliac or anything, right?"

"Gross, Chels!" Violet shuddered. "You're disgusting."

"Me?" Chelsea sounded shocked at the accusation. "And you're trying to tell me that *that* . . ." She waved her hand toward the newly mounded soil in front of them. "That *that* isn't disgusting?"

Violet thought about it for a second, then half shrugged. "Well, sort of. I guess. But in a completely different way. It's

230

not like I wanna make out with the bodies I find. I'm only drawn to find them. And only if they've been . . ." She hesitated, uncertain how to explain this part. "Only if they've been murdered."

Chelsea's eyes grew three sizes larger. "So you're saying that thing was *murdered*?"

"I'm saying it didn't die of natural causes. Something killed it, probably a coyote or a cat or something."

"Okay, okay, okay," Chelsea said, as if she were glitching. She took a breath. "Okay," she repeated. "Let's start at the beginning. How long have you known about this?"

Violet tried to remember the first time she'd realized she was different, when she knew that she was doing something other kids didn't do. She was little, that much she remembered. And she'd been with her father, walking in the woods around their house.

She remembered her father telling her, even then, how important it was for her not to tell anyone about it—what she could do.

And here she was, confessing everything.

"Forever," she said at last. "For as long as I can remember."

Chelsea's mouth dropped open. "And you never said anything . . . to anyone?"

"Except my family. And Jay," she admitted guiltily.

Jumping up from the rock, Chelsea pointed her finger accusingly. "Oh, *come on*! Are you kidding me? *He* got to know and I didn't? How long, Vi? How long has he known?"

Violet couldn't stop her laugh. She knew Chelsea wouldn't like the answer. "Since the summer between first and second grade. He used to help me bury animals in my graveyard."

"Your what?" Chelsea asked, her brows and lips all pinched and puckered. "Is that what that thing in your yard is? By the woods?" When Violet just nodded, Chelsea grimaced. "Burying animals in your backyard, isn't that one of the signs they look for in a serial killer? That, and, like, bed-wetting or something?"

"I think it's torturing animals, not burying animals in a graveyard, Chelsea. *Big* difference."

Chelsea sat back down, still shaking her head. Still not happy that she'd been left out of the circle of trust all these years. "Yeah. You're probably right," she said, sounding serious now, and Violet wondered if she should be offended that Chelsea had said "probably," like there was still some doubt. But she'd already moved on to her next question, and she leaned forward, captivated. Morbidly curious. "So, how does it work anyway? How do you know where to find them? How did you find that family at the lake?"

She'd had to explain this before, but for some reason, trying to find the words to tell Chelsea was harder. And infinitely more important.

She bit her lip as she lowered herself to the ground in front of the boulder, sitting in front of her friend. She drew her knees against her chest and hugged them tightly. "It's weird," she started. "It's like an itching under my skin at first, like everything inside of me is tingling. Sometimes I don't even realize it's happening, I'm just *pulled* in a certain direction, almost against my will." She glanced up, stealing quick glimpses at Chelsea as she leaned her chin against her knees. "As I get closer, it changes, and every body develops a unique energy all its own. It's like a signature. I call it an echo, but only because that's what my grandmother called it."

"Your grandmother knew too?" Chelsea asked, her voice small and awed now.

"My grandmother *had* it too," Violet told her. "These *echoes* can be anything, a taste, a smell, a color, a sound, a sensation. No two are alike, at least that I know of. And here's the weird part . . ."

"Dude. There's a 'weird part'?"

The corner of Violet's lip pulled up. "Right?" she said, agreeing that it had already reached maximum weirdness. And then she plunged ahead. "Whatever that echo is also attaches to the killer too, exactly the same. I call it an imprint."

Chelsea only missed a beat before she quietly said, "*Now* you blew my mind. So there are freaky killers walkin' around out there that you can smell and taste? And they don't even know it?"

"Totally." Violet nodded. "But not just bad-guy killers. Cops and hunters, too. And people who've been in wars. I can't tell them apart."

"And animals?" Chelsea asked, already sorting through the pieces.

"My cat always comes home with imprints. Drives me crazy sometimes."

Chelsea took a breath and leaned back on her hands as she studied Violet through brand-new eyes. "Is it weird?" She shook her head, as if trying to imagine it.

Violet scowled playfully. "I find dead bodies, Chels. How could it *not* be weird?"

Chelsea nodded, as if realizing how stupid her question had been. "Were the people at the lake the first . . . you know, *humans* you've ever found?"

Violet thought about how to answer that. She didn't want to lie, not anymore. But she didn't want to tell the whole truth either. There were still things she didn't want to share, things she shouldn't—and couldn't—share. Like about her team.

She waited too long and Chelsea leaned forward, waiting expectantly, knowing there was more.

"When I was eight, I found a girl buried in the woods near my house," Violet finally answered, skirting the issue by giving part of an answer. "And you already know that Jay and I found that body in the lake last year." She didn't tell Chelsea about all the other bodies she'd found.

"Oh yeah . . . the floater. Gross." She wrinkled her nose. "So I'm guessing that wasn't an accident. You didn't just *happen* to see it while you were out on the lake the way you said you did?"

Violet shook her head.

"What are they like, the bodies? Does it freak you out?

234

I gotta admit, I think I might pee my pants if I were in your shoes."

Violet stifled a giggle against the tops of her knees. "Well, I haven't peed yet, but I'll definitely keep you posted." And then she shrugged. "It's definitely not like on TV. There, the bodies still look"—she struggled for the right way to describe it—"like real people. Like they could just sit up and start talking to you. But *real* bodies, the ones I've seen at least, are *obviously* dead. The girl in the lake was so bloated that her skin didn't look like it even belonged on her anymore. It was shiny and blistery looking, and didn't sit right on her features. And I could see right through her skin in places. It was like looking at a water-logged roadmap." Violet kept her gaze on Chelsea, making sure she wasn't being too graphic. "The girl who was buried near my house when I was little already had bugs on her when I found her. They were *eating* her."

Chelsea cringed, and Violet thought about the family at the lake house, about their wounds, and wondered what Chelsea would think if she knew how their necks had looked, about the way the edges weren't smooth and clean the way they would have been if it had been on television. Instead they were ragged . . . as if they'd been gored rather than sliced.

But Chelsea didn't need to know such things. No one did.

Violet got up and held her hand out to her friend. "Come on, Chelsea. We should get back, it's been a long day."

Chelsea followed Violet's gaze, looking up at the sun through the filter of leaves overhead. It wasn't late. Not really. But it felt like it was.

It felt like they'd been out there forever.

236

BIRDS OF A FEATHER

"PLAY IT AGAIN." KISHA CLAPPED, HER ENTHUSI-
asm making her look younger, less tired. Less strung out.

Evan grinned back at her, laying his guitar aside. "Maybe later,
Kish, I'm tired."

He wasn't really; he could play all day, especially in the park
where his playing drew attention . . . a real audience.

Except that today they had another purpose. Today was meant
as a scouting mission.

He looked over to where Butterfly tried to get comfortable on
the blanket Boxer had spread out for them. She squirmed, her body
racked by an unexpected, relentless tremor, and he wondered if she
even realized what was happening to her as she reached down to

237

resume picking at the scab on her hand. It was easy to recognize the nervous energy she was trying to release, easy to spot an addict craving a new high.

When they'd first found her, less than a month ago, she'd been pretty and fresh faced. Despite her attempts to look urban, he'd pegged her for what she was: a bored rich girl who was trying to rebel against her parents, to prove there was more to her than spray tan and strawberry lip gloss.

To look at her now was like a study in contrasts. Her hair, which had once been a soft shade of reddish-blonde, had since been dyed black, but was now faded and dirty. Her skin, which had been clear, was now marked with pockets of acne, and her cheeks were hollow. Her eyes, although sunken and ringed with dark circles, were the only giveaway to the girl she'd once been, big and silvery green-gray, made more mesmerizing by the pining that tormented her.

He couldn't help her now though. He had to save enough for Bailey, who was getting progressively worse, her tolerance getting harder and harder to satisfy. Kisha and Boxer and Colton, at least, could function on small hits here and there. Bailey could no longer get up in the morning without the needle. And he couldn't bear to watch her tweak the way he was watching Butterfly do now.

Bailey had been the first to call him "family." The first to let him take care of her.

He refused to let her down, but at the rate she was going, she'd used up most of their stash. And he couldn't afford to let the rest of them come down for too long. He couldn't risk not having them need him. Not having them depend on him.

He'd need to score some more cash soon. And more cash meant finding a new mark.

"What about them?" Colton said, pointing with one hand while biting a nail on his other. "They look like they have money."

He watched the picturesque family, spreading out their picnic on the checkered blanket. This was the strange part about being out of the city and in the suburbs: Everyone looking like they'd walked straight out of the pages of a catalog, like they were props or paper dolls. All of them pretending that people like him—and his family—didn't exist. He scrutinized them for several long minutes, trying to decide if they could be right . . . analyzing their body language, the way they interacted with one another, the way they talked, laughed, and even breathed. He was a lion, stalking his prey, waiting for his chance to pounce.

After several long moments, he shook his head. "No. No good, man."

"Why not?" Colton whined, his voice fraying at the edges as if he were unraveling right before their eyes.

Something gentle and protective unfurled within him. This was what family did, he told himself. This was his purpose, to protect them. To teach them. "See her purse? It's a knockoff. And check out her hair. See her dark roots? That kind of grow-out says she hasn't been to whatever second-rate salon she goes to in months . . . way too long. Even the kid's shoes are from Wal-Mart or Target."
He pointed at the girl, a preschooler with the kind of golden blonde hair that the mommy had probably been trying to cling to with her discount highlights. "Parents don't usually skimp on the kids' shit. Not if they don't have to." He looked away from them, no longer

interested in what they had to offer. "Nah, they're no good. We need to find someone else."

"Dude, you sound like a fag when you talk about handbags and hair salons. You know that, don't you?" Boxer laughed, shoving him. "So who then?" he asked.

He realized then that Boxer wasn't shaking as badly as Butterfly or Colton, and he wondered if his old friend had gotten into their stash when he wasn't looking. He wondered if his authority might be slipping.

But Colton demanded his attention as he still strained toward the picture-perfect family. "We could still do 'em."

Kisha bit her already chapped lip until it bled. "What's the point, Colt? Why bother if they don't have nothing we want?"

Colton grinned, a smile so huge it was almost menacing. It was menacing. "For fun. We could still have fun with 'em. What d'ya say, Butterfly? You wanna have some more fun, don't you?"

Something flashed behind Butterfly's eerie greenish eyes, something close to comprehension, as if she nearly understood what he meant. As if she nearly remembered what they'd done to her family.

Not that he cared, really. She hadn't stopped them. She'd participated with the rest of them as they'd yanked the parents from their bed and dragged them down the stairs. She'd helped tie her mom's and dad's hands behind their backs, never even flinching as they'd begged for their lives. As they'd begged their daughter not to do this.

She'd hardly blinked when Colton had pulled his knife out. She'd giggled, even, as Boxer had sliced her mother's throat.

She was high as shit, but she was there.

He knew, because he was the one who'd given the commands.

240

He'd been the one carefully orchestrating the blitz on her family. And then he'd stood back and watched as his plans were carried out, each of his own family members following orders to a T while he looted the house for stuff that could be sold easily for cash.

He'd been surprised, though, by the intoxicating rush he'd felt at pulling the strings, despite letting the others have all the real "fun."

It was also when he realized he had a new calling. That he wanted people to see what he'd done, to know what he was capable of.

There were other ways to achieve fame. Other ways to make the world bow at his feet.

When the kid had come down the stairs and recognized his sister, he'd asked her what was wrong, what was happening. It wasn't until he saw his parents, when his face had twisted with fear and he'd screamed, that Butterfly had lost her shit. That's when she'd wanted out. That was when the high wore off and reality kicked in.

But it was already too late. She was in it. She'd joined their family then.

Boxer had hauled her into the other room and dosed her again, making sure she would either cooperate, pass out, or die. It didn't matter which, as long as she'd shut the hell up. As long as she'd stop fucking crying.

The kid had been tougher to watch. Not impossible, just tougher. Especially when Colton had decided to take a souvenir.

Watching as Colton had gutted the kid like that . . .

It wasn't like in the movies where someone just reaches in and pulls out a still-beating heart. No, Colton had had to work at it, sawing at the kid's chest to get through.

*It was messy. And the sounds of knife grating through bone . . .
it was disgusting.*

*He watched Butterfly now, as she frowned, trying to make sense
of Colton's words. And then he turned to Colton, staring into his
cold, emotionless eyes. "Leave her alone, will ya? I said no. We
need someone else."*

*Colton held his gaze, and he wondered if this was it, the chal-
lenge he'd been waiting for, the moment someone would decide that
he wasn't their leader. That he wasn't calling the shots. But then
Colton waved his hand, as if batting away a fly. "Whatever, man.
You're no fun sometimes."*

*He smiled then. "I didn't say we weren't gonna have fun today."
He lifted his chin, nodding toward a couple who were just getting out
of a silver Mercedes at the edge of the parking lot. The purse draped
over the woman's shoulder probably cost more than his parents' house
had, and they both wore designer sunglasses with big garish logos on
them. "What about them?"*

*Butterfly followed his gaze as her body was racked by another
spasm.*

*Kisha leaned up behind him, whispering softly against his ear.
"She looks like she deserves it, doesn't she, baby?"*

*Colton answered before he had a chance to. "She totally does.
They both do."*

CHAPTER 12

"GET IN." VIOLET'S VOICE WAS PRACTICED AND
steely as she met Jay's startled expression.

She wasn't surprised to see the look of shock on his face;
she was probably the last person he'd expected to find sitting behind the wheel of his car, engine running. But she
was tired of waiting for him to figure things out and come
to her, tired of drowning in her own self-despair, and she'd
decided to take matters into her own hands.

Plus, she'd known he kept a magnetic hide-a-key under
his front passenger wheel well. It wasn't *exactly* like she'd
broken into his car, or anything. Not technically at least.

"Violet . . ." he started to say, but she cut him off.

"Get in," she repeated, testing her foot on the accelerator and revving up the engine, hoping to make an impact on him, letting him know she was serious. "Now," she insisted.

He didn't jump at her command, which was sort of what she'd hoped for, and he didn't open the door and haul her out, burying her in his arms and begging for forgiveness. She'd imagined it that way too—along with about a hundred other scenarios, some good and some not so good. The begging-for-forgiveness one ranked right up there with the ripping-his-shirt-off-and-dragging-her-to-bed one. She smiled wickedly to herself.

She supposed she'd have to settle for his soft sigh of resignation and silent acquiescence, as he rounded the front of the car and climbed mutely into the passenger seat. At least he hadn't insisted she get out of his car and leave.

She'd been waiting in the dark for almost an hour, sitting in the parking lot of the auto parts store where he worked, knowing he'd be off any minute and find her there—borderline stalking him. She'd nearly changed her mind a dozen times as her heart climbed higher and higher into her throat, anticipation threatening to get the best of her. But each time she'd remind herself of how miserable she'd been the past few days without him, of how badly she wanted to fix this . . . this mess she'd made. And how sorry she was she'd let it get this far in the first place.

No more lies, she told herself. *No more secrets.*

Yet here he was, sitting right beside her, and suddenly all she wanted to do was bolt. To run away and hide so she didn't have to face him right now.

"What are you—?"

"Shut up," she insisted, not wanting to stray too far from the plan she'd formulated, otherwise she might just chicken out after all. She slammed the car into reverse, still expecting Jay to stop her at any second . . . especially since he'd never let her drive his car before. But he didn't. He bit back any questions he had as she pulled out of the parking lot, leaving her car behind in a darkened corner, just out of sight.

Violet pretended to concentrate on the road, and the traffic lights, and the steering wheel and turn signal, and everything else she could pretend was significant as she drove. Anything in order to ignore how uncomfortable the silence inside the car was. She stole glimpses of Jay whenever she was sure he wasn't looking, as he too seemed to find the signs and streetlights and storefronts fascinating. Entirely too engrossing.

She wanted to reach across to him, to touch him, let her fingers weave through his, but she couldn't. Not until she could talk to him, explain things.

She gripped the leather wheel, which suddenly felt sticky beneath her hands as she drove, following the path she'd mapped out in her head, wondering at what point he'd realize where she was taking him.

But if realization dawned, he never said so. He just continued to watch as stoplights turned into stop signs, and then were replaced by nothing but trees . . . all around them. Trees and deserted stretches of roads and night skies.

When Violet pulled off the pavement and the sound of gravel replaced the glaring silence, Jay finally spoke. "Why here?" he asked.

But Violet still wasn't ready to answer him. She stopped the car, putting it in park and turning off the ignition. She pocketed the key, and without looking his way, ordered, "Get out."

From the corner of her eye, she saw the faintest hint of a smile. "I have my own set, you know?"

Her stomach dropped, heavy like it was filled with lead. She hadn't considered that. Of course she didn't have the only key . . . she had the spare.

She squared her shoulders and got out anyway, slamming the door behind her, deciding to play this through anyway. He wouldn't just leave her out here, would he?

Without the headlights, it was darker. The only light came from the bridge about a quarter of a mile away. And it was too high up to be all that effective.

Violet stood there, waiting, straining to hear above the rushing water of the river for the other sound she so desperately wanted to hear—the passenger side door. It took far too long for it to come, but when it eventually did, her heart swelled with relief, like a balloon filling with helium. The sound of his footsteps, coming closer, made her feel like she could soar.

"Violet," he said, this time sounding more determined than before. "Why are we here?"

His voice wasn't soft or apologetic, or even filled with

the kind of lustful desire that would give Violet the impression he might *actually* rip his shirt off at any second, but he didn't sound angry either. She turned to face him, looking at him in the pale light that shone down on him from the bridge. The sound from the water, just steps away, was alternately trickling and gushing, as the river pushed and splashed and parted for both smooth and jagged rocks in its path. At the edge, where it was shallow, the water was cool and almost tranquil. But farther out, it could be treacherous; the perilous currents had been known to pull full-grown men beneath them, trapping them. Drowning them.

Yet it didn't stop people from fishing, swimming, rafting, and tubing this very same river. The shore where she and Jay stood now stretched into a long sandy beach along the water's edge, and still had the charred remnants of summer bonfires.

"Beer Bottle Beach . . . don't you remember? Your mom used to drop us off here? We used to go inner tubing in the summer." The beach probably had an official name given to it by the county or the parks department, but everyone called it Beer Bottle Beach . . . a name it had had for as long as Violet could remember.

His voice was low and husky. "Of course I remember. What I meant was, why are we here?"

Her feet sunk into the sand as she faced him, tears stinging her eyes. "Jay." She hated that she sounded like she was pleading now, and she wished that she could be tougher . . . stronger. "I told Chelsea everything." She wanted to tell him

247

the rest, to explain what she meant by that, but already her voice was wobbling, on the verge of breaking. She took a breath, trying to collect herself.

A soft breeze spilled over her skin, and above them headlights shone down on them as a car crossed the bridge. Just for a moment, she could see him clearer, and she knew that he could see her too as the tears she'd fought against spilled onto her cheeks.

He looked stupefied. "*What* . . . what do you mean, you told Chelsea?" His voice no longer sounded husky or quiet. "What are you talking about, Violet? You didn't tell her what you could do? Not about . . ." He frowned, as if just saying it, even here, while they were all alone, was too much to share. "Not about the bodies?"

But already she was nodding, and even in the faded lights, she knew he understood. He raked his hand through his hair. "Are you crazy? That's not what I wanted. That was *never* what I wanted. I want you to be honest with *me*. *With me*, Vi. Not to put yourself in danger by telling other people."

He took a single step away from her, and then seemed to think better of it and came back, positioning himself directly in front of her. If he'd had any notions about being aloof and cool, they were gone now, vanished with the admission of what she'd done.

"Dammit," he cursed.

"Jay . . ." She closed the distance as she reached for him. When her fingertips brushed the coarse hairs on his

248

arm, heat flushed her face, rushing all the way to her belly. Suddenly *she* wanted to rip his shirt off, regardless of how inappropriate the timing seemed. "It's just Chelsea. I trust her." She let her fingers move down, feeling their way along the sinewy muscles of his forearm, letting her thumb trace a circle around his wrist bone, moving until her hand was beneath his, their palms touching. "*We* can trust her."

He moved then too, his fingers snapping closed around her hand in a sudden, swift movement that startled her, making her breath catch. Her pulse hammered against the base of her throat. "It's not that you told *Chelsea* that bothers me," he said warningly. "It's that the more people who know—no matter *who* they are, no matter how trustworthy they are—the more likely it is to get out. Don't you get it?" His grip lessened as he tugged her, so softly she didn't even realize at first that she was being tugged. She was standing so close to him that she could practically *feel* his heartbeat across the distance. His eyes, normally playful and gentle and ready to smile, were on hers, brimming now with something intense and urgent as he willed her to understand.

Violet held her breath as she frowned. "I didn't want to lie anymore," she tried again.

But Jay was shaking his head. "No, Vi. You're wrong. You've got this all wrong." And suddenly they were no longer standing apart; they were no longer separated by the breadth of their heartbeats. Jay was squeezing her against him, crushing her. Not hugging or stroking her, but *crushing* her. She felt his fingers clawing at the back of her shirt, balling the thin fabric in his fists as he clutched her to him, and she could feel the days and weeks and months of frustration and fear and whatever else he'd been holding back come pouring out of him as he groaned achingly into her curls . . .

. . . *And he crushed her.*

She might have complained—needing to breathe and all—but instead she remained still, and silent, waiting for him to regain himself as he rocked and squeezed her. She concentrated on the fact that he was touching her at long last, and that through the small gasps she was able to take, his T-shirt smelled of car grease and Irish Spring soap, exactly like it should smell. Like him. And that she'd missed that smell more than she'd ever thought possible.

After a few agonizing minutes, he exhaled, dropping his chin against the top of her head. "I want you to lie. You *need* to lie, Violet. Just not to me."

She wanted to nod and tell him she would, that she would lie her ass off . . . whatever he wanted her to do as long as he'd keep holding her like this. And maybe if he'd take his shirt off too. But she knew that wasn't an option. "I can't. No more lies. No more secrets, Jay. Besides, Chelsea already knows. There's no going back now."

He shook his head, but didn't let go. "Fine," he said, and she swore his grip tightened again when he said it. "But that's it. Swear to me that Chelsea's the last one, you won't tell anyone else."

"I can't do that either. I might have to tell someone else," she said, but she was grinning now because it was hard to take him seriously when he'd let go of her shirt and his hand was moving low across the base of her spine. He was making it hard to think about anything but the path his hand was taking. She wiggled against him, and he groaned again, but this time for an entirely different reason than he had before.

She stopped then, realizing that she still had things she needed to tell him, and if she didn't tell him now, she'd feel like she was still keeping secrets from him. "Wait," she said, taking the barest step back and reaching for his hand, forcing him to pay attention. "I need you to know something. My imprint . . . it's gone."

It was his turn to go motionless, his hand falling away from hers. "Gone? How is that . . . ? How?"

Without waiting, Violet told him, before she could change her mind. "It was Rafe. Rafe got rid of it for me." She explained to him about her grandmother's journals, about the way the echoes and imprints vanished when the heart was separated from the body. She described what Rafe had done to Caine's body for her.

She told him, too, about Dr. Lee, his involvement in the Circle of Seven, the sleeping pills he'd been giving her. Everything.

And Jay listened. Wordlessly.

When she was finished, she reached up and absently smoothed a stray hair away from his forehead. He stopped her, catching her hand and her awareness. "Why do you think he did it?" he asked, and Violet strained to see him better in the dull light.

"Dr. Lee?" she asked back, being intentionally obtuse. She knew exactly who he meant.

"Rafe." He said the name with obvious distaste. "Why do you think he would risk so much for you? He'd get in a lot of trouble if he got caught."

Violet shrugged, still warring with that part of herself that wanted to avoid the truth. But she couldn't be that girl anymore, not with Jay. Shaking her head, as if her internal struggle had reached the surface, she said, "For a lot of reasons, I guess. Because he's my teammate. Because he's my friend." She shrugged again as she glanced away from him. "But mostly because he likes me. I think he's always liked me." Her voice had gone soft, and was muffled by the river behind them.

Shame filled her like the icy waters beyond.

She remembered once, when she and Jay had come to the river on a clear May day—far too early in the year for the sun to have warmed the waters that were just beginning to melt off the glaciers, trickling down from the mountains. But they'd decided it was warm enough to go swimming, and they'd searched the shoreline for a good spot, finally finding a place where the water pooled away from the rocks, where it was still and deep and calm.

They'd stripped down to their underwear under the late spring sun, and had climbed up into a tree that hung over the spot. Without so much as testing the water with their toes, they'd clutched each other's hands, and on the count of three, they had jumped.

If their parents had known what they'd done that day, they'd have been grounded for life.

But Violet could still remember how the too-cold water had felt when they'd plunged into it. The way a million frost-tipped needles had skewered her skin all at once, making her want to gasp even as water filled her nose and mouth. The way her lungs had compressed in on themselves, feeling as if they would shut down and might never breathe air again. The way every muscle in her body had felt paralyzed and her legs had refused to kick even when she'd started sinking toward the bottom.

She felt that way now. That's how the shame of not telling Jay about Rafe's feelings sooner felt . . . like needles and squeezed lungs and useless muscles.

And just like that day in the bitter waters of the river, it was Jay who saved her, who dragged her to the surface as he held on to her.

His hand on hers was safe and solid . . . and lifesaving. "And what about you, Vi?" he questioned, pulling her gaze back to his just like that. "Who do *you* like?"

She would have come up coughing and sputtering, the same way she had when he'd pulled her out of the river, but this answer was easy and came to her lips without a second thought. "You, Jay. It's always been you. It always will be you."

He reached for her then, and she was off her feet in an instant, giggling breathlessly as they landed in the sand beneath them. "I knew you'd say that," he told her as he buried his face in the hair that curled wildly around the side of her face.

The sand was still warm from the late summer day, and it molded around them, cradling them. "Then why'd you ask?" she insisted, already breathless and surrendering to his touch.

She could feel him grinning as his lips brushed over hers. "Because I wanted to hear you say it." And then he kissed her, his tongue slipping past her lips, and the sounds of the river faded, along with the light of the bridge and the worry of secrets kept and those revealed.

"Wait," she gasped, whispering as she reached up and pushed him away from her. She tried to sound serious as her heart hammered painfully inside her chest, but it was so terribly hard with him watching her like that, his eyes wide and expectant.

"What is it?" he asked, his breath hot against her own.

She grinned back at him, feeling devious and wanton. "I'm gonna need you to take off your shirt now."

CHAPTER 13

"GRADY! *GRADY*, WAIT UP!" VIOLET SHOVED HER way through the crowded hallway, hoping he could hear her above the ruckus. Hoping he'd care enough that it was her calling for him to stop.

She doubted he really wanted to talk to anyone at the moment. He hadn't exactly received a warm "Welcome back!" from the student body. It was more like the cold shoulder with a side of "What are you looking at, creep?"

It didn't matter that the police had exonerated him, and that no charges had actually been filed against him. The damage had already been done. In the eyes of the White River student body—maybe in those of everyone in

Buckley—Grady was a murderer. Or at least close enough.

Violet was panting after chasing him up a second flight of stairs, weaving her way in and around students in her path. When she heard Grady's name being passed between two girls who weren't even trying to keep their voices down, Violet glared at them.

"Get a good earful?" one of the girls sneered at Violet. "This is a private conversation, why don't you mind your own beeswax?"

Violet thought about stopping, about confronting the two of them right there in the hallway, but she hesitated on the words *beeswax*, giving them each a second glance. They were young . . . freshmen probably. *Ninth graders*. What kind of bully would that make her if she lit into them, even if they deserved to be set straight?

She shot them an impatient glare, deciding to ignore their ignorance. "Grady," she called again, when she saw him lingering in front of a bank of lockers.

He glanced up when he heard her, and she saw the look in his eyes—the one that said he wasn't sure whether to stand there and wait for her, or to dart away. To disappear into the crowd and avoid her—and everyone else—altogether.

She couldn't blame him really. She was sure it had been rough so far . . . and it was only halfway through his first day back.

Opening his locker, he shuffled through papers and books as she approached.

"I was starting to wonder if you were ever coming back,"

she said, suddenly feeling awkward and unsure. She wanted him to know he had an ally, but she also remembered that not so long ago she'd wanted nothing more than to avoid him. The same way everyone else was doing now.

"Me too," he said, digging a book out of his backpack and shoving it in his locker. "I probably wouldn't have if my parents hadn't'a gotten sick of watching me play Call of Duty all day. But, hey, lucky for me everyone's excited to see me." His voice sounded flat . . . empty. "Look at them. I'm, like, some sorta pariah." He nodded down the hallway, and almost all the kids in the vicinity pretended they hadn't just been watching him seconds before as all eyes shot in different directions. "They won't even look at me."

"That's not true." Violet touched his arm. "*I'm* glad you're back."

"Yeah, well, you might be the only one. No one'll even talk to me." He rummaged around in his locker some more. "I might as well have done it."

Violet tried to imagine being in his shoes, to have everyone talking about you, wondering what kind of person you are. Wondering whether or not you really were a killer.

She watched as he pulled out the same book he'd just put into his locker. He held it in his hands, looking at it as if it were foreign, as if trying to remember what he'd come there for.

"Come on," she told him, reaching out and slamming his locker door shut. "Come have lunch with me. With us," she insisted. Jay would have to accept Grady's presence. At least until some newer, better, juicier bit of gossip came along and bumped Grady back out of the limelight.

She thought he might argue with her; in fact she'd expected it. Instead, he looked down at her gratefully. "Are you sure?" he asked, and she just nodded.

She chatted the entire way, mostly to draw his attention away from the fact that everyone was staring.

But even more unsettling were the gapes and stares they got from the people at her own table when she and Grady sat down. Together.

"Really?" Gemma leaned in, getting close enough to her ear that Grady couldn't hear her. "Now the two of you are BFFs?"

Violet shrugged the other girl off, the way she'd tried to do with everyone else all day. She didn't need her own friends making things worse. She didn't need *their* judge-y attitudes too.

She leveled her gaze on Claire and Jules and Chelsea, daring each of them, as pointedly as she could, to say something. Anything. And then Jay joined them, and she directed it at him too.

Not a word, she hoped the look conveyed, in no uncertain terms.

But Rafe didn't get the memo, and he was right at Jay's heels. "*Killer* jacket, man," he told Grady as he dropped down next to Chelsea, directly across from Violet.

Chelsea choked on the chocolate milk she'd been chugging, and came up sputtering. Jules reached over and patted her on the back, entirely too hard to be any kind of serious attempt to help her friend.

"Oh my god, Rafe, did you have to go there?" Violet admonished.

Rafe shrugged. "What? It's a nice jacket."

Violet glanced at the letterman's jacket Grady was wearing and tried to imagine a world in which Rafe might actually envy it. This certainly wasn't that place.

"It's okay, Vi," Grady said, rubbing the back of his neck nervously. "Might as well get it over with. I figured I'd get some crap about what happened. But being back here was way worse than I expected. At least he's talking to me."

Rafe lifted his brows at Violet as if to say, *See?*

"A little warning, next time? I think some of that milk went up my nose," Chelsea complained, pretending to scowl at Rafe. But she wasn't fooling anyone. A scowl from Chelsea was as good as an eye-bat from any other girl. She was definitely flirting.

"Must suck to be back," Rafe offered Grady. "This isn't exactly the most open-minded place I've ever been."

Grady shrugged, taking a bite of his sandwich. "It beats the hell outta going to juvie, I guess."

Rafe half shrugged, half nodded. It probably was better than juvie, the gesture said, but also, *whatever.* Rafe's usual response to just about everything.

Gemma caught Rafe's attention then, from the other side of the table, and whatever message she was trying to convey to him, Rafe seemed to understand. He nodded and reached into his pocket. Violet watched as his hand dropped to his lap, his focus directed downward. He was checking his phone.

Gemma elbowed her too, a quick, discreet nudge that no one else should've noticed.

Except that someone had. Someone who'd been watching Violet a little too closely all day. Someone who was a little too fascinated by her, and what she could do.

Chelsea.

"What the frik was that all about?" Chelsea asked, falling into step beside Violet.

Violet glanced up at Jay, who was on the other side of her, and he looked back at her, puzzled. "What was what, Chels?" he asked.

"Okay, one," she started, ticking off her list of complaints, "I wasn't talking to you. And two," she continued, looking meaningfully at Violet now, "I'm talking about that weirdness between you and Rafe and Blondie. That's what."

Inwardly, Violet sighed. Outwardly, she braced herself. This was exactly the part of her ability she'd avoided discussing with Chelsea: her team.

"It wasn't anything. I don't know what you mean."

Chelsea stopped, and Violet considered forging on and pretending they'd lost her in the crowded hallway. But this was Chelsea she was talking about. She'd have to deal with this mess sooner or later.

Besides, Jay stopped too, and was now looking from

Violet to Chelsea. "I'm pretty sure I missed something. Are you two fighting or something?"

"Nope," Chelsea stated, frowning now. "And apparently I was the one who missed something." She leaned close to Jay, so close that Violet had to backtrack in her steps to hear what she was saying. "But don't worry . . ." Chelsea poked him with her elbow. "I know everything now. Violet told me her little secret. Or"—she narrowed her eyes at Violet, who was right beside them now—"I *thought* I knew everything. So what gives? Don't tell me Rafe knows too. And that girl?"

"*Shh!*" Violet hissed, dragging Chelsea by the arm away from the rush of students, not wanting anyone to overhear what they were talking about.

Violet turned to Chelsea then, her words coming from between gritted teeth. "I told you, it's a *secret*," she stressed.

Chelsea nodded. Eagerly. Wide-eyed. "Okay, yeah, and *I* was thinking we should have a secret handshake. Like a gang." She held her hand out to Violet, palm out, but Violet slapped it away.

"Are you kidding me with that? A secret handshake? Are you *five*? Come on, Chelsea, this is serious. You have to be careful." Her voice bordered on hysteria. "You promised I could trust you."

Chelsea straightened up, dropping her hand. "And you totally can, Vi. I was just kidding about the handshake. I mean, kind of. You can count on me. I swear I'll never tell anyone." She met Violet's gaze directly. "Swear."

Violet watched her, studying her, considering her words and the earnestness of her expression. And then she sighed, her shoulders sagging and her stomach unknotting, just a little bit. "Thank you," she said softly.

"So tell me then," Chelsea said, stopping Violet before she could go.

Violet turned back. "Tell you what?"

"Tell me if Rafe and Gemma know too."

Violet chewed the inside of her cheek, and she saw Jay watching her from the corner of her eye. She wondered what he would do, what he'd tell Chelsea if he were standing there, in her place.

Finally, she just said, "They do, Chels. But I can't tell you why."

Krystal waved enthusiastically as Violet got out of her car. She wore purple knee-high boots over black-and-white-striped tights that had a kind of, like, jailhouse chic to them. The streaks in Krystal's black hair were nearly as glaring as the purple of her boots.

Krystal sprinted across the parking lot to meet Violet. "You okay?" she gushed, her arms squishing her friend fiercely. "I heard what happened last week. Rafe said it was *grue*-some. Said you totally lost it. Puked and everything."

"Nice. Tell Rafe thanks for sharing." Violet winced, wishing everyone didn't have to know every little detail about her.

Krystal released her. "Aw, don't be that way," she coaxed.

"That's what we're here for. Teammates, right?" It was hard to be bothered by the statement though, not when it was coming from Krystal with her big, guileless brown eyes staring back at her. "Oh," she exclaimed then, reaching into her pocket. "I brought you something." She held out a tiny blue velvet bag that was cinched at the top with a narrow length of gold cord. "I left it in the bag so it wouldn't touch my skin. I didn't want any of my mojo to accidentally rub off on it. It's called merikanite obsidian, but some people call it Apache Tears. It's for luck."

Violet pulled the black stone out of the bag and rubbed her thumb across its smooth, polished surface. It had a tiny metal clasp affixed to one end of it. She could use some luck, she supposed.

"You can add it to the chain . . . with the others," Krystal told her, pointing to Violet's chest, and Violet wondered how Krystal had known she was wearing the necklace she'd given her. She always kept it tucked away, hidden beneath her shirt.

Already, there were two healing stones dangling from the chain. One that Krystal had given her just after Rafe had crashed his motorcycle, when Violet had first gone to visit Krystal at The Crystal Palace—the psychic shop where she worked. It was a slick black onyx, meant for protection. Violet had never pointed out to Krystal, who believed implicitly in the power of the healing crystals, that she'd given it to her right before she'd been assaulted by a gang member outside the Center.

So much for protection.

The second crystal had been a welcome-home present of sorts. Krystal had given it to Violet the day she'd come home, after her abduction. As a medium, Krystal claimed that she'd known where to find Violet after being contacted by the ghost of her abductor. *After* Violet had killed him, of course.

Krystal had brought her a pretty blue crystalline stone meant for healing. Violet had strung it on the same chain as the onyx. Unlike the onyx, the blue crystal was jagged and rough, but felt warm pressed against her skin, and Violet hated to admit how much she'd grown to depend on it. How badly she wanted to believe the stone would work. That it would heal her, make her better—both inside and out.

Violet pressed her hand to the place where the other two stones covered her heart. "Thanks, Krystal," she said, feeling suddenly awkward about accepting the gift from her friend. "You really don't have to do that."

Krystal punched Violet in the arm. "Don't be stupid. I know I don't."

Violet followed Krystal inside. She was always surprised by the way she felt when she stepped through the doors that led into the Center. Even after everything with Dr. Lee, she'd never felt . . . *uneasy* being here.

It still felt more like walking through her own front door.

It was no different today, when Violet slipped inside, that same sense of coming home.

When Sam saw her, he jumped up from the table, as

if he'd been waiting for her to arrive, and he rushed over to meet her near the entrance. They stood apart from the overpolished conference table, where Gemma and Rafe were already seated. Krystal didn't wait for them; instead she dropped into an open chair and began bouncing impatiently.

Rafe shot an indifferent glance in their direction, but Sam moved to block his view, not wanting anyone to overhear whatever he had to say.

His expression was eager and hopeful, reminding Violet just how young he really was. "I think I have something for you," he said, glancing around nervously, as if he expected to catch someone spying on them. "Let's talk. Afterward."

Violet had nearly forgotten about the photo she'd slipped to Sam at Dr. Lee's office last week. She wanted to know what he meant when he said he *had something for her*. But when she peered past him, Sara was already standing at the head of the table, watching her, and Violet knew it would have to wait for later.

She stole a quick glance at Rafe on her way to the table. He was reclining in his chair, making an effort to look as unfazed as ever by everyone and everything around him.

Taking the open seat by Krystal, Violet couldn't help smiling when Krystal threw her head over the back of the chair, leaning so far backward she was practically upside down as she grinned at Violet. "What was that all about?" she asked, not realizing that Sara had already started the meeting.

Violet pointed toward the front of the table, just as Sara's ice-coated fingers held up the first image.

"These," Sara explained on a gust of crisp air that only Violet could see, "are the first photographs of the crime scene I texted you all about this afternoon."

As soon as Violet saw it, she understood why they'd all been called down here. There were two victims in this picture, a man and the woman, lying side by side, and both of them had their throats cut in the same way the family at the lake had.

"And *this*"—Sara held up a second photo—"is why we were called."

Goose bumps peppered Violet's skin, as déjà vu tickled her senses. It was an image of the same strange cross as the one from the other house. It had been drawn on the wall in blood or red paint.

"It's called a brimstone cross," Sara went on. "It was adopted as a satanic symbol by Anton LaVey in the sixties. But it's also called the Leviathan cross, and is the alchemic symbol for sulfur. We're working on possible connections in other cases, places where it might have shown up before. But for now, at least we know what it's called.

"There was this, too." She held up another picture. The words, DO YOU WANT TO SUFFER? had been written on a wall, also in the same dripping red substance that Violet was certain must be blood.

She glanced sideways at the others, to see if anyone winced or looked away. But everyone stared forward, watching as Sara flipped through the photographs. It was easier to look at pictures, Violet realized, remembering the way she'd felt when she'd stood in the middle of the crime scene. The way she'd puked into the planter on the front porch from the sight—and smell—of all that carnage.

Beside her, Krystal twirled her chair from side to side. "Who were they?" she asked Sara. "The people in the pictures?"

"Young couple from University Place in Tacoma." Sara's blue eyes found Violet then. "But they found another body at the couple's home. A girl named Veronica Bowman."

Violet stiffened, every muscle in her body going uncomfortably rigid. She recognized that name, just as Sara must have known she would.

Sara frowned and nodded slightly, the hint of an acknowledgment, and Violet watched as the lights above them reflected off the frost that coated Sara's features . . . her lashes, her lips, her cheeks. Sara kept talking. "The girl was the sixteen-year-old daughter of the family Violet found," she explained to the others.

Sara slid another photo down the polished wood table, past Krystal and toward Violet. "This was her."

Violet felt as if Sara had just thrust her ice-cold hands around the base of her spine and squeezed. Icy pinpricks of horror seized her.

The girl didn't look anything like she had in the pictures Violet had seen hanging on the refrigerator in her house. Even if she had been alive, Violet doubted anyone would have recognized her if they'd seen her. She was older than she had been in the pictures, but she was also emaciated and her hair was dyed. She was haggard and worn, and bore the grim expression of death.

Yet her body didn't have the same gaping neck wound as the couple—or that her parents and younger brother had. Instead, in her left arm, dangling from the crook of her elbow, was a hypodermic needle, its plunger pushed all the way in.

"Drugs?" Violet asked, her throat entirely too dry, and she marveled that she'd managed to speak at all.

"We won't know for sure until the tox screen comes back, but it looks that way."

The chill slithered all the way down to her bones and she fought the urge to physically shiver as she turned to Sam. She wondered if that's what he'd been planning to tell her, that he'd somehow known—from touching the school photograph she'd given him—that the girl was dead. That she'd been murdered too.

Judging from the expression on his face though, Sam was just as stunned by Sara's announcement as she was. More so, maybe. He shook his head, and Violet glanced away quickly, not wanting anyone else to see their brief exchange.

But she caught Rafe watching her, and saw that she was too late. He didn't bother trying to hide the interest that flickered just behind his usual veiled countenance. She reminded herself to breathe as she forced herself not to even blink in response. Instead she smiled, hoping it made her look innocent rather than tense—wound painfully tight—like she felt. If only her lips weren't sticking to her teeth. If only Rafe would stop looking at her like he knew she was hiding something.

Violet pushed the picture away, not wanting to see it anymore. She got up and left the table, unsure her stomach could handle any more.

She retreated to the restroom, the one place where Rafe wouldn't dare come after her, and she studied her image in the mirror as she washed her hands. When the door opened behind her, she watched Krystal from the reflection, marveling that the harsh overhead lights didn't wash her out the way they had Violet. Krystal still looked vibrant and flamboyant, her hair sticking up from the coil at the back of her head in magenta and black spikes, making her look like some sort of goth peacock. Violet didn't want to look at herself again. She'd already seen how she looked . . . sickly and pale. Too much like the corpses she'd seen during her lifetime.

"Hey," Krystal said, approaching hesitantly, making an effort to sound light. "That sorta sucked, didn't it? Are you okay?"

Violet shrugged, rubbing her hands a little too vigorously. "Yeah, it sorta did," she agreed. And then, because it was Krystal, and because Krystal would open up to her if the roles were reversed, she said, "I don't know why it bothered me so much. I think maybe because I was sure we'd find the girl, and it would suck for her because she'd lost her family, but at least she'd be safe." She shrugged, wishing she had a better explanation. "Do you think . . . could you try to talk to her? To see if she can tell us who did this to her?"

Krystal snickered, and then straightened up, trying to look repentant for laughing at Violet's suggestion. "Sorry. I know you're serious. But, really, Vi, you know it doesn't work like that. I've tried to tell you I have no control over who comes to me. They just"—she raised her hands, which were closed, to her reflection and then opened them both at once, spreading her fingers wide and making it look like her ability to talk to ghosts was a magic trick—"*appear.* I wish it were that simple. I'd ask her in a heartbeat, you know I would."

"I guess I just wanted her to have a happy ending." Violet's voice was filled with remorse.

Krystal turned around and leaned against the counter, facing Violet. "I know you did. We all did," she said, commiserating as she chewed her bottom lip thoughtfully, getting neon lipstick all over her teeth. "Sometimes I think it'd be better if we didn't have to see the things we see, or know the things we know. Then again, if we didn't . . ." Her dark eyes were wide and honest and open. "If I couldn't do the things I do, we might not have known where to find you when you were missing. *You* had a happy ending."

Violet's heart stuttered. Krystal was right. There were other reasons she was here, putting her abilities to use. Reasons that had nothing at all to do with Dr. Lee.

Still, it didn't seem fair that she was okay while that other girl—Veronica—had ended up dead.

But life isn't always fair, her mom used to say.

And it certainly isn't always easy, Violet thought as she tried to wipe the images of the crime scene from her mind.

She ripped a piece of coarse brown paper towel from the dispenser and dried her hands.

Maybe Sam had discovered something that might help even the odds, that might make things a little fairer. Maybe he could help Violet figure out how to give the girl's death some meaning.

Suddenly, she had to find out what he knew.

It was getting cooler in the evenings now, and the late-summer-almost-autumn air clung to Violet's skin—not entirely uncomfortable, but not exactly balmy once the sun started to set.

Krystal and Gemma had already gone home, and Violet was beginning to wonder if everyone else had too.

She hadn't missed much after she'd excused herself from the meeting. Sara had managed to get some belongings from the family at the lake house—family photos, birth certificates, pieces of jewelry, a cell phone. But none of her teammates had picked up on anything right away. It was like that sometimes, just as Krystal had told her when they were in the restroom, they had no control over when and what came to them.

It was, Violet supposed, a little like magic after all.

She'd been waiting in front of the Center for nearly half an hour, and was starting to think that maybe Sam had ditched her. That maybe he'd snuck out that mysterious back entrance she'd heard Sara mention . . . the one that no one had ever actually bothered showing her.

She thought about walking around to the back of the building, about creeping down the alleyway to see if she could find it, but something stopped her.

Memories. Memories of the day she'd been attacked by James Nua in that very alley. Memories of his fatal shooting.

Violet's phone rang and she checked it. It was Chelsea . . . again. The third time she'd called since Violet had been out here. She couldn't help thinking she'd made a mistake confiding in her friend because now, suddenly, Chelsea was sort of . . . *preoccupied* with Violet and her body-finding ability.

It was weird, like Violet was a bug, and Chelsea was examining her through a magnifying glass. But she was worried that Chelsea might inadvertently burn her if she held that lens on her for too long.

She hit Ignore and shoved her phone in her purse, then whirled on her heel, deciding to wait in her car instead. As she turned back, she gasped when she ran into someone who was standing right behind her.

"Holy . . . geez, Sam, you scared me half to death!" Violet wheezed, clutching her chest and trying to catch her breath. "I thought maybe you'd ducked out the back."

"Sorry, Violet." But he didn't look overly sorry. Instead, he was grinning in that too-eager way that made Violet forget he'd nearly given her a heart attack. "I didn't realize you even knew about the back entrance."

"I don't. Not really." She frowned, wondering when

she'd stop being the *new girl* and start learning all the "cool secrets," as Sam called them. "So what do you have for me? Did you figure something out?" she asked, impatient now that he was standing here. Despite the sudden rush of adrenaline, she rubbed her hands over her arms.

Sam reached into his back pocket and unfolded a piece of paper. He held it out to her.

She glanced at it, and then back to him. "*Okaaay* . . . you have a flyer," she drawled. She peeked again. "For what? A band?"

Sam nodded. "Yep." He reached out and tapped the paper. "See that? They're playing tomorrow night." Violet looked at the date. "I want you to meet me there," he told her.

Violet scanned the rest of the flyer. The band was called Safe Word, and from all the skulls and eyeballs, and the font that looked like it had been carved with the blade of a knife, she guessed they played some sort of heavy metal or grunge, or maybe some form of alternative. The overall feel of the flyer was dark and lurid and menacing. "*Why?*"

Sam shifted on his feet. "I don't know, exactly. I just know that when I touched that picture you gave me . . . of the girl . . ." He pulled out the picture, too, and passed it back to Violet. "I see this band. I think they might have meant something to her. I think if we go there, we might . . ." He reached up and tugged at his collar. "I don't know, maybe figure something out."

Violet considered that. She thought about the kind of

place they might be walking into, and the kind of people who might be there watching a band called Safe Word, and she weighed that with the fact that they might actually find a clue there, something to help them figure out who's been doing this. Who killed the girl . . . and her family.

She looked at the address and frowned. "Do you know where this place is?"

Sam nodded, looking more eager, more confident now. "It's an all-ages club, near the Space Needle. And the show starts at eight, so don't be late." Before Violet could say anything, he said, "Did ya hear that? It rhymed."

She reached out and shoved Sam in the shoulder. "I think the fact you just pointed that out tells me you're not ready for a club like this—all ages or not."

Sam smirked at her. "You're just jealous 'cause you didn't think of it first." And then he sauntered away from her, heading toward the corner as he checked his phone for the time. Violet saw a station wagon turning down the street, an older one with fake wood paneling strips on the side of it. "Gotta go," he said. "My ride's here."

Violet lifted her hand to her eyes as she watched the car come closer, a woman with a full head of white hair sitting behind the wheel. "Is that your mom?" Violet asked casually.

Sam grinned back at her. "Nah. My folks work late, so my gram gives me a lift when I can't get a bus."

"Your gram?" Violet teased.

"What? It beats walking." He turned to go, but Violet

stopped him one more time.

"What's your gram's name?" she asked, trying to sound only mildly interested even as her heart began to beat a little too hard. Behind him, the station wagon was waiting.

"Her name . . . ?" He looked puzzled, and then shook his head, as if mentally shrugging it off. "Thelma," he said. "Why? You wanna meet her?"

Violet made a face, scoffing at the idea. "That's okay. I gotta go too." She waited while Sam climbed inside, and then she waved politely. Really, she was trying to get a better look at the woman behind the wheel. Trying to decide if she'd been mistaken.

She stood there as the car disappeared in the opposite direction, and waited for her pulse to return to normal again before she looked down at the flyer once more. She wasn't as confident as Sam had been, not about the place or the band or about finding a clue there. She concentrated on the large skull in the center of the creased paper, the one with a knife protruding from its eye socket.

She hoped Sam was right. She shook her head as she started to fold up the flyer to put it away.

But then something stopped her. Something in the bottom corner caught her attention. Something small and buried in the layout, obscured by the busy font and the floating, disembodied eyeballs that seemed to be watching Violet from the page.

At first she thought it was her mind playing tricks on her. And if she hadn't known what she was looking at, she most certainly would have missed it. But then she leaned closer, holding it up to the light and squinting.

It wasn't a trick, though. It was definitely there.

A small brimstone cross, just above the address to the club.

Exactly like the one from the crime scenes.

A HOUSE DIVIDED

IT WASN'T SUPPOSED TO BE THIS WAY. TOGETHER,
they should be strong, united, cohesive. Instead, they were splintered.
Fractured.

Just like his other family had been.

Before . . .

He wasn't sure where he'd gone wrong.

No, not him, Colton. It was all Colton's fault. And now,
because of what Colton had done to the girl, they were all at risk.
They were in danger of losing their family.

He'd have to figure a way to fix it. To make Kisha stop cry-
ing and to make Boxer stop glaring at Colton like he wanted to rip
his throat out with his bare hands. He had to find a way to keep

Bailey comfortable, and to make them all remember why they'd come together in the first place: Because they needed one another. Because they had no one else.

It wouldn't be easy though. But that's why he was there. That was his job, to fix things. That's what leaders did. What fathers did.

And he understood his role. He'd known from the beginning that the others—his lost children—looked up to him, that they needed him.

Without him, they were nothing.

With him, they were a family. His family.

They'd already had to get rid of one member, their newest member . . . their little Butterfly. All because of Colton. Because he'd wanted a girl. Because he couldn't be patient.

They couldn't afford to lose any others.

He needed to stay clearheaded and focused. It was his job to keep them on track.

Boxer would get over the girl. Kisha too. But he'd have to watch Colton. Colton was getting out of hand. He couldn't allow Colton to jeopardize them again.

He couldn't let Colton think he had the upper hand.

He was the father . . .

Maybe Colton needed a reminder.

278

CHAPTER 14

"I'M SURPRISED YOU CALLED. YOU DIDN'T LOOK so good back at the Center, I thought you'd probably go home and crash."

Violet surveyed Krystal's striped tights and her bright purple boots. She imagined herself trying to pull off the same look and knew she could never do it, that she'd only seem ridiculous. Yet Krystal rocked it, wearing her black lace-up bustier dress with the deep purple ruffles that peeked out from beneath the thicker layers of black that covered them like sable clouds. "I was hoping we could talk," she said, looking around The Crystal Palace.

Usually it was quiet here, a place where people came to

get their palms read, and shop for incense, healing stones, and massage oils in peace. But tonight, there was something going on, and the place was more packed than Violet had ever seen it.

"Oh yeah, sorry about that. Séance," Krystal said, nodding toward the crush of people milling together among the shelves and tables and displays.

Violet took a closer look at their faces, and noted their shared swollen eyes, and the way they clung to one another, holding hands and offering whispers of support.

Krystal lowered her voice into what should have been a whisper, but was still too loud, drawing more than one set of eyes her way. She pointed at a couple standing together, and Violet realized they were at the center of the congregation. "They're trying to figure out why their son killed himself."

"Uh . . . oh, sorry, is this a bad time then?" Violet asked, shifting nervously now as even more of the people turned to look their way. She felt suddenly like she was interrupting something very private. "I can come back . . . you know, later."

Krystal scoffed at the idea, dismissing it with a wave of one of her fingerless-gloved hands. "Nah. I'm not performing the séance. Mystique is doing it." She pointed again, indicating a small woman who was seated on a pile of colorful throw pillows surrounding a short, round table.

Violet had done her best to avoid Mystique—the shop's owner—ever since their first unfortunate meeting. Krystal had introduced Violet to the woman, who was older than both of the girls, closer to her mom's age, as a "friend," never mentioning anything about the team or that Violet had an unusual ability of her own. Not that she'd expected Krystal to share that kind of information with her boss . . . those matters were meant to stay private. Secret.

But Mystique had misunderstood Krystal's use of the term *friend*, deciding that Violet must be Krystal's latest *girlfriend* . . . of whom, apparently, there had been more than a few. She'd started asking Violet all about her background, her family, where she'd grown up, and where she went to school. It wasn't until she'd started asking about Violet's former "friends," and what her intentions toward Krystal were, that Violet realized what she was really getting at, and by then she'd backed Violet all the way up against the counter and was practically breathing down her neck.

Trapped, Violet had searched for Krystal, hoping her friend might bail her out of the sticky situation. But Krystal, Violet realized when she spotted her leaning against a rack of lotions and body sprays designed to open up your chakras, was grinning back at her, amused by Mystique's interrogation techniques.

It seemed to Violet that a woman like Mystique, who claimed to have psychic abilities, should have realized that Violet was freaking the hell out . . . *and* that she wasn't Krystal's girlfriend. You know, just for the record.

Now, as Violet caught sight of the woman hunched in front of the table, she felt trapped again by her black, weasel-like eyes. She wanted to search for a way to escape that beady gaze, feeling like Mystique was trying to peer inside of her. She was grateful for the mass of people who surrounded the table. Mystique had other matters at hand to contend with that didn't involve questioning Violet about her sexual history.

"Come on," Krystal said, reaching for Violet's hand and dragging her through the plastic beads that separated the cluttered storefront from the even more cluttered storeroom in back. "I needed a break anyway, that kid wouldn't shut up. All he wants is to be left alone, and for his parents to stop blubbering over him." She plopped down onto a stack of boxes and reached for a can of Diet Coke that was already opened, a straw with a purple smear of lipstick circling its top sticking out of it.

"Wait, do you mean he's in there . . . the boy who killed himself? With his family?" Violet asked, waving away the can when Krystal held it out to her. "Does Mystique know? Will she tell them, you know, to . . ." She made an uncertain face, not sure what, exactly, Mystique should tell the grieving parents. "To move on or whatever?"

Krystal nodded, as if that much were obvious. "I told her. She'll pass the message along to them. It'll make 'em feel better to know he's okay."

Violet cocked her head. "But *she* can't . . . or *can* she . . . ?"

Krystal waited for her to finish her sentence, but when she didn't, Krystal filled in the blanks for her. "*Hear him?* No. I'm not sure what Mystique does or doesn't hear, but she definitely didn't hear *this* kid, otherwise she'd've needed a break too." She sighed, taking another long sip from her straw. "So, what's up?"

"I wanted to ask you something." Violet reached into her purse and drew out her grandmother's journal. "Actually, I wanted to *show* you something."

She plucked the picture from beneath the cover and held it out to Krystal, watching as Krystal took it from her. "What am I looking for?"

"Just tell me if anyone looks . . . *familiar.*"

Krystal looked back down, and Violet waited. Krystal's eyes moved over the image, starting from one side, the side where Violet's grandmother was, and moving across it. Within seconds, she glanced up, a sly grin on her face, as if she'd just solved a complicated riddle. "That's Dr. Lee, isn't it?"

"Yeah, but that's not who I meant. Keep looking."

Frowning, she turned to the picture again. And then she froze, her face creasing with concentration, or maybe it was confusion, or disbelief, Violet wasn't entirely sure which. "That's my mom," she said, reaching out to tap the photo of a soft, nondescript-looking woman with mousy blonde-brown hair and full hips. She looked nothing at all like Krystal, who was garish and bold, and was at least partially of Asian descent. "Where did you get this?" And then as if puzzling it out, she asked, "Why is my mom in a picture with Dr. Lee?"

Violet reached over and took the photograph, not comfortable with anyone else holding it for too long. She didn't want it destroyed—the only piece of tangible evidence she had that the Circle of Seven had been real. "That's what I wanted to talk about. Your mom. Dr. Lee." She pointed to the picture. "My grandmother." She moved her finger. "Rafe's mom. They all knew one another. They all belonged on a team that called themselves the Circle of Seven." She glanced up at Krystal, who still wore the same bewildered expression on her face. "They all had abilities, I think. Like us."

Even after spending nearly an hour talking the whole thing over with Krystal, who was as baffled as Violet was by the discovery that their family members had known one another, Violet didn't have any more answers. She'd already known that Krystal's mom had been able to talk to ghosts the same way Krystal could. Krystal had told her that back when they'd first met.

She was sure now that it wasn't just chance that her grandmother, and Rafe's and Krystal's moms, were all on the same team as Dr. Lee. And that now she and Rafe and Krystal were all working together too.

She also didn't think it was a coincidence that Sam's grandmother had looked familiar . . . as impossible as it seemed.

Her team had been brought together, the same way their relatives had been.

But by whom? And why?

When she got home, she called Rafe and told him about Krystal's mother. He needed to know everything she did. She could no longer pretend she was in this alone. If Dr. Lee wanted her to be on a team so badly, then she'd stop fighting it and be the best darn team member she could be.

No more secrets . . . no more lies.

At least as far as those she trusted were concerned. And right now that list included Rafe and Krystal and Sam. Gemma, she still wasn't sure about, but Violet had no doubt that, whether she knew it or not, Gemma had a family member in the photograph that she kept hidden inside her grandmother's journal. Growing up in the foster system meant that, whoever Gemma's parents had been, they'd either been unwilling, or unable, to care for her.

Violet wasn't sure which would be more difficult to accept. No wonder Gemma had such a chip on her shoulder.

But for now, at least, Violet wasn't exactly ready to confide in Gemma.

Sara was also on the iffy list. Sara had saved her life on more than one occasion, but she couldn't get over the feeling that Sara might be withholding information from her. Crucial information about why she'd been recruited in the first place and who ran the Center.

Until she knew for sure, she decided it was better to keep Sara on a need-to-know basis.

She broached the Sara subject carefully with Rafe, feeling a twinge of guilt. "How are things going on your end?" she asked, after she'd finished telling him about her meeting with Krystal at The Crystal Palace. "Did you talk to Sara, or . . . find anything . . . helpful?"

"I told you. I don't think she knows anything." After a

slight hesitation, he added, "But I searched her room this afternoon, while she was still at the Center, and I came up empty." Violet knew Rafe didn't want to spy on his sister like that, but she also knew he understood how important it was to figure out who they could trust. "I found some of our mom's things, and I even went through those, but . . ." There was another pause. "Nothing. All I get when I touch Sara's things is this sense that she believes in what she's doing, and sometimes I get flashes of old memories. I feel like I'm eavesdropping on things I shouldn't be watching—personal moments. But nothing incriminating. I think she's clean, V."

"I'm sure she is," Violet agreed, and meant it. "But we still need to be careful."

He laughed. "You're paranoid." It was an accusation, but Violet didn't respond. She didn't have to, because Rafe was talking again before she could defend herself. "So now that we've got all that outta the way, you ready to tell me what the hell was goin' on between you and Boy Wonder back at the Center?"

SPARE THE ROD

EVAN STAYED BACK, HIDING IN THE SHADOWS. HE
*knew he wouldn't have to wait for long; Colton would be out of cash
soon. He'd only had twelve bucks going in, and twelve bucks didn't
go very far in place like this.*

But it would be just enough to keep him off balance.

*He knew that much from years of watching his mother scrape
together change, searching beneath couch cushions and under floor
mats, even raiding his piggy bank, before she'd drag him down the
street to the crumbling house, the one on the corner that even a six-
year-old knew was where the drugs were sold. She'd make him wait
outside on the sidewalk while she went in with her pockets jangling.*

*And when she'd come back out again, she'd be a whole differ-
ent person. Not the mom whose face had been tense and sweaty
and gray, the one who'd given him an almost indifferent peck on the
cheek. No, this mom would be flushed and would kiss him with lips
that were too wet and too enthusiastic. It was her eyes that always
got him, though . . . they were far too shiny. These were not his
mother's eyes.*

That was on the days when she actually came back outside.

*The other days she just left him there, out on the street by him-
self. He would wait and wait for her, too afraid to creep to the door
and ask for her. Mostly, he would hide in the bushes and watch,
hoping that the next time the door opened, it would be her . . . that
other mom.*

*Eventually, night would fall, and he'd get tired and scared. He
was old enough to know he shouldn't be out that late, and the people
who came and went from the dirty house where his mother was
became louder and more boisterous and more daring if they saw him,
hidden among the shrubs. When he wandered home, he'd sneak
inside as quietly as he possible, hoping he wouldn't disturb his dad,
who was already passed out in front of the television.*

But he wasn't that same frightened little boy anymore.

*And unlike his mother, he knew Colton would come out. This
wasn't the kind of place that took kindly to junkies crashing on their
couch. This was a place of business, and they couldn't have tweakers
littering their floors. No, Colton would get his fix and leave.*

*He ducked when he saw the boy emerge from beneath the
neon sign that cast a blue pallor over his skin. It was that familiar*

288

shit-eating grin plastered on Colton's face that nearly made him reveal himself too soon. He knew that look, it told him that he'd already used. He was already high.

Good for him. Bad for Colton.

Colton never even glanced his way. Of course he didn't. He had no reason to suspect he was being followed. He had no reason to suspect he'd overstepped his boundaries and needed to be taught a lesson.

Sauntering down the sidewalk, taking wide, zigzagging steps, Colton didn't bother to hide that he was stoned. Yet another strike against him. How many times had Evan warned them, those in his family, that they needed to be discreet? That drawing unwanted attention would only cause trouble, would only bring them one step closer to getting caught?

Colton was a liability.

He tamped down the urge to strike now, right here in the open. To beat the stupid grin off Colton's face.

A couple walking hand in hand saw Colton coming their way and crossed to the other side of the street to avoid him altogether. Smart. Apparently they could see what he had, the lack of inhibition, that wasted-ness about him that said he didn't care what anyone else thought, and decided they didn't want to tangle with him.

Colton called after them, "S'matter with you? Where ya goin . . . ?" His words were slurred as he listed toward them, nearly staggering off the curb before catching himself and shaking his fist in their direction.

289

The woman dropped her gaze and they both sped up their pace. It didn't matter really, Colton could never catch up with them, not in the state he was in.

He yelled again, but it was almost impossible to tell exactly what he'd said. It sounded something like, "You think you're too good for me?" But it might have been, "Y'fin yer two goo fer me?" It was that distorted.

He didn't exactly feel sorry for the couple; they had no business being out here, not in this neighborhood at night. This wasn't the kind of place people went out for a casual midnight stroll.

Once they were past though, Evan sped up, closing the distance between him and Colton. He could feel his blood pounding, could hear it pulsing in his own ears now.

It was the same way he'd felt the night they'd gone into Butterfly's house, the same rush of adrenaline that had taken him over . . . taken them all over when he'd set his plans in motion . . . when he'd set his children loose. As they stabbed and sliced and drew messages with the blood of that other family. Butterfly's family.

Yet even then it had been Colton who'd escalated things when he cut the boy's chest open.

But like any good father, he'd cleaned up after them, positioning the bodies just so, setting the scene. Creating the image of the ideal family.

And now he had to clean up again, a different sort of mess.

He waited until Colton turned the corner, just past a house with boards across the windows and front door. Like so many houses in this neighborhood it was either condemned or had been foreclosed on.

Something about seeing this particular house though, here and now, made him move faster, made his rage almost unbearable. He might have waited a few more blocks if he hadn't remembered what it had been like, all those years ago, waiting behind those very bushes for a mother who might, or might not, come out to retrieve him.

"Colton," he ground out. "Colton, wait!"

The boy in front of him swayed. It might have been comical to watch, except this was no laughing matter. "S'up, man?" Colton's words were sluggish as he turned and saw who it was who'd called out to him. "Wha're you do'n ou' here?" He backtracked, taking long, lopsided steps over the cracked sidewalk.

"We need to talk." He didn't wait for Colton to respond, as he looped his arm around Colton's waist and dragged him toward the bushes. The same ones where he'd once taken cover. The same ones that would hide them now.

But that smile was still there. Stupid and cocky and . . . there.

"We shoul' go out," Colton drawled and then poked him in the chest, as if emphasizing his point. "We shoul' stay out all night, jus' like the ol' days."

He wanted to hit him, to unleash all of his pent-up fury on him now. Instead he grabbed a handful of the other boy's shirt, trying to make him understand. Hoping there was still a chance for reason. "No, we shouldn't. That's exactly why I'm here. You can't do this shit. You can't stumble all over town, just waitin' for the cops to come and pick you up. Stop acting like an idiot, Colton. This isn't just about you anymore." Spittle flew from his lips as he shrieked in Colton's face. He would've worried that someone might overhear

291

them, that he might be the one drawing attention, but this wasn't the kind of neighborhood where others paid attention. This was a place where people kept to themselves.

Shock, and then understanding, changed the planes of Colton's face, and his smile mutated, becoming something less than cocky, less than smug. He bared his teeth, showing his true nature. Even his words were clearer now. "Then who's it about, Evan? You?" He slicked his hand over his greasy hair, shoving it out of his eyes as he stood upright. "I'm not one of your mindless followers like that moron Boxer or that cunt Kisha. What're'ya gonna do, dope me up like Bailey? Make it so I don't have a thought'a my own anymore?" There was a flash of fear behind his mud-colored eyes, almost as if he'd realized he'd gone too far, but it was gone almost as fast as it had appeared. Replaced by defiance. "You can't tell me what to do, Evan. You're not my father."

And that was it, everything he'd been holding inside, everything he'd held back was unleashed. Those four simple words: You're not my father.

Because he was. And Colton needed to understand that. Needed to realize he had to respect him as such.

His first blow was enough to drop Colton to his knees, and blood began immediately gushing from his nose. Evan's knuckles ached, but it wasn't satisfying, so he hit Colton again. And again. And again.

He felt removed, almost euphoric, as he released his anger, as he let it go on the boy beneath him. He pounded until his fists hurt, and then he pounded some more. He was only mildly aware of a *whimpering sound, coming from somewhere far away, and of the words* I am your father *being repeated loudly—hoarsely—over and over again.*

When he was out of breath, and his shoulders and back and arms ached so badly he couldn't possibly lift them even one more time, he slumped forward, collapsing onto Colton. Only then did he realize that the whimpering was coming from his son—from Colton. But it wasn't whimpering, it was wheezing.

He raised his head then, and surveyed the scene. He dropped the bloody rock he'd been holding, clutching, in his fist.

"You made me do this," he said. "Why couldn't you just behave?"

He waited for a response, for Colton to say, or do, something. But there was nothing. Just stillness . . . and wheezing. And blood.

He thought about the first time he'd seen Colton at the park, bruises under both of his eyes and a chip on his shoulder. He was just thirteen. Yet even then, Colton had looked up to him, had needed the older boy to watch his back out on the streets.

And he had. And when Colton had run out of places to stay, he and Bailey and Kisha and Boxer took him in.

He didn't like that Colton had pushed him to this, that he'd given him no other options, but it was what it was. Sometimes parents had to make the tough decisions. Sometimes they had to do things for the greater good.

He leaned down, peeling away the hair that had fallen back over Colton's eyes, hair that was now wet and sticky and red. He smoothed it away and caressed the boy's forehead, and then he leaned forward and pressed a kiss there. He wanted Colton to know that, even though he'd had to be punished, they were still family . . . no matter what.

This happened in families sometimes. They fought and they made up.

And this was one of those times.

CHAPTER 15

"AW, GEEZ, WHAT'S *HE* DOIN' HERE?" SAM ASKED
petulantly as he eyed Rafe with apprehension.

"Take it easy," Rafe told Sam, trying to sound as friendly
as Violet had ever heard him. It was completely false, like
Mr. LeCompte's accent, but she appreciated the effort nonetheless. It was her one caveat when she finally confessed what
she and Sam had been up to . . . that Rafe try to at least set
Sam at ease. She didn't want him scaring the younger boy
with his surly attitude. Sam had, after all, been doing her a
favor.

"Don't worry," Rafe said, putting up his hands. "I

promise not to get in the way. I'm just here to make sure no one gets hurt."

Sam's eyes narrowed. "So you don't think I can protect her?"

Rafe laughed, but it wasn't bitter and mocking, like his usual laugh. "Yeah, that's exactly what I'm saying." And then he chucked Sam in the arm, playfully.

Sam might not have wanted to, but he couldn't help smiling back at the older boy. Rafe could be sorta charming when he wasn't being a total jerk, Violet realized.

"Whatever, man," Sam said, rubbing his arm. Then he tossed his head toward the entrance. "There's been a steady stream of people going in already. Whoever this band is, they seem pretty popular." He looked at Rafe. "And from what I can tell, you'll fit right in."

Violet took in Rafe, in his worn jeans and threadbare T-shirt, his leather jacket and black boots.

Then Sam's gaze fell on her. "We're gonna stick out like sore thumbs."

As she glanced toward the entrance, Violet realized what he meant. There were other girls there, but none were dressed like her, and suddenly she felt out of place in her jeans and fleece jacket and sneakers. Sam was just as bad, wearing a button-down with a collar and khakis. Already they were drawing unwanted attention.

Rafe looked at the two of them and rolled his eyes. "Here," he said, stripping off his jacket and handing it to Sam. "At least try not to look so . . . collegiate. And you," he said to Violet, shaking his head. "Throw your North Face in the car and lose the ponytail. Try to look like you're here for a good time."

Inside the club it was just as bad . . . if not worse. They were so obviously out of place it was almost laughable. At least her and Sam.

Everyone around them seemed to be wearing black. Or leather.

Or black *and* leather.

And there were piercings and tattoos, and a sea of dyed hair and heavily lined eyes . . . not all of them belonging to the girls.

Even wearing Rafe's jacket, Sam didn't look like he was a day older than twelve.

The only plus side of the club was that it was dark in there. And the strobing white lights that pulsed from the stage made it hard to focus on any one thing for too long. The music was also distracting. It was fierce and nearly ear-shattering, but that was the reason everyone was there, wasn't it?

Violet studied her surroundings with the same cautious eye she would any potentially dangerous scenario, carefully trying to assess if there was anything out of the ordinary. Anything in the pulsating, alternating light and dark flashes, among the screams and pounding beats of the music, that didn't belong in this place.

Any echoes or imprints.

"That's the opening band," Sam shouted above the noise of the cheering crowd, drawing her attention. The band on the stage was just finishing up. "Safe Word's up next."

Violet nodded, still glancing around her. She caught a giant man watching her. Glaring was more like it. His head was shaved and practically polished, his scalp shone beneath the flashing lights. His neck was wide—nearly as wide as his head—making it hard to tell where jaw became neck, and neck became body. His massive arms were crossed in front of his chest as he stood against the wall by a doorway.

He looked like a bouncer, and probably was, Violet realized, as she guessed that the doorway might lead backstage. Or maybe outside, to another club entrance, and the giant was meant to keep stragglers from sneaking in the back door without paying their admission.

Violet couldn't imagine anyone trying to sneak past him, though.

She smiled at the enormous man, and was just about to raise her hand—to wave possibly—when Rafe nudged her. "Knock it off, V. I thought the point was to go unnoticed."

The bouncer frowned at first, and Violet wondered if she wasn't supposed to bother him while he was working, but then his expression changed, and he flashed a huge grin back at her. There was nothing menacing about him then. He was just a guy, a *big* guy, standing by a door.

"Oh, for God's sake," Rafe muttered, dragging her away. "What kind of detective are you?"

Violet shrugged, letting Rafe lead her toward the front,

near the stage, as the next band was setting up. "You never know who can help." And then her eyes widened and she lowered her voice. "Besides, maybe he knows something . . . about the symbol."

She felt Rafe's grip on her wrist tense. "What symbol?" he asked, and for the first time she realized she hadn't told them, either him or Sam, about the brimstone cross she'd noticed on the flyer.

"That one," Violet said, drawing Rafe's attention away from her as she pointed at the drum set already onstage. It was there too, in the center of the large drum that faced outward. That very same symbol . . . the brimstone cross.

She heard Sam draw in a sharp breath from behind her.

"Violet," Rafe said, using her full name now, his voice quiet and filled with warning. "Tell me what you feel. Right now, when you're looking at those guys up there . . ."

He didn't point, didn't move so much as a single muscle, he just held on to her, his fingers clamped around her wrist. But she knew who he meant.

Them . . . the band.

She turned her gaze upward, her eyes roving over each and every one of them as they took their positions, taking in everything about them. She spent time on each of them, studying them individually, making sure to separate them not just from one another, but from anything around her that might interfere. It was easier now, with just the prerecorded track playing in the background—still loud, but not shattering her eardrums.

There were five of them in all. Five possible suspects wearing leather and spikes and chunky boots and tight jeans. They looked like everyone else in the club.

Everyone but her. And Sam.

She took a step back, Rafe's hand still clutching her as she shook her head. "Nothing," she whispered at first, and wondered if they'd heard her. "I don't feel anything at all."

Violet washed her face and changed out of her smoke-infused clothes. For a nonsmoking club, there'd been a *lot* of smoke in the air. Short of showering, there was nothing she could do about the smell that clung to her hair, so she pulled it back into an elastic, keeping it as far from her face as she could.

In her room, she huddled in her bed, nesting in the jumble of blankets as she started poring through the pages of her grandmother's journals once more. She'd already read these entries—in fact, she'd already read all of them now—but she hoped against hope that maybe she'd missed something the first time through.

After nearly an hour of scanning the same entries and not learning a single new bit of information, she slammed the book she was holding shut.

It was useless. There was no more mention of the Seven in her grandma's diaries.

In fact, after that ominous entry about Muriel, *Muriel is dead*, she'd never mentioned her team again.

Not once.

Ever.

It was the strangest thing, Violet thought, trying to imagine what possible reason her grandmother could have had for not writing about them.

Had she quit the team? Had it disbanded after Muriel's death?

Had she been too afraid to put anything else on paper?

Whatever her reason, there was nothing more about them, just page after page of mundane entries about her everyday life, including Violet's mom's graduation and her move to college, her wedding to her dad, and the birth of Violet herself.

Okay, so it wasn't all mundane.

There was another section that interested Violet as well—or rather a non-section. A large chunk of Violet's grandmother's life that seemed to be missing, when she'd stopped journaling . . . just after Violet's grandfather had died.

It was nearly a year before she'd journaled again, and when she did it was just a quick entry about a doctor's appointment she'd had that day. They were all quick and sporadic after that, nothing significant or interesting, until it was more like looking at a calendar than a diary.

As if she'd lost that passion she'd had for documenting her thoughts and emotions and the events that shaped her life.

Violet finally gave up and laid the diary on her nightstand. As she did, her hand brushed the silver turtle Jay had given her. She picked it up, holding it up and inspecting it.

As strange as it seemed, she sometimes missed the intrusive imprint that used to fill her every waking thought. Times like now, when it was quiet. When her mind was restless, flitting from one place to the next.

The imprint had at least given her a place to land.

She turned the silver key at the turtle's belly and lifted the silver lid, closing her eyes as the first lyrical notes of *Moonlight* Sonata enveloped her.

And her thoughts, which had been harried, tripping over one another uneasily, settled at last, onto the musical bough of the familiar song.

LOVE IS ALL YOU NEED

"WHAT ABOUT HER?" EVAN ASKED, LIFTING HIS
chin toward a girl wearing a sundress and sandals. She looked young,
especially in the flowered dress, fifteen at the most. But young had
never stopped Colton before. "Colton'd like her, don't'cha think?"

Bailey touched his arm. "Evan . . ."

He scowled at her hand. "If you don't like her, just say so,"
he snapped. And then, because he recognized how curt he sounded,
he softened his tone. "You're right. She's not really his type. We'll
keep looking."

He turned, but not before catching the look that flashed between
Bailey and Boxer. A look laced with meaning. He told himself to
ignore it . . . to ignore them. But he couldn't. His temper soured as

he got to his feet, reaching for his guitar case. "You're wrong," he shouted down at them, not needing to hear either of them say it out loud to know what they meant. "He'll be fine. He's a fighter. This is Colton we're talkin' about . . . he's a fighter," he repeated, but his voice cracked as their doubts started to creep into his conviction. He shook his head, backing away from them, from the uncertainty on their faces.

"Evan," Bailey said again. She had to struggle to get to her feet, but this time she came after him. She clasped his hands in hers. "You can't know that for sure."

He ignored the way her fingers trembled and how skeletal they were, telling himself she was fine, that she wasn't getting sick again. She had to be okay because he didn't have anything to give her right now. "He's family . . ." He'd meant to say more, but he couldn't. Words were insufficient to describe how he felt about losing another member of their small clan. Losing Butterfly had been hard enough, and he'd barely known her. Colton was another matter altogether.

Boxer stood too, joining them, turning them into an unusual trio as they huddled together near the edge of the park. "You're right, he is family. But he's hurt. Bad. We can't know he'll make it."

Evan thought of Colton back at the apartment, unconscious on his mattress. Struggling for each and every breath. Somehow, he'd managed to haul Colton all the way back, even through the narrow sewer drain, where he'd delivered the nearly lifeless boy in a bloodied heap.

None of them had reacted to Colton's blood the way they had the night at Butterfly's house. This wasn't a cause for excitement, for celebration.

This was a time of sorrow.

Yet no one asked who'd done this to their friend—their family member.

And none of them had even mentioned taking him to a hospital where he could get real care from real caregivers.

Instead, they'd rolled up their sleeves and cleaned him up as best they could, mindful of his moaning, and taking it as a sign of his discomfort. They'd given him drugs, not the legal kinds the hospital would provide, but ones that were just as effective for the pain. More so, maybe.

And he'd lain quiet ever since, receiving his doses as regularly as they could manage, with both Boxer and Kisha sacrificing their shares for Colton. Because that's what family did.

Bailey gave up what she could, but he couldn't have both of them sick. Not at the same time.

Colton had to make it, Evan told himself. He had to so he could tell him they were good now. That the slate had been wiped clean between them.

And maybe the answer was to find Colton that girl he'd always wanted.

CHAPTER 16

"VIOLET? WHAT ARE YOU DOING HERE?" DR. LEE asked, looking around the small parking lot in front of his office.

She was glad he sounded confused; she'd meant to catch him off guard.

"I wanted to talk to you. Alone." She stepped away from where she'd been waiting for him near his dark sedan—not quite black, but not really blue either. Nondescript. The kind of car you'd have a hard time describing in a pinch.

"You could've made an appointment," he told her, still frowning. "Do you want to go inside?"

She shook her head curtly. "It's not that kind of talk."

306

Today he looked like the old Dr. Lee, wearing his cozy cardigan and canvas sneakers. This was the doctor who'd persuaded her to open up to him, to share her deepest darkest secret with him. This was the doctor she'd trusted.

But she knew the truth . . . this Dr. Lee was a fake.

His eyes narrowed, and even his stance changed as he approached her, his posture becoming more rigid and self-assured. "What kind of talk is it then?" His voice was lower too, laced with warning. She understood the meaning well enough: *Watch your step.*

But she was past watching her step now.

"Who are you, Dr. Lee?" She didn't tell him why she was asking, or reveal what she knew, she merely asked that simple question. *Who are you?* "Or should I call you Jimmy? Who are you really?"

He stopped where he was, and his body tensed. Violet realized she'd crossed a line and was now wandering into tricky territory. She watched him as he considered her question, and she couldn't help noting the way his nostrils flared ever so slightly, and his hands—probably without even realizing it—curled into fists.

She felt every bit as strained as he looked, and she wondered if her nostrils flared too. Her chest was constricted, squeezing the very breath from her lungs.

"What do you know?" he asked, his words whisper quiet. "What is it you think you know, Violet, because, trust me, this isn't a road you want to go down."

Without meaning to, she took a step back, stung by the

vehemence in his tone. Maybe he was right, she thought. Maybe this was better left alone.

But then she remembered how her grandmother had been trapped, the same way she was. "No," she mouthed at first. And then, this time louder, with more conviction. "It's exactly the road I want to go down," she insisted.

She reached into her purse and drew out the photograph, her heart hammering loudly, painfully. "This," she said. "This is what I know."

Dr. Lee stared at the image, and Violet waited.

Her hand was trembling, and she knew he noticed it too, but she continued to hold the photo out, and continued to wait for him to speak first. The ball was in his court. She was the one who needed answers now.

Eventually, he moved, his hands unclenching as he reached for the picture, taking it from her fingers. And still, he remained silent. Still, he just stared at the faces in the photograph.

"She was a lovely woman"—he didn't look up when he said it—"your grandmother. Funny and warm. Irreverent. People liked her. *I* liked her," he added.

Violet wasn't prepared for the flood of emotions that discussing her grandmother would cause. She'd thought she was ready for whatever he threw her way—threats, warnings, challenges, even anger. But what she hadn't expected was the kind of tenderness she heard in his voice.

She had to remind herself that he was a master at manipulating others, that he'd fooled her before.

"So that is you? In that picture? You were part of the Circle of Seven?"

He let out a derisive laugh. "The Circle of Seven? I haven't heard that name in years. What a joke. They had no business naming themselves . . . *naming us*. We weren't a club or a team, not the way they wanted us to be. We were just a bunch of people with uncommon abilities."

"Like us?" Violet bit out. "Like the team you won't let me quit?"

Dr. Lee seemed to snap out of whatever reverie he'd been lost in, as if remembering he wasn't alone with his own thoughts, that Violet was still there too. "No." He said it quickly, with a jolt of finality. "Not like you kids at all. We had no idea what we were capable of, what we could do with our abilities. No one did, really. We were floundering then, struggling to figure out how to work together. You kids are better at it. You kids have found a purpose and are using your abilities to help people. To stop killers and solve crimes."

She nodded, not sure why she was agreeing with him. But in the back of her mind she reminded herself of what he could do. She couldn't let him manipulate her emotions.

"Does Sara know? Does she know that her mother was in the Circle with you? With my grandmother?"

Whatever advantage Dr. Lee felt like he'd regained slipped as his composure faltered. "Sara's . . . ? How did you . . ." And then his lips pressed together. "Rafe," he whispered menacingly.

He didn't remind her about his warnings, but cold sweat broke out on her upper lip as she waited for him to tell her she'd broken the rules, that her family was in imminent danger.

"Who else have you told?"

She couldn't lie. There was no going back now. "I know that Krystal's mom was in the Circle too. I know that it's not a coincidence that you found all of us. And I know . . ." she said, her eyes flitting nervously to his. "I know that Muriel isn't dead." Violet held her breath as she waited for his response, expecting the worst.

But he simply nodded, his expression smoothing, growing solemn. "Yes . . . Sam's grandmother. I remember when I first heard the news that she was dead. I went to her funeral, you know, just like everyone else did. Officially, we were told it was a car accident. Unofficially, it would have been impossible *not* to hear the whispers of the others in the Circle; I knew what they believed. And their suspicions were the beginning of the end for us. As trust disintegrated, we began to turn on one another. I tried my best to . . . *ease* their worries. But my reach only extended so far. Eventually, we had to disband."

"But why fake her death?" Violet asked, still wanting to know.

She expected him to tell her to mind her own business, that she'd overstepped. On the contrary, he answered as easily as if she'd always been permitted to know such things. As if he'd never threatened her in the first place. Or maybe he was just tired of keeping the lies to himself. "As it turns out, Muriel had learned too much about our organization—about what those in charge were up to: blackmailing industry leaders, corrupting corporations. She was *persuaded* to relocate, and to never contact anyone in the Circle again." Violet hated the way he emphasized the word *persuaded*, and she couldn't help thinking of old-time thugs with trench coats and broken noses.

He continued, unaware of the way she shuddered inwardly. "She was kept away for years; even her name was changed. But when we discovered that her grandson was *special* too, we contacted her. When Sam's parents agreed to our terms . . ." His voice drifted off, and again, Violet got that sick feeling of Sam being haggled over, like a commodity. She waited a long time, while she considered all the things he'd just told her. "Violet—" he started to say, then stopped himself. "I'm not the one you have to worry about," he said at last, his voice no longer filled with menace. "I'm not in charge; I only do what I'm told. I know it's hard to believe, but I'm trying to help you." He frowned. "Don't you get it, your team has done some great things? Look at what you've been able to accomplish."

He sighed, his shoulders falling. "I'm warning you, Violet, the fewer people who know, the better. I'm saying this for your own good."

"Can I ask why you stayed . . . when everyone else split up? Why did you stay on?"

A wan smile tugged at his mouth. "My father. He was

the one who started this whole thing. My ability—whatever you call it, this thing I can do—my father had it too. He had grand ideas about finding a way to use it. About finding others and gathering them together to form some secret society, so we could use our abilities to . . ." His smile spread into a slow and twisted grin. "To take over the world, you could say."

"And now?" Violet asked, feeling uneasy, like she already knew too much.

Dr. Lee sighed. "Now he's dead. Now things have changed and it's a different organization. I'd like to think that those changes are all for the better."

She was cautious with her next question, not sure she was ready to hear the truth. "Would they have hurt my family or *relocated* me, the way they did Muriel? If I hadn't stayed on the team like I was warned?"

Dr. Lee was quiet, that same kind of long pause that made her think she might not like what she heard. "I can't answer that, Violet. I don't know everything."

She'd read enough of her grandmother's journals to know that if he'd wanted her to feel calm, she would have. But he didn't. She knew because of the way her pulse raced, and how her stomach twisted in agonizing knots, and the chill that shivered over her skin.

"Go home, Violet," he said at last, surprising her by handing the photograph back to her. "Just"—he shook his head, turning to unlock his car—"go home."

★ ★ ★

After her meeting with Dr. Lee, Violet continued to turn the information over in her mind until she realized it didn't really matter. He'd told her all he was going to . . . revealing half-truths and doling out vague advice.

Violet wished her grandmother could have lived long enough to know the truth: that Muriel hadn't died after all.

In her bedroom, she set her purse down, and noticed the flyer Sam had given her poking out from beneath it, right where she'd left it on her dresser. She pulled it out and examined it, momentarily forgetting all about Dr. Lee and the Circle of Seven.

The night of the concert, Violet had lain awake for several hours, thinking she must have missed something crucial, some bit of information that would link the band to the girl. She felt as if she had all the right information—all the pieces—she just couldn't make them fit.

The brimstone cross.

The band . . . Safe Word.

Veronica Bowman.

Even the missing echo seemed to taunt her, despite knowing the reason for its absence.

But there wasn't much she could do, at least not from the solitude of her bedroom, about the girl or her brother, so she decided to go online, to get as much information as she could about the cross and the band.

When she typed *brimstone cross* into Google, the first entries that popped up referred to its symbolism in satanism, just as Sara had mentioned. There were plenty of images to scroll through—drawings, jewelry, tattoos. But nothing more than what she already knew.

When she'd finished reading through the articles she could find, she typed in the name of the band, *Safe Word*. This search was harder, and had to be revised several times, since *safe word* was a bondage term, and brought up hundreds of images, including guys in leather masks, handcuffs, and whips.

When she added the term *Seattle band* to the search, she found what she'd been looking for.

There were Facebook and MySpace pages, and YouTube videos. She clicked on the videos, and immediately realized she was watching the right guys. This was the same band she'd seen at the club the other night. The same group with the brimstone cross on their drums.

She watched each video closely, trying to search for anything that might tie them to Veronica or her death. She searched for the girl during the crowd shots, pausing and going back and rewatching them as she studied each face.

It took her close to an hour to watch all five of the official videos that were posted, and another two hours to go through the fan-posted ones.

When she finished, she felt like she was no closer to an answer than when she'd started.

She clicked over to their Facebook page.

It was the first post on their Wall that made her stop, her fingers hovering over her mouse.

They were playing again. Tomorrow night in Tacoma

at another all-ages club.

The decision was easy: She was going. And she was taking someone with her, although not Rafe or Sam. This time she'd be taking someone from a *different* team.

When the phone was picked up on the other end, Violet grinned. "Hey, remember when you said you wanted to be my sidekick?"

Violet tugged at her black shirt, admiring the hot-pink skull that dripped down the front of it. It wasn't bad to look at, but it stretched too tight across her chest, like she was wearing a child's size version. "We look ridiculous, Chels."

"Are you kidding me? We look awesome! I might just make this my regular style." She stood behind Violet at the mirror, and Violet glanced back at her, appraising Chelsea's black eyeliner and combat boots. Somehow Chelsea managed to make the look work, and her toned legs looked hot in the fishnet tights, even if her skirt was entirely too short. The leather bands on her wrists were a nice touch too.

Violet looked back at herself, studying the makeup Chelsea had painstakingly applied on her to go with the outfit.

Smoky eyes, Chelsea had called them.

Whore-y eyes, Violet had joked, staring at the raccoon effect Chelsea had created.

"Besides, we can't just walk in there in our regular clothes . . . we need to try and blend. Otherwise everyone'll know we're there for clues," Chelsea countered.

"Clues?" Violet asked, unclasping the spiderweb

necklace, deciding it was a bit much. "This isn't an episode of *Scooby-Doo*. We're not there to unmask the ghost of Old Man Wheezer or find out who's haunting the abandoned amusement park. This is serious."

Chelsea puckered her black lips, her reflection staring back at Violet indignantly. "And I'm taking it seriously. Dude, stop worrying. I've got this."

"I hope you're right. Besides, I doubt we'll turn up anything anyway. I just didn't want to go alone."

Chelsea turned on the chunky heel of her boot, wrinkling her nose. "Yeah . . . about that . . ."

Violet frowned, not liking her friend's tone, or the implication that she was withholding something. "About what, Chels?"

"That thing about not wanting to go alone . . ." The end of her sentence lilted up, almost as if she were afraid to finish it.

Violet's face flushed and she could feel her cheeks turning red. "*Who?* Who did you tell? Did you invite someone to come with us?"

Chelsea bit her lip, wincing dramatically. "Well . . . yes and no. I mean, yes, I told someone. And, no, I didn't, technically, invite him." She grimaced as she rushed through her last words. "But he *is* coming. He insisted."

Violet threw her hands in the air. "Oh my god, spit it out already! Who then?"

"Rafe," Chelsea admitted guiltily. "It wasn't my fault really. I thought . . . since he knew . . . it was no big deal. So

316

I was telling him about the band, and he got all weird about it, and asked me how I knew about them. Then he made me tell him when we were going, and he . . ." She lifted her shoulders, trying to look innocent, but looking anything but. "He invited himself."

"Geez, Chels," Violet groaned. So much for her plan of making Chelsea her sidekick, she silently mocked herself. "I knew you liked him, but I thought you *got* that I didn't want anyone else to know. That was kinda the point here."

Chelsea sighed, an overly loud and theatrical sound. "Yeah, well, I don't think it matters whether I like him or not," Chelsea said, her expression turning momentarily serious. She didn't look accusatory, or even dejected, just matter-of-fact when she said it. "I think we both know who Rafe likes."

Violet blinked as she faced her friend, wondering how she'd known. She wanted to deny what she knew Chelsea was saying—to say that she hadn't noticed Rafe's feelings toward her—but somehow she couldn't muster up the lie, no matter how hard she tried. She'd worked too hard to be honest with Chelsea.

Before she could come up with anything, there was a knocking at her bedroom door, three quick raps that Violet would recognize anywhere. Her eyes widened as she stared at Chelsea.

"Are you kidding me? Jay too?" she asked Chelsea, before turning to the door.

Chelsea made a face as she nodded. "Rafe told him."

★ ★ ★

Violet stomped down the front steps that led to her driveway as she glared at the two boys who were waiting for her and Chelsea. "Since when are you two working against me?" She ignored the fact that they were both studying her a little too intently, taking in her tight jeans and even tighter top. She suddenly felt very exposed, ridiculous even. Like she'd dressed up for Halloween when no one else had. "I think I liked it better when you hated each other."

"We still do," Rafe quipped, flashing a grin in Jay's direction. "We're just trying to keep you from getting yourselves killed. You have no idea if you'll run into trouble down there."

"What are you talking about, killed? All we're doing is going out for a girls' night!" She draped her arm around Chelsea's shoulder. "Right, Chels?"

Chelsea ducked out from under Violet's arm. "Yeah . . . whatever she says." She wiggled her brows, and her butt, on her way to her car.

"*Right . . .*" Rafe drawled, not bothering to sound convinced. "And you just happen to be going to see the same band we saw the other night."

"What, and you think we need you two tagging along in case we get into trouble?" She managed to add a fair amount of cynicism to her voice as she glowered at each of them in turn.

"We think," Jay said, sounding considerably more reasonable, and far less flip than Rafe, "that it couldn't hurt to stick together. Especially since we have no idea what we could be walking into."

Violet shrugged. "I don't see what the big deal is. It's probably no different than the other club."

"Oh, and you did great down there," Rafe interrupted. "You practically made a pass at the bouncer."

"What?" Violet sputtered, as Jay raised an eyebrow at her, begging for an explanation. "*I did not!* I was just being friendly. Besides, he seemed . . . *nice.*"

Jay just shook his head as Rafe shot back, "Yeah, I'm sure he was thinking the same thing about you. *Such a nice little girl.*"

Violet glared at him as Chelsea shouted from over the top of her car. "All right, ladies, stop your bickering and get in. We don't have all night. Show starts in t-minus-thirty. Don't wanna be late, do we?"

It wasn't as far to Tacoma as it had been to Seattle, and they were there in plenty of time. The area was dirtier than the place in Seattle, though. A little scarier, Violet couldn't help thinking. The crowd out front didn't seem to be in a huge hurry to get inside, and there was still a short line, but there were also several people who were just milling around, talking and smoking. More than a few homeless people camped out in nearby doorways.

Suddenly Violet wasn't so sorry that Rafe and Jay had crashed her plans. Maybe a little backup wasn't such a bad idea.

After they circled the block several times, Chelsea finally

managed to squeeze her car into a space that may or may not have been legal, and they made their way past a row of decayed storefronts . . . businesses like nail salons, a liquor store, a place for check cashing and payday loans, and a smoke shop. It had a seedy feel to it, and Violet grew jumpier and less confident about her decision to be here, with each step she took.

Chelsea, on the other hand, grew bolder and *more* confident, as if the clothing itself had infused her with a new jolt of courage. "What d'ya think we'll find? You think the killer will be there? You think someone in the band knows something?" Her voice dropped as she hooked her arm through Violet's. "What do you do when you find them?" And then her eyes widened as a new possibility dawned on her. "You don't carry a gun, do you? Can you . . . *arrest* someone?"

Violet shoved her, laughing now. "Of course I can't. I'm not a cop, Chels. I call the police, just like anyone else."

Jay scoffed. "Yeah, because that's what you always do, right, Vi? You'd never go after a killer on your own."

He was right of course. She had been foolish enough to chase echoes—or imprints rather—before. And she probably would be again. No matter how hard Dr. Lee had tried, no matter how many warnings Sara had given her, she just couldn't seem to stop herself.

"You've done that?" Chelsea gasped, but it wasn't the kind of gasp that said she was shocked and appalled. It was more like she was impressed. Like she had a newfound respect for her friend.

"Not on purpose," Violet answered, hoping to defuse the situation . . . and the attention.

When they reached the entrance, Violet fished out her ID and her hand was stamped. Since the person at the door had two different kinds of stamps, Violet guessed that hers was the one that marked her as underage, limiting her selections at the bar. Fair enough, she realized. It wasn't like she'd been planning on drinking anyway.

Before they went in, Jay stopped her, his hand firm and warm as it closed over hers, pulling her back a step. The worry in his face drew her back another.

"What?" she asked.

"Just . . . don't do anything stupid, 'kay, Vi?"

She looked at him, at his serious expression. At the T-shirt he wore that wasn't black and the jeans that weren't ripped or held up at his waist with a spiked belt. He didn't belong in a place like this or, really, with a girl like her, one who was always dragging him into sticky situations. Yet here he was. And the creases etched across his forehead said it all.

She smiled. "Don't be an ass-hat." But her words were quiet and reassuring, and she leaned up to press the lightest kiss against his lips as she stared into his eyes. "That's why you're here, right? To keep me out of trouble."

He shook his head, surrendering to the fact that she wasn't going to listen to him, no matter how hard he tried. And then he wrapped his arm around her shoulder and dragged her through the door. "You're hopeless, you know that?"

Inside, the music was already playing, and Violet

recognized the song from the other night—the same opening band.

"Not really what I expected," Chelsea shouted as she surveyed the tall ceilings and the wide-open space that lacked any real sense of décor. It had a cold, industrial feel, with exposed metal heating ducts and concrete walls that were probably some shade of gray or tan or taupe when the lights were on. Right now, however, everything was black, except when the strobe lights flashed.

Violet shrugged. It was exactly what she'd expected, almost the same feel as the place in Seattle she'd been to just days earlier with Sam and Rafe. Even the people were the same, lots of steel spikes and chains, leather, tattoos, and piercings and gauges of all sizes and shapes. It was like a heavy metal rainbow.

"Now what?" Jay asked, staying at Violet's other arm.

Violet looked around, feeling as helpless as she had the other night. She supposed she'd been hoping for an easy, obvious answer, but there wasn't one. "Let's get something to drink."

They pushed and shoved and elbowed their way to the bar, where they ordered three Cokes and a root beer. Not surprisingly, it was Chelsea who had to be different, and she drew a strange look from the bartender.

"I'm not sure I have that," he said when she made her request.

Cocking her head, she placed her hands on her hips. "Well, you should probably start looking then, shouldn't you?" It sounded like a command when she said it.

The man behind the bar had hair that was long and curly and would have been almost like Violet's if it weren't so wild and unkempt, and if it wasn't so bushy and dyed to a deep shade of ebony. But it was his eyebrows that made Violet pause, holding her interest. His actual eyebrows were fine— normal, from what she could see of them—but black ink had been tattooed over them, and they'd been remade so that when the ink reached the center of them it flared upward, giving the man a permanent scowl. Making him look angry, even when he laughed. Which he did, howling at Chelsea's outrageous statement. "Yes, ma'am," he said, giving her a mock salute and turning to go find her some root beer.

"Root beer, huh?" The guy who'd asked Chelsea the question was cute enough. He wore a beanie and nervously used his tongue to toy with the ring in his lip as he leaned against the bar beside her.

Chelsea turned away from the bartender to face the boy, who was probably about their age.

She lifted a shoulder, looking at him, bored. "Mind your own business, will ya? Besides, I'm here with someone."

The boy shot upright and glanced uncomfortably toward Rafe, holding his hands up in surrender. "Sorry, man. No harm in trying, right?"

Rafe didn't correct the misunderstanding; he just shrugged and threw a bill down as the bartender set a glass down in front of Chelsea. "That's three Cokes and *one root beer.*"

"See?" Chelsea grinned back at the bartender, with his perma-scowl. She was no longer demanding, but practically giddy instead. "I knew you had some hiding back there."

Violet rolled her eyes as she followed Chelsea, who'd taken the lead, through the crowd. Chelsea knew how to use her new look to draw attention, which was exactly the opposite of what you'd want in a sidekick—someone whose job by definition was to help the hero go unnoticed. Already more than a few heads were turning to watch her short skirt as it hiked higher and higher up her thighs.

Perfect.

"Hey, why do you think that guy automatically assumed Chelsea was with Rafe? Why couldn't she've been with me?" Jay asked as they cut a path through the crowd.

Violet glared at him over her shoulder, but then turned ahead again, concentrating on where she was going, trying not to spill her drink as she was pushed from both sides. "Have you seen yourself? You don't exactly look like her type. At least not tonight," she teased. And she wasn't lying. Jay hadn't dressed for the occasion, not the way she and Chelsea had. Not the way Rafe pretty much always did. Jay was just Jay. If his T-shirt and jeans were good enough for school, they were good enough for this place.

Fine by her. She liked his T-shirt and jeans.

"Besides, are you sayin' you *want* to be with Chelsea?" she asked slowly, mockingly.

"Are you kidding? Have you looked in a mirror tonight?"

He leaned down, his words tickling her ear. "Have I mentioned how hot you look all death-metaled out? I kinda like the new Violet."

"Yeah, well don't get too used to this Violet," she shot back at him. "Because *this* Violet could totally kick your ass."

Jay's arm snaked around her waist, drawing her to a stop. "Yeah, well maybe I like it rough."

Violet giggled as she struggled out of his grasp. "Oh my god, you're so stupid sometimes."

They stopped at a long tall table where Chelsea had managed to squeeze in, after shouldering her way through a minuscule opening, giving them just enough space so they could set down their drinks.

Violet glanced around, but it was Jay who asked, "Now what?"

"I don't know, exactly," she admitted. "Maybe we should split up and scope things out." It wasn't a great plan, but it was the best she could come up with. Besides, the band—Safe Word—was just getting started, and Violet was dying to hear them play. Now that she recognized their music—after listening to it for hours on end—she had a new appreciation for them. She felt a little like a groupie, wanting to get a better look at them, even as she told herself it was only to see if she'd missed something the other night.

"I'll stay here," Chelsea announced. "To guard the table."

Violet followed Chelsea's gaze, which had landed on a guy standing near the other end of the lengthy table, and

Violet knew *exactly* what Chelsea planned to "guard."

"Awesome plan, Chels." Violet set her glass down and left the rest of them there to decide where they would go, as she beelined toward the stage.

FINDERS KEEPERS

HE STEPPED INTO THE CLUB AND FELT THE MUSIC
even before he heard it, the way he always did. The way any good
musician would.

Kisha was at his side, calmer now that he'd managed to scrape
a little extra cash together for her . . . to medicate her for the night.
She hadn't yet noticed his guitar was missing.

Didn't matter, though. That dream was dead. He was making
new dreams now, forging a new life for himself. Being a rock star no
longer mattered.

He was going to be a legend. A god.

Kisha squeezed his arm, whether from the excitement at being
out or from the euphoria of her fix, he wasn't sure, but he was glad

to have her back. "This is great!" she squealed enthusiastically. "I love this band!"

He glared up at the stage, to where they were playing, grating out the metal sounds of a song he used to love too. One he'd played for his new family.

"Look," Kisha gushed as she dragged him closer to the stage. "He sees you." She pointed indiscreetly to the lead vocalist, who clutched the microphone to his mouth, his eyes falling on Evan in the crowd below. His expression never changed, but Evan could feel the subtle shift in his eyes as he glanced . . . what? Nervously? Uneasily? Toward the guitar player beside him.

The new guy. He turned to Kisha, ignoring everyone on the stage now. He didn't need them or their insignificant band.

What he needed was a girl. For Colton.

"I'll be right back," he shouted, straining to be heard above the riffs from the stage and the screams of the crowd around him. "Stay here."

Kisha just nodded, her attention already fixated on the band as she swayed, her eyes glittering with delight.

When he first saw the girl he knew two distinct things about her.

First, that she didn't belong in a place like this. Even as far as all-ages clubs went, this one was rough and dirty and seamy. The people who ran it rarely paid attention to the teens who passed through their doors, so even though the bartender wouldn't serve minors, it was easy to sneak in booze. And even easier to score if you needed something stronger. It was his kind of place, but definitely not hers.

He could tell the girl had tried to fit in though. That her makeup was heavier than she was probably used to, and that she'd gone for the death metal vibe of the club with her short black skirt and fishnet tights, and a T-shirt with a cat—like Hello Kitty—but with a skull head instead. He'd seen plenty of suburban kids trying to fit in by shopping at Hot Topic, and this girl was no different from the rest.

The second thing he noticed about her was less obvious, but he'd recognized it anyway. It was something about the way she carried herself, despite being from the suburbs. Something about the way he'd seen her glare at the boys she caught watching her, and the way she lifted her shoulder in an I-don't-give-a-fuck shrug. This girl was bold, even though she was a fish out of water.

He knew right away that this was Colton's girl.

She wasn't alone, though. She was with a friend—a pretty girl with curls who was just as out of place as she was, although much less brash about it. The curly-haired girl looked apologetic, and even grimaced as they squeezed through the crowd, trying not to spill their drinks—sodas most likely, since these didn't look like the kind of girls who brought their own flasks. There was another kid too, a boy who hadn't bothered trying, and gave off an Abercrombie vibe that didn't generally sit well among the metalhead crowd. He practically hovered over the curly-haired girl.

The other guy, the dark-haired one who trailed in their wake, was never really close enough to be with them, but not so far away that he could be overlooked either. Unlike the others, this guy could easily blend in with the crowd at this club.

Evan watched the girl as the song came to an end, as the audience blew up, shrieking with applause, and he forced himself not to picture Kisha among them, cheering for the band that had cut out his heart.

When the next song started, he saw the curly-haired girl slip away from the others at their table, and then Abercrombie went after her, disappearing into the mosh pit just as quickly as she had. The other guy left too, but went in the opposite direction, and he wondered if he was ever really with them at all.

Didn't matter, really. Because they'd just given him a golden opportunity. One he was prepared for, he thought, as he wound his way toward the table, his fingers toying with the tiny plastic bag in his pocket.

He had a chance now. To get to her.

Colton's girl.

CHAPTER 17

VIOLET STOOD BACK FOR SEVERAL MINUTES, maybe longer. She'd gotten caught up in listening to them, like some lovesick fan. But the song they were playing now wasn't one she'd heard before, not one of the ones on their YouTube page or their website.

Everyone knows
I can't see
Innocence
Do you want to suffer?

The lead singer's voice was hypnotic, guttural and war-bling, and she felt like he was calling out to her, and her alone. The pulses continued to flash in her eyes, making it harder and harder to see, which seemed odd in a way she couldn't quite put her finger on.

Still, that voice called to her.

Eyes brim with need
Pull me down
'Neath the dark
Scrub your sins away

Emptiness
One last breath
Baptized in blood
Do you want to suffer?

The meaning was almost as chilling as the vocals themselves, hitting a little too close to home considering why she was here. She turned once, to look for Jay or Rafe or Chelsea, but the bodies around her had swallowed her up, creating just enough space so she could breathe. So her heart could beat.

And then it hit her, almost at the same time she recognized the line in the song, "Do you want to suffer?"

She knew that line. She'd seen it before. Smeared in blood on the wall where the couple had been slaughtered . . . the place where Veronica's body had been found.

And now, right here in this club, there was that strange flashing, blinding her. Only it wasn't just the strobe lights, Violet realized. There was something else too, something closing in on the edges of her periphery.

Same as before.

From the lake house.

She rubbed her eyes, not caring that she was likely smearing her makeup. But it didn't change anything. The flashing, and the colors too, were still there. Still clouding her vision.

It was the imprint. The one that matched the man with the slashed throat. Veronica's father.

And the lyrics, *Do you want to suffer* . . .

It wasn't a coincidence.

He was here. The killer.

Violet shoved her way forward, straining to get to the stage to see if she'd missed something before. It didn't matter, though, if he was up there with them . . . if he was one of them. He couldn't hurt her now, not in the middle of his show.

She watched the lead singer, still listening to the haunting sound of his voice.

Silence the voices in my head
Tell me which road to follow

333

Silence the voices in my head
I'm under their spell

Am I deaf?
Or is it mercy?
She begs to be spared

It wasn't him, she was sure of it, even from here, she couldn't feel the strange colors, the swirling and shifting kaleidoscope coming from him, so she turned to the drummer, whose drums themselves bore the brimstone cross.

If I should die
Torch me on an altar of sacrifice

Frustration welled inside her as she moved to the next member and the next, ticking each of them off her list. Something wasn't right. It wasn't any of them.

Monster or human?
Drowning in doubt
The evil consumes me

So who then? She whirled around as the chorus started again, straining through the flashes in her vision to see those around her. If he wasn't onstage, then he was down here, in the crowd.

With her.

She searched and searched, stumbling now as the song started to wind down.

If I should die
Ashes . . . ashes . . .

She looked to her left and saw Rafe, but only the back of him as he moved in the opposite direction. She took a couple of steps his way but knew immediately that was the wrong way to go as her vision began to clear. Backtracking, it strengthened once more, but there were too many people, especially up here, near the stage.

The next song started, and this one Violet recognized. Screams erupted all around her, as everyone seemed to go wild. If it hadn't been for the imprint, she would've stopped to listen too, but there was only one thing driving her now.

She tried to move toward it, to follow the path that was calling to her, but instead she got tangled in a mass of bodies and limbs, all pushing against her at once, all shoving her toward the front. Her chest tightened as she became trapped, enmeshed in the human prison.

Hopelessly, she glanced up to the stage, to see if there was any other way out. But there were just more people in her way. More bodies. And not enough room to maneuver.

It wasn't hard to realize she had no option but to ride the

song out, and maybe the one after that, as she struggled just to remain on her feet. She was pinched and grabbed, and she elbowed and shoved back, but mostly she concentrated on the music.

Because that's all she could do right now.

STICKS AND STONES

AT FIRST HE THOUGHT HE'D MADE A MISTAKE.

She was as tough and as bold as he'd first guessed. But almost to a fault.

She was kind of a bitch.

He started to wonder if he'd chosen wrong. If she wasn't the right girl after all. Colton deserved better, didn't he? Colton deserved someone warmer, softer, at least in the right moments.

This girl seemed to be all hard edges, incapable of softness.

But he decided to wait a bit, to see if the roofie mellowed her out some.

It wasn't hard to slip the powder into her drink. She was barely giving him the time of day, and no one else was watching him as

Safe Word broke out into their anthem, "Fire and Brimstone." But she'd at least given him enough space to stand beside her at the table.

He'd tried to talk to her, even before she'd started sipping her drink, but what he realized was that the more irritated she grew by his attempts at winning her over, the more agitatedly she chewed on, and drank from, her straw. Until she'd downed half her glass.

Along with half the Rohypnol he'd been able to drop in there when he'd casually opened his palm as he'd reached across the table—and her glass—for a napkin.

She had no idea what hit her, but by the end of the second song, she was chattier. And far softer.

And he was far, far more hopeful as she leaned on him, draping one arm over his shoulder to steady herself.

Kisha found them like that, as she watched Evan from where she stood in line for the bathroom. But instead of being jealous to find him with some suburban wannabe who hung on him like a cheap whore, she just smiled, asking him with her eager expression if this was the girl.

His nod said, It's her, as he told the girl at his side, "Let's get outta here."

"Wha's yer name?" Her words were starting to bleed together, and he knew they needed to move fast, before he lost her altogether and someone started asking questions. Before her friends came back.

"Evan," he said patiently as she led him to where Kisha was waiting. "But you can call me Father."

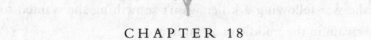

CHAPTER 18

THREE—POSSIBLY EVEN FOUR—SONGS LATER, when Violet finally managed to free herself from the confines of the crush in front of the stage, she took a deep breath, and focused. Her vision was still distorted, but not nearly as intensely as it had been just minutes earlier. As if whoever she'd been tracking had left the building.

She searched around frantically, not wanting him to get away as she tried to find that sensation again—desperately wanting to be blinded by the colors of death.

Yeah, because she wasn't strange. Who even thought things like that?

"Jay!" She jumped up and down when she saw him,

waving and trying to draw his attention. "Jay!" She hoped he could hear her above the music and the shouting, but somehow she doubted it. She could barely hear herself.

But he did *see* her, and that was enough as he, much more successfully than she had, shoved his way through the crowd. When he reached her, he was out of breath. "Jesus, Vi, I looked all over for you!" He had to yell to be heard. "One second you said something about splitting up, the next you were gone." He scowled at her.

But Violet just grabbed his hand and started dragging him away from the mob of people. "We have to go," she hollered back, hoping he wouldn't ask why. Telling him that she was following a killer wasn't something she wanted to scream in the middle of an audience.

There was a hallway to their right and Violet headed toward it, realizing that with each step the colors grew bolder, more distracting.

Once they'd ducked through the doorway, it wasn't hard to guess where the hallway led. There were three doors, two clearly marked with the universal stick figure signs that specified men's and women's restrooms, although the signs didn't seem to make a difference to the people waiting in line, as they took whichever room came available first. Apparently, when you had to go, you had to go.

Violet slowed as she passed the first door, but she could still see, making it more than clear that the person she was after wasn't in there. He also wasn't in line, she realized as she passed those who were still waiting. She and Jay got several strange looks as they squeezed by, and raised a few pierced brows.

Violet ignored them all.

"Damn," she cursed as she kept dragging him toward the third door.

This one was clearly marked: an exit. But she knew it was the right way to go if she intended to follow the imprint.

As she reached for the handle, Jay drew her up short. "Are you going to tell me what's going on?"

She pressed her palms against the long bar that would release the latch, the one that would let them outside. "He's out there, Jay. The killer. He was in here, and now he's gone. I know he's out there, just past this door. We have to go find him."

Jay stopped her, pulling her back. "Are you kidding? We're not going out there." He gripped her arms. "Violet, think about it for a minute. This is what I was talking about, you can't just chase after murderers." His voice became gentler, more persuasive. "Look," he said. "Let's go back inside and get Rafe and Chelsea. Then we'll call your uncle, or Rafe's sister, and tell them what you found. Let *them* go after this psycho."

Violet wavered, shifting anxiously on her feet. "But what if it's too late by then? What if he's already long gone?"

"Then he's gone, Vi. You can't put yourself in danger just because you're afraid the guy'll get away. Some things are out of your control." He started pulling her back inside. "Accept it."

She was only half convinced, and not at all happy, but she followed him because she knew he was right. It was the same thing Sara had been trying to tell her since she'd joined the team, teaching her the importance of putting her own safety—and the safety of her team—above all else. It was the same thing Dr. Lee had tried to teach her with all his stupid methods and techniques.

Yet here she was again, about to impulsively follow another imprint. About to put herself in harm's way . . . again.

Rafe was waiting for them at their spot at the table. Violet glanced up ruefully at two guys in her way as she squeezed past them.

"He was here," she told Rafe, looking around nervously to make sure no one else was listening to them. And then she added, "He must've slipped out the back though. I think we should call Sara."

Rafe straightened up from where he'd been slumped forward, leaning on his elbows. "Why didn't you go after him?"

"Because," Jay answered from over her shoulder, "I told her we should come back and get you and Chelsea first."

Rafe considered that and then nodded. "Good idea."

"Where is Chelsea, anyway?" Violet asked, her eyes raking the throng of people swarming the immediate area. She didn't see Chelsea anywhere.

"Dunno." Rafe shrugged. "I figured she was with you. Probably in the bathroom."

Violet knew that wasn't true. She'd just been by the bathrooms, and Chelsea wasn't there either.

"Hey!" she called to the boy Chelsea had been making eyes with when they'd left her. He was still sitting by himself. "Where's the girl who was here?" She tapped Chelsea's root beer, which was mostly empty.

He looked back at her indifferently, like he was going to shrug it off, pretend he had no idea who Violet was talking about, so she decided to jog his memory. "You know? Cute girl, short skirt, foul mouth? She was checking you out when I left."

He grinned slightly. "Yeah, I saw her. But she was more interested in that other dude."

Violet glanced questioningly at Rafe, but he just lifted his shoulder. "What other dude?"

"Dude she left with." His grin grew, knowingly. Leeringly. "She was pretty hammered though. You probably shouldn't'a left her alone. She could hardly walk—he practically had to carry her."

Violet's heart started pounding, beating at least five times its normal speed, and she felt like she was sweating through her skintight T. What was he talking about *hammered*? Chelsea hadn't been drinking.

She scrambled for a way to make sense of his words as she searched Rafe and then Jay for an explanation.

Her tongue was thick and dry, and she thought she might be sick.

She heard Jay asking the guy, "What did he look like,

the guy she was with?"

"Like everyone else, man. A little on the short side. Black hair." And then his eyes widened. "And a neck tatt. One of those cross things." He pointed toward the band. Toward the stage. "Like on the drums. Big black one." He traced his finger down the left side of his neck, showing where it was. "From his ear to his shoulder."

The brimstone cross.

The guy Chelsea had left with—had been carried out of here by—had a tattoo of the brimstone cross.

Violet lifted the root beer, her hand shaking so violently she could barely get the straw to her lips. Just as her mouth closed around it, just as she was going to take a long pull from the straw to quench her parched throat and hopefully soothe her stomach, she felt it being jerked from her hand.

"Don't drink that!" Rafe shouted at her, and Violet blinked back at him, wondering what the hell had gotten into him.

And then she saw what he was pointing at, what he'd been scraping into a small pile on the marred wooden table-top.

Fine white powder that could barely be seen between the flashes of light coming from the stage. Not much, but just enough to be noticeable. Just enough to make Violet take a second glance at the glass that was sitting on the table between them now.

At the bottom of the brown liquid, she could just make out a few of the same white granules settled in the base of the glass. Almost invisible. Almost all liquefied now, save those remaining few.

"That's not sugar, is it?" Violet asked.

Rafe shook his head, but it was the look on his face that made the knot in her chest tighten. It wasn't the look of someone who didn't care. He looked scared. "We have to find her," he told Violet.

Behind Rafe, she heard Jay talking to the other guy at the table, while her heart struggled to find its rhythm. "Did you see which way they went?"

The guy, who hadn't been paying attention to them as they'd figured out what had happened to Chelsea, turned back to them and pointed toward the exit. "They went out that way," he said. "But I doubt you'll catch 'em. That was a couple'a songs ago."

That way, Violet thought, thinking of the way she'd felt when she'd been standing at the exit.

She'd followed the imprint to that door, knowing he'd gone out there. The killer.

The guy with the brimstone cross tattoo.

And he had Chelsea.

They were running by the time they reached the door, and didn't stop as they burst through it. The cool night air was refreshing after the stifling atmosphere inside the club, and Violet hadn't realized how hard it had been to breathe in there. How suffocated she'd felt.

She hadn't stopped to think about what she'd do once

she was out here. Where they were going or what their plan was. All she'd thought about was Chelsea.

Saving her.

"Call Sara!" she screamed over her shoulder as she reached the small lot behind the club. "Tell her to call my uncle. To call everyone. We need help."

On the road in front of them, several cars zipped past and she was forced to slow down, to consider her next move. She had no idea which way to go next.

Spinning to face the others, she saw that Rafe already had his phone out and was dialing.

"What if it's too late, Vi?" Jay asked. "He's probably long gone. We don't even have a description of what he was driving."

Violet couldn't even consider that possibility, not when they had so much at stake. When she answered him, her breath came out in a wheeze. "*If*, Jay. *If* he was driving. We don't know he had a car. They could be on foot."

"Violet." Jay's voice tried to be placating, but Violet could hear the disquiet behind it.

Beside her, Rafe hung up.

"What'd she say?"

"She's calling the local police, and your uncle, and she's on her way now. She said to stay put."

Violet shifted nervously, barely able to stand in one place now. It didn't matter what Sara said, she couldn't just stand here. "I think we should split up. We can cover more ground that way."

She didn't have to convince Rafe—he was already nodding.

"But, aren't we supposed to stay put?" Jay countered. "Isn't that what you just said?"

Rafe grinned at Violet. "I said that's what Sara told us to do. I didn't say that's what we were *gonna* do." His attention shifted to Jay then. "You stay with Violet. Don't let her outta your sight." He started walking away from them, leaving them to decide which way to go, when he called back. "And keep your phone on!"

Violet only half nodded as she looked around, trying to decide which direction made the most sense.

Part of her knew Jay was probably right, that Chelsea was probably in the back of some guy's car right now, too far away for them to help her. But she couldn't just wait for Sara, or someone else, to arrive. Even if the police did show up in the next few minutes, she had no new information to give them. She'd already heard Rafe telling his sister about the club and the spiked drink and the brimstone tattoo, which was really all they had to go on at this point anyway.

She started pacing up the sidewalk, following the path along the street, certain Jay was right behind her. There was no way he'd let Violet out of his sight now.

"I should never have brought her here," Violet groaned, her steps speeding up now.

They reached the crosswalk and Violet repeatedly pressed the button for the crosswalk signal to turn with her thumb, as if the repetitive action might spur the signal along. It didn't and she grew more and more agitated, hopping from one foot to the other.

"There's no way you could've known." Jay tried to assuage her, but Violet didn't want to hear that now. The weight of Chelsea's predicament was crushing her.

"Except that's not entirely true, is it? I've gotten myself into jams before, why did I think this one would turn out any different? I shouldn't have involved anyone else. This is my burden, not hers."

The signal changed and Violet started jogging, and then running, not wanting to let Jay make excuses for what she'd done. For the situation she'd put Chelsea in.

This was all her fault. And if Chelsea got hurt . . .

She'd never forgive herself.

"Which way should we go?" Violet asked, her voice rising when they reached the other side. But the question didn't have an answer, not really, and she threw her hands in the air. "I have no idea what to do, Jay. She could be anywhere!"

She didn't want to cry. Not here, not now, but her voice trembled and the frustration of their dilemma overcame her.

Tacoma was a huge city. Sprawling . . . with thousands upon thousands of homes. Thousands upon thousands of places he could have taken a girl to hide her.

And Violet knew what he was capable of. She'd seen the proof firsthand.

Hunching forward, Violet swiped at the tears she couldn't manage to stop, rubbing her eyes. She felt helpless. Hopeless. Useless.

"We'll find her," Jay offered, but the conviction was absent from his voice. Even he knew he couldn't make a promise like that.

Sniffing, Violet stood upright again, and then she saw it.

She squeezed her eyes shut, trying to decide whether it was real or not. Or rather if it was only because her makeup was burning her eyes that the spot flitted into her vision. It was gone as quickly as it had appeared.

But she was almost sure she hadn't imagined it. That it hadn't been a trick of her mind . . . that single, tiny blue fleck.

She took a step one way, trying to re-create the effect.

"We should go back to the club and wait for the pol—"

"*Shhh!*" Violet demanded, trying to concentrate.

When it didn't come back, she took a step forward, and then another and another. Her heart seemed to match her paces now, quick and erratic, creating a staccato rhythm against the sidewalk, and inside her chest.

Nothing again.

She went back the way she'd come, to the place where she'd started, and still, nothing.

And then she crossed that threshold, moving one step farther. And again.

There it was . . . a quick burst of red.

And another step . . . a blast of yellow. Then one more . . . this time green.

The colors. They were back.

She laughed with relief, sounding deranged, unstable.

"He's here," she practically sobbed. "We can find her."

And then she was off, following a path that was gradually blinding her and could only mean one thing. That she was chasing a killer.

It was slow going, and they had to backtrack up and down side streets more than once as Violet would find the trail, and then lose it again. The neighborhoods they combed grew and more and more bleak, and more and more impoverished and menacing the longer they ran.

It felt like they'd been searching for hours, but according to Jay only five minutes had passed. Violet was worried. What if they were tracking the wrong guy? What if he didn't have Chelsea?

Or what if he'd had her and already disposed of her?

The image of Veronica Bowman flashed through her mind, discarded at a home that wasn't her own, a needle buried in her arm.

She'd been drugged too.

But Violet had something on her side that this guy didn't know about. Her ability.

She could track him. And she had no intention of giving up.

Turning once more, Violet flinched as a pair of dogs hit the chain-link fence that contained them. They were frenzied and tried their best to get at her and Jay. Jay's hand closed over hers as he drew her backward while the animals barked and growled, snarling and gnashing their teeth. There was nothing about the display that was meant for show. Those dogs would just as soon rip their throats out as let them pass.

"Holy crap," Violet whispered, still not letting go of him when they reached the streetlight on the corner. She took a breath. "That scared the crap outta me."

Jay's grip tightened. "You and me both."

They skipped that street, deciding to avoid Cujo and his friend. But they couldn't stop. They were close, Violet could tell, because her vision grew more and more impaired.

When they turned down the next block, Violet gasped as her eyesight nearly imploded in a shattering display. But through the eruptions she thought she saw an outline ahead of her, dark and shadowy and hard to make out among the colors bursting in her way.

People. They were too far away, and were obscured by the night—and her deteriorating vision. But Violet knew . . .

It was Chelsea . . .

And him.

"Chelsea!" Violet shouted before she could stop herself, nearly stumbling over her own feet as she rushed forward, trying to reach them.

Just before they vanished once more.

SEE NO EVIL

THE GIRL WAS SLOWING THEM DOWN, BUT IT *made no difference to him. He was anxious, sure, but Colton's condition probably hadn't improved since they'd left him. He was probably no different than he had been yesterday. And no different than the day before that.*

He was in no shape to appreciate his girl just yet.

Evan would have to wait to see the look on his friend's face when he presented him with his new toy.

In the meantime, it was a struggle just to get her home.

She fell, more than once, ripping her tights on the jagged-edged concrete of the broken sidewalks, and then laughing over the blood that oozed down her knees. He much preferred the drugged version of this girl, though, over the hard, prickly one he'd first met.

"C'ai tell yoo a seeee-krit?" The girl had her arms wrapped around each of their necks, as both he and Kisha dragged her along. The toes of her boots scuffed along the ground and her head lolled forward. He wondered how much longer she'd even be conscious.

He and Kisha exchanged glances over the back of her head.

"What's that, sweetie?" Kisha asked her, her voice taking on a motherly quality that he couldn't help being proud of. Ever since Colton's accident she'd stepped into the role without being asked.

It was what he'd always wanted, for them to be the perfect family.

"I . . . don . . ." She started to drift away, her words losing steam. "I don't . . . feel so . . . good . . ." The last words came out in a whisper.

Kisha was already panting, and he didn't know how much more of the girl's dead weight she could manage.

That's when the voice cut through the shadows, finding its way to them, and he knew they were in trouble.

"Chelsea!" someone called out from not so far away, and the girl in his arms perked up, lifting her head as high as she could.

Chelsea. Her name must be Chelsea, he realized, glancing once over his shoulder and making out the curly-haired girl and her Abercrombie boyfriend just beneath the street lamp at the corner.

"Drop her!" Kisha insisted, releasing the girl. "Let's get outta here."

He glanced at the girl's mystified expression, and wondered if she even knew where she was. Who she was.

But even with her dazed countenance and her smeared mascara she was beautiful. So very beautiful. She was perfect for Colton.

"No," he snapped, hauling her all the way back up, bearing all of her weight himself. He searched around them, scanning the houses up and down the street, surveying the ones closest to them.

Most had the same vacant appearance. A little too dark. A little too run-down, and far too empty.

But it was the one ahead of them that held the most promise. The one with the For Sale sign sticking out of the dead lawn, and the foreclosure notice taped to its front door.

There was no light at all coming from within, and he guessed that even if someone still lived there, they weren't home at this very moment.

He dragged the girl—Colton's girl—through the patchy, brittle grass. "Come on," he ordered beneath his breath to Kisha, who still looked uncertain, like she might bolt at any moment. "Get up here, Kish, I need you." At that she moved, suddenly darting toward him. They rounded the back of the house, still dragging the girl, but now Kisha was helping, trying to pull her along by her other arm.

When they reached the back door he kicked it open, and not waiting to see if it was actually someone's home still, they disappeared inside, closing the broken door as best they could behind them.

CHAPTER 19

VIOLET CLUNG TO JAY'S HAND AS SHE SPRINTED
up the street. Her vision had cleared, but only a little.

"You saw them. Tell me you saw them!" she cried, not
caring who heard her now. If it really was the killer she'd
seen—and the imprint was a dead giveaway—he already
knew they were following him.

Jay tried to hold her back, slowing her pace. "But I didn't
see where they went, Vi. Did you?"

Violet shook her head. "It doesn't matter though." She
glanced up and down the row of houses, and only one of
them stood out to her. Only one of them had a medley of
colors that erupted all around it. "That's it," she said, pointing

at the one just ahead of them. "They're in there." She dug her phone out of her purse and shoved it at him. "Call Rafe. Tell him where we are. Tell him we found Chelsea."

Watching as Jay fished out a flyer from the plastic box that hung on the For Sale sign, Violet waited just long enough to hear him reading the address to Rafe on the other end . . .

. . . before she slipped away.

NO REST FOR THE WICKED

THEY MOVED QUICKLY, PULLING THE GIRL AS HER
boots banged and clattered along the top of the old floorboards. There
were boxes strewn about and maybe a broken chair or two, hard to
tell for sure, but it was mostly garbage they had to maneuver around.
The house was definitely vacant. Probably only inhabited by rats at
this point.

He figured they'd be safe as long as they could just stay quiet.

Besides, there was no way the curly-haired girl and her boyfriend would know they were in here. No way they'd figure out
where they were hiding. Eventually, they'd get tired of searching for
their friend, and they'd move on to the next place.

Then he and Kisha would duck out again, and head for home.

He dropped the girl in a heap on the floor as he crept toward the front of the house. He was just about to peek out the window, between the boards that covered the broken glass, to try to see out to the street beyond, when he heard it.

The back door.

And the voice.

"Chels." She was quiet. Uncertain. But far too close for his liking.

"Kish," he whispered, swinging his arms in wide arcs in the dark as he searched frantically for her. When his fingers closed around her arm, he dragged her up against him, his mouth right at her ear. "Help me get her up those stairs."

It was hard to see the staircase in this kind of blackness. It was there, though, off to the side of what had once been a banister. But without a handrail, the banister was now just a row of pointed spikes that would more likely impale you than prevent you from falling.

Kisha didn't argue, she just reached beneath the girl's arm and heaved her up, using the last of her strength—probably more than she even had left—to help him. To get Colton's girl someplace safe. Out of the way.

To hide her.

CHAPTER 20

THE SMELL OF STALE URINE HIT VIOLET FIRST—
human or animal, she had no way of knowing, but it was
strong—and it burned a path all the way to her sinuses.
Instinctively her hand shot up and she covered her nose and
her mouth, trying not to gag as the urine scent melded with
the smells of mildew and old garbage and something else
that festered just beneath it all.

Feces, Violet thought. It was probably feces.

"Chels," she said timidly, hating that she was virtually
blind now. For all she knew, the killer was standing directly
in front of her.

Ahead of her, she heard voices, low and unintelligible

359

voices. He was talking, but who was talking back? Was it Chelsea?

She took another step and noticed something else, a strange sound, like the trickling of water. But not a faucet, not steady and driven by man-made devices.

No, this sounded more like a stream. Like the soft cascading waters of a mountain stream.

Right here, in this crumbling old house.

Violet knew what it was. It was another imprint, of course.

He was a violent killer, and it made sense that he carried more than one.

She tried to find the other, the one she knew from the lake house—the old coffee grounds—but she couldn't amid all the tangible smells that competed for her senses.

She heard more noises. Banging and thumping. They were moving away from her, making her feel braver so she stepped again, her hands out in front of her to keep from walking into walls. "Chelsea!" she called again, this time louder, bolder.

As the sounds moved farther, so did Violet. She knew they were upstairs now, she could hear them above her, but she had no idea where the stairs were. She fumbled around, feeling her way along walls, and straining to see through the narrow openings created between the imprints. But those glimpses were too brief, not giving her eyes enough time to adjust to the blackness.

Her fingers brushed over something sharp, a spike that

seemed to be sticking up from the floor itself. Beside it, there was another one, equally jagged. She struggled to make sense of them in her mind as she took another step.

But her foot caught on something and she careened forward, barely having enough time to process the fact that she was falling right toward one of those stakes.

"Jesus, Vi," Jay cursed as he caught her from behind. "What the hell are you doing? That thing almost impaled you."

"They're upstairs," she answered, ignoring his lecture.

His voice dropped. "And you just thought you'd sneak up there while I wasn't looking? Can you even see, Violet?" She felt a whoosh of air under her nose and she knew he was waving his hand in front of her face.

"Stop that!" she insisted, brushing his hand away, but as her hand passed through the air, she knew she'd missed, that her timing had been off.

His words were challenging now. "Violet, this is a bad idea. We can't just storm this guy. What if he's armed? We already know he's dangerous."

She reached for his hands, and finding them, implored him. "That's right, Jay," she whispered. "He's dangerous. And he's up there *with Chelsea*. We can't just leave her there, can we? Who knows what he's doing to her. What if he *is* armed? Maybe we can stop him before he . . ." She didn't finish, she couldn't. Jay hadn't seen what she had.

The pause was short, much shorter than she'd expected. "You're right. We can't just leave her. You wait here, I'm doing this alone."

It didn't matter what he said, though. Because what she was really listening to was where his feet hit the stairs.

She followed almost immediately, never really intending to stay behind. He could be pissed at her later. For now, she had a friend to save.

"You never listen," Jay grumbled quietly, but he didn't stop, and she could sense the determination coming off him in every step he took. He was less cautious now, less worried about each creak beneath their feet.

Suddenly it seemed he wanted to find Chelsea as badly as she did.

He kept Violet behind him, which was good, because she needed to use him as her guide. Him and the imprints only she could sense.

The water sound grew clearer, stronger. It drew her as surely as the flashing kaleidoscope that blocked her view.

But as they reached the top of the stairs, Violet knew something was wrong.

Terribly, terribly wrong.

The imprints split there. Right there at the landing.

One imprint—the colors—pulling her one way. The rushing water pulling her the other.

She heard Jay then, above the babbling sound of water. "Which way?"

Vacillating, she turned her head in each direction, trying to make sense of it all.

How could there be two imprints, leading her in two

different directions?

"I—I don't know." Her words hit the air at the same time they both heard it. The moan. Low and muffled and almost imperceptible, but there all the same.

"This way," Jay said, dragging Violet along. Dragging her toward the sound of the stream.

SILENCE IS GOLDEN

THEY WERE PRACTICALLY RIGHT OUTSIDE THE
door now. Right on top of him.

He glanced around, trying to figure a way out, but he was
trapped. If only she'd be quiet. If only she'd lie there and be still.

He thought about dosing her again, but there was no time.
Besides, he'd given the rest of his stash to Kisha right before hiding
her in the attic.

Better, he'd told her, if they split up. Abercrombie and the girl
were looking for him and Colton's girl, not for her. He'd told her
to stay there, no matter what happened, no matter what she heard,
until she was sure it was safe to come out again. She could stay quiet
as long as she wasn't dope sick.

Colton's girl whipped her head to the side, but was still unaware of anything around her. She'd passed out halfway up the stairs.

He heard their voices. And even farther away, much farther, he heard sirens.

And then she moaned.

Damn! Damn, damn, damn! He dropped to his knees and covered her mouth with his hand but it was already too late. He could hear their footsteps now too, and it was only a matter of seconds before they busted down the door. Before they found their way inside.

Before they caught him.

He bent forward, pressing a gentle kiss on the girl's cheek. "I'm sorry," he said almost sadly as he released the blade on the knife in his hand.

And then plunged it into her gut.

CHAPTER 21

WHEN JAY HIT THE DOOR WITH HIS SHOULDER, it didn't splinter beneath his weight or anything quite so dramatic. The handle, which was probably old and in disrepair anyway, fell apart on impact, and the door shot open, banging against the wall on the other side. The crashing noise filled the house, echoing off the walls.

The sound of rushing water was stronger in here, as was the urine smell. Violet recoiled, again covering her face. She could see fragments of the space around her, tiny pieces of the room: an old bureau with a cracked mirror, its jagged shards catching bits of light from outside and reflecting it around them; a window with dingy-looking curtains billowing in on either side of it; a mound in the center of the floor that could only be one thing.

"Chelsea," Violet whimpered, falling to her knees at the same time she caught a glimpse of another person—the killer—emerging from the darkened corner. Above his head there was something glowing, a blur of light that Violet couldn't make out . . . he was moving far too quickly now.

"Jay," she tried to warn, but it wasn't necessary.

Whoever he was, he was already launching himself toward the open window, throwing himself over the sill just as Jay was about to reach him. And with him went both the trickling of water *and* the stench of old urine.

Two of his imprints.

"We did it," Violet breathed. "We found her." Outside, the shrill sound of sirens came closer, and she no longer cared about anything except that she'd found Chelsea.

And then, before she could stop him, before she could even shout his name, she watched as Jay, too, hurled himself over the window's ledge.

She started to get up, to go to the window to see if he was okay. To see if he'd landed safely, but a hand stopped her. Chelsea's hand.

Relief rippled within her and spread outward.

"It's okay, Chels, I'm here now. I'm here."

She heard it then, a wheezing sound, and she felt frantically for Chelsea's face, her hands stroking her friend's cheeks. "It's okay," she repeated, but this time she was no longer sure. Something was wrong.

She kept going, her hands searching the girl beneath her as the sirens outside grew nearer and nearer. When her hands reached Chelsea's belly, she felt something warm and sticky and wet.

Her first instinct was to draw away. She didn't want to touch it. Not this. Not Chelsea's blood.

But that moment passed quickly, and then Violet was screaming as she heard the commotion below her, just outside the window. *"Help! We need help in here!"*

She pressed her hands as hard as she could to the wound, it was all she could remember from the abbreviated first aid course they'd had in PE. She thought that maybe she should do something more, but she wasn't sure what that something might be.

And then Chelsea went still beneath her.

Not the kind of still that happens when someone falls asleep, when you continue to feel their breaths, when you know their blood is coursing within them.

No, this was a different kind of still. The kind that Violet had only seen in death.

She heard footsteps that seemed too far away. Voices that were disjointed and sounded nonsensical to her ears.

Nothing made sense. Nothing was real.

Hands pulled her off Chelsea and she struggled against them, fighting to stay with her, fighting to remain at her friend's side so she could save her. So she could protect her. To stop whatever was happening.

But when she first saw the smoke coming up from

Chelsea, from her hair, her skin, her mouth, as insubstantial and wraithlike as the air itself, she realized . . . she knew . . .

She was too late.

Heat . . . smoke . . .

This was Chelsea's echo she was witnessing.

"No!" She heard someone screaming. "No, no, no, no . . ." It went on and on and on . . .

She didn't realize it was her until they were dragging her from the room so the paramedics could work in peace. Behind her she heard the sound of the electrical paddles charging, and then voices and scuffling, followed by more machines. She heard all of those things repeated more than once. More times than she could count.

She huddled on the floor in the hallway unable to catch her breath, unable to do anything but pray, and she wasn't even sure she was doing that right. After either a minute or forever, she had no idea which, a man's face appeared in front of her. She had no idea who he was, and frankly, she didn't care. He asked her question after question, none of which she could answer:

Did she know what her friend had taken?

Did she know how to reach Chelsea's parents?

Was she injured? Had she taken anything?

She couldn't talk, she couldn't think.

Was there anyone else in the house besides the two girls?

Somewhere, in the back of Violet's mind, something clicked, as if a switch had been flipped. That one—that question—meant something to her.

It took her a minute to work through it, to make the words make sense, but when they did, Violet stared back at him and nodded.

"Someone's in here? Who?" the man asked, signaling to someone behind him, and she saw his uniform then and realized she was talking to a cop. "Where? Can you tell me where?"

She nodded again, reaching up to wipe her eyes and realizing that's what was bothering her. There was still another imprint in the house. The colors were still swirling and spinning and blurring her eyesight.

She pointed up.

Another officer joined the first one, and they exchanged a glance. "Upstairs? But we're on the second floor," he told her, and she nodded once more.

"He wasn't alone," she said at last, her voice rasping as she hoped she made sense. She tried to look past them, to see through the slits in her vision. "An attic, maybe? There." She pointed now, finding it in the ceiling. "The opening."

"Someone get her out of here," one of them called, and then she was being pulled down the stairs. She tried to see into the room, where they were still working on Chelsea, but all she could see were bodies swarming, and all she could hear were the sounds of chaos.

She watched as the officers converged on the attic door, weapons drawn, and she rejoiced in the fact that, as she was pulled away, her vision began to clear.

★ ★ ★

Outside, she hugged herself as she was ushered toward one of the big red ambulances. She'd been in them before, she knew the drill.

There were so many lights flashing it was nearly as blinding out there as it had been inside the house, where the imprint had been. She had to shield her eyes just to see where she was going.

She felt numb. Cold and numb.

Hysteria began to creep in, and she wondered if this was what it felt like to go mad. This sense of nothingness.

She saw Rafe, already giving his statement. He started to say something to her as she passed, but she ducked her head, not wanting to have to say anything in return.

It was too soon to talk.

She let them lead her into the back of the van and she dazedly accepted the blanket, although she just let it fall from her shoulders, not caring whether she was cold or hot, or anything really. She waved away the water, not even able to say no thanks.

She closed her eyes when she saw Rafe approaching. "That boyfriend of yours is way more badass than I thought. He's got one helluva right hook."

"Jay?" she gasped. She hadn't thought about him since she'd watched him jump out the window.

Rafe nodded. "I saw that guy come flying out that window, and I thought what a dumb mother . . . Well, you know . . ." He shrugged. "And then I saw that dumbass boyfriend of yours come right out after him. When he hit the

371

ground I thought for sure he must've busted both his ankles."
He shook his head as he recounted the story for Violet. She
struggled to focus on his words. "But then he jumped up and
started beatin' the hell outta that guy. I swear if the police
hadn't gotten there when they did, dude would'a been on his
way to the hospital instead'a jail."

Violet nodded, trying to keep up. "They got him? He
didn't get away?"

Rafe indicated one of the police cars, and Violet looked,
seeing that there was a guy sitting in back. He had black hair
and a straight nose and skin too smooth to be considered
a man just yet. If it wasn't for the brimstone cross running
down the entire length of his neck, Violet would never have
realized it was him.

Except that now that Rafe had pointed him out, she
could sense those other things too. The water. And the scent.

And one more thing, something she hadn't been able to
make out in the room.

He had a halo. A ring of light around his head that
almost . . . *almost* made him look angelic.

But Violet knew better.

This boy was no angel.

"Where is he? Where's Jay?" she whimpered, wanting to
see him now. Wanting to touch him and hold him.

She heard him then, and realized he must've been near
her the entire time. "I'm right here." Leaning forward, she
glanced into the back of the ambulance parked beside the

one she was in. Jay was there, holding a thick piece of gauze to his cheek.

He nodded at her. "I would've come find you, but I was told if I try to leave the back of this rig again, they'd tell the doc to sew my stitches in the shape of a heart."

"Stitches?" Violet asked, jumping down and going to him.

He hooked his arm around her waist, drawing her close. His breath was warm and comforting against her cheek, and his voice was soft. "It's nothing. I'll be fine."

She would've asked more, but just then she heard the commotion behind her, and there was a stretcher coming out. One of the paramedics was calling out orders and she heard something about a girl who'd OD'd. But somewhere in there, in all that chatter, she heard the words: *Vitals are stable.*

Her heart sped up, hope filling her to overflowing. She left Jay and went closer, wanting to see for herself. Needing to know if it was true, that Chelsea had survived.

But then her vision clouded, and she realized it wasn't Chelsea at all. It was another girl.

One who must've been hiding in the attic. A killer.

Jumping out of the way, she let them pass as her hope faded. And then she saw the second stretcher. Paramedics were flanking all sides, making it impossible to see past them, and Violet scrambled to get closer, knowing it could only be one person on there.

"Is she . . . ?" she tried to ask as they passed. But the question hadn't been necessary, because she could see now.

And she almost fell to her knees again.

The imprint . . . the smoke . . . it was gone.

One of the paramedics nodded at Violet as they walked by. "She's stable," he said, and then they disappeared into the back of an awaiting ambulance and drove away.

CHAPTER 22

VIOLET SAT BACK IN HER CHAIR, STARING UP AT the ceiling tiles. She knew that it was daytime, and that Chelsea was out of surgery and was now in recovery, but other than that she had no idea what time it was . . . or even what day.

Time seemed to bend and sway and warp around her, distorting her every thought and making her head split.

It felt like weeks had passed since that night at the abandoned house.

Yet only hours had gone by since her best friend had died.

She'd opted against waiting with Chelsea's family—her

parents and her little brother and older sister—and with Jules and Claire, and the rest of the people who'd gathered in the family waiting lounge. Instead, she'd found this quiet stretch of hallway, too brightly lit, but entirely private from the stares of well-meaning friends and family.

Her own parents had come and gone, at Violet's insistence, giving her the space she'd claimed she needed. They were good like that. Patient.

"There you are. I've been looking everywhere."

Startled, Violet stopped humming, not even realizing she'd slipped into the old habit, as she glanced up at the familiar voice. She shrugged, not sure how she could explain her need to be alone at a time like this, when she should be clinging to others for support. "I've been here."

Sara sat down next to her, and the temperature dropped at least five degrees, at least in Violet's estimation. She drew in on herself, wrapping her arms around her as she turned to face her fearless leader.

"The girl came to, the one from the attic. Couple of hours ago. She was dazed but she told the officers who escorted her that they needed to find someone named Colton. She said he was hurt and needed help. Most of what she said didn't make much sense, but they were able to get a location from her." Violet watched Sara's blue lips, wondering at the sheer beauty of them. The frost that coated them sparkled beneath the glare of the too bright lights. "When they got there, they arrested a boy and a girl, and found another boy severely beaten, barely clinging to life." She winced as breath gusted from her mouth on a sigh. "They'd been treating him with heroin. He may never regain consciousness."

"One of their victims?" Violet asked.

Sara shook her head. "One of their own. As far as we can tell, Evan Schulte, the boy who hurt your friend . . ." Her expression was grave. Sad. "Evan Schulte, the boy we have in custody for hurting Chelsea, was using his friends for home invasions, where they would steal enough to pay for drugs. Apparently, the Bowmans weren't their first victims, just the first situation that got out of hand and turned deadly. Evan hasn't said a word, so unless we get the other kid, or one of the girls, talking again, we won't know much more until forensics start coming back."

"Unless one of us can help sort things out," Violet said, smiling a little now. Glad the killing spree was finally over.

"Yeah, you should be able to sort out who killed who at least," Sara agreed. "With this many suspects it'll be hard to know for sure who's to blame. As far as the why and the how, well, I'm hoping to get my hands on some of their things so I can let the rest of the team start working on it."

There was a long quiet moment, and Violet felt time slipping once more. She couldn't tell if it was too long, the silence, or if just enough time had passed.

"How's Jay?" Sara asked at last.

As if conjured by her words, Jay appeared, carrying a Styrofoam cup. There was a bandage on his face, covering the stitches he'd gotten in the emergency room.

"It's not Starbucks," he said, handing the cup to Violet.

"But it was the best I could find." He looked ruefully at Sara. "I'd've gotten you one, but I didn't know you were here."

Violet sipped the bitter liquid, tasting the powdered creamer and wishing he'd have been a little more generous with the sugar.

"Here," Jay said, reading her thoughts. He unloaded his pocket, which was stuffed full of sugar packets. "I had no idea how much you'd need."

She smiled at him, as she tore into three of the packets, dumping them into her coffee.

Sara was watching Jay, watching both of them, when she told him, "I'm really sorry you got dragged into this. Both you and Chelsea."

Jay sat down on the other side of Violet and leaned forward, so he could look Sara in the eye. "I didn't get dragged into anything. I'd do anything—go anywhere—for Violet. I'm glad I was there, glad I could help stop that creep."

Violet was glad too. She'd already wondered what might have happened if Chelsea hadn't told Rafe where they'd been planning to go. Things might've ended very differently.

But Jay was still talking. "And as far as Chelsea, I gotta be honest. That girl doesn't do anything she doesn't want to do. No one dragged her into this mess. She went willingly. She wanted to be part of Violet's life. I think she was just glad the secret was finally out in the open."

Apprehension wrenched her gut as Violet watched Sara's reaction. Sara didn't know Violet had confided in Chelsea.

378

Or at least Violet hadn't told her. And she was learning that Rafe didn't tell Sara everything.

He hadn't told Sara about Dr. Lee. Or about their mother being part of the Circle.

Sara didn't flinch from the news, didn't respond at all. Still, Violet was grateful when a nurse wearing pale pink scrubs came toward them, interrupting the tense silence.

"You can see your friend now," she told Violet. They were the sweetest words Violet had ever heard.

"Hey there . . . how ya doin'?" Violet asked, easing her way inside the hospital room. The antiseptic smell stung her nose, and she winced when she heard the incessant beeping of machines all around her.

She stopped short when she saw Rafe there too, standing by Chelsea's bedside.

"Oh . . . I, um, I'm sorry . . . is this a bad time?" Violet took a half step backward, hating the surge of resentment that rose up her throat like bile.

Chelsea's head rolled over on her pillow, and her half-lidded eyes widened. "No, don't go."

"It's okay," Rafe said to Violet, his actions jerky as he rubbed at his neck. "I was just leaving." Then his gaze fell on Chelsea, and his voice lowered . . . softened. "I'll come back later, okay?" His hand dropped, and the back of his fingers brushed over the back of hers in a gesture that was far too intimate.

Chelsea smiled blearily up at him, and Violet swallowed hard, forcing herself not to watch the two of them.

"I'll see you later," he told Violet as he brushed past her on his way out.

It was true, Violet thought. They would see each other. At school, and at the Center, and maybe even outside both now that he and Chelsea seemed to be . . . *getting closer.* So why did that thought make her stomach churn? Why did she want so badly to keep them apart?

Didn't they deserve to be happy?

"I heard I have you to thank," Chelsea said, drawing Violet's attention, her lips moving slower than usual. She seemed to have difficulty peeling her tongue from the roof of her mouth. Each word was sluggish and hard fought. "I told you you were a hero."

Violet forced her smile to remain in place, but inwardly she cringed. "Don't say that, Chels. I'm just glad my stupid stunts didn't get you killed."

Chelsea frowned, her entire face collapsing. "Are you kidding? Look at me. I'm bulletproof."

Violet looked. At the tubes coming in and out of Chelsea's arms. At the machines lining both sides of her bed, making noises and monitoring her vitals and who knew what else. Leave it to Chelsea to try to sound tough even when she was half conscious in the hospital.

"Too bad for you it wasn't a bullet, I guess."

Chelsea laughed, which turned into a cough, which made her moan and set off a round of monitors, causing a nurse to come rushing into the room. The woman glowered at Violet, who had the good sense to look shamefaced about what she'd done.

"Yeah," Chelsea said, while the nurse peeled back the sheet and checked the bandage beneath Chelsea's blue-green hospital gown. A fresh wave of guilt washed over her. "I guess I'm not *stab* proof."

The nurse flashed Chelsea a disapproving look, and then shot another one at Violet.

Violet understood the meaning well enough, but the nurse voiced her thoughts anyway. "You need to take it easy. If you can't, then we'll have to restrict your visitors. I doubt we'd have a hard time persuading your parents to agree." Her already arched eyebrows raised almost to her hairline as her warning sank in.

She was probably right. Chelsea's parents had always liked Violet . . . but that was before. What would they think of her now, after what had happened last night at the club? After Chelsea had almost gotten killed?

When the nurse was gone, Chelsea dismissed the notion. "My folks'll be fine. They don't hate you or anything. I already told them it was my idea to go down there. And it's not like *you* were the one who drugged me."

Violet knew Chelsea was right about all of those things, but she also knew parents. Fear could trump logic.

She reached for Chelsea's hand, thinking how strange it was to hold one of her friends' hands like this. When they were little, everyone held hands. Everyone hugged and shared Popsicles and sang songs, never caring if they were off-key or that everyone might be listening.

Now, they kept their hands to themselves and didn't say things like "I love you" even when it was true.

"I'm so sorry, Chelsea. I can't tell you how sorry I am. I would never have let you go with me if I'd've known . . ."

Chelsea's fingers twitched, and Violet wondered if she was trying to squeeze her hand. "Shut up, Vi. That's messed up if you think I'm gonna let you take the blame. I knew what I was doing." She smiled then, a small un-Chelsea-like smile with not enough oomph behind it. "Well, except for that whole stabbing part. That, I could'a done without."

Violet shook her head. She had no idea what more she could say.

But she didn't have to, Chelsea wasn't finished yet. "Can I tell you something?"

"Anything, Chels."

"You know in that room? When you came in and I . . . well, right before I . . ." She tried to shrug, but she grimaced when she tried. ". . . died?"

"Yeah." Violet nodded, wondering where Chelsea was going with this.

Chelsea's face scrunched up, her brow wrinkling as she concentrated. "This is gonna sound weird, but I thought I saw something. I swear I saw an angel. . . ."

Violet's eyes widened as she waited for her next breath to come. It felt trapped, caught in the space between her lungs

382

and her mouth. Stuck in the denial she wanted to voice, but couldn't.

"I felt warm all over, and then saw this weird flash of light, and then, right before I closed my eyes," she added, her voice so quiet Violet had to strain to hear it over the blood rushing past her own ears. "He just *flew away*."

Chelsea's eyes flitted closed then, and Violet just stood there, waiting to see if there was more. If Chelsea was going to open them and tell her this was all a hoax. That she was playing some sort of practical joke on her.

But there was none of that. Just Chelsea lying there, her breathing growing quieter, her eyelids flickering back and forth beneath her closed lids.

Violet waited a few more minutes, and then realized that she should go. Chelsea needed to rest, and it wouldn't do Violet any good to hover over her and watch her sleep. She should probably get some rest too.

But how could she? After what Chelsea had just told her?

An angel. Chelsea thought she'd seen an angel.

But was that really so weird? Didn't people who'd died often say they saw angels? She couldn't have meant Evan Schulte, the boy who'd drugged her. She couldn't have seen the same halo of light that Violet had seen.

Violet started to go, barely noticing the flowers and balloons that sat on tables and trays, already lining the wall near the door. But then something caught her eye. She took a step closer as she saw something peeking out from beneath one of the arrangements. Something familiar, something she'd seen too many times before not to recognize. She wandered closer and plucked it free, turning the small business card over in her hands.

On the back was a handwritten annotation:

PTSD Therapy

Violet shoved the card in her pocket and left the room.

EPILOGUE

My Sweetest Violet,
I've tried to sit down and write this letter so many times.
And so many times I've given up, not quite sure where to
start . . . or where to end it. I have so many things I want
to say to you, about what you can do. About what we can
do. But you're still so young, and I don't want to frighten
you.

I used to fear my ability—hate it even. I used to wish
I'd been born like everyone else, unable to sense the death
all around me. I prayed for nothing more than to not pass
this trait on to my children . . . on to you.

But I know better now. I know that this . . . this gift

is part of what makes me who I am. That being different is never a bad thing. I've learned that unique is something to be treasured, to be valued.

I have no idea if this letter will ever find you, but if it does, I want to tell you to hold your gift close. To cherish it. And if the opportunity arises, to use it. Help others with what you can do; because you <u>can</u> help others, I just know it . . . even if I wasn't able to find the way myself.

You, my dear, have something special. Something important. And don't let anyone tell you otherwise.

Forever,
Grandma Louise

Violet folded the note and tucked it inside the pages of the diary where she kept the photograph of the Circle of Seven. She'd found the letter when she'd been repacking the box, poking out from beneath one of the cardboard flaps . . . hidden from view.

She wasn't sure why, but the letter from her grandmother didn't make her misty-eyed or nostalgic, the way it probably should have. Instead she felt empowered.

Her grandmother understood her like no one ever would. Her grandmother was telling her, even after everything she'd been through with the Circle, to find a way to make her ability useful if she could.

And Violet could.

She picked up her phone and pressed Call.

"Are you sure you don't want me to go with you?" Jay asked, zipping his jacket all the way up to his chin.

The temperatures had dropped quickly, plummeting from brisk to downright chilly in the past several days, making it clear that summer was long gone as autumn bore down on them with a vengeance. Violet watched his breath as it hit the air in a cloud and then dissipated once more.

"Why? Are you scared?" she challenged, only half teasing.

She couldn't help herself. She liked watching the way his pink scar puckered when he scoffed at the idea that he was afraid of being left alone in the cemetery, even though she'd only be a few steps away.

"Me? Scared of a few ghosts? Are you kidding?" His breath gusted again as his chest puffed up. "I don't know if you've heard, but I'm kind of a hero around these parts. I singlehandedly caught a killer, you know?"

Violet shoved him, laughing at his stupid joke, one she'd heard about a million times already. And then she saw the man in the trench coat picking his way among the gravestones, searching for one in particular. "Stay here," she told him, slipping out from behind the tree. "I'll be right back."

Instead of going to him, Violet went to their designated meeting spot and waited. Dr. Lee was just a few steps behind her, and he glanced down at the grave markers Violet stood in front of.

He shook his head. "It's a shame, isn't it?"

Violet looked too . . . at the markers for the Bowman family. Their imprints were at rest now that they were buried. She could see through the beautiful array of colors, and could barely smell the hint of coffee that hit her nose as she'd approached. She couldn't see Veronica's—the girl's—echo but she was sure that if she could, it would have been the halo.

She stood in front of Tyler's grave, though. The only one missing an echo altogether.

It didn't matter—Violet knew he was at peace too. He was with his family.

As it turned out, Grady had been holding the key to the connection between Veronica Bowman and Evan's unusual "family" all along. It had been on the iPod the police had recovered at his house. It was the band, Safe Word. Veronica had become obsessed with their songs, and had started slipping out to the clubs to see them perform live.

It had been at one of those clubs where Evan noticed her in the first place.

"What's this about, Violet?" Dr. Lee asked, getting right to the point.

"I want you to know I'm staying. On the team." She turned to watch him from the corner of her eye. "Without the threats. I'm doing this because I want to."

A satisfied grin tugged at his lips, making him look far too smug. "What changed your mind?"

She closed her eyes. "Everything," she answered. "But not you. It wasn't because of anything you said or did. It was . . . other things. I still don't trust you, and if I find out the Center is doing anything shady, I *will* expose all of you."

He tilted his head, appraising her. "Is that it? Did you bring me all the way down here to tell me that?"

Violet squeezed her hands, her palms sweaty. Her heart fluttered, but not in a good way, and her vocal cords were paralyzed.

Dr. Lee took her silence as his cue to leave.

But Violet had one more thing, and she chased after him. "Wait!" she shouted, freeing her voice at last. She reached into her pocket and fumbled for something. She remembered that day at the park, not so long ago, when he'd come to her with an ultimatum . . . a warning. Now it was her turn. "There is one last thing." Her fingers closed around the business card she'd looked at a hundred times since that day at the hospital, and she threw it on the ground between them as he turned back to face her. She bared her teeth at him, caution laced in her voice. "I don't know what you think you're doing. But I'm warning you, stay the hell away from my friend."

And then she swiveled around on her heel and left him standing there.

ACKNOWLEDGMENTS

As a writer, I love all of my books. But this one became even more personal for me when I lost my grandmother—my granny Kelly—while I was writing it. During the scenes in which Violet is reading her grandmother's journals, I found myself thinking of my own grandmother and feeling that sense of loss alongside my character.

Rather than live the way that was expected of a woman of her generation, my grandmother traveled, fished, painted, and, to be honest, cursed like a sailor. She was tough and determined, and raised her daughters and granddaughters to be as strong-willed as she was. So to my granny, thank you . . . and I miss you enormously.

I also want to thank the students from the real-life White River High School, who have tolerated me putting their school through the wringer—I've made them targets of serial killers and caused them all kinds of mayhem. Thanks too for not complaining that I gave your school lockers in my books . . . and yes, I know your school doesn't actually have them, but I really, *really* wanted *my* White River to have lockers!

To those of us who grew up in Kent, Auburn, or anywhere in the vicinity of the real Beer Bottle Beach on the Green River . . . thanks for letting me move it to Buckley for Violet and her friends!

I also need to thank those people who are responsible for making all my dreams come true in the first place: Laura

Rennert (the best agent ever!); Farrin Jacobs, Sarah Landis, Catherine Wallace, Kari Sutherland, Hallie Patterson, Cara Petrus (for this *breathtaking* cover!), and the entire team at HarperCollins who have worked on the Body Finder series (I love you guys!); Gretchen Hirsch, Marisa Russell, Melissa Bruno, Sasha Illingsworth (for all the other amazing covers), and the rest who are no longer at Harper but who still played incredible roles in these books (I can't thank you enough!).

I also have the most awesome go-to team when it comes to research, and I'd be remiss if I didn't thank Bryan Jeter, John McDonald, and Randy Strozyk for letting me pester you with my outrageous hypothetical scenarios—you guys truly are the best! To Erin Gross for your continued support with the Body Finder Novels fan site . . . and for being awesome! To Shelli for letting me brainstorm *and* whine. To Amanda and Tammy, for always helping me come up with names when I feel like I've hit a creative wall. To the Hildebrand family for all of the terrible things you let me do to your family members in this book. To Carol, Tamara, Shawn, Karma, Candy, Pam, and Susan, for never bothering to be quiet (this is why we'll be friends forever) . . . and to Jacqueline for shushing them anyway. And to Linnie, Annette, and Gaylene, sometimes when I'm writing about Violet and her friends, I'm reminded of the way we were in high school . . . I love you all so much!

Lastly, to my family, I'm not sure what more I can say, except to thank you again and again and again for being here for me. So, thank you. Again.

Read on for a sneak peek of
KIMBERLY DERTING'S
new series

PROLOGUE

WE KILLED THEM.

Crushed, to be precise. Crushed to the point that the other team left the field in tears, like a bunch of five-year-olds, falling into a defeated huddle in their grass-stained blue-and-gold uniforms and offering one another the lame consolations of runners-up. They did their best to avoid making eye contact with us as they had to go down the line and slap our hands, congratulating us on our win on their way to their dugout. On our massive, season-ending victory.

We, on the other hand, had hoarse voices and couldn't stop jumping up and down and grabbing everyone within arm's reach and gripping them to our filthy, sweaty selves as we screamed into their ears, again and again, that we'd done it. We'd done it. *We'd done it!*

Cat caught me in her tough, wiry arms and squeezed me so hard she nearly crushed the breath out of me. "It was all you, baby! All you!" She didn't bother keeping her voice down, and everyone heard her. I could feel the dampness that soaked her uniform all the way through.

My face blazed in the wake of her comment, and I giggled nervously. She never seemed to understand the whole "there's no *I* in team" that coach was always drilling into us. As far as Cat was concerned, *I* was the team. "Shut up," I insisted, shoving away from her.

"You saw him, didn't you? The scout?"

I didn't have to answer her or try to explain that I was sure he wasn't there just for me, because we were caught up in another round of cheers and congratulations, and after a moment I forgot all about scouts and embarrassing best friends and focused solely on the fact that we'd just won the championship.

That was how Austin found me, still wearing my ear-to-ear grin as I nearly walked right past him on my way to the parking lot to meet my dad. It had taken almost half an hour to finally disentangle myself from my teammates, and another ten minutes for coach to stop congratulating us, and herself, and then us some more, before excusing us so we could get on the buses to meet up for the victory celebration. Of course, my dad had asked coach to make an exception. To let me ride with him instead of the rest of my teammates on the bus. He had *things* he wanted to discuss on our way to the pizza party.

Austin was propped against the fence, offering me one of his signature smiles. It was a smile I'd known almost my whole life, and in it I could picture our entire summer spreading out before us. Long days spent on the riverbank as we stretched our damp towels over sunbaked rocks. Climbing through his bedroom window after his parents left for work so we could sleep till afternoon in his cramped twin bed with its worn Batman sheets that he should've outgrown years ago but that he still hadn't parted with. Late nights at the drive-in theater, staring up at the stars instead of watching whatever dollar movie was playing on the giant screen as we talked about our future and all the things we would do together once we were free of our parents and high school.

And kissing. Lots and lots of kissing.

Austin pointed playfully at my chin. "You got a little something. . . ." Then he grinned as his finger flicked downward to indicate the rest of me.

My eyes followed as I smiled wryly. "Ya think?" I was practically wearing the softball field: grass, dirt, chalk.

He reached for me, his fingers twirling around the orange and black ribbons, our team colors, wound through my hair. "You sure you don't wanna catch a ride with me? I promise I'll take you straight to the Pizza Palace so you can celebrate." He leaned close, his Tic Tac–fresh breath tickling my cheek, and I only briefly wondered if I smelled as ripe as Cat had; but I knew he didn't care. He never cared.

Glancing past him, I saw my dad watching us from in front of his silver Prius, clutching a stack of shiny new brochures in his hands. He didn't wave me over with them or anything, but I could see it in the way he looked at me—the hurry-up look. The I've-got-something-to-show-you look.

I closed my eyes before answering but gave the only response I could. I pressed my cheek against Austin's, transferring some of my grime to him in the process. "How 'bout you meet me there?" I leaned against him meaningfully. "We can celebrate later."

My dad is probably my number one fan. He could outshout any peppy cheerleader when we were winning and could outscream any ump when I got a bad call.

My dad was definitely a bigger fan than my mom, who often worked too late, like tonight, to make it to my games. Apparently, an escrow closing on a foreclosure was more important than your daughter's championship game.

"He gave me some pamphlets," my dad announced from the front seat.

Pouting might be immature, but every sixteen-year-old girl has mastered some form of it: the silent treatment; crocodile tears; eye rolling; the fake, nothing's-wrong response. The list goes on and on.

For me it was sullenness. Not pretty, sure, but effective.

Sullen sometimes forced a sixteen-year-old to banish herself to the backseat like a little girl. It was worth the payoff, I decided as I avoided his eager gaze in the rearview mirror.

But my number one fan wasn't about to give up that easily. "It's a great school. Big Ten. He was talkin' full ride."

I crossed my arms. We'd had this discussion. More than once.

My dad stiffened, sensing, if a little late, that I was digging in my heels. Again. "You don't have to stay in-state, Kyra. You have more options than anyone else on that team. Hell, probably more than anyone else in this town. A good pitcher is hard to come by. A great one is damn near impossible to find." I knew what he was doing. My dad, who knew me far too well—better maybe than anyone else—was searching for the right thing to say, something that would coax me into seeing his side of things.

Gritting my teeth, I turned to stare out the window. It was dark outside, so there wasn't much to look at, but it was better than catching my father's hopeful glimpses staring back at me.

I heard him sigh, and then there was a silence—not long and not short either—and then he added, "I don't know why the two of you think you have to go to college together."

That was it. He'd definitely found my hot button. "It's not your decision," I snapped as if I hadn't said this a hundred times before. "We've already decided where we're going. I don't know why you keep talking to these scouts. Stop encouraging them."

"Oh for chrissake, Kyra. College doesn't have to be a

'we' thing. It doesn't have to be a joint decision. It wouldn't be the end of the world if you and Austin went to different schools for a few years."

My fists clenched in my lap. "You and Mom went to Central Washington. It's a good school. Why do you have such a problem with this?"

"Your mom and I didn't go there together; we met there. And I don't have a problem with the school. It's just that you can do so much better."

I met his eyes now, daring him to lie to me. "Are you talking about the school, or about Austin?"

He only held my gaze for a split second before turning back to watch the black ribbon of road that stretched out ahead of him. "Both, I suppose." Before I could let the gravity of his words sink in, he tried to explain. His voice was softer now. "It's not Austin. You know I like him. Hell, he's practically family. It's just that you've known him your entire life, Kyr. You've never had a chance to meet anyone else. To know any different."

This was new, this argument against Austin and me. It was no longer about my education; he was talking about my future . . . my real future. The one Austin and I had been planning forever.

I blinked hard, not wanting him to know how betrayed I felt by the sting of his words. "Stop the car," I stated, and hated the way my voice cracked when it finally cleared the barrier of my throat.

"Kyra . . ."

6

"I mean it. Stop the car!"

We were in the middle of nowhere, on Chuckanut Drive, still miles away from Burlington. My dad slowed but didn't stop, his tires crunching on the gravel on the side of the road. "You're not getting out. There's nothing out here."

"I'll call Austin," I insisted. "He'll pick me up."

The car was still moving, but only barely, as his words tumbled into the darkness, finding me in the backseat. "I just don't want you to settle. I want you to experience the world. To go big." It was one of my dad's catchphrases: "Go big or go home."

Only this time he was wrong. I didn't want "big." I didn't want to live a catchphrase at all, none of them. I wanted to live my life.

And I wanted out.

Opening the car door was easy, and even though the Prius felt like it was moving in slow motion, the road I stared down at looked as if we were racing in the Grand Prix. I thought of what breaking my ankles might mean to my dad's precious full-ride scholarships, and suddenly I didn't care about scholarships or scouts or full rides.

"I said stop!" I yelled at my dad, and when I heard the screech of the Prius's tires skidding to a complete stop, I leaped out of the car.

By the time my feet hit the ground I was already running, but I was moving too fast, and I was crying now too. I couldn't see where I was going, and I tripped on the unforgiving asphalt.

I barely registered my dad's voice coming from behind me, and I definitely didn't feel pain, at least not yet. But I knew from years of sports' injuries that adrenaline could mask the initial discomfort, and you would always feel it later.

I was still getting up, brushing away bits of rocks and gravel from my uniform and from my hands, which had taken the brunt of the skidding part of my fall, when everything around me went white.

White, like blinding white.

It came in a flash, all at once, from somewhere that seemed both far away and right on top of me at the same time. In that moment I couldn't see anything, but I heard my dad.

He was screaming this time. Screaming and screaming. My chest felt tight, and my eyes burned as I tried to find him, tried to see through the light that scorched my retinas.

All I knew was that one moment I was in the middle of a deserted stretch of highway, arguing with my dad about scholarships and boys, and the next minute my limbs were tingling and I felt weightless and dizzy.

Then . . .

. . . nothing.

CHAPTER 1
Day One

MY HEAD WAS POUNDING. BUT NOT LIKE A HEAD-ache. More like someone was using it as a basketball against the pavement. Or for target practice.

That was it, I realized, prying my eyes open at last. Something was hitting me. Pelting, more like.

There was still too much light to make out anything clearly, but after blinking several times, I was at least aware of shapes around me. I dug my fingers into the ground beneath me and recognized the gravel and sand and asphalt at my back. All around me the smells of oil and gasoline lingered with something sickly sweet—like the smell of warm rot—sparking my gag reflex.

Another hard thing pegged me in the side of the head again, and I flinched, lifting my hand to try to shield myself from the assault.

This time I heard a sound. A giggle, maybe?

I squeezed my eyes, blinking harder, willing them to focus.

It was daylight that blinded me, which seemed wrong for a reason I couldn't quite put my finger on. But it wasn't just that—this whole situation seemed wrong. And now it wasn't just my head that was pounding; it was my heart too. My brain felt scrambled as I grappled to make sense of where I was and why I was waking up here, outside, instead of at home in my bed.

The silhouette of a little boy stood above me, shadowed by the glare of the sun behind him. I blinked harder, still trying to sort it all out, and I could see his expression then, a look of delight. He held one hand behind his back.

Spread out like marbles in front of my face, I saw an array of brightly colored candies that looked suspiciously like gum balls or mini jawbreakers.

"What are you doing here?" the boy asked, the hint of a slight frown shifting the planes of his freckled face.

I searched for an answer, and when I couldn't find a suitable one, I asked one of my own, "What are *you* doing here?"

The boy looked back over his shoulder. "Waiting for my mom." Past him, I saw the gas pumps and a small convenience store behind them. I squinted against the sunlight and read the sign: *Gas 'n' Sip*. A woman was at one of the stands, filling the tank of her red minivan.

What the—the Gas 'n' Sip, really? How the heck had that happened? *When* had that happened? I shoved the base of my palms into my throbbing eyes, trying to crush the pain away. Eyeing me curiously, the boy absently popped a piece of the candy or gum into his mouth from the hand behind his back as I struggled to sit upright.

It wasn't easy. Apparently, I'd slept outside all night. And behind a Dumpster at the Gas 'n' Sip no less. That panicky feeling shook me, and I glanced around uneasily, wincing as I realized that the rotting smell had been garbage.

"Robby!" The woman yelled, and the boy's head whipped around.

"Gotta go," he whisper-told me as if we'd developed some sort of bond and I required an explanation for his departure. "You want these?" He held out his hand, palm open to reveal his remaining candies: three red ones, a green, and four yellows.

I thought about turning him down. They looked sticky. But my mouth tasted like I'd just licked home plate, so I nodded instead.

He held them toward me, and I accepted his gummy offering as they peeled, rather than dropped, from his skin. "Thanks," I said before he skipped away.

I popped the candies into my mouth, letting the sour jolt of them awaken my saliva glands and wash away the tang of dirt that seemed to cling to my tongue.

As always, I got impatient and bit down on one of the

11

candies. Despite their gooey outer shell, inside they were rock hard, something I discovered the moment I felt a chunk of my right-side molar chip away.

Cursing, I spit the rest of the candies in a messy wad onto the ground and ran my tongue over the new, rough edge of my tooth. I'd just been to the dentist last week, something I hated doing, and now this would mean I'd be forced to see him again.

Fishing my cell phone from the front pocket of my uniform pants, I decided it was time to call for backup. I still couldn't believe I'd ended up behind the Dumpster of a gas station last night. My parents were probably freaking the hell out. I was freaking the hell out.

Not to mention Austin . . .

I dialed him first, not caring that my decision was sure to set off another round of arguments when I got home.

I held the phone to my ear and waited. After a moment I pulled the phone away and inspected it.

NO SERVICE, the screen read.

No service—how was that even possible? I knew exactly where I was. I'd been at this gas station hundreds of times; it was maybe a mile from my house—well within our coverage map.

Whatever, I thought, getting tentatively to my feet and waiting till my legs felt steady. I did my best to ignore the headache that continued to pulse behind my eyes. The walk would probably do me good.

I wasn't sure how much good the walk had done me, but at least my head had stopped throbbing. I still felt off and couldn't quite pin down what, exactly, was bothering me.

I had this strange sense of déjà vu that clung to me. It was like a wet second skin, all itchy and maddening, making me glance, and glance again, at everything I passed. It all seemed familiar yet *not* at once. Like I'd been here before but was seeing it all for the very first time.